A Tender Thing

A Tender Thing

Emily Neuberger

G. P. PUTNAM'S SONS

New York

PUTNAM
— EST. 1838 —

G. P. Putnam's Sons
Publishers Since 1838
An imprint of Penguin Random House LLC
penguinrandomhouse.com

ISBN 9780593084878
ebook ISBN 9780593084885

Printed in the United States of America
1 3 5 7 9 10 8 6 4 2

Book design by Elke Sigal

For my parents, Loretta and Carl

My heart wants to sing ev'ry song it hears.

OSCAR HAMMERSTEIN II

A Tender Thing

ACT ONE

The "I Want" Song

Chapter One

The O'Hanlon farm was devoted mostly to pigs, with stalls for breeding and a large slaughterhouse on the west edge of the property. They also owned a horse barn, an apple orchard, a coop for chickens, and a field where they grew food for the animals. The farm was like a large body, clear yet relentless in its needs. While the animals' appetites stayed consistent and the chores of the day never changed—only occasionally growing more difficult, due to weather or workers' illness—Eleanor, who had spent nearly every day of her life on this farm, made mistakes. As often as she brushed the horses until they gleamed, she would also bring the chickens the wrong feed. She had a tendency to grow dreamy while picking apples and let too many wormy runts into the mix. She was not a stupid girl. But the place did not allow for a lack of attention, and though it had been her family's farm since her grandfather bought it forty years earlier, Eleanor was never interested enough to learn its rhythms.

Still, while Eleanor dreaded all of her farm chores, she never once neglected to feed the pigs. On sterile winter mornings, she resisted the pull of her bedclothes and stepped onto the chilled floorboards. It was easier in summer, when she woke with the sheets sticking to her back.

On her twenty-first birthday, the June sun was hot. She carried heavy pails with rag-wrapped handles that wouldn't cut into her palms. When the pigs noticed her approach, they swarmed the edge of the sty, their noises layering into a fugue of desperation.

It was early, and dew still shone on the soybeans in the neighboring fields to the east. The land was flat and pale green, the sun sending rays straight into her eyes. Pink, fatty bodies rammed her legs; snouts nudged her hands and pockets in search of food. She greeted them each by name and dumped feed into the trough, rubber boots sinking into the mud. Eleanor was the one in the family who'd named the pigs. The names were born from a desire to bait rather than sentiment. It enraged her father. She hated the sows most—gelatinous, sedentary bodies reserved for reproduction and consumption, bellies already resembling Christmas hams. When Eleanor saw them, her tongue rose with sharp nausea.

She slid out of the gate, using her thigh to keep the animals inside, and returned to the barn. A cat uncurled from its place on the supply shelf and darted away. The hay all around her was dry from the heat, which was good. Sometimes, on humid days, it was stuffy inside the barn. She closed the door so only a seam of light glowed through, inhaled, and began to sing.

Even surrounded by the muffling hay, Eleanor's voice filled the space. She always warmed up with ascending scales. Her voice was a strong soprano with a persistent rasp, as if she had just woken up. She'd learned to sing in church, but despite her talent she was passed over for solos. Her mother said everyone was jealous; her best friend, Rosie, said it was because her voice was too sexy for Jesus.

As soon as Eleanor had gotten old enough to manage the morning chores alone, she'd started rushing through them to make sure she had time to sing before breakfast. Some days, her barn mornings were all the practice time she got. So even when she did not want to wake up, she did, because the only thing worse than rising at dawn to feed the pigs was a day without singing.

After her warm-up, she chose a song: "If I Were a Bell" from *Guys and Dolls*. It had opened on Broadway eight years earlier, and she'd memorized it off the record. It was a bright song, tipsy and fun, and reminded Eleanor of New York, where she had never been but burned to go. She loved to imagine what the actress might have looked like onstage—how could a woman make a song come to life with nothing but her body and voice? How would she move her fingers, her eyebrows, her shoulders? Eleanor pretended she was singing to a man, her scene partner, and stepped as far into the character as she could. For half an hour, she lost herself in the material. Alone, she performed.

Singing was innate to her, like walking, speaking, or sensing the temperature of the air. Her body had learned to sing before her mind caught on. Music was everywhere. Television jingles had enchanted her as a baby. Mass was fascinating—as long as the priest kept quiet. What was background noise to everyone else was a life-giving pulse to her. At parties, she had trouble keeping up in conversations, distracted by whatever record was spinning.

She sang in the barn until her parents would come looking for her. They knew she liked to sing but would be angry if she were distracted during chores. Her practicing was private; she didn't allow herself to feel ashamed that she was performing for bales of hay. She knew she could never become a performer, but in the barn, she trained as if she had a real chance. She found dignity in the rigor of her practice. Through routine and dedication came improvement, which awarded a satisfaction otherwise absent for her on the farm. Every day she worked, and during those minutes, she allowed herself to imagine that practicing might lead somewhere. It was impossible to work so hard without wanting to sing for an audience, though such a desire was dangerous to encourage. The possibility for heartbreak was overwhelming, but the fantasy was irresistible. But when she sang, she imagined herself selected from a pool of girls to perform on Broadway. Today it was *Guys and Dolls*. Yesterday, *The Music Man*. And Gershwin, and Irving Berlin, Richard Rodgers, and Cole Porter. This time was hers.

Eleanor walked back toward the house, its paint peeling, the sun displaying the spots that needed repair. The family dog, Lou, galloped toward her and butted her with his head. She pushed him down. Normally singing energized her, but today she felt a heavy pall. Perhaps it was because she was another year older—and each day that passed was another spent in Wisconsin and one less she might spend in New York. Another day with the pigs. She had a desperate, breathless feeling in her chest that morning, as she realized that however young she might be, her life was progressing in place. The barn mornings were hers, but they were not enough. Eleanor faced the possibility that they might have to be.

She left her boots on the porch and opened the screen door, letting it slam behind her.

Her mother was at the stove, sleeves rolled up as she poured grease into a tin on the counter. Eleanor's stomach turned; she hated bacon.

"There's the birthday girl!"

Eleanor could have rested her chin on top of her mother's head. Instead, she poured coffee.

"Rosie and I are going to the movies tonight."

Her mother made a noise. "With anyone special? Might be nice to dress up."

Eleanor pulled bread from the box and ignored her. Growing up, Eleanor's mother had described her as "the marrying kind." She was tall, with a solid figure softened by large breasts and bearing hips and reddish hair, the tone enhanced by her freckles and a tendency to blush. Her features were pretty but generic. Her appearance called to mind sensible girls rather than stunners. The only thing that distinguished her was her voice. It was low and husky, and made men turn around when she spoke in stores. When she was speaking, it was more interesting than average, enough to earn a double take. But when she sang, for all of her uncertainties, even Eleanor knew it was something.

It was not, however, enough for her mother.

"You know, your father and I will be the only people without grandchildren."

"Surely not the only ones."

Her mother intensified her whisking, scraping against the metal bowl. With another slam, her father entered, forehead already shining. "Another hot one!"

He presented her with a flat, light package that Eleanor knew would be a record. Probably one she already owned. She guarded against disappointment and tore the paper. *Guys and Dolls.*

"Saw it in Green Bay last month." He was so proud; she felt embarrassment for him. "This is the one you wanted, isn't it?"

She had hoped for *My Fair Lady*. Her parents understood only so much about musicals and failed to grasp any differentiation. At first Eleanor had accepted this, but lately she felt as if it was a willful decision not to learn more and engage.

After breakfast, Eleanor took the truck into town to Miltenberg's Music. Owned and curated by her friend Pat Miltenberg, it was the only music shop for miles around.

Eleanor had first visited when she was nine. Her mother was getting her hair done and Eleanor grew fidgety. Armed with a nickel for candy, Eleanor passed Miltenberg's. Aisles of records were lined up like rows of corn. The shop owner was behind the desk, penciling notes in a ledger, squinting despite his small glasses. The place smelled dusty. Her footsteps were swallowed by the cardboard record sleeves and sheet music. Her parents put on a record of Christmas carols a few times each December, and apart from the occasional pop tune, Eleanor didn't even know there were other kinds of music.

She read the cards stuck between the records: *Opera, Classical, Jazz, Popular Music, Hymns, Show Tunes.* She flipped the records one by one, awed by the colorful cardboard sleeves, amazed there was enough music to fill an entire store.

"Can I help you find something?"

Eleanor pulled her hands to her sides when the owner approached. "I'm only looking."

He was graying and plump, a larger man than the farmworkers she was used to, and wore a pilled blue sweater with corduroy pants light at the knees. He smelled of tobacco and something sweet and herbal. Though he was middle-aged, he gave off the energy of someone even older. Eleanor was told to be quiet in the company of adults, but he crouched to meet her eyes. "That's all right, dear. What kind of music do you like?"

Eleanor beheld all the rows of records, quivering.

"My name is Pat." He shook her hand like she was a grown-up. "Let's find out what you like."

Eleanor followed as he browsed different genres, debating for long moments before selecting which record to present. No one had ever taken her so seriously.

When he was searching Irish Ballads, she spoke up. "Sometimes I sing in church. I like that a lot."

"No doubt you do." He pulled his glasses down. His nose was round, spongy with pores. "I have an idea." He led her back to the show tunes and picked through a stack. He freed one from its sleeve, pulled the needle off a turning record, and set the new one to spin.

Eleanor swayed on her feet, unsure of herself. She mimicked Pat's posture: leaned against the counter, ankles crossed, eyes closed.

Then the music came through. The moment it hit the air, Eleanor straightened her back, skin turning bumpy. It was a brassy sound, modern, spirited but sincere, with humor and vulnerability. Her body reacted instantly—it was like eating a sweet, or petting the new spring kittens. She didn't need time to decipher her feelings. The pleasure was instant and right.

"What's this?"

"'They Can't Take That Away from Me' by George and Ira Gershwin." Pat must have seen how her eyes brightened. He began to gesture, his voice growing more animated. "Pair of brothers who got their start in Tin Pan Alley—do you know where that is?"

Pat told her about the writers in New York, collaborating in tiny apartments. He told her about vendors selling frankfurters on the street and how thousands of people lived on top of each other in buildings taller than church steeples. Writers and musicians lived there, but also students, fashion designers, finance moguls, chefs, and people who enjoyed living someplace where interesting things happened every moment. He'd been there once, years earlier. "I loved it," he said. The wrinkles around his eyes deepened. "But it wasn't for me." Eleanor imagined Tin Pan Alley as a factory, with actresses going down the assembly line, men switching out their lyrics as they passed. Pat said it was more human than that. New York was the place to be if you loved musicals. Lyricists partnered with composers until they found a match, writing for stage works filled with drama and dance. People built relationships, and out of them, the art was born. Each word, each note, each harmony was as deliberate as a surgical stitch. Eleanor had seen just one musical on television—*The Wizard of*

Oz. By the time her mother found her later that afternoon, Pat had gifted her three records and awakened her to a whole world of music and stories.

From then on, she spent all of her pocket money and free time at Pat's, leaning against the counter, begging for more of all he knew. He told her anecdotes about actresses, stories gleaned from newspapers during years when he'd had no one to discuss them with. As Eleanor grew older, she memorized every lyric to more than forty shows. Instead of attending school football games and corn mazes and dances in the town hall, she listened to music. No peer-approved pleasure could rival the thrill that rose in her body when she placed the needle down on a new record. In order to afford them, she worked as a babysitter, music teacher, and seamstress. New records were not objects, but events.

Today, her twenty-first birthday, she found Pat unloading a box of sheet music, one hand on his lower back as he lifted. His store had grown gradually more packed, since he could not stand to throw away music. Every year, he squished his inventory to accommodate the swell. It was tidy if one looked closely—Pat took meticulous care of his merchandise—but at first the place appeared shambolic. Every time she smelled cardboard from the inventory boxes, she felt calm. Eleanor loved this place. Pat was one of the few people she'd met who abided musicals at all, and the only person who loved them as much as she did.

"Eleanor! My favorite customer." He left the stacked boxes and met her by the register.

She showed him the *Guys and Dolls* record. "Could you sell it?"

He turned it over, looking for bends. "We certainly can't let it go to waste. Ah—look what I got in Monday." He presented her with the *My Fair Lady* record. Eleanor gasped and held out her hands. "I saved it for you. Happy birthday, my dear."

Flipping to the back, she read the cast list. Julie Andrews. Rex Harrison. Brooks Atkinson had called Andrews magnificent. She was very young—twenty. She'd starred in the television version of *Cinderella*, which Eleanor had watched with her face a foot from the screen. Hadn't Ms. Andrews been unknown before all that? Did regular girls have places on the stage?

She pushed the record back to Pat. "Put it on! I want to listen with you."

He slipped it out of the sleeve. "Ms. Andrews is astonishing."

"And practically an unknown!" Eleanor said.

He made a face. "From the vaudeville circuit, I think. One of the kid hoofers."

"That's right." Eleanor knocked Pat's desk with her fist. So this Andrews girl had been on Broadway before—a child star with parents who knew the ropes and brought her up to act.

Pat crossed his arms, and folds of skin scrunched up at his elbows. She never tired of watching him: Pat listened like it contained an entire meal.

It was too early to tell anything else about the music, but she loved Andrews's voice. Eleanor needed at least three listens, straight through, before music began to digest in her brain. Only after she sat away from it, and a melody lingered in her head, did she know if it had caught. Then she could return to the record, warmed to it, primed for a deep listen. So far, Rodgers and Hammerstein had done that with *Oklahoma!*, *Carousel*, and, her favorite, *South Pacific*. She adored them, but they were second best. The man whose work she would follow to the ends of the earth was Don Mannheim.

His sound had called to her since his first musical, 1948's *Fifth Avenue*. Something about his rhymes—he loved to vary a scheme, so she never knew when the ring would come, it hit her like a surprise, thrilling, every time—and his observations about humans, so fresh, often mean, made his musicals unforgettable. He incorporated his classical training, blues, jazz migrating down Manhattan, and even the new rock-and-roll licks other Broadway composers wouldn't touch. He could write any kind of music but often preferred a pared-down sound: the singer, a piano, perhaps a muted drum kit, the lyric. He distilled everything she liked about musicals into one voice.

According to the reviews in the *New York Times*, which she had to drive ten miles to buy whenever he had a musical opening, his scenes were as good as the score. Mannheim was one of the few writers around who penned the music, lyrics, and all the lines. But Eleanor had only ever heard the soundtracks.

She fell in love with his works as she discovered them. First Pat introduced her to *Fifth Avenue*, Mannheim's debut, with a second act not quite as good as the first but still precious, in its own way. Then there was *The Birds and the Bees*, which according to the *Times* was Don's "attempt to rival Ziegfeld." He didn't venture back.

Charades was his fifth musical and her favorite. It was still running on Broadway after six years. Mannheim spun together seven characters' stories with finesse that took her breath away and assured his genius status. The whole score sounded like the city—heavy brass instruments, tinny percussion, strings that made her think of the sun glinting off skyscrapers. It wasn't typical material for a musical—a pregnancy, a dying woman searching for a last affair—which made her love it all the more. No one in her town talked about those things.

Don Mannheim wrote about the peculiarity of being surrounded by family and friends and feeling unknown. So often, Eleanor felt her love of musicals overflowing, bursting within her, and when she expressed it to her mother and father, they said something like, "What a fun little song." When she saw other young people, apart from Rosie, she was sneered at or ignored; they didn't know what to do with her. These dismissals broke her heart a thousand tiny times. She was off, but couldn't help it. Her obsession lifted her from the group. Though she had an escape with Pat, Eleanor often felt strangled in the daily battle of suppressing herself. Don Mannheim turned the feelings in her soul into lyrics. That meant he felt them, too, and understood this particular loneliness well enough to finesse it into a useful, beautiful line. When listening to his music, she heard her own pain echoed.

She'd torn through his remaining works—*Pillow Talk*, *The Ladies of Sheridan Road*, *Candy Apple*—and loved everything he made, like unique children. Mannheim blended commercialism with the catharsis of classic dramas and the wit of a French salon. He wrote with the snap of Porter and Hammerstein's sensitivity. Eleanor clipped every review and hung them on her wall. She ran her hands over his picture until the pads of her fingers were inky. He was forty-one, a hulking, virile man with shiny black hair, a self-made musician who'd composed his way out of a factory town and made it to New York on scholarship. He was a veteran who'd fought in Japan in World War II. He had a brilliant smile, and in her favorite picture, he grinned openmouthed, hands spread across the piano keys, midlaugh. Eleanor adored him.

Once Pat and Eleanor reached the song where Eliza Doolittle mastered her speech, singing in a clear soprano about rain in Spain, Pat lifted the pin on the record. His eyes were wet.

"You are the rightful owner." Pat slid the record back into the sleeve and presented it to her with pride. "And now for your real present." Pat reached under the desk and produced a page from a newspaper, folded over. "Look there, honey."

She leaned over the counter and read.

MANNHEIM/FLYNN DUO TURN TO PUBLIC FOR NEW LEADING LADY

Eleanor's face went hot before she read the rest.

"What's this?" Her hands shook, so she hid them under the counter.

Eleanor didn't want to read more. She knew what an open call was: a way for ordinary girls to get on Broadway. Already, she felt jealous, excited, terrified, as she read the article. The number of girls would be staggering. The back of her neck started to sweat. Hordes of girls would line up in character shoes. Gorgeous girls, girls who'd had dance lessons. Her chance, and it was a thousand miles away. She wanted to vomit.

She tried to keep her cool. "That theater will be a madhouse."

A quote from Don followed the announcement of the audition: "We've had a string of wonderful young starlets in the role but Harry [Flynn, Mannheim's creative partner and the director of *Charades*] and I want to take this opportunity to find someone fresh."

Pat stared at her. Blood rushed to her ears.

"Guess they ran through everyone good." She squared her shoulders and slipped the article across the counter.

Pat pushed it back. "You should go."

She made herself laugh, though her heart pounded.

"Eleanor, you're good." His voice was energetic—he believed she could get the part. When it was too cold to practice in the barn, Pat lent her his store after closing; he'd heard her practice for years, noticed her improvement, her dedication. But that didn't mean he was right.

"Every girl with a smidge of talent hears that," she said. "Especially in small towns. I've heard enough musicals. They're fantasies, not real."

"It's a cliché because it happens. Not every star is born in New York."

"It won't happen to me."

"Don himself is from Indiana."

"Don studied music at Juilliard."

"That was his ticket out. This is yours. Eleanor, your voice is special."

Eleanor's love of theater was a flame inside her—she guarded it, and no matter who was cruel to her, no matter how dull her life, the music and lyrics brought joy. Only Pat knew just how deeply she loved it, and not even he would understand how humiliated she would be if her talent was ever put to the test and found lacking. She'd lose herself. An audition in New York was a gamble, risking everything she had.

"Please. Eleanor, how much can a train ticket be?"

A lot; she'd looked it up many times. Eleanor handled her family's sales to the market and butcher shop. She knew what things cost, the days of work involved. A train ticket to New York was more than her family could spare, even with her parents' support.

"Eleanor, listen." Pat removed his glasses and set them down. She could see the lines on his face as he ran a hand over the scruff on his jaw. "It would break my heart to know that your only friend is an old man in a music shop."

She kept her eyes on the record. "I have Rosie."

"You are an artist," he said. "You need that in your life. Without it, you'll shrivel up."

"You're being silly." But his words flustered her. Pat was a person who was invited to other families' Thanksgivings. As far as Eleanor knew, he might be one of those who, as Rosie said, "preferred the company of men," but this was something Eleanor scarcely understood. Their friendship was based on a shared love. In all the years she'd come to discuss musicals with Pat, she'd never encountered anyone else doing the same. Sometimes when Eleanor thought of him and his little house, filled with the records and reviews he couldn't fit into the shop, she felt desolate, and then afraid. She looked at the shop, his life's work, and for the first time saw it as a desperate grip on a part of him that he needed to survive.

Pat offered her the article and squeezed her hand. "Eleanor, you have a chance. Go."

Her throat had gone tight. But she folded the article and put it in her pocketbook.

Thoughts of the audition tipped life on its side; suddenly everything looked temporary. What if she never had to feed pigs or chickens again? Never had to hide her practicing? Spent Fridays with composers and singers instead of at the movies? But then she thought of the open call. All those girls wanted what she wanted. Eleanor thought of them as slender and clear-skinned, trained in ballet and acting, bred like racehorses. They would have years of coaching. How many girls in there had grown up with shit under their fingernails?

Was even one of them self-taught? Did they stay up all night with the record turned low, listening again and again to a perfectly enunciated syllable? Hold their breath and let it out as slowly as possible, keeping track of the seconds they'd added to their lung capacity? Did even one stand among the hay in her family's barn and attempt to focus her voice until it buzzed high in the center of her face, along her nose and forehead, because she had an instinct for resonance?

Of course not. They'd been trained—while Eleanor had earned her voice, slowly, with daily practice and careful study. But no one would see that. It was such luck, those young girls who were plucked for Broadway. And they all had whatever constituted "good legs." Eleanor's legs were fine, but served mostly to get her from the barn to the slaughterhouse, where she held the runts while her father slit their throats.

Who would be able to see past her Midwestern blandness when there was a knockout raised overlooking the lights of Broadway, ready to step onstage? When, for God's sake, there was a girl who had already seen a Broadway show?

It was too much. Traveling to New York only to watch her dream go to some sink-bleached blonde? Worse, to watch Don Mannheim make that decision himself? No, thank you.

✳

Eight minutes after Rosie was due, a horn blared from the driveway. Eleanor plucked the curtain back from the window and groaned when she saw a pale blue Studebaker.

Rosie opened the door and wiggled out of the front seat, turning back to make a face at the driver. Eleanor's stomach knotted. She heard Rosie's enhanced laughter and pictured her: wide grin, back arched to best highlight her assets, a piece of hair between her fingers, maybe even tickling her mouth. New Yorkers weren't the only girls who could act.

Eleanor opened the door before Rosie knocked. "You brought a boy."

Rosie dropped her perky stance. She was, as usual, coiffed and made up, her short, curvy body dressed in a matching two-piece set she'd sewn herself. Rosie checked her hair in the mirror. She never left the house without putting on her face. "I ran into John Plutz at the drugstore. I was buying Daddy his Bromo and got embarrassed, so I gave a rambling explanation." She shrugged. "I think he thought it was cute. Who am I to say no?"

Rosie was usually fun, but sometimes she was aggravating.

"I didn't want a boy around on my birthday." Boys did not like Eleanor. Most made this clear by ignoring her, but some couldn't handle that she was more interested in something they did not understand, and punished her for it with cruel words said to her face or behind her back. She would rather have pretended they didn't exist, but Rosie refused to accept this.

"Don't worry." Rosie reached in her purse and uncapped her lipstick, before handing it to Eleanor. They'd both worn Cherries in the Snow since ninth grade. "I brought two boys."

John drove with his hand on the bottom of the wheel, the other hand on Rosie's knee, and chomped on his words like they might run away. "Twenty-one? *Wow.*"

All these boys had been making noise in the background at school for sixteen years and now, after they graduated, the ones who hadn't married or gone to college endlessly reminded you why. Eleanor's date, Steve Macdonald, planted a wet kiss on her cheek as she slid into the back seat. The only memory she had of Steve was from three years earlier, when he'd knocked over a rack in Pat's store accidentally-on-purpose. Eleanor made sure he noticed her wipe the saliva with her thumb.

"So, I don't know what you ladies did all day, but Steve and I have been working at the mill and we're starved. Mind if we swing by Hersh's?"

"We'll miss the movie," Eleanor said. "*Auntie Mame* plays at eight. After that it's *The Fly*."

"Well, I couldn't sit through a movie without dinner!"

Eleanor wondered why John's appetite was her problem. "I don't want to see *The Fly*."

Steve glanced across. "Why would you want to see *Auntie Mame*?"

"Why would I want to see *The Fly*?"

Steve turned to face the window, already giving up. Eleanor felt a flash of pain, then satisfaction—he couldn't even handle three sentences between them.

Rosie jumped in. "Hersh's is fine—as long as you boys buy us a milkshake."

Eleanor recognized every single person inside the diner. They filed into a red plastic booth, and Eleanor ordered grilled cheese, extra pickles. Rosie ordered a milkshake, extra whipped cream. Steve surprised them all by ordering pancakes. "With bacon, please."

"Well, I for one need a real meal." John ordered a burger, pleased with himself for maintaining the status quo.

At the thought of bacon, Eleanor lost her appetite. She leaned against the vinyl with a sigh.

"You all right, Ellie? You look a little . . ." Rosie pushed her soda toward Eleanor.

She held up a hand, hoping her suffering was apparent. "I'm fine."

Rosie turned to the boys. "Eleanor doesn't like bacon because she lives on a pig farm."

"You can only name so many pigs before you lose your appetite for them." Eleanor stood. "I have to use the ladies'."

Rosie leapt to join her. When they were alone, Eleanor turned to her. "He's got the brain of a sardine."

Rosie plumped her breasts in her brassiere. "He's nice."

"Oh, well then. Doesn't he just razz my berries."

"In case you haven't noticed, all the good ones are taken," Rosie said. "Soon I'll have to go to Madison for a typing course to meet someone."

"Your daddy would never let you go to Madison. Too commie."

"So don't ruin this for me," Rosie said. "I'll be single forever!"

Compared to life with these fools, Eleanor didn't think that sounded so bad. Men! How could the same word describe John Plutz and Don Mannheim—the latter so vital and handsome, and able to spin lyrics that wrenched her very soul? They didn't seem the same species.

"I wouldn't mind being single forever." Eleanor thought of Pat, putting on a record as he set the table for one, maybe adding candles to heighten the evening, and her hands went numb. But wouldn't she be just as lonely, married to someone who stifled who she was?

"It's not about John," Rosie said. "It's about kids."

When they returned to the table, Eleanor tried to talk to the boys. But she couldn't be so unfaithful to herself as to laugh at John's jokes. Eleanor watched Rosie, who didn't seem nearly as torn apart by the act of pretending, who could act happy despite it not being true. Eleanor sat against the vinyl, aware she was pouting, feeling sorry for herself as they stopped including her. She watched them, wanting to be someone who could participate, lost as to how, feeling nothing but a persistent anxiety that put her off even pickles.

They skipped the movie and stopped instead at a bar, where the conversation got bawdier and John and Rosie disappeared for long minutes, during which Eleanor pushed her bottle cap along the sticky tabletop while Steve talked to a group of girls she had known in high school but no longer pretended to be friends with. Then, at midnight, Rosie and John dropped her home, John harping on about doing this again next week. "Wouldn't that be fun?"

Eleanor left it at good night.

Chapter Two

In her bedroom, Eleanor took the false bottom out of her jewelry box and removed the money she'd amassed during the last twelve years. It wasn't enough. She had counted many times and knew there wasn't enough to get her to New York. She flung herself on the bed, but the tears didn't come. Instead, she went to the old fantasy that she often played in her head: A spotlight. A costume, a crowd. All the people in Wisconsin talking about how she'd done it, really made it to Broadway. Don Mannheim, holding a dozen roses, watching from the wings.

Rolling onto her stomach, she reached for her pocketbook and retrieved the audition notice from Pat. The open call was in five days. An eastbound train came through the Wisconsin Dells on Sunday mornings. She could arrive Monday afternoon for the Tuesday audition. Eleanor knew her voice was good, and it wasn't because of what people said, nor was it ego. She knew because of how good it felt to sing. Her voice rang in her face, her throat, her chest. The sound vibrated between her molars, up the socket behind her tongue, in her forehead. Resonance. No breathy, wispy sound; it was full and powerful and a real, solid thing. It wasn't something just anyone could do. She didn't have money or experience, but she could sing.

She'd sing a Gershwin song, wear her blue dress, and borrow Rosie's red pumps. Her résumé was blank and she had a school photograph instead of a headshot, but she had talent. Enough that she deserved a chance. Maybe her life didn't have to be filled with distant obsessions about the latest record in Pat's store. Maybe she could spend her mornings inside rehearsal rooms instead of pigsties. People would respect her instead of offer ridicule. She'd spend evenings memorizing lines instead of out with boys who ignored her if she didn't pretend to laugh at their jokes.

Her body tightened with anger until she was wide awake, her skin hot. She sat up. She wasn't a farmer; she was a singer. As Pat had said, an artist. When had she decided that this place—Hersh's, the boys, her parents' harping about grandchildren—was what she deserved? Here was a chance, a slim but real one, to get out.

In a year she'd have saved enough.

But in a year, there wouldn't be an open audition for a Don Mannheim show.

Blood pounded in her ears. She slipped out of bed. Suspending herself from the two railings, she shimmied downstairs without touching a step. In the living room, she retrieved the box where her mother stored the war bonds.

She spread them on the carpet, moonlight shining through her mother's hand-tatted curtains. During the war, when Eleanor was a girl, her parents had scrimped along with everyone else and, whenever possible, loaned $18.75 to the federal government. Eleanor's mother still talked about how good she felt, counting up coins to protect their freedom, in Eleanor's name. Each bond would appreciate. Eleanor would receive the money upon her marriage, to help her husband buy a house or land.

She put them down. It was as good as stealing. Her parents had designated this money for one purpose. Abandoning her parents with two fewer hands on the farm, and the shame of a renegade daughter, was a betrayal.

The bonds were for her future. But Eleanor could not imagine living the future her parents had planned for her.

She went to the kitchen and dialed Rosie.

After many rings, Rosie's father picked up.

"Who's calling after midnight?"

"I'm sorry, Mr. Hughes." He always made her nervous. "I need to speak to Rosie."

"You can talk in the morning."

"Please. It's my birthday."

She heard the phone click down on the counter. A few minutes later, Rosie got on the line.

"I'm going to New York," Eleanor said.

Eleanor could imagine her friend's face. Rosie always twisted the cord around her arm when she talked, until it left a red mark on her skin. She'd endured countless hours while Rosie giggled with beaus on the phone, then hung up and rolled her eyes. But she wasn't giggling now. Eleanor knew Rosie would take this seriously.

"On Tuesday, there's an audition for a Don Mannheim show." There was a pause. Eleanor could feel her future hanging in the balance. What if Rosie tried to talk her out of it?

"I'm coming," Rosie said.

"Rosie, it's expensive."

"If you think I'm going to wait here while you have an adventure in New York, you're batty. How much are the tickets?"

Eleanor told her. Rosie hissed in her breath. "I've got thirty in savings."

"There's a train at ten a.m. on Sunday."

"Daddy's home all day Sunday," Rosie said. "He'll notice."

"It's the only train that'll get me there in time."

"Are you chewing?"

"Pickles help me think."

"Sunday it is."

"I love you." She jumped up and down as quietly as possible.

"You'd better."

Eleanor hung up. The thought of her parents upstairs brought an old sadness over her, like homesickness. She could handle that later; she couldn't allow herself to lose her grip on her decision. The audition was too important. The war bonds waited on the living room floor. She replaced the ones in her parents' names and took the rest.

In the morning, Eleanor wore her best dress and swept her hair back from her face. Even so, her heart accelerated when she arrived at the bank, as if she were about to rob it. Eleanor was shown to a desk, the name placard reading "Mr. Paul Farrell."

A gray-suited man with a pinched mouth approached.

"I heard you're thinking of cashing your war bonds."

"Yes, sir." His eyebrows were raised. Eleanor deepened her voice. "In twenties, please."

He put on his glasses, shaking his head. He held out a hand. Eleanor scrambled for her pocketbook and retrieved the bonds. When she gave them to him, along with identification, she felt nervous, as if, for some reason, he might tear them up.

He examined each one. "You know, dear, your parents saved for these. The money should go to something important."

Eleanor nodded, but he looked up, wanting more information.

"It's very important, Mr. Farrell." She took care with her tone; without a bank account, she feared he wouldn't relinquish her money at all.

He glanced at her left hand. Eleanor regretted not slipping on a dummy ring before leaving the house. "Many parents save these for their daughters' husbands." Eleanor kept her mouth shut. Finally, he sighed. "I'll be right back."

Sweat gathered under her arms. It took a long time. Three customers received service from a teller. She wondered if there was more she needed to do to receive the money. Then Mr. Farrell returned. He spread the bills on the desk.

Eleanor's neck prickled with shame, but she refused to buckle. She reached out.

"Ah, not just yet—I need to count it for you."

Eleanor bit down on the side of her cheek. The money could get her to New York and keep her there long enough to figure out her next step. Without the open call, she'd never have the nerve to go. It felt like Don Mannheim had reached through the newspaper with a personal invitation. All she needed was a train ticket.

"Two hundred."

Before Mr. Farrell could inquire after her plans, she snatched the stack and clicked closed her pocketbook.

"Be careful with that, now," he said. "Go straight home."

When she walked onto the street, she was reminded of the first time she'd driven, or when they took the sleds out in winter and skimmed across the icy fields. But this time, it wasn't a taste of freedom, it was real, and with that came an awareness of all she'd leave behind. Her house, Lou, the farm, even the pigs—she couldn't yet imagine her parents. But, she reminded herself, she wasn't only leaving home. She was going to a new one—and not coming back.

When she told Pat her news, he went to the back of the store. At first, she feared she'd made him angry. But when she followed him, she saw his hand pressed to his eyes. She embraced him. He patted her head, extricating himself as he cleared his throat.

She recalled again Pat's time in New York, how he'd left, how it wasn't for him, despite the draw of the theater. What kind of place was she going to?

"Pat." She felt doubt and gripped the counter. "Pat, I can't."

He met her eyes. His mouth was set in a line, the corners falling, his brow pulled down and heavy. "You must, Eleanor."

He took her by the hands, pressing paper into her fist. "Off you go."

When she got to the street, she looked. Pat had given her one hundred dollars.

By ten o'clock on Sunday, Eleanor and Rosie were exhausted and pale. They'd packed all night, then snuck out just before sunrise, Eleanor's heart pounding as she carried her suitcase a quarter-mile down the road. There, far enough from the house to hide the headlights, John Plutz picked her up—he couldn't be counted on for secrecy but loved the idea of a heist—and drove to the Dells. By the time they started to see the winding river passages for which the city was named, the excitement had worn them raw.

"My father is going to kill me," Rosie repeated for the third time since leaving. Eleanor had already asked her to stop whining; Rosie was coming by choice, and there was no theft on her part. Eleanor had left a note for her parents saying that she had to follow a dream and would write from New York. *I'm going to be on Broadway,* she'd written, boosted by the mischief of running off. Hours later, she felt sick imagining their reaction.

"You'll be back home in just a few days," Eleanor said.

In truth, Eleanor couldn't imagine facing her family again. She'd shoved as many of her belongings as she could into her suitcase. She was getting out, with or without a Broadway role. But she knew Rosie would never have agreed to go with her if she knew this move was permanent.

Rosie smiled at her, wiggling in her seat. "Two girls on the way to New York! Oh, we're going to be in so much trouble!"

After a night on the train, they were spat out onto a concrete platform, still underground. Eleanor hadn't slept. How could she, knowing she would see New York in the morning? Her body was tightly coiled, and she felt neither fatigue nor hunger. Even the air on the platform felt different. Droves of sleepy passengers flowed toward a door up ahead. The whole place smelled of oil and steam, though as she walked she caught snatches of something cooking up ahead. Nuts, and maybe meat. She memorized every detail. She would get just one first day in New York.

Rosie grasped her hand, losing her pluck now that they were in such a crowd. There was a map in Eleanor's purse, as well as a list of everywhere they were due to be: Mrs. Horton's Hotel for Girls Traveling Alone (Eleanor thought it sounded like the title of a gothic novel); Bowling Green, so they could wave at Lady Liberty; and finally, the Plymouth Theatre, where she would audition for Don Mannheim.

They reached the edge of the platform and went through the rotating doors into a gold-and-stone palace of a hall. The ceiling was magnificent, cerulean, decorated with constellations. It was so high above that Eleanor couldn't tell if the designs were made from paint or tile. Briefcase carriers crossed the space with routine in their movements, but even they glanced up, the beauty of the room holding fast despite the dulling effect of daily commutes.

"This is the train station?" Rosie's mouth was open, her head bent back. "Holy cow."

Eleanor's heart felt swollen. The floor was dirty, the lines in the marble stuffed with filth. Across the expanse was a sweeping staircase to a restaurant dressed in mahogany and golden light. In Manhattan, even the train station was glorious.

"I love it here." Suitcase in hand, Rosie began to spin, never taking her eyes off the blue masterpiece up above. "I'm in New York!"

Rosie's suitcase collided with a passing someone. She skittered to a stop and caught the glare of a man in a trench. "I'm so sorry!" She reached for Eleanor's hand. "I can't wait another moment—let's go outside, Ellie."

But Eleanor couldn't move.

Rosie grasped Eleanor's hand ever harder. "We're supposed to get a frankfurter from a street cart, Pat says."

Without answering, Eleanor walked with Rosie toward one of the exits. Her body thrummed with an excitement for what was to come, trembling with the nearness of it all. Broadway was here. The studios that produced the records she so loved, here. Don Mannheim.

She stopped at the door long enough to feel the anticipation for one last moment, then pushed it open.

The city roared.

A driver was leaning on his horn somewhere nearby. Taxis idled outside the station, their bright yellow bodies angled close to the curb so traffic could pass. Eleanor and Rosie stood under a viaduct, cars rushing above, and on either side, skyscrapers erupted from the concrete. Cigarette smoke and vehicle exhaust came from all sides. People shouldered them as they passed. Eleanor's heart pounded, and she allowed herself a moment of panic before she breathed again and watched the masses curl around each other, sidestepping, lunging for taxis, crossing the street in sling-backs. There was a rhythm. She watched a child duck a man's arm as she trotted to her mother, who continued forward with her hand stretched back, scolding her daughter to keep up. Eleanor's heart stopped rushing. While it appeared chaotic, this place was organized.

Eleanor scurried to the curb and raised her face to see the top of Grand Central. It was the most ornate building she'd ever seen. Animals were carved into the corners of the building—gargoyles, which she had seen once, on a cathedral in Milwaukee. A glance around her revealed four buildings with gargoyles just on this block.

A man knocked her to the side. "Look out, miss!"

Rosie laughed out loud. Head tipped, one hand securing her hat, she too looked at the buildings, her mouth wide with joy.

Eleanor couldn't speak, or even smile. She'd done it. All around her, the honking, the shouting, the slamming car doors—she was here.

Rosie took her hand. "Is it how you imagined?"

Eleanor squatted down and touched the sidewalk with her palm. Straightening, she looked over the crowd for a street sign, trying to get her bearings, then gasped and gripped her friend's shoulders.

"Oh, Ellie, don't—that's filthy."

"We're on Forty-Second Street." Eleanor waited a beat. "Rosie! This is the street! It's famous! Forty-Second Street—oh, couldn't you die?"

Rosie looked back at her, blank.

"This is where the theaters are, Rosie. We must be close."

Rosie set her suitcase down on the dirty concrete and sat on it, inspecting a soggy half-eaten roll in the gutter. "I don't think we should wander about."

"Tell you what. Let's stop in a diner. We'll wash up and have lunch, then make a plan. How's that sound?"

"Neat." Rosie smoothed her hair. Eleanor noticed then that her friend's hands were trembling and felt a rush of affection for her, that she had taken a risk to join her on this adventure.

"I'm starved," Eleanor said.

They couldn't waste money on taxis and had elected to avoid the subway throughout this trip, imagining shadowy figures that they both claimed they didn't fear. So they walked and found a corner diner. It was packed—they had to wait by the hostess stand, and Rosie had to turn sideways to make room for a group of girls to pass, giggling with the novelty of it all.

"I think we should order corned beef," Eleanor said when they were finally seated. "It's the special here."

"We have that at home!"

"Then what about a Reuben?"

When the waitress returned, they ordered two of them, and then settled with their map to plan the rest of the day. When the sandwiches arrived, Eleanor declared hers the best she'd ever had.

They split the bill and left, passing a group of navy men sitting at the counter drinking coffee. Rosie blushed in their presence, but Eleanor waited until they were out on the sidewalk before she teased her.

"Just passing a group of men sends you into a tizzy now?"

"My mother says navy men'll seduce you without a second thought!"

Eleanor looked up at the street signs. They were on Third Avenue. They'd escaped the bulk of the crowds, but the city seemed heavier here, like it was pressing down around them. Everywhere she looked, metal and rock. It took her a moment to realize why she felt unmoored; then she noticed there was no horizon. For most of her life, when she was outside, she had been able to see the horizon.

"But I thought we were on Lexington," Eleanor said. "We need to head east, since we're going to Sixth Avenue."

Rosie turned the map over. "If you say so."

In fifteen minutes, Eleanor had a blister on her palm from her suitcase handle. They crossed a street and reached a highway. Beyond that, water.

"What on earth?"

"The river!" Rosie moaned. "That can't be right!"

"But which one?"

"The East, knucklehead," Rosie said.

Eleanor sat on her suitcase and consulted the map and groaned. "We made a wrong turn."

"Well, don't flip your lid."

They went back in the other direction. Eleanor felt another blister forming on her heel. It was too hot in New York. The pavement reflected the heat back up so it wafted beneath her skirt, like she was baking in an oven. By the time they reached the diner again, sweat pooled between her legs, her thighs burning as they chafed together.

"We're just blocks from Grand Central," Eleanor said. "We can ask directions there."

Rosie watched the passersby. "But that will let people know we're from out of town."

"We are from out of town. And you said—"

"Do you want to get mugged, Eleanor?"

She didn't answer. Admitting defeat was like saying she didn't belong. Wasn't New York the benchmark for success? She refused to be the kind of person who didn't like it.

Eleanor looked through the window of the diner.

"We'll ask one of the navy boys." She spoke loud to cover her doubt and opened the door before Rosie could stop her.

"Excuse me." Eleanor approached the men and pitched her voice down and stilled her body, thinking if she didn't advertise her femininity, they wouldn't notice.

No such luck. Three men in olive drab swiveled around on their stools. One was still chewing.

"We're new here," she said, glancing at Rosie next to her. "Can one of you gentlemen please point us in the right direction?"

"Why don't you take a seat right here?" the tallest man said, blond and gangly. He patted the seat next to him and winked at Rosie. "Have a milkshake."

Eleanor would kill her if she said yes. "We're actually on a schedule? On our way to a hotel, and have to check in by a certain time?"

The man in the middle stood up. He was stockier than the other men, less boyish. He had a wide face and a strong jaw, dark hair that curled like an Irishman's, and startling blue eyes. He had the look of a gentleman, a man who would call a skirt a dress and a bow a thingummy.

"My name's Tommy Murphy." He wiped his hands on a napkin before he shook Eleanor's. She noticed his shoulders moving beneath his uniform. He had calluses on his palms. His friends made coy noises that he ignored. "Where are you ladies going?"

Eleanor surveyed his friends. Should she give the address in front of them? Didn't people say it was dangerous to do that?

Tommy pulled out his wallet and thumbed bills onto the counter. "C'mon, I'll walk you."

Her scruples dissolved along with their convenience; this young navy man could be as randy as the gossip said, but he wasn't likely to leave them bleeding in an alley. She resisted the urge to turn to Rosie and raise her eyebrows to gloat.

"Thank you, sir," Rosie said. "Or should we call you something more professional?"

"I'm a yeoman," he said. "Tommy is fine."

He didn't look like the type to push papers. Her mother would approve of a young man who did his duty but made sure he came home at the end of it.

When they stepped out of the diner, they gave him the address and he offered his hand. "Which of you has the heavier suitcase?"

"Rosie," Eleanor said. "She always overpacks."

"Eleanor!"

But she held on to her own luggage; if Rosie knew how much she'd shoved into it, she'd know that Eleanor had no intention of returning on the Thursday train.

"I'm Eleanor O'Hanlon." She nodded at Rosie. "This is my friend Rosie Hughes."

"How nice to meet you." Tommy spoke so politely that you could hear the training behind it, as if his mother were manipulating the words right out of him. "Where are you ladies from?"

"Wisconsin."

"Hmm. So which one of you wants to be an actress?"

Eleanor's heart flared. He would assume it was Rosie, because that was what people did.

"How did you know Eleanor wants to be an actress?" Rosie asked.

"Girls like you only come through here to visit family, get married, or audition for the shows." He turned his head to check the traffic, and Eleanor caught a whiff of tobacco.

"Girls like us?" Rosie said, her practiced flirt coming out.

"Nice girls," Tommy said, "with no idea what they're doing."

"That's not true," Eleanor said. "Women must come here for other reasons."

"But you are auditioning for a musical, am I right?" He winked.

Eleanor shut her mouth and focused on her surroundings. They were coming up on a park that was about a city block long on each side and surrounded by tall buildings. When they crossed the street, they entered to cut through it.

"Don't ever come here at night," Tommy said.

"Is this Central Park?" Rosie asked. "Because I know we're not supposed to go there at night."

"Central Park is up farther," Tommy said. "This is Bryant Park."

It was nice of him not to point out how obvious this was; Eleanor hadn't known its name, but even she knew this place wasn't big enough to be the famous Central Park.

The Broadway theaters should have been just a block away. Eleanor felt their proximity. Would they be enormous or small? It would be lovely if they were small.

"Can we keep going?" Eleanor asked.

"We're supposed to take Sixth Ave uptown," Tommy said.

"I know, but we're so close. I want to see them." He gave Eleanor a curious look, and she was impatient with his confusion. "The theaters."

"She okay?" Tommy asked Rosie.

"You might have seen other girls audition for Broadway shows," Rosie said, "but you haven't met Eleanor. She lives for the theater."

Tommy acquiesced, and they continued walking and were soon coming up on Broadway. Eleanor felt the moisture leave her mouth. All down her arms, her skin prickled, and her hands went cold.

"Look to your right, Eleanor," Tommy said with a smile in his voice. "Times Square."

In the movies, the ingénue always lifted her arms as if she could take in the whole world. Eleanor herself had planned to spin and yelp when she reached Times Square. She'd directed her first entrance to New York dozens of times in her mind.

But all she could do was stare. Her eyes filled with tears. She raised her hands to her mouth.

It was the most colorful place in the world. There were painted signs covering every surface. A giant Canadian Club Whiskey billboard stared her in the face, but it was blocks away. Neon letters mounted on scaffolding advertised beer, cigarettes, Kleenex, televisions, clubs with names that made Eleanor blush. Enormous statues of Pepsi bottles sat on the roof of a clothing store. It was as if she'd walked onto the pages of a catalog. Then she looked at each of the storefronts and saw the marquees. Even just seeing the theaters, sleepy during the daytime, made Eleanor feel like she'd met her heroes.

"The New Amsterdam," Eleanor said. "That used to be where Ziegfeld had his *Follies*. It's a cinema now."

"I thought you said you haven't been here before."

Eleanor had quite forgotten Tommy was there.

"I've read about it." Eleanor's feet wanted to move, and her skin itched. There was a tugging feeling in her stomach. She walked ahead and waved at her companions to hurry up and cross the street.

"This one still operates," she said, hustling them down Forty-First Street. "The National."

"I didn't think anyone knew the names of these places," Tommy said.

"Eleanor knows all the names," Rosie said, "and their intersections. She memorized the map when we were fourteen."

"I remember when I first learned that they weren't all on Broadway." Eleanor shook her head. "I couldn't believe it!"

"I never thought about that," Tommy said.

Rosie raised an eyebrow. "If you spend more time with Eleanor, you'll hear buckets of things about theater you didn't care about before."

Tommy smirked. "Or since."

Then Eleanor stopped in her tracks, suddenly quiet. "There it is," she said. "A real theater."

The Broadhurst was an unassuming building to anyone else, but to her, it was holy. It was large and square, with a balcony lining the front top floor and a marquee hanging over four sets of double doors. Every night, a thousand people filed through those doors. What would it be like to go backstage? It must have thrummed with activity. The crew, the orchestra, the director, the wardrobe personnel, the actors. An entire building filled with people living their dream. Dozens of people who loved the theater as much as Eleanor did.

Rosie reached for her hand and squeezed.

They stood there for a long while before Rosie convinced Eleanor it was time to move. They turned west. Eleanor looked behind her, watching the bright colors slip behind the cold steel of the skyscrapers, until it was gone.

Tommy walked them the rest of the way, growing more animated as they went. He liked being a tour guide. He told stories about fun nights with his buddies and pointed out places to get a cheap dinner or where they might find a kind shopkeeper if they ran into trouble at night. Eleanor felt a flurry at his words, at the idea that they would stay a lot longer than three days. Eleanor listened as if she were hearing a preview of her life. The thought of her parents gave her more than a pang, but she refused to bow to the guilt. When Tommy dropped them off in front of their hotel, he wished them both luck and kissed Eleanor on the cheek.

"Next time I see you," he said, "you'll be a Broadway actress."

Eleanor watched him go. She'd convinced at least one person.

Chapter Three

Eleanor knew she had reached the Plymouth Theatre when she saw a line of girls wrapped around the block. Most of them stood in twos or threes chatting animatedly, even though it was seven o'clock in the morning. She stopped on the opposite street corner to take it all in. Many of these girls had what she imagined were Broadway legs—long and slim, made to wear those beaded leotards she'd seen in pictures of revues. In Eleanor's experience, there were pretty girls and plain girls, fat ones and thin ones, but that was the limit of the qualitative assessments. But in the face of her competition, she became aware of a hundred new ways to feel inadequate. Eleanor was neither fat nor thin; her body was strong and substantial. Her complexion was smooth but freckled. Her copper hair was all that distinguished her in this crowd of beautiful girls. She'd never been the loveliest girl, nor the plainest. But once in line, she felt the thickness of her thighs, the stubbiness of her hands, the roundness of her cheeks. As though her origins could be read on her face, Eleanor was sure she looked like one of the pigs on her farm. But none of these insecurities would hurt as much as whatever way she fell short against the girl who would win the part.

Eleanor wished she didn't want the role so desperately. It pushed her into fear and disquiet, out of the town where she had the best voice and into an audition with hundreds of others in New York.

Eleanor thought of returning to Wisconsin—facing her father's disappointment, listening to her mother recount every time she'd risen early to sell pies at the market to afford the bonds that Eleanor had taken in one selfish blow. She thought of John Plutz, who had been so tickled when she said she was auditioning for a Broadway show that she may have led him to believe she'd been personally invited. What would Pat think of her, giving up after she'd made it all this way? *It wasn't for me*, he'd said.

Eleanor needed this place to be for her. If she returned home, she would never live down the shame or regret. And then what was left? Managing Pat's store, growing old with only the records as company? Dodging comments from the people in town who had always made fun of her ambitions and who now had even more of an excuse? Eleanor could not allow that to happen.

The early morning air gave a touch of freshness to the otherwise smoggy Times Square. It was cool without humidity—back-to-school air. Eleanor let it work on her, then stepped across the street.

Two girls beat her to the end of the line. For some reason, Eleanor felt more threatened by these two than all the rest, as if watching them assume her spot in line was foreshadowing for what would happen in the audition. One of the girls was a short redhead, her hair more brilliant than Eleanor's, the other tall and reedy.

"I hope they make us dance," the redhead was saying. "Though you'll be better than me."

Dance? Was that even an option? Eleanor had memorized the *Charades* audition notice. Dancing wasn't mentioned. Sixteen bars of your best musical theater ballad, the ad had specified. Eleanor had brought three choices. In addition to "The Man I Love," she'd brought a Don Mannheim selection called "Somebody" and a piece by a composer called Marc Blitzstein titled "I Wish It So."

The auditions began at ten. How early had the first girl in line arrived? Eleanor shuddered at the thought that there were girls here who might do more for a role. Vague images ran through her head of experience she didn't have and games she didn't understand. She had heard of the casting couch. She'd never done more than kiss a boy. In the privacy of her mind, she admitted she would do anything for the role if she knew how.

After an hour, a young man holding a coffee in a cardboard cup came by with a sign-up list. Eleanor gave him her brightest smile.

After another hour, the line began to move.

"I thought the auditions were at ten?"

The redhead in front of her turned. Eleanor noticed her whole face was freckled, in an uncommon but pleasing way. She held herself like she wasn't even embarrassed about them, as Eleanor was about her own. This girl had the high-volume version of Eleanor's looks: her hair flame, her eyes bright amber. She looked at Eleanor like she could not have been more bored with her question, shrugged, and resumed her conversation with her willowy friend.

The line continued to move slowly. Eleanor was now even with the marquee. It wasn't lit up because it was daylight, but she could see the bulbs. The logo was bright blue with yellow accents, and in the morning sun, the artificial colors and modern font clashed against the sky. Everything in Times Square did. Standing there, looking up at the blue and remembering she was on Earth, the same place that held trees and creeks and Wisconsin, she felt vertigo.

The line moved again, and she was at the box office door. Through it she could see deep-red plush carpet, the walls beige with golden accents running along the bottoms. Behind another set of doors was the actual theater. Before she could stop herself, she began to cry.

Crying was terrible for singers. Talking through tears was hard enough; sustaining notes was a trick, and controlling vibrato was next to impossible. Eleanor shut her eyes tight and tried to breathe, too loud. Once again she attracted the attention of the girls in front of her.

"Are you all right? You look like you're about to keel over."

"I'm fine," Eleanor said. "Just overcome. I've never been to New York before."

The girls softened, as if she were a child. "How do you like it?"

None of the words that came to mind were enough. "I want to live here."

The redhead touched Eleanor's arm. "Darling, no you don't. I've lived here my whole life and I can tell you Manhattan is on the way to the dump."

Eleanor thought the girl was lucky to be worldly enough to hate this place.

"I've never been in a Broadway theater either," she said before she could stop herself.

The girls looked surprised at this. Eleanor didn't know why—if she hadn't been to New York, then she hadn't been to a theater.

"My name's Maggie Carmichael, and this is Lisa." Maggie, the redhead, nodded to her friend. "I grew up on the Upper East Side."

So close to where Don Mannheim lived. "Where are you living now?" Eleanor asked.

"Excuse me?"

"You said you grew up on the Upper East Side," Eleanor said. "Do you still live there?"

"No. Two friends and I have an apartment in Hell's Kitchen, on the corner of Eighth and Forty-Third."

Something rang a bell, until she remembered Tommy's warning about Eighth Avenue. "Do you like it there?"

"Sure. A girl's gotta audition, and the apartment's close to the theaters. Where are you from?" Maggie's eyes looked expectant. Something inside of Eleanor turned over and rose up, like an animal awaking from sleep. This girl was a predator, and Eleanor must not let her take a bite.

"The Midwest. Near Chicago."

"I've always wanted to go there," Maggie said.

Me too, Eleanor thought. The line began to move again.

Eleanor alternated between checking her watch and lifting her aching feet off the ground, and panicking as she got closer to the front of the line. If she weren't so nervous, she'd have been hungry; after four hours in line, she had left just once, to use the ladies'.

Then the young man returned.

"Name?"

"Eleanor O'Hanlon."

He held out his hand. Eleanor shook it.

He blinked in annoyance. "Headshot and résumé, please." Maggie turned and giggled.

Eleanor realized her mistake and pulled out her résumé, a typed-up list of her choir solos, with a photograph paper-clipped to the top, and handed it to him.

The man scanned her paltry résumé but did not offer opinions.

"You three can go in." He indicated Maggie, Lisa, and Eleanor.

Eleanor felt a twist. It was time. Don Mannheim was inside.

She stepped through the box office doors, then to an open door off to the side.

Backstage at the Plymouth. Her skin prickled with awareness. It smelled like sawdust. The hall was bright, with tile floors and beige-painted walls. Facing her was a cork bulletin board, where a sign-in sheet hung. She peered and saw scribbled initials of various members of the cast, starting yesterday and going back two weeks. Eleanor recognized some of the names from the newspapers.

The stage, according to large white letters, was beyond a pair of double doors. All of her senses reeled. Despite her feelings about her companions, she couldn't stay quiet.

"He's in there," she said. "Isn't that amazing?"

Maggie smiled with half of her mouth, but in her expression was true excitement even she could not conceal. "It's the scariest thing in the world, when what you want is so close."

Eleanor agreed so much that she couldn't respond.

"It's so hard when the role is an ingénue," Maggie said. "You know?"

Eleanor didn't.

"Every girl thinks she's an ingénue. Anyone under thirty or a hundred fifty pounds comes out for these auditions." She rolled her eyes. "Some people don't understand type."

Eleanor had not weighed herself in years and took in that number with some trepidation. "Type?"

Maggie looked at her like she was an idiot. "You know. Ingénue. Soubrette. Siren. Matron. Et cetera."

Eleanor knew those words but hadn't realized they were so ironclad. The roles themselves might have been confined that way: the beautiful young lover, the flirt, the very sexy woman, the comedic older-woman character. But were actresses, too?

"Do you mean people can only play certain roles?"

"Well, I mean, people can play whatever roles the director casts them in," Maggie said. "But for the most part, directors look at a girl and know who she should play. For example, I always play ingénues."

Eleanor felt a rush so powerful that she clenched her fists. She smiled. "So do I."

She faced the wall so she could ready herself for the coming moment. This close to the stage, she could hear another actress's audition. The girl was terrible. She pushed her voice past its comfortable point, so she yelled rather than sang.

Maybe I have a chance, Eleanor thought. Her fear melted away in favor of bullheaded pragmatism. She turned to the young man with the clipboard. "Water?"

He pointed around the corner at a cooler with paper cones. Eleanor warmed the water in her mouth before swallowing so as not to contract the muscles in her throat. Next she gargled, then massaged her throat, face, shoulders. Enunciating silently to warm up her facial muscles, she clenched her fists hard, then let go and touched her toes, breathing as deep as she could. It was amazing how preparation could quiet her mind.

The music was in her body; she could no more forget the lyrics than forget her own name. The places where she'd stop to breathe or crescendo were ingrained. Eleanor was talented, but moreover, she was prepared.

Maggie went in when the other girl finished, but Eleanor knew better than to listen. If Maggie was good, all this mental centering could be disrupted. She continued to stretch and think through the song in her head.

In less than two minutes, Maggie emerged from backstage.

"That's it?" Eleanor asked.

Maggie did not seem upset. "I sang, they asked me about my dancing, then I left."

"Who was in there?"

"Harry Flynn and Len Price," Maggie said. "A producer."

"Don Mannheim wasn't there?"

"Guess not. It doesn't matter. Harry Flynn is the one to impress, if you ask me. He is the director, after all. They say he's the meanest man in the business."

Even Eleanor had heard that. His bitter tongue was so infamous it was mentioned in reviews. She tried not to think about Don's absence—she'd burned to see him, but if she won the part, she'd see him all the time.

Maggie flipped her hair. "Break a leg."

Eleanor took deep breaths before Lisa emerged next, looking upset. Eleanor didn't even have time to pretend to be polite before the clipboard man returned.

"Eleanor?" he asked.

Eleanor felt something in her throat. She needed more water, but there wasn't time.

"Go in, give your music to the accompanist, and stand center."

She barreled through the doors and almost missed that she was backstage at a Broadway theater, then stopped. Set pieces were tucked off to the side, and on an ordinary day she would have killed to explore all of them. The smell of sawdust calmed her. It reminded her of Pat's store and his cardboard inventory boxes. She took in her surroundings for another moment, and then walked out of the wings, onto the stage.

"Eleanor?"

The lights were too bright to see. Harry Flynn was in the middle somewhere. Her eyes adjusted enough to spot him in the audience. She recognized his thin face from photographs. He was a long-boned man with a background in ballet. A large gray-haired man sat beside him.

"Where are you from, Eleanor?"

Was he supposed to ask these questions?

"Wisconsin." Her voice was too soft. She repeated herself and waited for him to ask something else. He didn't.

Her feet were sweating; they slid in her pumps, and she knew her walk was funny. The pianist was downstage on the lip, behind an upright.

She crossed to him and plopped her music down.

"I'll be starting with 'The Man I Love.'" Leaning over the piano, she conducted a tempo, humming along.

The man paged through her music, passing the Gershwin piece and stopping at the Blitzstein. Was he listening?

She tried not to sound nervous. "That's my second choice."

He looked up and speared her with a stare. "I know."

Eleanor's body recognized him before her mind. She felt a drop in her stomach, coolness in her hands and feet. The man at the piano was Don Mannheim.

Behind the piano, he was both smaller and larger than she'd expected. Smaller because the idea of him had swelled enormous in her mind. Larger because Eleanor always imagined intellectual men to be slight and thin wristed; Don had broad shoulders and a burly chest. His jeans and a sweater were so regular they looked wrong on him. Coffee stained his cuff. His hair, almost as dark as it was in the black-and-white photographs, was mussed instead of slicked back, and shadowed his chin and cheeks. There was tightness in his body when he sat, and even though she knew he was a talented piano player, he lacked the ease of a pianist. He looked tense and volatile, his leg jiggling. His demeanor was of anxious impatience, as if he were being scratched by the air around him. This was so noticeable, and so opposite what she had imagined, that Eleanor had to recast him in her mind. Don Mannheim, the genius, was a nervous man.

He nodded, acknowledging her recognition without any performed kindness, then looked at the music. At once, his awkwardness made sense. He wasn't timid or jittery; when Don looked at the music, his eyes took on the tight focus of a man with augmented concentration. He flipped through her pages and then looked at her, as if imagining her performing each song. He was so intense that she understood now why his musicals were so good. Don Mannheim was at home in his area of genius.

"I love Blitzstein." Black hair crept up the backs of his hands and grew on his knuckles. His nails were cropped short, and he had a bruise under one of them, like he'd slammed a finger in a door. She was glad to know these intimate details and ran her eyes over his body, collecting more to replay in her mind later. His legs were thin. Beneath the neck of his sweater, she saw a furry chest. She watched his irises move back and forth, reading the music like it was a sentence in a book.

He played the first measures, thrilling her. As soon as he pressed the keys, the tension in his body was directed toward the music. His eyes were intense, but he swayed with the melody. Eleanor felt a flip in her stomach, watching him move.

He stopped abruptly. "Sing this."

"What?"

"I want to hear you sing this." His voice was quiet and deep. When he looked up, she was aware of having all of his attention, but he didn't meet her eyes. "What is your tempo?"

They were so close, his gaze boring into her, before his eyes flicked away, then down. He was real, and he smelled like soap. It was difficult to move her body, as she was so struck by Don's presence. She hummed the music. He played a section. "Like this?"

"Yes."

"Whenever you're ready."

She crossed to center stage.

"Come forward," Harry Flynn called from the audience. She stepped downstage. "Good."

She looked toward the back of the house, black beyond the lights, and centered herself. For one moment, she tried to forget where she was. The song was about wanting something so much you can't sleep. She took a breath, took one more step, and Don began to play.

The first three notes, the sorrowful sound, froze her, and she was sure she would forget the lyrics. But then he kept playing, and she continued, the words coming from her as if her mind had nothing to do with it. She sang, and her breath came full and easy, infusing her voice with depth and power. At her best, she felt her voice resonate in her head, her neck, her stomach, even where her lungs opened up against her ribs in her back. The music came from every inch of her.

As the music swelled to the bridge, she took a breath and stepped forward, her hands reaching out. Everything vanished except the music and the story she was telling.

Then Don stopped playing.

"Thank you," Harry said.

Eleanor blinked.

"That was great," Harry continued. "Thank you for coming in, Eleanor."

Her cut had three more phrases left, but she gathered herself enough to smile, then infused her voice with as much happiness as she could. "Thank you!"

How did one walk across the stage like a star?

She took the music from Don's outstretched hand. He watched her as if he wanted to ask her something but said nothing except, "Thank you."

By the time she reached the wings, she had started to cry.

"You were in there a long time," Maggie said, voice sharpened by jealousy. "You sounded beautiful."

Eleanor was already walking to the door. "So did you."

When she returned to their hotel, Eleanor found Rosie on the bed reading a guidebook.

She tossed it aside as soon as Eleanor was in the door. "How was it?"

Eleanor felt like she'd lived an entire lifetime in a few hours but wasn't ready to speak of any of it yet. "What did you do all day?" she asked instead of answering.

Rosie barely hesitated before continuing. "I went to the Metropolitan Museum of Art! I could have spent all day in the Egyptian wing, but then I found the medieval armor . . . I've never seen anything like that. Of course I've heard all about knights and such but seeing their suits of armor—to know someone wore that, and died in it—it was another thing altogether."

Like auditioning for a Broadway show and meeting one's idol— another thing altogether.

Rosie sighed. "I never want to go back home."

Eleanor had not let herself think beyond today. She had stopped her thoughts outside the door to the audition, as if her life would hover there in perpetuity.

"You look like you need to eat," Rosie said. "Do you want a nap?"

"No." She'd given two phone numbers on her résumé: one for the hotel, the other for Pat's store. She didn't want her parents to pick up. Her eyes fell on the phone that sat between the narrow hotel beds. "Let's go."

Shopping was out of the question, so they explored the neighborhoods they'd circled on their map. Eleanor was glad Rosie had gone to the Met without her, since wandering galleries seemed like a waste of time when there was so much city to see. They walked until their blisters opened up again. Eleanor made Rosie stand outside the theaters with her at intermission. She'd heard about "second-acting"—sneaking into the theater with the smokers in order to stand in back—but at the last moment, she lost her nerve.

They ended up at another diner, trying matzo ball soup.

"You still haven't told me anything about the audition."

Eleanor put down her water glass and shrugged.

"We came all this way and you won't even tell me." Rosie looked perturbed.

How could she explain it? The experience was neither letdown nor triumph. If Eleanor tried to define it in words, she'd end up on one side of the issue and either get her hopes up or condemn herself.

"Was Don Mannheim there? Did he hear you sing?"

In Wisconsin, you couldn't see outside at night; the windows would turn black. Her mother always pulled the curtains closed so people couldn't see in, even though no one was ever in their yard but the pigs. In New York, the streetlamps were bright enough that the people were bathed in an orange glow and could be seen from inside the diner. A girl wearing jeans and a turtleneck that didn't cover her stomach accepted a cigarette from a young man outside. She kissed his cheek, her mouth lingering over a day's growth of beard.

"No, he wasn't there," Eleanor said, turning back to Rosie. "I don't think the audition was as important as we thought."

Rosie's expression dimmed. "Really?"

Eleanor shrugged. "It was a waste of time and money."

Rosie straightened her shoulders. "Well, there are two days left, and we won't let this ruin them."

But the trip wasn't ruined. When they returned to the hotel that night, the front desk presented Eleanor with a written message.

She was due at the Plymouth Theatre the following day, ten o'clock. Prepare nothing. Wear high heels.

Chapter Four

This time there were only ten girls at the Plymouth. Impossible not to compare herself in a crowd this small. Eleanor was, without a doubt, the stockiest one. Three had long legs. One was thin as a rail. Another was Maggie.

"Hi," Maggie said, a moment of panic showing on her face before she could mask it with a smile. "Glad to see you here."

"You as well." They were lined up in the hallway. Each of the girls stood like a giraffe in her highest heels. Eleanor had shoved her feet into Rosie's red size sevens. "What do you think we're going to do today?"

Maggie shrugged. "I've been off book since I was called in to audition last time."

"Last time?"

"I've been in for this role before," Maggie said. "Made it to the final round last time. I'm sure they'll have us sing from the show, read some lines. Do you know the music?"

Eleanor did know it but hadn't thought about the script. She'd never even read the lines. "Will they give us copies of the script?"

"You mean sides?"

Sides? "I mean I'm not memorized."

Maggie touched her arm. "I'm sure that's fine," she said. "I'm always memorized, but that's just me. I like to be prepared."

"And you auditioned for *Charades* before?"

"Sure. I audition for everything." Maggie checked her lipstick in a compact mirror. "Listen, I don't mean to be rude, but I need to take my time before I go in there. I don't want to mess this up."

Eleanor should have been doing the same, especially if she didn't even know the script. Maggie had made it to the final round before—did that mean she stood more of a chance or less? On one hand, they liked her. But she'd lost the part once. Eleanor scooted farther away and closed her eyes, hoping that calm would come over her. It didn't. She had no music to review, no lines to memorize, nothing to ease her nerves.

Each girl was called into the theater for a different amount of time, but it was clear the longer, the better. A girl with stunning blond hair emerged after two minutes, in tears. Another did not come out for forty minutes and smiled at everyone, refusing to mention what she'd had to do inside. Eleanor's adrenaline had prevented her from eating breakfast, and her nerves had a muting effect on her hunger. But by one o'clock, her stomach growled. Maggie had gone in an entire hour earlier.

When Maggie emerged, she looked exhausted but happy. The first real smile Eleanor had seen shone on her face. There was an innocence hanging over her as she glowed, happy with herself. "I hope we both get in, some way."

She meant she hoped Eleanor would be her understudy. "Me, too."

Eleanor waited to be called. After five minutes, the door to the stage opened. A man came out and glanced her way without saying anything. It was Harry Flynn. He passed her, slim legs taking him down the hall long before she mustered the courage to speak.

Eleanor looked around until she saw the young man with the clipboard who had supervised both of the auditions.

"Excuse me," she said. "When is it my turn?"

He looked down at his papers. "Are you Eleanor?"

"Yes." Eleanor clenched and unclenched her toes in Rosie's shoes.

"I'll bring you in when they tell me to."

"I saw Harry Flynn leave."

"Time for lunch."

"So what do I do?"

"Whatever you want."

Eleanor leaned against the wall. Five minutes went by that felt like twenty, and then another five. Then the door to the stage opened.

"Eleanor?"

Don Mannheim emerged.

Her mouth went dry.

He was wearing a gray sweatshirt. Apart from the audition the previous day, Eleanor had only seen him in photographs from the openings of his musicals, wearing a tuxedo. His body looked warm and masculine, his fingers drumming on his leg. His gaze was so intense she had to look away, but again, he didn't quite meet her eyes, just examined her face and body. He would notice her hem had been let down.

"Come on in, Eleanor."

"What about Mr. Flynn?"

"I called you in here myself." He spoke in a crisp manner. When he met her extended gaze, he looked away, calling to mind a child uncomfortable in the company of adults.

She followed Don inside and he crossed the stage, his shoes making no sound on the floor. She felt goofy in her clacking heels. The house lights were on, so every empty red seat stared back at her. With the spotlights off, she could see down into the orchestra pit. The chairs were empty and haphazard, like the whole orchestra had abruptly stood up and left. The larger instruments had been left behind: a bass leaned on its side, a grand piano with its lid closed, a harp balanced on its stand. She stopped and breathed.

Don watched her. Eleanor waited for him to reply with something understanding, some appreciation of the empty theater.

"This is not a callback." He sat behind the upright piano that had been wheeled onstage.

The thoughts flooding her head embarrassed her with their eagerness. Don wouldn't waste time calling her in for no reason. What if he was as captured by her as she was by him? What if he was going to offer her the part, right here, right now?

"I like your voice," he said.

Eleanor crossed the stage as fast as possible until she hovered by his shoulder. Sheet music was spread against the piano, with handwritten notes on the staff.

"You have an interesting sound. The Blitzstein was a good choice."

"Thank you."

"Did your teacher give it to you?"

"No, sir," she said. "I haven't had a teacher."

"Good. Don't get one. You have a rough sound. There's that dangerous warble at the end of your phrases. No teacher could resist smoothing it out. You'd be a good student, too, wouldn't you?"

Eleanor had no idea what he was asking.

"Don't let them ruin your sound. It's fascinating."

"I do even better on the Gershwin," she said.

"No. That's not a good song for you." He pointed to the music on the page, hit a chord with both hands. "Here's the key, Eleanor. You read music?"

His handwriting was horrific. He worked in a felt-tip, so she couldn't see whether some of the note heads were open or closed, and had to guess how long to hold them.

"Good sight reader?"

"Your handwriting—"

"Don't worry about the words. Sing 'la' if you can't read them. I want to hear you sing the music. Start at measure eight. I'll play a two-bar intro. Follow along."

He played a slow Alberti bass with his left hand, sustained chords with his right. It was a touch below walking tempo, slow enough that she could get her bearings. He played very loud, slamming the keys, in his customary dissonant style.

She felt herself falter. Her ears were good, but without knowing the melody, the notes coming from Don's right hand were close enough to her vocal line that she was mixing them up, until she felt her voice dipping under the pitch.

You're messing this up, she thought. *Don must be laughing at you. You're screwing up your one chance. You're going to have to go back to Wisconsin, and that will kill you.*

"Thanks, Eleanor." Don took his hands off the keys. He didn't look at her yet and seemed to be thinking about something.

Eleanor waited for what she hoped was a reasonable time. "I can try again," she said.

"No," he said, still thinking. "That's enough. Thanks for coming in, Eleanor."

This time, she didn't wait until the hallway to start crying.

When Eleanor told her she was not going back to Wisconsin, Rosie was unsurprised.

"But where will you live?"

"I met some girls at the audition," Eleanor said, the idea coming to her as she spoke. "They're looking for another girl for their apartment."

Rosie did not look convinced. "What about a job? Your parents?"

"My parents will be upset." Eleanor tried to think of a "but" and none came. Rosie didn't even know what Eleanor had done to come here.

"And a job?"

"I got a gig working at a tailor shop." This, at last, was almost true: Eleanor had passed one on her way to the hotel and inquired about the Help Wanted sign in the window. She'd go back the following day to meet the owner.

The owner, an old man named Mr. Rabinowitz, had written down her name. "Can you sew?"

"I made clothes for my whole family." This was also true; she wasn't as good as Rosie but knew her way around a seam. "Men's, too. I'm good with shirts and hems."

Rosie chewed her lip, making her look even more like a squirrel than usual.

"They pay enough."

"New York is dangerous."

"I can take care of myself. Besides, it's only been three days. My street smarts will come." She shook Rosie's arm. "Come on, Rosie. Did you really think I was going home?"

"I knew you wouldn't. But that didn't mean I liked it."

Rosie was so dear; her small, oldest friend. Everything about her—the dark hair on her arms, her pressed cotton blouses, the neat little earrings she took care to wear—tugged at something inside Eleanor.

Eleanor thought about the callback, the way she had failed in her one chance with Don, and wanted to tell Rosie. But the weight of what had happened sat on her, until she felt her tongue swell and her eyes fill with tears. It was too horrible. Grief unlike any she'd ever known was setting in. Her dreams, they were all gone.

"I'll die if I go back home. I'll grow old in a record store selling Perry Como. Even if this doesn't work, even if I never set foot on another stage in New York, I have to be here."

Thursday, Eleanor woke early to take Rosie to the train station.

"You promise to write?" Rosie said, fiddling with the strap of her pocketbook as they walked.

"Of course."

"But people say that and then don't." A crease had shown up between her eyebrows. "Promise me, Eleanor. You're my best friend."

"I promise. I already told you."

"What am I going to do in Wisconsin by myself?"

It hadn't occurred to Eleanor that Rosie might also have wanted to stay in New York. With only a few blocks left before they reached Grand Central, she felt her stomach clench. She hadn't been listening to her friend this entire week.

"You can marry John Plutz. After all, he did provide our getaway car."

Rosie looked disappointed. "We might not all dream of Broadway," she said. "But that doesn't mean I ever wanted to marry John Plutz."

"But you said—"

"I'm not so dull and small-town as you think, Eleanor."

Rosie did not look any less miserable by the time she boarded the train. Eleanor kissed her cheeks, feeling guilty. She knew she had the tendency to drive right over people and didn't like doing so to Rosie.

"Come back and visit?"

"If I can."

"Lock the door to your train car."

Rosie hugged Eleanor once more. "I love you. I'll miss you."

"Tell my parents—"

"No, darling. That's your job."

Eleanor kissed her again. "I'll write to them today."

To keep herself from crying, Eleanor stepped into a souvenir shop and poked through postcards. Now that Rosie was gone, a terrible feeling had rolled in like fog. Eleanor had a dwindling supply of money and nowhere permanent to live. She was due to start work soon, but other than that, she had no plans. By the time she had selected a Statue of Liberty postcard, she was in despair.

When she cried, she liked a milkshake to cheer her up. Remembering the diner, she walked east and sat at the counter. Already this lifted her spirits, knowing a familiar place to go.

She had settled in to read the ads on the back of the menu when she felt a tap on her shoulder. A smiling face appeared over her shoulder; it was the naval pilot from their first day.

"Hello," she said. His grin eased her. "Johnny?"

"Tommy," he said, but didn't sound offended. "It's Eleanor, right? May I join you?"

She hesitated, then nodded. "I guess I've invaded your regular place."

Last time they'd met, Eleanor had been too nervous to notice the openness of his face, the way his eyes were clear and blue, or the crinkles on the outsides of them when he smiled. "How's the theater?"

Eleanor dropped her head in her hands. "Oh, I don't know what I was thinking."

"Maybe we need something stronger than a milkshake?" He held his palms open. "I'm a gentleman, I swear. I'd be otherwise, but my mother would kill me."

She smiled. "Sure, but I'm going to finish the milkshake first."

Four hours later, Tommy walked Eleanor home. She swayed on the sidewalk, pleasantly drunk, until he grasped her arm in his hand.

"I don't know why I stayed," she said around a hiccup. "What has it gotten me? My friend left, I have no place to live, and now I'm drunk in the middle of the day. I'm a wreck."

"Maybe so," he said, touching her chin. "But an awfully cute one."

She grimaced. "I think that's the problem. Too Midwestern." She'd told him everything, from the audition to Rosie's departure, even lingering on her love and fear of Pat and his shop. Tommy was a good listener.

"No problem for me." He twirled some of her hair around his finger, and it glowed red in the setting sun. "Can I kiss you?"

When boys in Wisconsin asked, it was with a smarmy and false chivalry. When Tommy asked, his voice rasped, desire clear. His hand moved to her waist, indicating his intentions in a way she found more persuasive. She lifted her chin.

Right before his lips touched hers, another face flashed in her mind. She thought of Don, the fool she'd made of herself in front of him. What would he think of her, the country girl, kissing a boy on a dirty New York sidewalk?

Chapter Five

Eleanor waited at the corner of Eighth Avenue and Forty-Third Street for two hours. She held herself stiffly, afraid of a man propositioning her, but no one approached. As she was getting hungry, she saw Maggie Carmichael turn the corner. Eleanor hustled over to her.

"Maggie!"

She turned around, confused and annoyed. When she saw Eleanor, she widened her eyes.

Before she could get too nervous to ask, Eleanor said, "I was wondering if I could live with you."

Maggie offered the kind of grin that comes out when one can't settle on an expression. "Come upstairs?"

The apartment was messy but not dirty. There wasn't enough room for all the girls' things, so shoes cluttered the whole length of the entry hall. A bookshelf with plays, family photos from three different clans, and a stack of audition magazines made up one wall. Maggie scooped up a few dresses that had been laid across the couch and gestured that Eleanor should sit, hooking her finger to pick up a mug with a dried tea bag stuck to the side.

"So tell me! What's going on with you?" she asked on her way to the kitchen.

"You must think I'm crazy."

"I have water and gin," Maggie said.

"Gin."

Maggie appeared with two glasses in hand.

"I'm staying in New York," Eleanor said. "I can't go back to Wisconsin."

Freckles covered the tops of Maggie's feet and ankles, going up her calves until they disappeared beneath her skirt. "It happens to the best of us."

"Do you have room on your couch?" Eleanor asked. "If you go from splitting your rent three ways to four, it will be better for everyone. I'm clean and I'll be working or auditioning. What do you say?"

"I have to ask the other girls."

Eleanor ran through things she could say, high points she'd left out, benefits to her presence that might convince Maggie, but saw that Maggie didn't want to hear them. "I'll write down the hotel number."

"Don't go ape," Maggie said. "I haven't asked yet."

Eleanor blushed. The gin had sloshed over her hand, and she felt clean coolness where the liquid touched her. "How much alcohol is in this?"

"In gin?"

Eleanor sampled it for herself. "Maggie, did you get the part?"

Maggie's smile stabbed Eleanor right in the gut.

"I start rehearsals Tuesday," Maggie said, the businesslike tone dropping away. She gave a wiggle that reminded Eleanor of Rosie. "I am so excited!"

Eleanor tried to drink and smile at the same time.

Ten days after her request—and, Eleanor suspected, about five more than were necessary—Maggie called to say they had space in the apartment. Eleanor didn't have enough money to be prideful and moved in that night. Every morning, Eleanor shuffled around the kitchen making an egg salad sandwich while Maggie left empty-handed because she could afford to buy lunch. At night, Maggie roped Eleanor into running lines with her. Eleanor seethed and rejoiced each time Maggie missed a line—might the creative team grow disappointed in Maggie and let her go?

Walking in New York helped scrub *Charades* from Eleanor's mind. With a hundred people rushing past, coffees in hand, hailing cabs, breaking up, losing their jobs, it was difficult to be self-centered. What was one more actress? Far from being comforting, this made her seem even more foolish for thinking she had a chance. Yet the decision to leave Wisconsin felt more right as each day passed. Even when Maggie hogged the bathroom in the morning, unrolling the curlers from her hair and commenting that perhaps Eleanor should do something with hers, it was better than the pigs and the farmhouse. In New York, she felt free to be herself.

With a place to live and a job, Eleanor mustered the courage to slip a nickel into the hallway phone and call her parents. She waited until evening, when rates were cheapest.

When it started to ring, she nearly hung up. But then she heard the phone lifted off the cradle, and a second later, her father's voice. "Hello?"

"Dad, it's me."

"Eleanor."

Even though she'd left without a word, her father sounded more relieved than angry. It cut her.

"I'm calling to say I'm sorry."

"Your mother has called every hotel in New York. Eleanor, why didn't you tell us you wanted to go?"

"You would never have let me."

She twirled the cord around her arm. Perhaps this was why Rosie did that—the twirling gave her something to do during an unpleasant conversation.

Eleanor told her father she'd found girls to live with and a job. "In a costume design studio."

"Fancy that."

"Yes. I even got to work on the ball gowns for the opera singers at the Met." Eleanor had no idea where these lies were coming from. "I'm helping him construct the costumes—sewing on beads, ribbons, that kind of thing."

"He? Is it just you and this man?"

His disapproval of her fictional job chafed at her. "They're gorgeous pieces. I'm learning a lot. I'm very busy. Sorry I haven't had a chance to call."

"What kind of girls are you living with? They aren't Italian, are they?"

"Dad."

"Your mother will want to talk to you."

Her father was one thing. Consumed by the farm, he didn't care what she was up to so long as the tasks got done. Her mother was something else. In the O'Hanlon family, her mother had the temper and all the fear to fuel it. "Is Mama home?"

"She's at church group tonight. It's Wednesday, honey."

"Sorry. I'd forgotten."

"I know it's expensive, but could you call tomorrow?"

A rustle came on the line, and then a loud, raspy voice came through. "Marty—Marty? Is that you?"

"Hold on, Eleanor. Mrs. Leery, could we have five minutes?"

The damn party line. Eleanor had always hated it—especially living next to Mrs. Leery and her inexhaustible list of conversation partners. But that night she leapt at the interruption.

"It's all right, Dad. I should go, too. I haven't eaten dinner yet."

"Not had dinner—it's nine o'clock."

"Marty, I need to call my daughter. She's expecting me."

"One minute, Mrs. Leery—"

"I'll talk to you soon, Dad. I love you."

"I love you, too, Eleanor. Now, tomorrow—"

She hung up before she had the chance to promise another call.

Work at the tailor shop was better than she'd expected. Though she already had calluses on her fingers, Mr. Rabinowitz was kind. He let her go home before dark. Mornings were busy, passing quickly as she numbered items and handed back tickets. They cleaned as well as mended clothes. The rush slowed by eleven, when she could sit behind a row of coats wrapped for pickup and eat her pastrami. Tommy had turned her on to it; they'd seen each other four times more, and the second time he'd brought deli sandwiches and they'd fed the ducks in Central Park. Being with him was like nothing she'd ever experienced or thought to want. It was a paler, steadier pleasure than performing, but Tommy's company was startling in its niceness. She started to do things like examine the pins on naval officers for their ranks, or look for the baseball scores when she passed a television.

The second phone call with her parents never happened; in letters, she could better control the information. She mentioned Tommy. Her parents had always been nervous about the fact that she never talked about boys. Tommy looked great on paper, so she didn't even have to lie about him. She didn't bring up the war bonds. They were gone, and after a few weeks, so was the money. It was a breach of trust that couldn't be regained by a few words. A stiffness and chill lingered. She was ashamed; it fueled her to stay in New York.

Meanwhile, Eleanor nursed her rejection. Despite her resentment, she would not let Maggie's success stunt her own. Maggie had worked steadily in the chorus of several revues and supper clubs around the city. According to Maggie, she'd done everything onstage short of taking her clothes off. "You have to pay your dues," she told Eleanor. "Success doesn't come easy."

Eleanor recognized that, obnoxious as Maggie was, she had much to learn from her. She practiced daily, memorizing Maggie's role in *Charades*, riding on her last hope. She eyed the newspaper for more auditions. None of them ended in either casting or embarrassment—just a simple thank-you. But the novelty of singing for a part on Broadway was still seductive. Every time Eleanor saw something about Don Mannheim in the papers, or one of his three shows running on Broadway, she felt an attack of desolation. Instead of rehearsing for his show, as she'd planned, she steamed armpit stains out of dress shirts while reciting lyrics in her head. Maggie regaled her apartment mates with stories about rehearsal, and though Don did not come in every day, she met him once, and told the story of his compliment to each roommate individually. "Such arresting charisma," he had told Maggie. Eleanor wanted to vomit. Charisma? What about talent?

Then the night of Maggie's debut rolled around.

Thanks to Eleanor's short time in New York and only three weeks of work, she had no money for a ticket. It was a relief. But all day in the tailor shop, she shifted from foot to foot, wondering whether Maggie would earn a standing ovation.

By eight, Eleanor could not handle the agony any longer and went to the theater to wait outside. At nine fifteen, the doors opened for intermission. Eleanor took in the women in their furs, their smoking, suited men. Before she could think about it, she slipped through the doors.

She clenched her fists, convinced people were watching her. What had she done? But she was inside the Plymouth and would not lose her nerve. This was her opportunity to act in a Broadway house. She raised her chin and lowered her shoulders. What would it be like to belong here, even in the audience? She walked through the crowd in the lobby, the high-pile carpet springy under her shoes, and tried to appear at ease until the bell rang, signaling the show's recommencement.

Eleanor followed two older ladies back into the theater. The second bell was already ringing by the time she was up the stairs, thinking the balcony might be less conspicuous. To her dismay, it was full; only Don could sell out the balcony a year into a show's run. She looked left and right for an empty seat, hoping she didn't appear too obvious. If she ended up in the wrong seat, someone would ask to see her ticket, and she'd be thrown out. She would not be able to stand the shame.

She felt a hand on her elbow and jumped. "I'm just looking for my seat!"

She stared into the smirking face of Don Mannheim. He wore suit pants and a white shirt, sleeves rolled up. The bruise on his finger had healed.

"Eleanor O'Hanlon."

That he remembered her name affected her more than she would ever admit. "Yes."

He offered her an awkward nod that she already recognized.

"Sit with me? I'm assuming you have no ticket."

"No—I do!" she said, but when she tried to think of more support, she had none. "Why are you in the balcony?"

"I like to save the good seats for the paying customers," he said. "Kind of you to do the same."

"I swear I've never done this before."

"Shocking." He gave her a look. "I'd snuck into forty shows before I'd seen New York a year. I can see so much more from up here," he said, looking down the railing at the rest of the theater. "If the cast is lazy, if someone isn't in their place. Down there you only see the principal players, not the whole picture."

He led her to seats near the side of the balcony, in the back. The entire stage was visible below them, all the way to the backdrop. Eleanor adjusted her purse in her lap, but not quick enough; Don's eyes landed on her trembling hands.

She told him it was her first Broadway show.

To her surprise, he grinned with real pleasure. The mocking gleam she had grown used to seeing in the eye of every girl in her apartment was nowhere to be found. "You're in for a treat. Of course I would have recommended something else for your first time—there's a lot wrong with this one. *My Fair Lady* is a true masterpiece. I'm sorry you missed *Guys and Dolls.*"

He spoke faster, his controlled tone gone. She felt a flip in her stomach. Don was a fan, like her. What if they could become friends?

Eleanor leaned in. "I love *My Fair Lady.*"

"Better than my work?"

Eleanor looked up at him, surprised. His voice was tentative, maybe even nervous. Was he looking for a compliment? "Your musicals are the reason I want to sing. I've devoured all of them. When I first heard *Fifth Avenue*, it was like I was meeting myself. I must sound terribly silly. But all your characters, what they sing about . . . the loneliness, the isolation. It's beautiful."

Don looked away from her with a twist of discomfort. Eleanor had begun to notice he moved this way often, as if the spotlight of a person's gaze burned him.

"People never talk about that sort of thing," she said. "Sustained isolation. Perhaps lonesomeness, missing someone or loving the wrong person or whatnot. But that feeling so many of your characters have, of being separate from the world . . . I'd never heard that before."

"I'm hardly the first."

"But you must know you write differently," she said. "People have told you."

The lights dimmed and the spot shone on the curtain.

"People say things," he said. "But I find the masses often love things for the wrong reasons."

She had so much to say, saved up from years of loving his material, but the orchestra began to play.

Maggie had the eleven o'clock number. Even Eleanor had to admit she had stage presence—her body was free and loose, the sparkle in her eyes visible from the balcony. But she was so performative, like an animated wax figure. She winked like a ham, shuffled her hips, even added cutesy girlishness to her voice. The audience ate it up, according to the applause and laughter, but Eleanor found her cold. There was no truth. Her performance was all about the moment—no depth, no humanity. Her song was dazzling, but once she left the stage, it evaporated into steam.

When the lights went up after the bows, Eleanor waited for a prompt so she could unleash her opinions.

"What did you think of your first show?" Don asked.

"It was wonderful," she said. "The entire production . . . magic."

He waited for her to finish, eyes on the stage. He was hanging on her words in a way that she had not expected. "But?"

"But nothing."

"You have something to say," he said. "What is it?"

"It's not your work," she said. "It's Maggie. Maybe I'm jealous."

"How could you not be? This is Broadway, and you're not up there."

She regarded the stage below. Even empty, it thrummed with significance. "True," she said. "You made sure of that. But . . . Well, she's very talented."

"Yes."

"But she's a mask." The words, unleashed, came quickly. "She doesn't understand what she's singing. There's no truth there. Your words, your lyrics . . . they should live in her body. Why did you choose her? She was fake."

Don looked toward her. At first she thought she had offended him, but then he spoke. "Harry liked something about her, and I trust him. The audience adored her."

"But they won't think about her tomorrow."

He stared at the stage, unblinking. Eleanor wanted to say more to fill the silence but felt galvanized by her admission. If this was her last chance with Don, she was going to remain controlled.

"If you understand all this, why didn't you do it in the audition?"

"I was nervous."

"I don't need to tell you that working under pressure is part of the job."

"Let me try again." She was conscious of where she was, of whom she was speaking to—what if this was her chance? Didn't artists fight for an opportunity and figure the rest out later? She grasped his arm. "I can do it."

"No. Your voice is gorgeous, but this part is wrong for you."

"Then let me try something else."

Don stood up.

Eleanor, sensing the end of the conversation, jumped to her feet.

"You're so brilliant, you are supposed to see everything," she said. "But you can't see me. I'm not some girl who wants to be on Broadway for the fame or glamour. I *understand* this. I understand *you*. There's something vulnerable in your musicals, all of them, and you need an actress who can sense that as much as she can sing the music. If you hire me, you won't get an actress, you'll get a girl who loves the theater as much as you do. I'll give it everything. Give me another chance and you'll see I'm not some pretty thing that blows away the second a man offers her a ring. This is my life, and if you don't give it to me I'll find another way."

Her words hung between them, and he looked her up and down, examining her face with an intense gaze that didn't quite meet her eyes. She felt ill. He was uncomfortable. Eleanor didn't blame him. But when he was quiet too long, she couldn't resist saying more.

"I promise to surprise you."

He reached out and took her chin in his hand, turning her face up to his. He was handsome in an ordinary way—long, unkempt brows, a large jaw, pale eyes. Yet not ordinary; nothing about him was ordinary. The fact of who he was infused his features with significance. He met her gaze this time, but she encountered a strange concentration there. Like he was looking at her eyes, not into them. She couldn't breathe. Finally, he released her.

"Eleanor, you already have surprised me."

Chapter Six

It was a good thing Eleanor was supposed to meet Tommy that night, because she was far too keyed up to head home. She smeared on lipstick and met him at a pub near Times Square.

"Say," he said. "Why do you look so down?"

"I'm never going to be on Broadway," she said. "How can that be?"

"I hate to say it, honey, but I think that's the case for most girls."

Tommy squeezed her hand. She finished her beer, then excused herself for the ladies'. When she wobbled, grasping the back of her chair, Tommy was looking at her funny.

"Oh—I suppose I'm tight."

Ten minutes later a plate of mashed potatoes and boiled meat sat in front of her. She ate obediently, like a child, the weight of the last few weeks heavy on her. She felt coddled; her misery was insignificant in the context of New Yorkers. She liked that Tommy took it seriously.

"Can you walk me home?" she asked.

"Sure," he said, but fumbled with the bill. "I wanted to ask . . . would you like to come to my parents' for Sunday dinner?"

"Why?"

He stared. "To meet them?"

Her face warmed. "I'm sorry. I meant . . . I didn't know you felt that way."

Tommy looked pained. "My mom makes great lamb," he said. "Don't worry. It's a full house on Sundays with all my brothers and their wives and kids. No one will even notice you."

She smiled, stomach fluttering. "All right then."

Mr. Rabinowitz was already absorbed by a hemline when Eleanor arrived the next day. She hung up her purse and greeted him, flipping the sign at the door to open.

As usual it was a busy few hours. She took four shirts and a jacket from Mr. Hunter, a dress from Mrs. Gold, and a whole stack of clothes from the Fannings' maid. Eleanor stood at the register and handed out tickets, hanging the clothes on the rack, then turning back when the bell rang for a new customer. Around two, Mr. Rabinowitz left for a late lunch at home. He wouldn't be back for hours, as he liked his long nap. As soon as he was gone, Eleanor went to the back of the store. People sometimes picked up their clothes during lunch, but now that rush was over, too, and the store would be slow.

Mrs. Jefferson had dropped off her garments that morning. Eleanor had gotten a glimpse as she numbered them but had been looking forward to exploring more all morning. She rehung them on the rack so they draped across the other clothes, the better to be touched and appreciated. Mrs. Jefferson bought all her clothes at Bergdorf's and Saks. This time she'd dropped off a wool houndstooth jacket, a black sheath—both Chanel—and a cashmere cardigan with pearl buttons that grew warm under Eleanor's fingertips. After she concealed herself behind the racks, Eleanor unbuttoned her blouse and skirt. Mrs. Jefferson was one size bigger, which was perfect because she could slip everything on without fear of tearing a seam. She smoothed the dress over her hips. The silk lining poured cool over her skin. The darts on the waist lay perfectly, as if Coco herself had ensured her garments flattered each woman who wore them, with or without alterations. The dress looked ridiculous with Eleanor's worn-out saddle shoes, but that couldn't be helped. Sling-backs never came through the store. She turned this way and that, imagining herself as a woman who wore these clothes. They felt right on her. She extended her hand as if a man had asked for it, then turned away, re-jecting him.

The bell behind her jingled.

Eleanor whipped around to face the door. It took her a moment to recognize him out of context, but then she lost her breath.

"Miss O'Hanlon." Don Mannheim looked stiff but amused.

Eleanor pretended to unlock the register to give herself something to do with her hands. Their last interaction came to mind, her impetuousness seeming ruder in retrospect. "How can I help you, Mr. Mannheim?"

He leaned against the desk. "New outfit?"

"Mr. Rabinowitz likes me to dress nicely."

He chuckled. She never would have thought him capable of such levity. For a moment of privacy, she shuffled through the inventory book. First sneaking into the show, now this. He must think her a thief.

His eyes strayed from her and looked toward the clean garments waiting for their owners. "Quite a mix of wealth at this corner," he said. He pointed at her jacket. "That's pure wool, isn't it? But that, hanging up over there, that's a blend."

She followed his eyes as he pointed out the different articles.

"That color doesn't look right on cheap fabrics," he said. "So, I'm guessing it's silk? But that shirt"—he pointed at another—"has been washed so many times it's the wrong blue. My guess is it used to be more like a lapis." He speared her with a look. "And anyone who's opened a magazine knows that jacket's a Chanel."

She ran a palm over the houndstooth. "How do you know all that?"

"A lifetime of wanting better things," he said. "And a career in the theater. I know what fabric looks like from far away."

The clothes felt hot against her skin, as if she were allergic. The brightness in his eyes was still there; a swooping hope came through her, that maybe he was flirting with her. She blushed even thinking it. What a foolish idea.

Don tapped his knuckles on the desk. "Eleanor, can you cut out early?" He looked uncomfortable, and his boyish expression came back, like he wanted to go home. "I'd like to discuss something with you."

"You came here to find me?"

"Your friend Patrick mentioned where you worked."

"Pat!"

"His was the number on your résumé." He gave her an odd look, then asked, "Who is he? A boyfriend?"

Was he curious? "Oh, goodness. No. My, did you mention your name? He would have fainted."

Don picked up a pen and tapped it on the counter. "Lock up. Tell your boss you're sick. Unless you don't want to come?"

She grabbed a pen and ripped out some blank receipt paper.

"Give me a moment to . . ." She looked down. "Change?"

"I'll wait outside."

When she emerged, Don had a cab waiting. Though she braced for it, he did not comment on her old skirt or Peter Pan collar. She felt even younger than she was.

"Seventy-Fourth and Central Park West, please."

Eleanor looked out the window so she could avoid looking at Don. He was a large man, and she was conscious of his form next to her on the leather seats. Her heart was pounding, and she kept her hands clasped in her lap. In a moment of weakness, she inhaled, trying to smell him. She caught soap, light spiciness like cologne, but nothing human.

"Have you been to the park yet?"

"Pardon?"

"The park. Been yet?"

"Oh—no." She was so flustered, it took her a moment to remember she'd been there with Tommy. By the time she remembered, it was too late to correct herself.

"It's quite lovely. I enjoy walking there in the mornings."

Eleanor opened her mouth, thinking that it was an invitation, before she caught herself.

"I'm sure."

"Clears the head."

"And I'm sure your head must need a lot of clearing." She turned to the window. Why did she speak like an absolute ninny?

"Yes. Too much rattling around."

Finding she did not trust herself to contribute further, she slumped against the seat and dedicated her next minutes to worrying that she had upset him. They climbed Broadway, through Columbus Circle onto Central Park West. The car turned left onto Seventy-Fourth and stopped outside an enormous apartment building.

Eleanor opened her door and stood staring.

"It's a castle."

"No," he said, "just home."

Eleanor expected Don Mannheim's apartment to be sparse, everything in service to his work. In a way, that was true; the apartment was meticulous. Don opened a door into a sunken living room with a leather couch and ornate rug. The walls were hung with art that even Eleanor knew was expensive. Without ever having been in a professionally decorated place before, Eleanor knew that this was one.

Through a door, she saw his bedroom, and a plain white comforter. She turned away and faced the bookshelf that made up the wall closest to her, fighting for something to say.

"Do you read a lot?" Sweeping her eyes over the shelf, she found what she was looking for: a Tony Award, the little circle tilted to the side. She wondered where he kept the others.

"No time." He passed the kitchen and dining room and walked through a door without looking to see if Eleanor followed.

It was his music studio. In the original design this must have been the master bedroom; a bathroom was attached. This was the only room that looked used. There were papers everywhere covered in musical notation, drawings of a stage floor, lyrics.

The moment could not have felt more intimate if he'd brought her into his bedroom. Eleanor stopped at the threshold. This was where the musicals had been written; this was the piano, his piano. She wished she had a camera. He did not keep the place neat: a box of tissues on the piano bench, a pair of slippers cast off on the floor, dirty dishes scattered about.

"I thought pianists were supposed to be fussy about things touching their pianos."

"I'm not so fastidious," he said, patting the Steinway. Behind the piano, his shoulders dropped. That uncomfortable look he'd sported for most of the afternoon went away, and he relaxed. "Thank you for coming, Eleanor. I suppose you'd be interested in learning about my next project?"

Eleanor straightened like someone had shoved a rod down her spine.

"I am working on something unlike anything we've ever seen onstage. Lots of people will hate it. Some people will love it. But it will challenge everything that's come before."

"What is it?"

"A new musical," he said. "With a fully integrated cast."

She waited. Hadn't *Show Boat* had an integrated cast, decades ago?

"Onstage and off," he said, holding up a finger. She earned a smile, like he knew what she was thinking. "There's going to be none of the face painting like *The Mikado*. We're going to delve much deeper than *South Pacific*. No silent characters here. It's going to be a full-blown checkerboard, half black, half white."

Don was talking about something that had never truly been done before in Broadway musical theater. Even for Eleanor, who was game for anything he wrote, this was scandalous.

"What is it about?"

"That's the best part. It will be a love story."

Her cheeks went warm. "Really?"

"A Negro and an Irish girl in Chicago. They meet and fall in love. They sleep together, then elope. It will be called *A Tender Thing*."

Eleanor looked down to hide her reaction. Don wanted her to be unfazed by this. But it was shocking. Where she came from, boys and girls didn't even spend the night together. Getting pregnant out of wedlock could shame a girl's family for decades. Eleanor had been taught that being fast and easy was as shameful as being a liar—worse, even. All that without adding race into it. Had she even spoken to a black man before? Had she ever had a reason? No. The idea of a girl like her with a man like that, making love to him no less, shuffled something in her. It wasn't disgust she felt, necessarily, but a slippery, unsure fear. Whites and blacks didn't mix. But with just a few sentences, Don had thrown a wrench into that. A white girl could sleep with a black man—Eleanor had been foolish to think the idea impossible. It was possible, but not done. She had never considered that before. Eleanor felt unbalanced. She could hardly imagine being nude in front of a man, even Tommy. She tried to imagine reaching that level of intimacy with someone so unlike her.

Don watched her face. Conscious of the heat in her cheeks, Eleanor focused on the sheet music. There were no song titles yet, just notes scratched onto a staff.

"I've never seen anything like that before."

"No," he said. "*South Pacific* had an interracial couple, but we won't be doing it like that. This is no wartime infatuation, not a soldier imposing boyish savior ideals onto a Polynesian girl. It's true love. Passion, sex, desire. It's people sacrificing everything to build a real life together. And she's a white woman. The ultimate affront. Her family would never be able to suffer the idea of a Negro in her bed."

Eleanor's stomach flipped, and she wasn't sure if it was in fear or excitement.

"Do you know why I brought you here?"

She'd been so wrapped up in hearing about the musical that she had honestly forgotten to wonder. But with his words, she was slammed by anticipation, excitement, and, the most terrifying, hope.

Don continued. "The main character is named Molly. She's innocent but strong, a girl who follows her heart but knows the practical way of the world. No drippy thing. A girl who knows when to nurse an animal back to health and when to put it out of its misery."

Eleanor tucked her hands behind her back, clasped them together until her fingernails dug into her palms.

"The show wouldn't work if she was too innocent." Don turned his gaze to the half-finished work on the piano. "We won't be making her a stereotypical ingénue. The audience needs to feel like Molly is in control, they can trust her to make this work. She's naïve enough to believe in true love and strong enough to fight for it. Molly's not sophisticated, but she's not silly. Even so, society's reaches are strong."

He continued to outline the character, the arc of the show. Molly and Luke meet when she gets lost in the wrong neighborhood. It's love at first sight and he walks her home. At the end, she steals a kiss despite the risk.

Soon they're meeting together, until at the end of act one, Luke crawls through Molly's window and proposes. She agrees and invites him to spend the night in her bed. The second act opens on a city picnic. The couple tries to elope, but her parents find out. But at the last moment the couple gets away for a happily-ever-after.

Eleanor heard everything he said, but the words slipped over her. As he spoke, she searched for what she wanted to hear, heart beating so hard the blood in her face felt hot. Don began to lose himself in his work, and Eleanor grew impatient. She curled her toes in her shoes to keep from tapping her feet.

"I want you to play Molly."

She closed her eyes to prevent the tears.

"I saw you at the audition for *Charades* and I thought, *There she is*. I prayed you could sing. You could. When you couldn't sight-read I was crushed. New musicals are a lot of work, throwing songs in last-minute. You were too green. But that evening at the show . . . You *were* Molly. Sneaking your way in, nervous, foolish but determined. I thought, *Green is good, if she's strong*. And you are. You're perfect. Your voice. Everything, down to your freckles. Your body."

He slid his eyes over her form as if seeing something being constructed in front of him. Everything that might have once caused her grief—her farm-girl hands, her height, her sturdy shoulders and legs— suddenly seemed new. She was strong, substantial, not something to blow away in the wind. His gaze had transformed her.

"I knew I could make it work. I had to."

All along, she had been right. Don didn't want an ingénue. He wanted a woman.

"You like my voice?"

"You have the right sound," he said. "It's sturdy yet pretty. Then there's that roughness, vulnerability. I need to hear you sing the music, but I know it will be right. I'm never wrong about these things."

"Let me try."

He hit a chord, startling her, reached onto the back of the piano to riffle the papers. He found what he was looking for: three pages of handwritten music.

"I've got about eight songs finished," he said, "and the musical language of the characters is in my head. This one is new, I wrote it last night. It's Molly's duet with Luke when they decide to run away. End of act one."

Don's music was never easy to sing, and sight-reading it was even more difficult. He tended to pack lots of words into the musical line and used notes that didn't commonly follow each other. He liked to surprise the ear.

But when he began to play, Eleanor stilled. It was sweet music. The right-hand notes, legato and simple over a churning bass, seemed to ache. She took a breath. Perhaps it was the confidence he instilled in her, but she followed along. She missed some of the lyrics but filled in with nonsense syllables and never broke the vocal line.

The lyrics were simple, but combined with the deep blue tones of the music, they felt significant. Eleanor responded to the push and pull of the harmonies and felt herself relax into the melody. It was a tonal, lyrical line that spanned over an octave with a dramatic rush that expressed the heated determinacy of Don's young lovers.

It was like nothing he'd written before. "Morning 'Til Night" was a real love song. None of his previous musicals had them; those songs were always about unrequited love, or desire, or jealousy. Don played Luke's parts and Eleanor hung back, reading her upcoming lyrics before she breathed and came in again. "Morning 'Til Night" had yearning, had sensuality, warmth, and desire. He had turned into sound the very feelings she had for the theater, for Don. If she hadn't been singing, she would have blushed. But Eleanor was an artist, and rather than blush, she sang with all the more candid ardor.

"I feel your breath on my cheek / Your hand warm my skin / And I pray all day / That I can be with you again / From night 'til morning / Morning 'til night."

Her voice was full and available to her, even without a chance to warm up. She felt her sound resonate in her face, her chest, until it was full and clear and—she knew—beautiful and alive.

Chills shook her spine when he hit the last note, the chord different than the one her ear expected and all the more striking.

He looked up at her, and she was surprised to see vulnerability there.

"Well?"

"It's stunning."

"It needs work." Now he could afford to be rough. "As do you. You're green. That's good. We don't want to polish all that away, but you have a lot to learn, and Harry is going to be hard on you."

Eleanor bit her lip. She thought of Harry Flynn, the coolness of his gaze, the way he'd watched her audition like a scientist waiting for the correct chemical reaction.

"Did he like me?"

"He liked you fine," Don said, "but he defers to me on certain matters." He looked at her. "Matters like you."

Don stood from the piano and walked her out of the room. They passed the living room, where this time she noticed a tank containing a turtle the size of a paperback book.

"That's Sullivan," Don said, noticing her gaze.

"As in Gilbert and?"

Don chuckled. "Of course." He turned to her, the full force of his gaze hitting her. His eyes were pale gray and arresting. "So what do you say? Can you do it?"

Before he got the question out, she accepted. It wasn't until she was in the cab on the way home, Don's five-dollar bill in her hand for the fare, that she realized he hadn't asked would she do it. He'd asked if she was capable.

She decided he would never have to ask that question again.

ACT TWO

Love Songs

Chapter Seven

Eleanor went out to the hallway to call her parents. Whispering—she wasn't ready to share this news with the apartment girls—she told them what had happened. Her father wanted to know whether she had been alone with Don—"In my day you didn't invite a girl home unless you were married to her"—while her mother brushed past the acting job in favor of her preferred subject: Tommy.

Eleanor thought about snapping at her parents—she had achieved her dream, after all—but stopped. Was she ready to tell them what the show was about? She thought of saying the words but could barely form them in her mind. Instead, she lied and said she'd purchased a slow cooker with her first paycheck.

After hanging up, she tried Rosie, but she was out. Eleanor dialed Pat, knowing at least he would understand the significance of the news. She expected the conversation to flow like it always did with him but found it awkward to speak over the phone. Pat's voice was soft, and she often had to ask him to speak up. When she told him the news, she heard him pause, and when he congratulated her, he had tears in his voice.

Eleanor didn't know what to say; she knew he wouldn't come to New York to see her perform. She thanked him for pushing her to go. Dishwashing sounds clinked in the background, the sound of a record, and she said goodbye, oddly nervous about the exchange, like she had already left him behind.

In the kitchen, Lisa, the tall girl who'd accompanied Maggie to the audition, draped over the counter and picked her nail polish while Eleanor sniffed the milk. "How many auditions did you go to today?"

Eleanor poured cereal into the bowl. "I couldn't make it away from the shop."

Lisa sucked her teeth. "You do know it's a numbers game? The more you go to, the better your chances."

There were no clean spoons. Eleanor washed one. "And how many did you go to, Lisa?"

"Six." She picked up an apple. "And five yesterday. It's the only way to do it."

How she wished she could share her news—but not yet. She kept her face blank. "Thanks for the tip."

"Glad to help."

She was pouring milk when someone knocked. Lisa opened the door, and judging by the way her voice went up in pitch, it was a man.

Eleanor poked her head around the wall and smiled. Tommy.

He had his hands behind his back. "I have a surprise and couldn't waste it on the fellas." He leaned across the threshold and kissed her cheek.

"I have something to tell you, too," she said. "But what's the surprise?"

He brought his arms to the front. He had a live lobster in each hand, their claws tied shut.

"What in the world?"

He was laughing, looking both pleased and surprised at his bounty. "The admiral's pilot took me along today on his flights. We went to Maine. Here you are, my lady—fresh lobster."

"Holy cow."

"So? Shall we cook them?"

Lisa shook her head. "I'll be in my room," she said, taking her apple with her.

Neither Eleanor nor Tommy had ever made lobster before, but they found a cookbook of Maggie's and left it open on the counter while Eleanor filled a pot of water and he opened some beers. Though she thought she would burst with her news, she wasn't sure how to tell him. With

Tommy, she felt completely normal in a way she never had before; she'd always been removed from her peers. But with this news, she felt herself separated out once more. Would being on Broadway ruin their dates in the park, when they did nothing but talk and french? Those days felt quotidian now in the face of what she was about to do.

When it came time to kill the lobsters, Tommy plunged them one by one into the pot, manfully holding the lid down as they thrashed inside. He looked at Eleanor, perhaps waiting to receive praise or offer comfort, but found her leaned against the counter, serene.

"You aren't squeamish?"

"I grew up on a farm."

The lobsters succumbed to the heat. He approached Eleanor and put his hands on her waist, his lips on her neck. "Practical little thing."

"Hardly the most romantic compliment."

He nipped her ear; she shivered. "I like it," he said. "Sturdy girl." His hand dropped lower, to the swell of her backside. She was tense, and he left his hand there without a squeeze, waiting until she relaxed in his arms before he felt the shape of her. "I wonder what it would take to rock you," he whispered. "I wonder if you'd let me."

She pulled away. "Tommy."

"I like you so much."

She hid her face against him. She knew it was naïve, but Tommy's gentlemanliness had convinced her he didn't have the same needs that women had always told her in warning tones all men possessed. But after they'd been out a few times, they were kissing and he moved her hand from his arm to his erection. She jerked away, shocked, and by the time she'd gathered herself enough to want to try it again, he had apologized, mistaking her inexperience for modesty. She wanted more, but Tommy thought she was a certain kind of girl. Until recently she'd assumed she was, too.

"It's okay, Eleanor." He kissed her forehead. "Are you hungry?"

She nodded, still flustered but happy for the subject change. As many times as they'd fooled around, Eleanor had yet to think about him when she touched herself. Amorphous male images flooded her brain, erotic enough in their distance to help her stroke her body into passion. It was as if now that she had the option of making love to a real man, the reality frightened her so much that she clung harder to the fantasy. Evidence of Tommy's humanness, from the smell of his sweat to the hairs on his arms, made her nervous. Though she tried to think of him—and she did love the way he touched her—the scene gradually morphed, until she imagined being underneath someone else entirely.

Tommy retrieved a lobster from the pot with tongs, now brilliantly red, and presented it to her with a triumphant smile.

"I was offered a part on Broadway," Eleanor said.

Tommy was even better than she'd imagined. He picked her up, spun her around. He kissed her, whooped like a boy, and asked all the right questions. Unlike her father, he did not seem to find anything wrong with Don's having her in his apartment. This time it was the lack of suspicion that bothered her. Didn't Tommy, who claimed he wanted her so, think she was desirable enough to be seduced by someone like Don?

"So, I'm going to be very busy."

"We'll figure it out." He clinked his beer against hers.

"It won't be anything like your friends, with the girls who wait for them after their shifts," she said. "I'll have a job of my own. A big job."

"You'll be on Broadway." He smiled. "I'm so proud of you. You really did it."

She looked at the lobster, unsure how to open it. "You know, I always knew I would."

There was lots of business to get through before she could begin rehearsing. She met Harry Flynn, who gave her a look of such contempt that she was afraid the role would fall through, before Don mentioned that he looked at everyone that way. Harry encouraged her to find an agent and sent her away with names and business cards. Then she was measured for a costume. It would be a long process of rehearsals in New York so Don could finish writing *A Tender Thing*, then a run in Boston to get out the kinks. They wouldn't open in New York until March, seven months away.

Over the following week, she didn't see Tommy at all—she postponed dinner with his parents—but met with five agents. She chose a man named Geoffrey Bennett, who wore a bright green suit and was the only one who didn't act like she was terribly lucky to be in his office. He looked over her contract, which was valid for the first leg of rehearsals, and noted what they would improve when they signed for the Boston run. After that, she joined Actors' Equity, the performers' union. She wouldn't be allowed in a production of this caliber without joining.

Until they cast everyone else, Eleanor would rehearse privately with Don in his apartment. Her salary was small—she was, after all, an unknown—but it was more money than she'd ever seen and enough that she could live on her own. Because she could not open a bank account without a male relative, she had to cash every check and hide the money in a drawer. She parceled out a percentage right away and put it in an envelope addressed to her parents. With luck, she could repay the cost of the bonds in six months.

After the bank, she brought an African violet to Mr. Rabinowitz and broke her news. He kissed her cheek and wished her luck, and she left feeling like a girl in a fairy tale, adored by the townspeople and chosen by the prince.

Maggie took the news with grace. She even gifted Eleanor a pair of her expensive character shoes that she'd bought in the wrong size. She had expected that Maggie would feel the same rivalry, but she seemed happy for Eleanor. "Every actress dreams of originating a role," she said. "Good for you."

Tommy helped her move into her new apartment, a walkup with a tiny living room and galley kitchen, and a bedroom with a fire escape that she stocked with a tomato plant. He carried her suitcases up the stairs and went with her to buy a bed and dresser, assembling them for her. That night, she finally let him touch her breasts and was surprised again at his fervor, how the moment he touched her skin he lost himself. He bent down and used his mouth, and rather than dying of embarrassment, she began to lose herself, too.

He slept over that night, which more than anything else made her feel homesick. It was yet another thing she never could have done at home—

even Rosie had gone to second base in a boy's car—and when Eleanor woke up with a man's hairy leg against her own, she nearly cried. But then he pulled her to him, so they were slotted like spoons, and even with the stiffness of him against her backside she relaxed.

Don already had company when she arrived for her first rehearsal. The doorman let her in, and she heard music coming from the studio. A man was singing. Eleanor waited outside the door, afraid to interrupt and not wanting to stop the sound. His voice was a warm and rich tenor, deep in tone but high in range. Her favorite kind of voice.

He had a very slight rasp, like she did. She knew that their voices would blend. He must have been playing Luke. He sang with joy, though the song was sad. She could hear that he felt about singing the same way she did. His soul was happiest when he sang.

When the song ended, she became nervous. She had never had an extended interaction with a black man before but was about to meet a man she would have to kiss in public. Eleanor had kissed exactly three boys before, including Tommy. The other two were wet, nervous memories she wanted to leave in Wisconsin. What on earth would she say to this man? How soon would they have to kiss? She brought her hand up to knock twice before she could give it more thought.

"That you, Eleanor? Come in."

Don was already focused on the music. He was making a note in pencil and barely turned to acknowledge her. "Welcome."

The man at the piano was tall and thin. Unlike Don's steely focus, this man had an easiness to him. He was relaxed in his body, one hand on the music stand, turning to a new piece. He had something of Tommy's approachability, the same tendency to grin.

"Nice to meet you, Eleanor." He held out a hand. "I'm Charles Lawrence."

"I am." *Damn.* "I mean, yes, I'm Eleanor. Pleasure to meet you." A thousand thoughts ran through her head, the loudest being that she was shaking the hand of this man whom she would later kiss, and no one was acting like this was strange. What would her parents say if they saw her kissing a Negro? Would they think she was a slut, up onstage kissing a man they wouldn't even speak to?

But what did her farmer parents know, anyway? She was a New Yorker now; she would learn to be more modern. "You must be playing Luke?"

"Yes," he said. "I hear you're fresh off the farm."

"This is my first show."

He whistled. "You must be quite a protégée."

"Have you worked with Don before?" Eleanor was unsure whether to use his first name.

"I snapped him up years ago," Don said, smiling at Charles with a warmth she hadn't seen before. She wondered what it would take for him to look at her that way. "When he was seventeen, I put him in the ensemble of *Candy Apple*. Quite a voice on this young man. I've wanted to do something with it for a decade. The moment I saw him, I thought: *Romantic lead.*"

"You're making me blush." Charles grinned, his humility true but not self-deprecating. "I didn't think theater was for me, but Don followed me around for a month until I agreed."

Whereas Eleanor had followed Don. But looking at Charles, she could see why the situation was reversed. His energy was physical and grounded, magnetic. Eleanor knew immediately he would shine onstage; he had an engagement with his body that great performers had, a physical presence that transmitted emotion with every gesture. An everyman quality, rendering his expressions relatable and accessible, while still handsome. In a thought that embarrassed her, Eleanor noted that he seemed very at ease for a Negro with two white people. She was not similarly at ease.

"Have you always lived in New York?" she asked.

"I grew up in Harlem."

She noticed a thin band on his finger.

"Do you like it there?"

He nodded. "And my wife loves it, and I'm always happier when I'm in good graces with the lady." He smiled in a way that suggested she should be in on the joke.

He was bright and brilliant, and Eleanor fought to imagine what woman could be confident enough to be married to him.

Don nodded at a music stand in the corner. Eleanor retrieved it and took the sheet music from his outstretched hand.

"Stand there," Don said, pointing in front of the piano, "where I can see you both. Angle your stands together. Yes. I want you to get used to singing to each other."

Don dropped music in front of her, a song called "With You."

"This is their meeting song," Don said, "as well as the finale. It's about the magic of fitting together, finding each other, and then, at the end, it becomes a song of triumph when they run away."

Eleanor scanned the melody. Charles sang his verse first, and hers was a repeat. It was a bright, happy piece; it sonified the effervescence of falling in love. She had never sung a proper duet before. Don had to stop her multiple times for singing too loud.

"You're the woman," he said, slapping his hand on the piano. "Your voice is higher, it carries naturally. Don't force it or you'll swallow him up."

When they switched to "Morning 'Til Night," he stopped halfway through the chorus and didn't say anything at all.

"What did I do?"

"You breathed in the middle of a phrase," Charles said. His words held no condescension. "The line will sound better if you go all the way through 'Night 'til morning / Morning 'til night' without a breath."

"Right."

"You'll get a feel for it."

He was treating her like they were already friends. Somehow this made her more nervous. Was he offended that she was not doing the same? "Thank you."

She learned many things in that rehearsal. Some were musical facts, which she noted on the page, thankful that for all her inexperience, she knew how to read and notate music. But most were about Charles and Don. Her greenness was more evident next to Charles, who could apply corrections the first time. Don did not like to repeat himself, and when she made the breathing mistake twice, he raised his voice, asking if she needed her hearing checked. She marked the music with a shaking hand, writing in all caps not to breathe, hoping to frighten her future self out of messing up. Charles was also more comfortable acting than she was.

When they sang together, he looked at her like Luke would look at Molly—lovingly, fearful of the power of their connection and all that it meant. He engaged all of his body and mind, unafraid of looking stupid or doing it wrong. Despite how much Eleanor wanted to be good at this, she was terrified, and felt the vestiges of reality tugging at her when she tried to get into character.

By five o'clock, she was exhausted and had been taught so much that her head felt heavy.

"Are you hungry?" Don asked when they were done.

"Do you mean dinner?" she asked stupidly.

Charles raised a hand in a polite deferral. "I wouldn't want to keep Gwen waiting."

Don gave him another warm look and touched Charles's back with disappointment. "Say hello to the ball and chain."

Charles smiled again, and Eleanor liked him even more, as he allowed Don his joke without laughing at his wife. In that moment, Eleanor knew, in the way that every woman does, that Charles was a good man.

"His voice is beautiful," Eleanor said when he was gone.

"Wait until you see him onstage." Don looked toward the door Charles had just vacated. "You won't be able to tear your eyes away. And a real hard worker, too," he said. "They aren't always, you know."

Eleanor was confused before she understood what he meant, and then, unsure what to do, laughed.

"When I was twenty-three, I met Cole Porter. The poor bastard had just made it through the accident. His legs were in smithereens." Don reclined, wineglass dangling from his fingers.

Empty plates of what had been seasonal vegetables and chicken sat between them. Don refilled her glass. The bottle had grown warm over the course of the meal. Her bones felt soft; smiles came easy.

"I said, 'Sir, you can write a lyric, but you can't edit worth a damn.'"

Don widened his eyes in response to Eleanor's shocked look, his body shaking with laughter at his past audacity.

"Was he furious?"

He waved a hand. "The man's plots are as rambling as they are ridiculous. He knew it." He looked at her, winked. "Of course he was furious." Scraping back his chair, he stood and walked to the refrigerator. Eleanor watched him rummage through it. The intimacy of the act, the way he shouldered the door closed, sent a twist through her stomach. Dining with her favorite composer—her nerves hadn't stopped jumping for the whole meal. He brought back strawberries, setting the green cardboard basket right on the table. "I learned early on that I couldn't care what people said. Not even Cole Porter. I would never get anywhere otherwise."

Eleanor nodded, but she wasn't sure. She was an actress. Her career depended on what others thought of her.

"That's why I liked you." He wagged a strawberry at her. "Right away. You wanted it so badly, up there, trembling like a terrier with a bone. No one was going to tell you no."

Eleanor smiled. Don might have been a genius, but he was wrong. He had no idea of the doubt she held inside of her, a huge well that threatened to spill over any time someone looked too hard.

Don was relaxed now. Maybe the wine had hit him too—though he'd stopped at two glasses—but the nervous energy that usually electrified his limbs, fingers, seemed to calm. In the candlelight, even his jaw softened.

The conversation slowed. Eleanor did not dare look at the clock, in case he took it as a cue to end the meal. She leaned forward, her hair falling over her shoulder. "Why do you write musicals?"

"The same reason you're an actress," he said. "I could never do anything else."

That wasn't what she was asking. Something significant must have set him apart long before he even began writing. Eleanor knew what it was to feel different, to see the world through the lens of stories. But she looked at what Don did and it intimidated her. Even now, as relaxed as she'd ever seen him, his gaze was focused, his fingers precise as they drummed on the table. When he turned his head to speak, she sensed he already knew how she would perceive his words. Everything about him was deliberate but not contrived. His brain was ahead of his body.

He set down his glass. Finally, after she had started to worry that she'd offended him, he spoke.

"One summer when I was a boy, I stayed with my aunt in Sacramento," he said. "She lived next to the zoo there. At night, I could hear the lions roar. It was too hot for them. I had nightmares, thinking monsters were in my room. But once I was awake, I liked to listen." Don looked toward her, his gaze unguarded. "It's an incredible sound."

She had no confirmation to give. The animals she had grown up with emitted sounds that were so vulgar they turned her stomach.

"It amazed me. They were agitated and then out came this"—he waved his hands in circles—"sound. Humans don't do that. We hide everything behind these layers. Our frustration is harder to see, but it's there. Like right now." His stare was intense, probing. She felt taken in, like he was aware of every detail on her face. "You cover your mouth when you're afraid."

She dropped her hand. Had she been nervous? She had been so focused on his nearness, the hairs on his arms, the heavy weight of him leaned on the table.

By the time she'd scrambled for a reply, he had moved on. "We're not as obvious as the lions, but once I started looking, it was all there. I saw it all, then, back home in Indiana. Whole lives revolved around the factory, the fights for promotions, the wives and the affairs. It doesn't matter where you are; animals are all the same. You lived on a farm. You know what I mean."

Something in the evening had shifted. Don was confiding in her. Eleanor began to shake her foot under the table.

"Did you date at all, back in Wisconsin?"

"I didn't like the boys there." She worried he was growing bored with her.

"So you saw what I'm talking about." His voice was distant. "The animal mating ritual. The boys and their bravado, the girls and their tricks . . . the way people pretend it's about something more than sex, food, shelter." He shrugged and looked at her. "You understand."

How different was Tommy, really, from the boys back home? "I had to get out of there."

"Trouble is, it's like that everywhere."

"You're not like that." Her heart was pounding. She felt desperate to cross this line. For years she'd understood this about Don, or believed herself to; suddenly she needed to know if she had been right about him, if what she'd heard in his music had been true or only a pathetic reflection of her own loneliness. "You aren't."

"I'm not what?"

"Animal. Even talking to you the first time, I could tell you were different. You see it all—it's in your lyrics—but you're not enslaved to all that." He was on another plane; she wanted to know everything in his mind. She realized she was tipped far forward in her seat and returned to the back of the chair.

Don stood, gestured that she should follow. He brought her to the far end of the apartment, where a floor-to-ceiling window looked down onto Central Park, fifteen stories below. Eleanor had to reach out and touch the cool glass to fight the vertigo.

"I've never been up this high."

"What is it about humans, that we love to see things from above?"

Don stared out at the city. Eleanor sensed his mind was very far away. He was tired; his eyes were red and had circles beneath. It was moving to see something human in him.

"It's worse, not to be an animal," he said. "You, my dear, have one foot in both worlds."

She thought of Wisconsin, Rosie's dates, the pigs, and the way other people could bring themselves to care about the state fair. The memories had a dull brown wash over them, her entire mind rejecting them. "I wish I could live in musicals instead."

He didn't respond but draped an arm around her shoulders. He was heavy, and hotter than she'd imagined. She was too nervous to lean into the gesture but hoped he would pull her close. He cupped a hand over the roundness of her shoulder, the gesture comforting, opaque.

She closed her eyes, glad he couldn't see her.

"I've wished that every day of my life," he said. "And every day I get closer."

"I've never met anyone who understands," she said. "I thought I would, in New York. But they're the same here. The girls care about their parts, the photographs, and the costumes . . . but I haven't met anyone who really understands." She struggled for the words: how her whole being relaxed when she listened to a show, the plot rising and falling with a precise balance, the harmonies, the rhymes, everything accounted for, matched up, perfect. Every single part, from the costumes to the faces of the actors in the ensemble, would enhance another part. It was a perfect construction. "Except you."

"The world is never as clean as in a musical," he said.

Eleanor exhaled. It was exactly what she had always believed.

They went quiet again. Eleanor watched cars pass below. After a long time, Don smiled, his walls up once more.

"Thank you, Eleanor, for saving me from an evening with my thoughts. I'll get you a cab." He went to the closet and unhooked her pocketbook, draping it over her shoulder. "You are wonderful company."

In the cab going south, Eleanor buzzed. It was ten o'clock and the shows were letting out. She felt the Broadway lights seep inside of her, until she felt bright and full, as if she herself were shining. After their discussion at dinner, Eleanor knew that Don understood this joy she felt. His dreams were parallel to hers and yet unfulfilled; when he saw the lights of Broadway, he was still hungry enough to dream.

Chapter Eight

On Sunday, she had the day off. Tommy arrived at her apartment in the morning with keys in his hand.

"The admiral's pilot let me borrow his car for the weekend," he said.

Eleanor raised an eyebrow, the door still open between them.

"Well, I'm supposed to be taking care of it while he's out of town, at least. Have you been to Coney Island yet?"

Tommy drove well, albeit with a lead foot, and was excited to take her to Brooklyn. He looped around the Belt Parkway, taking her to his family's neighborhood, Bay Ridge. Eleanor had expected something dingy, since Tommy often mentioned how little money his family had, and she'd heard the stories her own family had about Irish immigrants. But when he pulled off onto Bay Ridge Avenue, she encountered a lovely neighborhood, if humble; he drove them past stone houses, pausing for children playing in the street. Some of them stopped and ogled their dark Cadillac.

He turned onto Ovington Avenue and slowed. Eleanor had been wondering if he planned to take her to meet his family and felt herself get very nervous. He idled outside a neat house in the middle of the street, with window boxes filled with bright flowers.

"Is that yours?" Eleanor asked.

"Indeed."

"All of it?" It was two stories, three windows wide.

"Shucks no. We have the top-floor front apartment. The building houses four families. But Mama does all the windows. The woman downstairs is getting on."

"That's nice."

"They'll be having Sunday dinner right about now."

She turned forward, avoiding his eye. When she didn't respond, he drove on.

Eleanor had never been to the beach. When they reached the Coney Island shore she found that the salty wind exhilarated her in a natural way. It was too cold to swim, but she dipped in her toes. On an impulse, she reached down and scooped some seawater in her hand, then brought it to her mouth. It tasted wild.

When she looked up, Tommy was grimacing.

"Why did you do that?"

"I wanted to know."

He then took them to the boardwalk, where they played games and rode the Cyclone, and she ate cotton candy.

"This all new for you, too?"

"Are you kidding?" she asked. "I'm from the Midwest. Land of the state fair."

They made their way back to the sand. She removed her shoes and dug in her toes. The cold sharpened the brackish smell all around her.

Tommy offered his jacket. She shook her head and he put an arm around her.

"I'm enjoying the air," she said.

He looked over at the ocean. "I love the sea. I know this isn't the best place, with the roller coasters and all that. I've heard the beaches in California or Mexico can bring a guy to his knees. But even this is beautiful.

"You know, when you cup your hands like this"—he brought his palms around his eyes—"and you block out all the tourists and umbrellas and things, we're looking at exactly the same thing the Indians used to see. I take the train down here a lot, early in the morning. Watch the storms come in. It's peaceful."

Eleanor dug some of the sand up and let it slip through her fingers until it formed a pile in front of her.

"Why did you want to be a pilot then?"

"What I do for a living is just one part of me. If I love to come to the sea on Sundays, it doesn't mean I have to be there all year round. I also like baseball, and hamburgers, and talking to you."

"I've known exactly what I want to do since the first time I heard a Gershwin record."

"Nobody knows anything for sure, though, do they?"

There was no way to explain it to him. "Don't you want things?"

"I want to buy a house someday. With a yard."

Eleanor went back to digging. "I'm never leaving the city," she said. "Ever."

She didn't look at him. She'd felt pleasure in needling him before. Now she felt clumsy and mean. She dug until she reached wet sand, deep down. It was so cold it hurt her fingers.

"I'm getting hungry," he said, standing up and brushing sand off his pants. "Shall we?"

Her hands were filthy, and she wiped them on her skirt, feeling childish.

"I have to get home," she said. "Lines to memorize."

Tommy was still smiling, but Eleanor sensed that he was upset. That, in turn, bothered her. She didn't want to hurt Tommy, and moreover, she didn't want him to be hurt by the things she wanted. But she couldn't help them. If she looked too hard at his pain, she might start to have regrets. That was not an option.

"Let's get you home, then," Tommy said.

Tommy stayed over that night, then walked her to the studio where they'd rehearse from then on. They stopped on the sidewalk outside the front door. Eleanor saw Don approaching from down the street out of the corner of her eye. Her heart picked up, but she didn't look at him. She wanted him to see her with a boy.

"Dinner tonight?" Tommy asked.

"I need more time with my lines."

He stroked her face. "Okay. I can wait."

Don was closer now; she felt his gaze on her face like a warm light. Tommy grinned, thinking it was his words that had earned her blush.

"Don't be shy," he said. "I think we're past that." He leaned down and kissed her. Don would see. She angled her face to deepen the kiss as much as was acceptable in public. Tommy laughed, deep in his throat.

"I'll call you," she said.

He grinned, that open smile that Eleanor knew girls must love. But her entire body was attuned to Don, who passed them without stopping.

Tommy touched her cheek. "Have a good day. Don't miss me too much."

She winked at him, then walked inside. Don was probably up the elevators already. Now that she was away from Tommy, she felt her shoulders drop. Music was already coming from inside the studio. She was ready to sing.

When she walked inside, Don nodded at her. Eleanor averted her eyes, embarrassed both by what he'd seen and that she was glad he'd seen it. He approached her, coffee in hand.

"I hope you're more careful in your own building," he said.

"Sorry?"

"The boy who walked you to rehearsal. I'm assuming you spent the night with him?"

Her cheeks flamed.

"You must have been at your own apartment, or else your clothes would be worn. Landlords here might seem different than your neighbors in the dairy state, but they aren't far off." He gave her a look. "And besides, you can't do the show if you're knocked up."

Eleanor stared back at Don. He did not seem scandalized, but every principle with which Eleanor had been brought up taught her she should be ashamed. She felt like a naughty child.

"Don, I—"

Don held up a hand. "Don't get distracted."

She swallowed over the lump in her throat, humiliated. Don met her eyes, and she was surprised by the sadness in his expression.

"I'm sorry," he said.

She took her things to the side of the room. Charles came up behind her, setting his bag down next to the mirror. She hadn't seen him since the first rehearsal and stumbled through a greeting. Had he heard her conversation with Don?

"Are you all right, Eleanor?"

She nodded. He didn't seem to believe her but smiled and patted the seat beside him.

They kept to small talk: the weather, how far along they were on memorizing their lines. More people entered the room one by one, but Eleanor didn't know them—were they the rest of the cast? A young white man greeted Don with a handshake. Harry kissed his cheek before he began to stretch beside the mirror. He looked over at Eleanor, and she turned away, too shy to introduce herself.

"He's the dance captain," Charles said, holding a hand up to wave across the room. "Freddie. Incredible mover."

Harry approached and clapped his hands. "Good, you're talking. I don't want to do all the work." He told them to leave and spend the day getting to know each other.

Eleanor clutched her script to her chest, feeling the need to hide her body. "You don't want us to rehearse?" She'd been excited to do more work.

"I can't do anything with you until you're comfortable together," he said. "Get out of my sight, and come back friends."

It was a tall order; Eleanor normally had plenty to say to people, but she was still getting used to Charles—his experience in the theater, his connection to Don, and their impending kisses. But she was grateful for a day off; she didn't think she could look Don in the face today.

"What about the Met?" Charles asked. It was a stunning September day.

"The opera?"

"No, the museum," he said. "We can look at the paintings, then walk through the park."

Since she had no other suggestion, and his saved her from the possibility of staring at him across a dining table, she agreed.

They burned through all the easy questions while riding the subway. How had Charles ended up in show business? He was born in Harlem and was plucked out of a nightclub by a music producer in Tin Pan Alley.

"The last gasp of the renaissance," he said, "but sometimes producers still go there. The clubs are great. Anyhow, the man wanted me to front a quartet. It wasn't exactly my style, pop music, but I loved to sing and it sounded great to get paid for it. Don heard the record and liked my sound, and came to the club to watch me sing. That was ten years ago."

"It must have been incredible, meeting him."

Charles made a strange face, then shrugged. "He has this way of watching you, do you know what I mean? Like he can see straight to your bones."

Eleanor nodded. She understood.

"I thought he was crazy, honestly—he followed me, asked me to sing for him, told me he could make me a star. When he didn't go away, I agreed to give him five minutes. Then he played his music for me."

He raised his eyebrows. Eleanor knew what it was to hear Don's music for the first time.

"What about you?" he asked. "How'd you make it? All I hear's Don plucked you out of an open call."

"I think I badgered him into it," she said. Other train passengers stared at the two of them, but Charles either didn't notice or ignored them. He looked over at her with an easy smile, waiting for the rest of the story. "My audition didn't get me into the show. It was all I wanted, to be in a Don Mannheim show. When I ran into him at a performance of *Charades*, I bullied him into taking me seriously."

"Nobody can make Don do something he doesn't want to do. You must have been good."

Good enough at convincing him. Good enough at singing, maybe, but acting? Don hadn't even asked her to read lines. Her personality had been enough to get her in the door. Who knew if she could follow through? She looked away from Charles, before he could read the anxiety on her face.

"Well, it's like Molly, isn't it?" When she spoke, now that she knew the script, she understood what Don had meant. "She did what she felt was right, damn all else."

"Don is a genius," Charles said. "He saw something in you. You're a star now."

He was right. If Eleanor was going to be a star, she would need to banish this feeling of being an imposter. She tossed her hair, straightened her neck until it was long and ladylike. "No matter how I got it," she said with as much dignity as she could, "it's my role now."

Eleanor had suspected the museum might be boring—paintings and sculptures lacked the dynamic emotion of music. But the pure grandeur of the museum affected her with its power: an homage to the greatness of New York, art, and people with enough will and money to put it all in one place. As they wandered from exhibit to exhibit, topic to topic, they attracted glances. It was a weekday, so the museum was filled with mothers and children, a school group, retirees, and tourists, many of whom raised their brows at Charles and Eleanor. But no one commented. The public space allowed them privacy in conversation without appearing intimate. Eleanor knew Charles had chosen it for that reason.

Charles had a surprising knowledge of religious portraits. "My mother collects prints of the saints," he explained.

"So does mine." The topic of her mother brought a mixture of comfort and disquiet. Eleanor wondered if she'd ever be able to think of her calmly again.

Charles laughed. "My little brother, Davey, broke the one of St. Theresa one day. He had to eat standing up for a week."

"Your saint day is coming up. November," Eleanor said.

He looked over at her, impressed.

"In my family, name days are more important than birthdays," she said. "We keep the calendar on the fridge." Her name day was August 18; her parents had sent a card, but she had not responded. Even their forgiveness made her feel guilty. She looked at Charles and the feeling intensified.

"You should come with us to church some Sunday," Charles said. "My mother always cooks a massive feast for after." Then a strange look crossed his face. "Well, maybe not. I don't know about you coming all the way up to Harlem."

"That's all right." They had been going along at such a clip; she didn't want this moment to spoil it. "But thank you for the offer."

"What about you?" he asked. "I'm married, we covered that. Do you have a sweetheart?"

"I'm seeing someone—he's a nice enough guy."

"I don't know one man who wants his girl to say he's 'nice enough.'"

"His name's Tommy. He's a yeoman in the navy. He can fly planes."

Charles whistled. "I always wanted to fly a plane. Is he all right with you doing the show?"

Eleanor clenched her jaw.

Charles looked at her with sympathy. "I've been in the business awhile. I've seen lots of girls drop out because their men take it hard."

"He's the first sweetheart I've ever had."

Charles just nodded.

"Does Gwen ever get jealous? Of the girls in shows?" She realized she was implying there was something to be jealous of and was about to backtrack when Charles shrugged.

"Not especially. I haven't done a romantic lead before," he said, "but it's just acting. Gwen is my wife."

His tone held a seriousness that made Eleanor feel silly. He sounded grown-up. She thought of Tommy again and the fun they had together, the way it made her feel good to meet a boy after rehearsals, to have someone to kiss. It didn't seem on the same plane.

After the museum, they walked through the park. They went to buy frankfurters and endured an awkward moment when the seller ignored them, helping two customers behind them first. Eleanor had to cough, then speak up, before the man served them without apology.

"You must have an interesting social life," she said when they finally had their food in hand.

"What do you mean?"

"I mean, you're always around . . ."

"White people?"

She blushed, but Charles smiled.

"It's all right, Eleanor. Sure, I spend a lot of time with white folks. What are you asking?"

There was so much to ask, she wasn't sure where to start. "Is it different, to be with us?"

"It never really goes away, that feeling of being the only black guy in the room."

She thought of their rehearsals, where she was the greenest one there. "What do you think of the show, then? Molly, falling in love with Luke. I think it's so beautiful, that true love would of course see straight through anything. Audiences always root for love. So they'll be forced to question what they believe about race." She crumpled her napkin. "I don't . . . I don't think race matters," she said. She worried Charles might laugh at her, but he didn't. "Maybe it's because of where I'm from in Wisconsin. I'm a Catholic, and my mother didn't want me to talk to the Lutherans. It's all so silly to me. Consubstantiation and transubstantiation—such silly things to dictate your whole life. So I guess I assumed it was the same, with race."

His face was gentle, but Eleanor flushed, conscious of the clumsy simplicity of what she'd said. "I think it's complicated," he said. "Even if on some level we're the same, our lives are so different that it doesn't matter. But somehow, the musical seems to understand that. How different their lives are, but that they see each other despite all that. Don understands that Luke is the one taking the real risk, not Molly."

She furrowed her brow. It was true; Luke had a song in the second act in which he debates running away with Molly. At the beginning of the song, he weighs sense against love. At the end, Luke realizes that allowing fear to dictate his actions would be locking his own handcuffs. So he chooses Molly, but it's calculated, and clear how frightened he is.

"That part gives me chills," Eleanor said.

"I was surprised, you know—a white guy writing this show. But he did a good job." Charles shrugged. "Some parts are off, but he clearly understands something about it all."

She was curious and asked, even though she thought it might not be a good idea, "Would you ever date a white woman?"

He waved a hand, showing his ring.

"I don't mean now," she said. "In theory."

They had reached the bottom of the hill, the gate to the zoo.

"I don't know, Eleanor," he said. "I guess I'd like to believe it's possible, but I don't know."

It was, she thought, an honest answer.

The following day, Eleanor hadn't put down her pocketbook before Harry beckoned her over to him. Charles was already there, changing out of his street shoes.

"Your meeting scene," Harry said. "Now."

The first kiss. She was unprepared.

Harry walked her through the scene. "Enter up right, Luke intercepts right of center . . ."

All Eleanor could think about was the kiss. Charles did not look embarrassed or fazed. She was waiting for someone to hoot or tease them, but it didn't happen.

"All right," Harry said, walking to the front of the room so he could watch. "Now, from the top."

While she couldn't descend into the character, she recognized the emotional beats she needed to hit. She entered, looking around for the street signs. Luke was already onstage watching her. In the production, there would be musical underscoring.

"You lost, miss?"

She jumped. "No. I'm meeting a friend."

"I'm not trying to frighten you." He held up his hands, palms out. "I don't normally see girls like you in this neighborhood. Can I help you call somebody? Walk you someplace?"

"No, thank—" She looked up. It was a quintessential musical-theater moment; Molly's eyes locked with Luke's, and she froze for a long beat.

She was overcome. "How do I get to the Blue Line?"

"It's too late for the train." Luke stared at her, his expression kind and mixed up with the same puzzled look she had.

Molly swayed. "Walk me?"

They "exited" in the rehearsal room, then walked around to where they'd enter again after a scene change.

Luke did not release her hand. "What's your name?"

"Molly. Yours?"

"Luke."

It was time. Harry was assessing her, and out of the corner of her eye, she saw Don watching. Charles was in character, and she felt moved by how good an actor he was. Under his eyes, she felt more beautiful than before. In a feat of intense bravery, she went up on her toes and kissed him. His lips were warm and chapped. That was all the information she could gather before Harry clapped his hands.

"Scene."

Eleanor broke away. She caught Charles's eye.

"Nice job," Charles said, then turned to Harry for notes.

Her insides felt like they were dancing. She could not stop herself from smiling. It was far more exciting than her first actual kiss.

Chapter Nine

The musical flowed from Don like wine from a barrel. During the first weeks of rehearsal, the cast, at first just Eleanor and Charles, swelled to include the other characters: Molly's parents, Luke's sister, the ensemble. Every day, the stage manager distributed new pages. Sometimes they were for songs the cast had never seen, other times they were edits on songs they'd just learned. Eleanor spent late nights memorizing the new additions, only to have them wiped away in favor of new material. It was exhausting—and fascinating.

Don was playing piano for the rehearsal, which was all but unheard of. Usually a hired pianist played rehearsals.

"Gives me more time to know the music," he had explained. "Going over and over sections, I'll see the problems. I want this work to be perfect."

Eleanor had always imagined rehearsals to be nuclei of creativity. In fact, they were, but the ideas generated from Harry, Don, and the designers, and the creativity demanded of her and Charles was more specific, a distributary of creators' visions. She was surprised to find her role as an actress increasingly disappointing. Her job was confined to the material given, her interpretation restricted to the lines and music. She felt silly for being put out by something that was obvious to most everyone. One morning, after they had run a scene no less than fifteen times with differing notes from Harry, Eleanor sat on the floor and rubbed her temples, not hiding her frustration.

"I thought I'd be allowed more interpretation. Not just act as a vehicle for Harry's," she said to Charles.

"We're paid to do the material. There's enough to keep you busy."

Eleanor had never thought of it that way, like she was doing a job the same way a schoolteacher might do hers.

"But what about the story?" she asked. "Do we ever get included in that part?"

Charles looked at her, confused. "Playing another person is complicated, honorable work. There's infinite material there, in discovering who they are."

Eleanor found that she was less interested in her character, Molly, than she was in the show as a whole: how all the characters fit together, how their actions affected the larger story. Hearing this, Charles shrugged.

"I don't know what to tell you. You're an actor. This is the job."

"All right." Harry clapped his hands for their attention. "Right before you begin 'With You,' Molly, Don is changing the line from 'I feel I've always known you' to 'When you called for me, I felt a chill, right here. Do you feel?' And, Luke, take her hands. Got that? Now again from the top."

"Yes, sir." She always soaked up the edits she got, trying to understand why he and Don might have made such choices, deconstructing the musical from the inside. Every decision Don made fascinated her; she watched him whenever she wasn't in a scene, anxious to learn all she could about the process, the building of a musical. Of course he never confided any of this to her, so she tried to read it all through his decisions.

Harry's reputation for cruelty was well earned, and she never would have survived even one rehearsal without Charles. Though she had gone into the show thinking her relationship with Don might protect her, it was Charles who offered her a comforting smile after a harsh adjustment. Don was all business, either correcting her with fastidious care ("Why didn't you enunciate both T's in 'meant to be'? It's not 'men to be,' it's 'meant to be'") or concentrating on the music as if staring long enough at the lines would fix the problems before his eyes.

During private rehearsals in his apartment, he was more generous with his time. Don loved discussing music, so asking a question about an accent or dynamic marking was a quick way to an actual conversation.

Once, after going on ten minutes about the dramaturgical significance of composing in the Lydian mode and how it connected the romantic and jazz periods, Don looked embarrassed.

"I'm sorry," he said. "I'm not used to people who care about this. I'm boring you."

He wasn't. Eleanor had so many questions, and Don was happy to have someone with whom he could deconstruct his work. He put so much thought into every piece that most people would never notice; he was delighted to share these details with her. Their rehearsals often ran late.

Where Don was technical, Harry was physical. His choreography was central to his directing, even in the nondanced sections. Character, he said, lived in the movement of the body. If she gestured with her elbow the wrong way, he'd stop the scene but refuse to tell her how to do it correctly. "It needs to come from you," he'd say. "But that? That's wrong." She spent breaks crying in the bathroom, though she did this with pride, as if crying in rehearsal meant she was a real actress.

Harry segregated the cast in order to keep the performers—who had to hate each other onstage—from becoming friendly. He kept the groups separate so they spent long days rehearsing dance numbers and creating relationships with only the people their characters cared for. When Harry complimented one group, the other tried harder. For her part, she and Charles were made to eat lunch together every day. She had nothing to do with the other cast members. They were allowed to speak when rehearsing, but only in lines from the script. Eleanor was privately relieved; she was overwhelmed as it was by keeping up with the social niceties.

But she couldn't resist Freddie, the dance captain, who drew her eye every time he moved. At twenty-five, he already had seven Broadway shows under his belt. He had years of ballet training, and Eleanor had never seen a professional dancer in person before. His body electrified the air around him. Harry's choreography seemed organic in his body, and Freddie tried things out on breaks, turning, stretching his leg, laughing when he flubbed a landing or did not prep a jump properly. His talents lived in his body, and even among the other dancers, he seemed impossible to ignore. Eleanor didn't have to dance in this musical and was relieved—she had no idea how, and watching someone as effervescent as Freddie was frightening.

A month into the process, Freddie was rehearsing a turn sequence. He tightened his stomach in order to get around another time, his back muscles moving under his shirt. Don approached her as she watched.

"Another kind of genius," he said.

"I can't imagine ever moving that way," she said.

Don watched Freddie a moment longer before shaking his head. He reached into his coat pocket and presented her with a 45. "It's Rodgers's newest song," he said. "Are you interested in taking a listen?"

"Yes, of course, yes!"

"I'm curious to hear your thoughts on a work in progress."

All day she thought of the demo—what would Pat say? Back in Wisconsin, she had dreamed of spending her evenings listening to new music. After rehearsal, she rushed home and put on the record. It was a crackly, muffled sound, and then a thin male voice. With a chill, she realized it was probably Rodgers himself. It took more than one listen before she could hear it as the song would really sound, sung by a woman, with an orchestra. She lay on her back in the middle of her floor listening to the song, then sat up and reset the needle when it ended. She liked the melody, though some of the lyrics were clunky, particularly a rhyme in the bridge. She noted down her observations and returned to rehearsal the following day bursting with thoughts, but Don was busy with Harry.

When they broke for lunch, Don stayed at the piano, working out a transition between numbers. She lingered beside him, but he didn't appear to notice, playing the same four measures again and again. Finally, she cleared her throat. When that didn't work, she spoke. "Don, I loved it." She handed him the 45. "I've always loved Rodgers's music."

He took it from her, looking almost disappointed. "Funny, I thought his earlier work was better. Anyway, enjoy your lunch."

She was struck by his dismissal but still thought it a win. After all, he hadn't asked anyone else to listen to the record.

Almost suddenly, they had six weeks before *A Tender Thing* moved to Boston. Apparently most other shows were put together with far less rehearsal, but Harry thought art was built slowly. He referred to the show as a piece of clay. It took him a long time to choreograph and he was not above making the cast work eight hours on something that he'd abandon the next day.

"Again," Harry said, the first cold day of the year. Eleanor was tired, her feet hurt, it was five o'clock, and she wanted to get out of the rehearsal studio. It was the first day she was unhappy to be there.

"Come on, lady," Charles said. "You've got one more in you."

She disagreed.

"You'll be mad at yourself if you let yourself quit now."

She leaned against him. After their day at the Met, she had become more comfortable with Charles, a mixture of their daily proximity and his kindness. Kissing and touching someone every day in rehearsal had a way of breaking down boundaries. He held her by the scruff of her neck and gave her a shake. "You're a professional now. Come on."

"I hope you aren't complaining," Harry said from the far end of the studio, where he was studying his notes. "One minute and we're going again."

Eleanor restrained a groan.

"Everyone's replaceable," Harry said. "Especially you, Eleanor." He looked up, making sure she'd heard him.

Harry's words made her hate him enough that she wanted to show what she was made of. The scene was from act one, right when they met. Luke was still terrified of being caught, afraid that Molly couldn't possibly love him.

"And now, with you / I waited so long for you / But here you are, and I've no words to say." Soon, Charles joined in. Molly put her hands on Luke's cheeks, feeling the roughness there. When she was singing, her mind moved slower. She felt instead of thought. After the last note, she rose on her toes to give him a long, slow kiss. It was stiff, coming in the right place with none of the passion.

"Good enough," Harry said.

Eleanor had never been happier to hear that.

＊

After that difficult rehearsal, Eleanor was nervous to attend her next one-on-one with Don. He let her into his apartment and offered her a piece of lettuce.

"For Sullivan."

She felt childish that he'd noticed how much she liked the turtle. "Thank you."

"You seemed down yesterday."

"It won't happen again."

Don nodded at the couch. So far, their rehearsals had been confined to the music studio. She sat.

"How do you think the show is going?" he asked.

Wondering if he meant her part, she was unsure how to reply.

"I'm having trouble with act two," he said. "I think the picnic scene is running long."

Molly and Luke were barely in the picnic number; realizing that he was asking her for her opinion, not critiquing her performance, Eleanor considered her words.

"I think it will be different once Harry finishes the choreography," she said. "But I agree. The audience will be wondering about Molly and Luke running away and might grow restless during a long dance number."

"Hmmm, I think I'll cut two verses." Don rubbed his chin. "You have good instincts."

Her tongue was dry. "Thank you."

Don nodded at the script in her hand. "Everyone has bad days. I didn't write at all yesterday. Tried for hours, nothing happened."

He met her eyes, without the careful deliberation he usually mustered up before doing so. Don covered her hand with his. She felt his touch all the way up her arm. "I have faith in you."

His touch and words rendered her speechless. He took his hand away and brought her to the studio. The rehearsal that followed was far better than the previous ones, distracted as she was by the memory of his hand on hers.

✳

On a Friday in November, Eleanor was to accompany Harry and Don to a party where she would sing a cut from "Morning 'Til Night" and promote the show for investors.

"You're new meat," Harry said over a lunch meeting. She'd ordered a burger, and he waved at the waiter, correcting it to soup and a salad. "The audiences might be excited for a novice, but the producers will hate the idea unless they think they've picked you themselves."

By now, Eleanor was getting more comfortable performing in the context of the show, but she was nervous to sing in a rich New Yorker's apartment. She glanced at Don, who was picking his way through a salad. He never ate anything that wasn't lean chicken or vegetables.

"You'll be fine," Don said. "You know how many hits Harry and I have between us?"

"Six," she said.

"Correct. So we know better."

"Is Charles coming?"

Harry gave her a look. "It's not that kind of party."

When they finished their meal, Don hailed her a cab.

"Head to the costume shop," he said. "I laid out some dresses. The girls there will alter them for you."

Eleanor imagined Don pulling dresses off the rack and envisioning them on her body. A warm flutter went through her.

"You have pearls?" Harry asked. "Pearls are good for young women. I'll bring some of my wife's."

Harry had a wife? Eleanor had noticed the way Harry chatted with the chorus boys, correcting their posture with open, slow hands on their backs and complimenting them like a prince distributing flowers to girls at a ball.

"You'll look beautiful," Don said. "I have good taste, remember?" He raised his eyebrows, smiling, and she recalled his knowledge at Mr. Rabinowitz's shop. She was thrilled that he also remembered that day.

"A car will pick you up at seven thirty," Harry said. "See you there."

As she sank into the seat of the cab, Eleanor's fear must have shown on her face, because Don reached over and grasped her hand quickly before leaning out to shut the door. She felt it all through the ride to the costume shop.

✳

At seven fifteen, Eleanor sat on the floor in her underwear in front of the mirror. She threw a pillow at her reflection. She'd tried several different lip colors and wiped them off until her lips looked twice their normal size. With a charcoal pencil, she'd attempted a flared cat's eye and ended up looking like she'd been punched. Who was she kidding? She wasn't cut out for the circus, let alone a Broadway musical. Rolling onto her belly, Eleanor knocked her forehead against the floor. This was going to be a disaster.

The phone rang. She ignored it, but it rang again. She groaned loudly before rising to pick it up. "What?"

"Heya, Eleanor."

"Tommy, I don't have time for any chitchat." She propped her hip against the kitchen counter. There were entire days when she did not think about Tommy. Since their time at the beach, his presence made her uneasy. Tommy was great fun—after the lobsters, he'd once brought a handle of rum from a navy trip to Cuba—but while he never complained about her rehearsal schedule, she sensed his exasperation. She often let the phone ring in case it was him and spent her free time studying lines. Moreover, Tommy's companionship did little to fill the void of Rosie's, which she missed more than she'd thought possible. "I'm having a crisis, Tommy."

"What's the matter?"

"I'm a disaster. A phony." She pouted, her reddened chin scrunched up.

"I wanted to wish you luck."

"I need more than luck. I need a miracle." She threw her hands in the air. "Clowns aren't allowed at parties."

"I'm sure you'll be fine."

"You know nothing about it."

"Well, have a good time, Eleanor."

She hung up without stopping to feel bad about being so rude.

Eleanor had thus far been able to fake her way through all the new experiences. She hadn't known what to expect from a Broadway rehearsal but stayed cooperative and professional. Theatrical jargon was foreign to her, but Charles was quick to whisper what things like "blocking" and "cheating out" were. When it came down to it, Eleanor felt in her bones that she deserved the chance to be the first person to sing Don's music. He had chosen her, and she trusted him. If she believed in Don, she had to believe in herself. So nothing in rehearsals would rattle her—she wouldn't allow it.

Parties were different.

To make herself feel better, twenty minutes earlier she'd begun eating pickles out of a jar. Now she lay on the floor with a stomachache. The doorbell rang. Wrapping a blanket around herself, she poked her head out the window to see who it was. She leaned over the fire escape and saw shiny black hair, a white shirt, expensive shoes.

She ducked inside. Damn. She pulled on a robe and took the stairs barefoot.

"Don," she said. "What a surprise."

He clicked his tongue when he saw her feet. "What if you step on a nail?"

A flutter at that.

He followed her up the stairs. Before she opened the door she cursed herself. Dirty dishes filled the sink, and if she remembered correctly she'd hung hand-washed panties over the shower curtain rod.

"Looks exactly like I imagined." Don examined her records in the living room, stacked against the player, then lowered himself to the couch.

"What are you doing here?"

He rested his arm on the back of her couch. Though Tommy was younger and fitter, Don—one leg crossed wide over the other, exposing dark dress socks over a thick, strong ankle—filled the whole room.

"I thought you might need bucking up."

"I can't do this." She flopped down, the robe opening and exposing freckled flesh before she tugged it closed. He was watching her. Too nervous to reopen the robe, she left her hand there, as if suggesting the option.

"I thought the same thing at my first industry party."

"You were a student at Juilliard," she said. "You couldn't have been unfamiliar."

"Only two years out of Indiana," he said. "And I barely knew society there. Most people don't know I was sickly as a kid."

"You were?"

"Weak heart. They only let me serve in Japan because I'm good with equations and details and could do paperwork no one wanted to. And growing up in Indiana, I was cooped up. My parents didn't know what to do with me."

"That's terrible."

"All I did was study and write musicals. By the time I was ten, I'd written three." He waved off her look of awe. "Garbage. The point is, I had more company inside my own head than with humans. My first industry party was a disaster. I couldn't speak to anyone, and when they spoke to me, I either laughed or said something rude."

Like insulting Cole Porter? Was the story he'd told her weeks before nothing but bravado, put on to impress her?

"I thought I was so brilliant that everyone would listen to my opinions," he said. "But it doesn't matter how brilliant you are if people don't like you." He leaned over so they were almost side by side. "You, Eleanor, are going to be a star. People need to like you."

She was wearing white cotton underwear and had mascara smudges all over her cheeks. Sitting there, she'd never felt less like a star.

"You are," Don said, though she hadn't spoken. "And I've written you a great show."

"Rehearsals are more difficult than I thought they would be."

"Of course. Making a Broadway show is one of the hardest things there is. But trust me, this is going well. And you, my dear, are doing exactly what you need to do."

"I don't feel prepared for any of this. I know how to sing. I don't know how to be an *actress*."

Don placed a hand on her hair. "You're going to dazzle them." Her scalp prickled where his fingers landed. "And it's nearly seven thirty. Put your dress on."

Eleanor wanted to groan again but didn't think that would help her appear the mature paragon. If she was going to be a star, she'd need to muster some mystique. She went into her bedroom and closed the door. Her dress was cherry-red taffeta with a full skirt that fell to her knees, sleeveless with a high neck. Youthful, elegant.

She appeared in the living room, shoes in hand.

He stood up to approach her. She felt a flip in the base of her stomach. He brushed her hair from her shoulders. "People always say redheads should avoid red. But you look like a flame."

She swallowed, unable to respond.

"Pearls are wrong for that," Don said, his voice returning to business. "We need gold. Nothing on the neck. You have such a pretty neck and arms; let them speak for themselves."

The compliment floored her. "The costume shop lent me some things," she said. "In case Harry forgot the pearls."

Don searched the velvet jewelry bag until he held out two gold circle clip-ons. "These. And a red lip. All the men will imagine kissing you."

If she were bolder—if she were Rosie back when she was fifteen—she might have asked if he included himself in that group.

"How do you know?"

"I told you in the tailor shop. I've been in musical theater my whole life. I know what people like. Unity, dear. As Oscar Hammerstein said, 'the orchestra should sound the way the costumes look.'" Don took her by the shoulders and turned her toward the bathroom so she could finish her makeup. "We're a unique breed."

Taking more care this time, she applied her makeup as he watched from the doorway.

"Careful," Don said. "Don't cover that fresh face with paint. Just that is perfect."

"Hair?" She gathered it in one hand, turning her neck, then let it down.

"Let me. You fix your lips." He took the comb. Eleanor tried to focus on applying her lipstick. She wanted to glance at him but was afraid of meeting his eyes in the mirror. Don ran the tip of the comb across her scalp above the inside of her right brow, creating a new part. She shivered. Gently, he combed her hair on either side and worked through the tangles until it hung around her shoulders.

"I've never seen hair this color," he said. She felt the warmth of his breath on the top of her head. "So many shades of red and gold."

She swallowed, hardly breathing. Though he was not touching her with his body, she could feel the heat of him all the way from the nape of her neck to the backs of her thighs. She had only had flirtations with boys. Eleanor wondered what things Don might know about, or have seen, that Tommy had no experience with.

She turned around, short of breath. Don stepped back, a pleasant grin on his face, and gestured for her to exit the bathroom first. It took her a moment to realize he was not going to kiss her.

She was glad she faced away from the mirror; she was probably as red as her dress.

"Are you all right?" he asked, casual as could be.

"I think I'm dizzy," she said.

"You lock your knees?"

She brushed past him to her bedroom. She found her purse on the bed and dropped the lipstick into it.

"It's past seven thirty," she said over her shoulder. "I bet the car is outside."

"You're probably right," Don said. She met him at the front door, and he gave her an appraising glance. "You look lovely."

"Thank you."

"Now," he said, offering his arm and opening the door. "The snake pit."

Chapter Ten

Harry made it clear during rehearsals, at lunches, and even on the sidewalk right before they entered the party that her role in the Broadway production was not a done deal.

"People have to sign off on you," he said. "Then their people have to sign off. Then their people. Do you understand?"

Eleanor wanted to tell him that she was not an idiot, but he had moved on.

"I like the flat shoes. Good choice."

"Don's idea."

"We're going to shove you down everyone's throats until people are talking about you in Scarsdale, Upper Saddle River, Garden City. The bridge-and-tunnel crowd has to like you. But we'll start with people whose opinions matter: rich Manhattanites."

Don took her arm and tucked it within his. He touched her chin with his knuckle and raised it up.

Eleanor was not sure what she'd expected—bite-sized food passed around on silver platters, maybe. Champagne. Expensive clothes. All of those things were present, but something was off. At first she wasn't sure what was strange. She followed Don and Harry through the crowd as they shook hands with people, Harry businesslike and magnanimous, Don more reserved, made jumpy by the numerous guests. They introduced her to many people, most of them wealthy business owners or theater producers, but a few other creatives. She recognized Meredith Wilson, the composer, talking with a young man near a window. Spotting him, Don touched her arm and excused himself to say hello.

After a moment, Don held out a hand to her, and she crossed the room, feeling chosen. A small crowd had gathered, asking him about the musical.

"My inspiration, right here." He tucked her hand against his arm and turned her to face the group of men.

"I am so excited for all of you to see the piece," she said. "I've always been a fan of Don's work, but this is something truly special."

The crowd continued to ask questions, and Eleanor—though her feet were sweating in her shoes—found more confidence. Don kept his hold on her arm and took her around the room, scarcely speaking. Eleanor felt astonished by her fortune: she, a young woman in a beautiful dress, on the arm of a brilliant man. It wasn't something she'd thought would ever happen to her. She felt alluring, which in the context of the party felt almost better than talented.

A tall young man with a classically handsome chin approached Don, showing off his dimples. He greeted him by first name. "It's been ages."

A smile hung around the corners of Don's mouth. "I'm sorry, I don't recall your name."

"Peter Whitman," he said. "We met at Lulu Martins's party out in the Hamptons, two years ago. The one where the daughter ran off with her mother's arm candy." He raised a glorious brow. "If I recall, there was a bit of a snafu with the hostess during the fireworks?"

Don kept his face blank.

"Anyway, I've been surprised not to see you around more. Those parties are so dull, there's never anyone to talk to. How's the new show coming along?" He drank his champagne as if he couldn't be bothered to hear the answer and was waiting to be asked a favor he could deny.

"We're in rehearsals now," Eleanor said. Peter turned to her, his lips pursed with surprise at her contribution. He reached out and tapped one of her earrings.

"You must be the starlet."

Eleanor felt heat on her neck. "I'm loving the process so far," she said, keeping her voice even.

Peter turned to Don. "The rumors about your project are rumbling through the audition studios, my friend. People say it's dead scandalous."

Don adjusted Eleanor's arm in his. "Dear Eleanor is about to sing for us," he said. "If you'll excuse us, I'm going to get her some water."

Eleanor followed him through the crowd. When they reached the bar, Don rolled his eyes.

"Did you actually meet him at that party?"

"Who knows?" Don said. "I can't walk down the street without some young actor auditioning for me."

Eleanor accepted the champagne. "I suppose that's what I did, during *Charades.*"

Don frowned. "You were never so false, my friend."

"No?"

"I would be naïve if I blamed you for taking advantage of such an opportunity. Young actors have to use every trick they have. The difference is you never pretended to be sophisticated enough to fool me." He drained his glass. "There are scores of young men and women like him, thinking if they play slick and bawdy I'll be dazzled into casting them. You, Eleanor, were too green, and too smart, to pretend to be anyone but yourself."

She wished someone were there to hear what he'd said. "Thank you."

"I didn't bring you here for the champagne," Harry said from behind her.

"Eleanor and I were escaping the hangers-on," Don said.

"Unavoidable minnows." Harry took Eleanor's arm. "Come, come. Get back to work." She followed him as he stuck out his thumb at her with phrases like "fresh from the country" and "green as a leaf." When speaking to investors, he sold her with more finesse: "Don and I were floored when we heard her sing for the first time. I've never heard a voice like hers. I can't wait to share her with you." He sounded so convincing that Eleanor even believed him, until he turned to her and said, "Marketing, toots."

It wasn't until Eleanor had a break and accepted a shrimp from a waiter that she realized what was strange about the party. There were hardly any women. Only a few investors had brought dates. Eleanor was the only woman there on business. The men talked in tight circles, trading industry stories and jokes, while the women perched beside them in brightly colored dresses. Eleanor, caught somewhat between, was unsure of herself. Even the waiters were pretty young men, passing napkins with slender hands.

Once the guests had been greased with champagne, Harry directed everyone to a library with a piano. Eleanor was afraid that these men would not like her performance, but a large part of her was eager to show them that Harry and Don were right. She was good. The closer she got to Don's material, the more she felt their connection. Out of her mouth, his words felt like her own. Even his music felt at home in her voice; she never had to stretch for a note.

"Thank you, everyone, for coming," Harry said, champagne glass in hand. "As you know, Don and I have been working together for years now."

Eleanor noticed Don's stiffness, the way his fingers twitched toward the keys. He wanted to play. She joined him near the piano.

"We've had some success," Harry said with an attempt at modesty that he abandoned halfway through. "But believe me when I say that *A Tender Thing* is different from everything we've done before. Ten years ago I promised Don I'd work on anything he wrote. But even if I hadn't, I would fight to work on this piece. Don has outdone himself. I'm sinking my teeth into rehearsals. But you're lucky because tonight you're going to get a glimpse behind the curtain."

Harry turned and raised his eyebrows at her. Eleanor smiled, her heart pounding, her fingers tingling. Her mouth was dry; she bit the inside of her cheek to moisten her tongue. Everyone was looking at her.

"You're in for a treat," Harry continued. "May I present to you one of my favorite numbers from the show, 'Morning 'Til Night.'"

Don began to play. The sparse notes of the introduction comforted her with their familiarity.

They had edited the song to skip Luke's lines. Eleanor allowed Harry's praise to lift her. She was ready to sing for new people. They expected greatness. She would ascend.

"From morning 'til night / Your face comes to me clear . . ."

At first, she focused her eyes on a painting on the back wall, so she wouldn't see anyone staring. But the music enveloped her in sensuality, until she was imagining Don's touch, the way he'd searched for her at the party like he needed her. She sang about holding Luke close; even in the packed room, Don's simple melody was intimate. The notes seemed to create threads between her and the listeners, drawing her nearer to each one. Though she didn't look any audience members in the eye, she engaged her body and felt herself grounded to the floor. Her hands rose in an unrehearsed gesture that felt right. The lyrics worked on her until she was as comfortable as Molly was with her lover.

When she finished, the room was quiet. She heard a murmur, then clapping began. A true beam felt like it was emerging from within her, and she looked around the library. People smiled at her, talking among themselves with raised eyebrows. Pride unlike anything she'd felt before, greater even than she'd felt when she was cast, crept up. So this was what it was to have an audience.

Soon after, Harry whisked her through the crowd for more introductions and felicitations. Even Peter Whitman complimented her beautiful voice. She was eventually spat out near the bar, where a black man gave her a glass of champagne.

"Thanks," she said, accepting it with a sweaty hand. She was still breathless from the performance. She wondered if this man had heard her sing.

He offered her a napkin.

"Do you always work the parties here?"

"No, ma'am," he said.

She smiled, her fingers fiddling with the glass stem. She thought about the show. Suddenly she felt a desire to connect with this young man, impress her openness onto him. "You know, both of us are misfits here," she said. "I don't have any money at all, really. I grew up on a farm. I've never been to a party like this."

Again he didn't say anything. She finished her champagne and, feeling uncomfortable all of a sudden, handed it back.

"You've probably been to more of these than me."

"Perhaps, ma'am."

Instead of engaging her in further conversation, the young man began to pull spare glasses from a shelf beneath the bar, setting them out for future use. Eleanor felt silly.

"Have a good evening," she said.

"You as well, ma'am."

Flushed with alcohol, she stepped away from the bar. The guests had vacated the library in favor of the living room, which had a wonderful view of the surrounding buildings. She looked at the crowd of men. One smiled at her, then turned back to his conversation partner. Someone passed, complimenting her on her performance once more. There was no one else to engage in conversation; the men were speaking to each other. She wandered over to the fireplace, where some of the women were talking, and hovered. A few glanced her way and smiled, but they went on among themselves. Two women discussed boarding schools in Connecticut. Eleanor waited a few minutes before she left them, too.

She looked off into the dark hallway and, checking that no one saw her, slipped into the library and shut the door before anyone could follow. She turned, looking about the room, until she saw the piano and jumped.

"Don," she said, hand over her heart. "I'm sorry. I didn't see you in here."

"It seems we're both hiding."

Though the party continued outside, she felt very alone with him. It sped up her pulse. "Do you want a drink? I could fetch one."

"No, thank you. I don't care for champagne."

"That's a good thing." He didn't ask, but she continued. "I can't have more. I'll get too tight." He still didn't look at her.

He set his hands on the keys and played a quiet chord.

Eleanor toyed with one of her gold clip-ons and watched him in the lamplight, in shirtsleeves.

"You did well tonight," he said. "Those earrings were the right choice."

She approached the piano, feeling the confidence of the compliment. "Can I tell you a secret?" She paused. "I felt like I knew you even before I did."

He chuckled again. "Many people think they know me."

The champagne stirred her blood, and she felt galvanized in the same way as she had back in the Plymouth during Maggie's *Charades* debut. She sat next to him on the piano bench. Body heat came off him in waves, and she felt it through her dress. His leg was close to hers, one shoe pressing down a brass pedal. He had loosened his tie. The notch of skin drew her eyes, made her feel warm.

"Do you remember when I told you I felt your musicals? I didn't fit in at all in Wisconsin. Then I heard your musicals and knew it wasn't just me who felt that way."

Don stopped moving his fingers on top of the keys. He was tense. Somehow he no longer seemed twenty years older. In the last few months, the mysticism had worn away, until he became a man she knew.

"It was you, too," she continued. "You felt like me."

"Everyone is lonely," Don said. "I hope you aren't like me."

"This discomfort inside of me—yours is the same. You said so yourself. We're apart from the rest. There's no one like us, Don."

His breathing was audible, rasping beside her ear.

"Darling," he said finally. "You think our pain is the same only because you can't imagine any greater than your own. You'd feel the same way of anyone outside the middle."

"No." Eleanor had never felt such kinship with another person. It was attraction, physical and mental. "You've said yourself we have something in common."

He looked up then, and his expression was hard. She had upset him. But then he softened. "In some ways, I suppose." He played an augmented chord, soft. "We worship the same gods."

Her fear had mixed with excitement until it had reached an intoxicating height. Her hands were shaking but she loved it.

More than anything, she wished to kiss him. Unlike with Tommy, when the option had been there from the very beginning, she felt that such an action was, with Don, unreachable. Perhaps it was because he was so shy. Everything about him was calculated, careful. He did not improvise or make mistakes.

His hands stayed on the keys.

Eleanor felt drunk and couldn't stop herself. She spoke low. "Did the lipstick work?"

He glanced up, amusement in his eyes. She felt both adorable and brave under his gaze, like when she watched the foals fight to stand for the first time.

She made her voice low. "Did all the men imagine kissing me?"

He chuckled in his throat.

Heat rose in her body.

He looked at her again, almost through her. "I'm confident they did."

Every bit of her called out to him. But while he did not move away, she felt no opening, no invitation.

Eleanor wondered if he had ever had a relationship. It was difficult to imagine him with anyone. The noise from the party was dull around them, turning the room into a pocket of intimacy. Eleanor felt the desire to kiss him, but also the desire to have kissed him—to possess the experience, to merge herself with this soul she knew so well.

Without any better idea of how to do it, Eleanor leaned forward.

Don retreated. He raised his eyebrows. Eleanor froze. Her neck and chest flushed, advertising her shame.

Don smiled a smile she had never seen before, soft with pity yet understanding. It leveled her. He blinked and looked down, and in that allowance of embarrassment, she saw a flash of the real him, one she had barely gotten to know. Eleanor understood at once that Don bowed his head before very few people. She felt a dropping of formality, a moment in which she saw a man apart from his achievements. Don looked back up. His eyes were wet. She kept still, afraid to move until she understood what was happening, lest she make a catastrophic choice.

He placed an arm around her. His touch was gentle, and he cupped her shoulder, pulled her close to his chest. She rested her head on his heart. He kissed her temple, breathed in against her hair. "Harry will be looking for us." He nodded at the wall, which muffled the party sounds. "We've been gone a long time."

"Oh." Eleanor sat up. "Of course."

"It's been a long night," Don said, his business smile coming back on. "Why don't I take you to say your goodbyes?"

Eleanor searched his face for a clue, for rejection or acceptance or any emotion at all. She found nothing.

✳

Outside, it was cold, but she barely cared. She'd run out of the apartment before Don could fetch Harry, terrified to hear what he'd say. All the tension that had knotted up as she sat with Don at the piano had stayed within her, hot and impossible to ignore. His rebuff of her seemed more complicated the longer she walked down Broadway, until she reached the fifties and the glow of Times Square. He hadn't allowed a kiss, but the warmth of his embrace stayed with her. With no way of interpreting the situation, Eleanor enjoyed the memory as she could and walked south with her arms around herself.

"Pretty baby." A man leered at her, then passed, chuckling. She shivered with a shock of fear that reminded her she could not stay out by herself. Taxis passed with vacancy lights on. She hailed one but stopped short of giving her address. It was Tommy's free night, she remembered. He had invited her out with his friends and their girls.

"McCloughan's on Forty-Fifth and Ninth, please," she said.

"There she is!" Tommy opened his arm when she arrived and drew her close, kissing the top of her head. "Isn't she pretty, fellas?"

She pressed against him. "How much have you had to drink, Tommy?"

He touched her nose. "Just one, baby."

She gave him a smile that she'd seen other women give and plucked the beer from his hand. The boys howled when she took a long sip.

"How was the party?" When he was drunk, he got happy eyes, holding a smile even when his mouth dropped it.

"Not as fun as this," Eleanor said. "Want to dance?"

"Absolutely not. But I'll watch you."

She giggled. His hand was hot on her hip. He angled her so she was partially concealed by the bar, then placed his palm on her backside. She squealed, not even having to play the flirt.

Tommy was affectionate, kissing the side of her face until she laughed. But then she heard one of his friends say, "You can stand to kiss her after that?"

Eleanor pressed Tommy's shoulder when he tried to kiss her again. "What's that?"

"They're just teasing me," he said. "Nothing to worry yourself over."

Eleanor looked at Tommy's friend again. He was talking to another young man but still looking at Tommy. She felt a creeping down her back. "Tommy."

"They're giving me trouble because you kiss another guy. Nothing I can't handle."

Eleanor felt heat all down her neck. How could they know what had just happened with Don? But then she realized he meant Charles. "I'm an actress."

"I know that." Tommy pulled her in. "Look, it's just something between the guys."

She heard more male laughter, louder this time. "Tommy, I'm not that kind of girl."

"I know that." His ears were pink.

Eleanor pulled away from him and went up to the friend, who was still watching them. "What's your name?"

His hand went slack around the neck of his beer. "Jeff."

"Okay, Jeff. Tell me, why are you laughing?"

Jeff turned to the other young man and raised his eyebrows. Tommy touched her shoulder. She shook him off. Tommy smiled at the other guys. "We've all had a few too many."

"I'm an actress," Eleanor said. "I have a job to do. I'd appreciate if you wouldn't make insinuations."

Jeff looked at Tommy. "This one's mouthy."

Tommy's grip tightened on her shoulder. She regretted his discomfort but continued.

"If you have a problem, come out with it instead of giggling like a little boy."

Jeff looked surprised, and then he straightened to his full height. "It's not the acting, sweetheart. You're running around town kissing Negroes. My friend deserves better than that."

Eleanor slapped him. Jeff put his hand to his face. He turned to Tommy. "What the hell?"

Tommy tugged her arm. "Let's go." He raised a hand at Jeff in apology. "C'mon, Eleanor, let's go."

She jerked from his grip but left the bar, knocking into a few customers as she went.

Outside, Tommy took her by the shoulders. "You do not get to slap my friends."

She poked him in the chest. "Me? What else could I do? You didn't stand up for me."

Tommy's face went slack, then he pulled his eyebrows together. "What the hell? You think people respond to that sort of behavior, Eleanor?"

"Maybe I got a bit carried away. But I was mad. Charles is my friend. Why didn't you stand up for me? For Charles?"

"And alienate everyone by starting a brawl in a bar?" Tommy shook his head. "I told you, I don't care what they say. It doesn't matter to me. I'm not so weak that I need to slug any guy who I have a problem with."

"But you should make them stop." She felt frantic. "He was wrong, Tommy."

"I know that. But I can't control everyone," Tommy said. "I can only control myself. You know I don't think that way about Charles. But other people will. It shouldn't be that way, but it is."

Eleanor was aware that she was upset because she had, in a private way, been unfaithful to him tonight. But that wasn't all it was. Charles had warned her about this. She wasn't at all sure she believed Tommy meant what he said.

"You should stand up for what's right, regardless of if it makes a difference."

Tommy took her in his arms. "Ellie," he said. "Jeff was drunk. He's not a bad guy. He just doesn't agree with you on this. Trust me, I know him better than you. He's a good guy."

"Are you going to stay friends with him?" Her voice sounded shrill.

Tommy looked surprised, and then angry, and Eleanor flushed. What was she doing, bossing a young man around like this? She'd almost kissed another man tonight, then slapped one of Tommy's friends for the very insinuation. She shook her head. She would never be able to keep a man, acting like this. Tommy's hands were warm on her waist. She leaned into his chest, inhaled his scent. "I'm sorry."

He took her in his arms. "I don't think it's right, either. But, Eleanor, I can't control him. I can be friends with people I disagree with. It's no way to live, cutting people off."

She felt ashamed, dirty, knowing she'd pushed too far. She nodded. "Take me home?"

As always, he obliged, but when they reached her door, she lingered in the goodnight kiss. She liked the look of him in her hall light. "Tuck me in?"

Her confidence stretched as far as the bedroom, where she led him by the collar of his shirt. Once inside, she stiffened. Tommy sensed the change in her and adjusted. He held her hands in his own and kissed her palms, then kissed her mouth until the tension left her shoulders, until she slumped against him.

By the time they were on the bed, Eleanor's thoughts were wild. Was she about to do this? For all of her New York adventures, no one, not even Rosie, would suspect she was capable of what she was about to do. She had been raised Catholic, raised to be "nice." Back home the only girls who went all the way were easy, lost causes. But this felt like it was happening to another person, a person she liked being. She was a free girl from New York, who kissed Negroes at her acting job and brought boys home to bed. Boys she didn't even love.

Tommy was good at what he did, and they quickly advanced past all they had done before. She trembled from nerves and probably adrenaline, but he touched and kissed her body in ways she didn't know to ask for, soothing and agitating at the same time. So this was being with a man. The sensations were surprising in their intensity. Everyone in the world could not possibly have experienced this; it felt too illicit, too appealing.

It was dark, but when Tommy asked to turn on the lamp, she said no. His momentary disappointment vanished the moment he found the zipper on her dress. He groaned, dragging a hand over her stomach until he reached her underwear, which he also removed. When he lay over her and their skin touched, something primal rose up in her. She rolled her head back in surrender, not to him but to her own desire.

With her body beneath him, Tommy changed, like every particle of him was drawn to her, awake and humming. He was both sweet and passionate. He covered her with kisses in places she'd never thought to appreciate—her shoulders, her navel, the sensitive backs of her knees. His mouth was warm and slow and she nearly wept from the tenderness.

Small groans came from deep inside him, more truthful than words. He pressed against her. That roughness, animalism, brought the world back into the room. She pushed hard on his chest.

"Tommy, we have to be careful."

"I know that." He kissed her again, until she worried he hadn't listened. She couldn't relax anymore, afraid that she'd have to stop, afraid he'd be angry, or worse, that she would make a mistake and lose her spot in A *Tender Thing* because of one night with a boy.

Eleanor squirmed beneath him.

"Tommy, did you hear me? I can't get pregnant."

He sat up. "I promise if that happened, I'd marry you."

She swallowed, her heart pounding now, sweating. "Tommy, I can't have a child now."

He didn't understand, and Eleanor knew that he would never understand.

"Are you frightened?" he asked. "We can stop."

She heard the reluctance in his voice, but also the honesty. She didn't want to stop—her arousal was demanding and loud. What had once seemed far off or impossible was now vital, like she would die if she didn't do it.

She waited in the dark a long time, until her eyes were filled with tears.

She felt for Tommy's hand in the sheets, found his leg instead. "I'm sorry."

Tommy didn't speak, just held her close. He kissed the top of her head, right where Don had. Eleanor felt something crack inside her, until she couldn't bear Tommy's touch any longer, couldn't bear his closeness or his normalcy. For Don had been right; she did have one foot in each world. There was a part of her that wanted this: a man's touch, a person in her bed, easy dinners and nights watching television, weekends in the park, companionship and sex and intimacy. Though the other part of her—the part that pushed her to chase her dream, the part of her that made her risk everything—was stronger, this was nonetheless a terrible loss.

She searched through the dark for her nightgown, then climbed back into bed. Tommy pulled her against him and kissed the back of her neck. Eleanor stifled a sob.

Eleanor woke with a start the next day, as if she'd been shaken. Tommy slept beside her. The sight of him roused anxiety, but not much. She felt that a turmoil had been resolved. It was still dark, but she rose. She turned on the shower and, while it heated, boiled a pot of coffee.

She could hardly stand to look at her body in the mirror, so she opened the medicine cabinet and looked at lipstick, soap, and talcum powder instead. Tommy would wake soon, and Eleanor dreaded it. She could not think of what to say.

She washed. Thoughts of what she would miss, the box she had put herself in, invaded her peace, but she focused on washing her hair. She ran through her day in her mind and the altered scenes she would need to know for rehearsal. The choice was made, and though she mourned, she did not regret it.

Eleanor dressed herself as quietly as possible. But when she finished fastening her buttons, she saw Tommy looking at her. He raised an arm to her, beckoning her back to bed.

She kissed him on the forehead. "I have to go to rehearsal."

Chapter Eleven

Eleanor had to count to fifty before she gathered the courage to open the studio door. She was quite early; only Don was in before her. He was leaning against the top of the upright, writing on sheet music. He glanced up, then continued his notation. "Where'd you get off to last night?"

Afraid someone might come in and hear them, she approached. Don did not ruffle at her presence. Eleanor had been expecting a lecture. She whispered, "I wanted some fresh air."

He spoke at a normal volume. "You arrived home safe?"

"Yes."

"Good." He sat down at the piano and played. Eleanor waited for him to finish and continue the conversation, but he played almost to the end of the overture, stopped, went back six measures, and began to reconsider the final modulation. Eleanor took a seat across the room.

She spent the morning against the studio wall, memorizing lines. Harry did not believe in letting his cast members have days off—there was always something to be learned by watching—so even though he was choreographing the second-act men's number, she had to attend. It was slow work, with Harry often spending ten minutes moving people around the room, standing back, then doing it again.

While Harry talked, Don leaned against the upright piano, making notes on a score, his hair unkempt and mussed on his forehead. Had she misread everything and made a grave mistake? She had a ready excuse: too much champagne. But Eleanor recognized that she had been his date to the party, even if he hadn't said so outright. And he had complimented her; no one had ever said things like that to her, least of all a man. Remembering him in her bathroom, his hands in her hair, made her stomach go quick. That meant something, even if he had held back. Don's reservation made her want him more; his fame and talent put him in a position of power and Eleanor respected him for not using it.

As Don played, Eleanor recalled the photograph of him that hung in her childhood bedroom, grinning openmouthed. That Don hadn't escorted her at the party, but he was there when he played. Eleanor watched him in rehearsal, searching for glimpses of this freer man.

When they broke for lunch, Eleanor hung back. After the moment between them at the party, she was afraid he would no longer include her in those long talks about the show. Eleanor wondered if she could smooth it over, perhaps by asking more questions about his writing process. She was drawn to his insights. The reality of the night before, and the choice she'd made with Tommy, was large in her mind. Yet somehow, it seemed that with Don it could be different. Taking such a risk with Tommy would be foolish. That same risk didn't carry the same weight against the chance of getting closer to Don.

But before she could approach Don, Harry snapped his fingers and beckoned her.

"Len wants to meet you and Charles. We have lunch at Sardi's."

"Len Price?" He was the show's lead producer and had been at her audition for *Charades*. Harry looked at her like she was an idiot and didn't respond.

She retrieved her coat and pocketbook and met Harry and Charles by the elevator. Don joined, nodding at Eleanor. She was devising what to say to him when Harry pinched her arm.

"Easy on the snacks, doll. Those canapés at parties aren't made of air, you know."

At once, she was furious.

"We can't have an ingénue with a big fanny." Then Harry turned and began speaking to Don.

"Don't let it worry you," Charles whispered. "He's being a bully. The only man who scares Harry is Len Price. At least we have each other at this thing."

They walked over to the restaurant, Don and Harry half a block ahead.

"I think it's nice that they are including us," Eleanor said to Charles. "We're just actors, they certainly don't have to."

"And don't think for a second it's for your benefit. Don't be dense."

Eleanor turned to him. "I'm not."

"Haven't you noticed no one making the decisions around here looks anything like me? And there aren't any ladies either."

Eleanor felt hot and uncomfortable. After their first day at the Met, Charles had thus far avoided discussing subjects like this, and she'd been grateful. She remembered her blunder in the park, about race's not mattering, and how foolish she'd felt.

She drew herself up. "I think we're quite fortunate to be working on a show such as this. Think of it—a woman star, a Negro, kissing."

"Don't kid yourself into thinking it would happen unless those two thought it would be profitable. People like scandal."

"Obviously things aren't quite as good as they could be," Eleanor said. "But the theater is far more accepting than other fields." She thought about the party, how few women had been there, and how Charles hadn't even been welcome. She pushed it away. "Why, in Wisconsin I'd never even met a Negro, and here you are, a star on Broadway!"

"Have you ever heard of a black director? A lady director?"

Eleanor had no words; her feelings were stirred up and unpleasant. She was so lucky to be in the show—she didn't want to think about everything else she might do, if the world were fairer. In all her life she had never imagined a woman composer, a woman director, a woman version of Don Mannheim, and doing so made her feel frantic, like she wasn't doing enough.

Eleanor felt trapped, like anything she said would be wrong. This whole time in New York, she hadn't felt so rural. It made her feel small and stupid; why was Charles pushing her?

"I think we're so much better off in the theater than other professions."

"I'm so behind that 'better off' doesn't even get me a seat at the table."

So the alliance was over now? "I don't know what you want me to say."

Charles sighed. "I don't, either, Eleanor. I guess I'm just a little scared."

She looked at him. "Stage fright? You're so talented."

"Eleanor." He gave her an odd look. "What do you think will happen when America finds out I'm spending my evenings kissing a white woman?"

"It's fiction," she said.

"Maybe that's what you need to tell yourself. But I know you're scared of the same thing. Your daddy can't be happy with what we're doing on-stage. But the fact is, we are really kissing. You asked if Gwen was jealous—she's not. But she's afraid."

Eleanor didn't mention that not only had she not yet had the strength yet to tell her parents what the show was about, she had stopped calling them altogether. Caught up in the excitement of it all, she hadn't thought much about the reaction of the audience. She didn't want anything to spoil her enchantment.

They'd reached a streetlight. Don and Harry were now an entire block ahead. Eleanor watched the two men, wool overcoats hitting their knees, a sheen of power hanging around them even in their relaxed state. She longed to join them, with a deep ache, and leave Charles to his brooding talk. Odd ones out—there was nothing she wanted less than being left out. There was so much to do with the show, so much to learn and focus on to make it better. But none of it would get done if all the focus was on sulky things like who got what and why. Eleanor wasn't interested in that. She had what she wanted.

They finally reached the restaurant. "Well, we have a seat at the table today, Charles."

Harry ordered for Eleanor, allowing her three shrimps from the cocktail and a Cobb salad. At least she got some protein. Len Price was an enormous man in gray plaid who ordered a steak and a martini. Don ordered water, grilled chicken, and broccoli.

After telling a few rehearsal stories, Len zeroed in on Charles.

"You ever been here before, son?"

"No, sir."

"Will you look at that. The boy's done four Broadway shows and never been inside Sardi's." He leaned an elbow on the table and winked at Harry, who laughed. He was sitting straight, and Eleanor remembered what Charles had said about his fear. "What spring chickens the two of you are. Skin like babies, milk and chocolate."

Eleanor stirred her iced tea. It clinked against the glass. Harry caught her eye, and she stopped.

Charles surprised her the most. Despite his talk beforehand, he clearly knew how to work a situation like this. He was courteous and urbane; he'd spread his napkin across his lap as soon as he sat down. He laughed at Len's coarse humor and listened to his stories as though they were fascinating. Len asked Eleanor just one question—how did she feel about the party the night before, had she been comfortable? Eleanor was surprised that he cared until he added that he needed a star who could sell the show as well as she could sing it. The meeting was clearly between Harry and Len—Don wasn't really a businessman and was content to eat in silence. All Charles and Eleanor had to do was smile and look young.

When the waitress arrived with their food, she leaned across the table to set a plate in front of Charles. But she stumbled, sending cooked spinach straight into his lap. Bolting straight up, she looked behind her, hand going to her backside. Eleanor caught Len's smirk, his hand headed back to the table. She looked away in shame. The waitress reached out to Charles with a napkin. "Oh my goodness—I'm so sorry. Please, let me clean this up."

"Don't you worry about it, darling," Len said, and winked at Charles, who picked the greens off his lap without looking up. "See? He's fine. Hell of a first impression, son, am I right? Sardi's—not the same anymore. Oh, toots, don't beat yourself up. He won't even know the difference."

The waitress looked at him, still unsure, then glanced at Eleanor. She knew that look, had exchanged it herself with women who went up against men in public. *Is this a joke? Or should I be scared?* Eleanor looked away.

Len pulled a twenty from his wallet and tucked it into the waistband of the waitress's skirt. She stiffened. "I don't want to hear any more about it," Len said to the rest of the table, brandishing his fork like a trident. "Let's eat."

The conversation went back to the three older men. She and Charles ate as neatly as possible. When the waitress brought the check, Len tucked in his business card along with a bill.

"Keep it," he said, tapping a finger on the leather book. "And give me a call sometime. I'll get you in front of some directors. You've got a great face."

In a short moment, Eleanor was furious; the waitress was pretty, far prettier than Eleanor. It made her want to toss another plate, this time at Len Price. So that was all it took? A great face?

On their way out, Eleanor refused to meet Charles's eye. She was afraid of seeing him in case he was going to gloat over having foreseen the other men's boorishness. So upset, she couldn't even look at Harry or Don, lest she risk them thinking that she was bothersome enough to get emotional after such a small incident. But when he walked away, ahead of the group, Charles didn't look smug at all, just tired.

That night Eleanor stopped to buy a bottle of wine and a box of chocolate cookies. She was due for her monthly in a day or two. Hang Harry and his observations about her weight. Hang Len and his pretty waitress. Hang Don for being infuriating. Why did Charles even have to bring all of this unpleasantness up to her? She didn't want to find fault with the experience. With her purchases under her arm, she trudged up the stairs.

When she turned to ascend the last flight, she raised her eyes and saw a pair of red pumps and slender legs.

She nearly dropped the cookies. "Rosie Hughes!"

Her friend raced down the stairs as Eleanor went up, and they threw their arms around each other. Eleanor had to grip the rail so they didn't topple over. Rosie's smell was lovely and familiar and it made Eleanor hold her tighter.

"What are you doing here?"

"You must think I'm nutty!"

"You have no idea how much I missed you."

"You missed *me*? I was stuck in Wisconsin. I thought I would die."

Words still pouring from them, they went the rest of the way up to Eleanor's apartment.

"I had to wait outside an hour before your neighbor let me inside the building," Rosie explained. "She thought I was a streetwalker!" Rosie erupted into giggles, and warmth flooded Eleanor's body.

"I have cookies," she said. "And wine."

Rosie patted Eleanor's cheek. "A better dinner there never was."

There was so much to catch up on that they attacked each topic at once, sentence by sentence, in a round-robin. Finally, Eleanor slapped her hands on the table. "I can't keep up. First, what are you doing here?"

Rosie dropped her face in her hands. "John proposed."

"Plutz?" In truth, Eleanor wasn't all that surprised. "And you said no?"

"I feel like I'm forty in that town, not twenty-two, that's how few options I had. But I couldn't do it. He knelt and I almost got sick right there. He went on and on with some canned speech and it was all I could do not to laugh."

Eleanor touched her shoulder. "Rosie, I'm proud of you."

She shrugged. "What now? Remind me to send my parents a postcard tomorrow letting them know my throat hasn't been slit yet."

"What will you do?"

"Is your tailor looking for a girl?" Rosie smiled, looking so distraught that Eleanor reached out and took her hand. Rosie's eyes were wet, but then a smile broke out onto her face. "You know, Eleanor, when I first came here, I loved it so much. But I thought it wasn't for me." She squeezed Eleanor's hand. "But you know what? I don't need to be an actress to love New York. It's like you said, not every girl in the city wants to be on Broadway. I can work in a shop and meet a fella and do everything I was going to do back in Wisconsin, except now it will be my choice."

Eleanor's words back then had served to comfort herself and make the competition seem less fierce. But she realized now it was true. Girls lived normal lives in New York, and Rosie could, too.

"I realize I haven't even asked if I could stay. I don't have any money yet but I'm sure I'll find work soon."

"Where else would you stay?" Eleanor said. "It will be like old times, except better. It'll be the life we never even thought to dream of."

So much had changed since they'd last seen each other. How could Eleanor explain the show, the rigor of rehearsals, Don, the kiss and his restraint, Tommy? Now that the conversation could happen in person instead of over a clipped long-distance call, Eleanor realized how badly she wanted to share all of this with Rosie. They stayed up half the night talking, until her voice was hoarse. Rosie wanted to know about the show: what the girls wore, how well they were paid, and if Eleanor really kissed her costar—"like mouth to mouth?!" Once they hit the topic of Charles, Rosie did not budge. Eleanor endured endless questions about the man, where he lived, whether he was kind, and what on earth they talked about.

"What does he kiss like?"

"Like a person," Eleanor said.

"Have you talked about it at all?" Rosie asked. "Him being black and you being white?"

"Rosie, I don't know what the big deal is."

Of course this was a lie. But with Rosie here, she felt the gaze of Wisconsin on her back. Eleanor needed Rosie to see how New York had changed her. "He's just a man."

Rosie did not accept that answer. With each of her probing questions, Eleanor thought about what Charles had said earlier that day about being odd ones out. Were they? The very thought that she was more like Charles than Don upset her. Even with these ungenerous thoughts, Charles was her friend, and Rosie's questions picked him apart like he was a concept instead of a man. Her words got under Eleanor's skin.

"We have plenty of time to catch up," she said. "Let's go to bed now, shall we?"

When she finally made it to rehearsal, Eleanor learned that Len Price had secured a theater for their Boston run of *A Tender Thing*, which would open in January. Eleanor pictured the program, her name on the posters outside the theater, maybe even in lights. They were to leave a week after Christmas, in about a month. The entire cast and creative team would live in a hotel for eight weeks. As a principal, she would get her own room. She flicked her eyes to Don. Perhaps some time in a hotel would foster intimacy between them? Surely there would be late nights, cocktails? Either way, they would be spending even more time together, and she would have a chance to prove that she wasn't just any actress. He would see her in a different light.

"We're running the first act today," Harry informed them, "straight through."

Running the first half of the show without stopping was challenging, but she was ready, itching to go without interruption. The show opened with a group number showing off the dancers and introducing the neighborhood, and she didn't appear for twenty minutes. It gave her time to watch the other players, feel the rhythm of the show for the first time. True to his word, Harry did not interrupt them. Even when they made mistakes, he didn't flinch, but stared forward. Eleanor could guess at the fury behind his held muscles.

When it was time for her entrance, she felt excitement in her fingers. In this first song, Molly wanted to get out of her parents' house and find something more in her life. It was too real; Molly even worked in a tailor shop. She thought about what Molly wanted, internalized it, stepped into the middle of the studio, and sang the song. Everyone was watching her, and this helped: the thrill of the attention allowed her to step outside of herself, push to show Molly's internal thoughts, intimate desires.

Then Luke entered. She let him work on her, and it wasn't hard; he was so handsome. Molly wanted him to want her, felt her power as a woman crackling like fire. They moved easily into "With You," their fingers interlacing, his hands warm on her waist. But when he moved to kiss her, her walls went up. She felt everyone watching. She was stiff. She missed a beat and flicked her eyes over to Don on the piano. Catching herself, she didn't think, and sang, "My love, with you / Forever now, with you / For every night and every day."

When they got to the end of the first act, when Molly and Luke plan to run away together, she was in tears. Kneeling, she clasped him around the neck and sang "Morning 'Til Night." Don had expertly blended blues and jazz with classical music, brassiness cutting through the sweetness of the melody. It was dark, a love song filled with sorrow, with the desperation of desire. She sang with everything in her, thinking of the party with Don, how badly she had wanted his kiss when they sat close at the piano. She clutched Charles, sang her heart out.

When they finished, the cast applauded.

It took her a moment. The world came back to her like it was being poured in through the top of her head. She sat back on her heels and caught her breath. Charles looked over at her and smiled. They'd done well, and he knew it.

"Nice job, everyone," Harry said.

"An hour for lunch," the stage manager said. "Meet here at one thirty."

She and Charles had no energy to go out, so they sat in the stairwell sipping water. For a long time they were quiet, tired from the run-through, hungry. But they were satisfied and excited. Eleanor asked if Gwen would be joining them in Boston.

"Yes," he said, smiling. "We have news."

From his expression, Eleanor could guess what it was.

"I'm going to be a father," he said. "In May."

"Oh, Charles, that's wonderful!"

"Thank you," he said, the smile still in his eyes. "We've been trying for a while."

"God's will, my mama says," Eleanor said, though she wasn't sure why. It wasn't what she believed. "I hope your baby inherits your voice."

"Gwen's a singer, too, you know," Charles said. "That's how I met her—we sang in the same club. I thought she was the prettiest thing I'd ever seen, with a rough hoot of a voice."

"Does she want to be on Broadway?"

Charles shrugged. "She's not as comfortable, down here."

Eleanor wasn't entirely sure what "down here" meant, but she was sure it had something to do with white people. "But you are."

He shrugged. "It's my job."

"You really seem to love it."

"I do," he said, but his voice was quiet. "But I like to keep it in perspective. Family first."

"But you must love the theater, too. You've been so successful so far.

But it's just a paycheck to you?" Thinking about a real career in theater made her heart race—she imagined being at the center of musicals for a decade. Even if acting wasn't what she imagined it to be, she'd endure it for the chance to work on new material.

"Sure I love it. But I can't afford to give everything to this business. I have to take care of myself. I'm not going to give everything to a bunch of fellas who wouldn't stand my friend if the tides turned, you know?"

A wave of loyalty for Don rose up. "Do you mean Don? He adores you."

"He doesn't know me. He adores my talent. He thinks I'm handsome," Charles said. "And I never trust a man who can't meet my eyes."

Eleanor looked away, her whole body hot, whether from fury or fear she wasn't sure. She wanted to argue, but she realized he was right. Don didn't look anyone in the eye. But she felt that it didn't come from shiftiness or conceit; Don was sensitive, uncomfortable. "He's shy. You know that. He's a genius."

"I didn't say he wasn't. And I'll defend his work to the grave. This show is special. All I'm saying's I'm not going to trust him. The man isn't totally honest. Do you understand?"

She assented like it was a question on a test she wanted to get right. But she didn't believe it. Every criticism of Don felt wrong; he was odd, but she didn't find him suspicious. Charles's warnings assured her that Don was misunderstood.

Charles didn't press the point, and reached over and patted her knee. "Boston will be tougher than New York," he said. "For me."

It wasn't fair to be upset, Eleanor realized, not if she cared about him. He was the one shouldering the burden.

"I'll have to be careful. I'll have a child to take care of."

In truth, Eleanor was afraid of the audiences, too. This show felt as exposing as if she'd been asked to take off all her clothing onstage. But she also knew it was different for Charles; by kissing him, Eleanor was stepping away from the safety of the crowd. Charles was venturing into a mob of enemies.

"The audience won't be happy."

He looked in her eyes; though they did this often onstage, she felt bare this time and had to look away. "I'm not worried about the audience," he said. "I'm worried about some nut job taking a swing at me outside the stage door. I'm worried about someone following me home. Following Gwen."

"You can't live your life afraid of some freak occurrence," Eleanor said.

"Freak? Eleanor, I'm a black man, kissing you, a white woman, in front of hundreds of people. At least one of them is going to have enough of a problem with it to want to punish me."

She twisted her skirt in her hands. "I hadn't thought of that."

"I'm just saying, I have to be careful." He stood up. "But then again, I've never seen anything like this show before. What if it changes someone's mind? What if someone sees it and thinks differently? What could that mean for my son?"

"You're brave, for doing this," she said.

He looked at her. "This show is important to me," he said. "But it's not nothing, being in it."

When Tommy came by the apartment, Rosie kept busy, poking her head out of the bedroom to say hello.

"Nice to see you again," Tommy said, then to Eleanor, "How long is she staying?"

"As long as she wants."

Tommy's annoyance clung to him even as they descended her stairs into the night.

He rubbed his hands together. "It's colder than a well digger's ass."

She couldn't help it; she laughed. But when he touched her, she walked forward, a step ahead of him. She couldn't look in his eyes, didn't want him so close.

"Something my dad says. Hey, you never let me know about Thanksgiving. It's this week, you know."

Eleanor kicked a piece of ice on the sidewalk. "Things are different now that Rosie's back."

"Rosie's welcome."

"I think it might be nice for the two of us to spend the holiday together."

He raised his eyebrows. "My family would miss me."

"I meant Rosie and me."

Tommy looked away. She could tell by the set of his shoulders that she'd troubled him. Suddenly, his presence was too much; she had to tell him she was going away to Boston soon but was not up to the task that night. It had been an exhausting day.

"You know, Tommy, I'm sorry. I'm really not feeling well."

He turned back. "Hey now. I came all this way from Brooklyn."

"It's not you," she said. "It's a headache. Long day."

The set of his mouth was taut, but then he took a breath and the tension went away. "Let me walk you back."

She nodded, tamping down her relief. "I'm sorry about Thanksgiving."

"That's all right. I know you want to be with your friend."

"Tell your mama thanks."

"I will." They reached her door. He took her in his arms. "Hey, we're all right, aren't we? I know things went pretty fast the other night."

Oh goodness. This conversation might be even worse than the one about Boston. "Tommy, we don't have to talk about this."

"I want to make sure everything's swell between us, Eleanor. I know it's a lot for girls. You know what I mean. I didn't think about that. I was so excited."

"Tommy, I promise I'm fine. I'm not rattled." Suddenly she thought of his apologizing to Jeff in the bar. "Tommy, I need to go inside."

"Look here, Eleanor . . . I haven't been going out with anyone else. I'm not good at this. Do you know what I'm trying to say?"

She turned and looked through the glass door at the mailboxes beyond. She'd never added her name to the front slot. Suddenly she felt a powerful urge to do so, as if her presence in the building would not be official until her name was inscribed there.

"I'm sorry," she said. "But I told you I had a headache. I don't want to talk about this."

"Jeez, Eleanor. What's a guy have to do? I'm standing here freezing trying to tell you I want to go steady. I like you. I think you're super."

The longer Tommy looked at her, the more sure Eleanor was that she did not want this. She remembered the heat of Don's body as he brushed her hair. Was that love? Was that what it meant? Her most passionate moments with Tommy evoked only the barest stir of the heat that, in Don's presence, overwhelmed her. Standing there looking at Tommy, she was hit with the knowledge that she had fallen in love with Don. She'd come to New York halfway there. It was natural. It made sense. This realization felt like something clicking into place.

When she didn't respond, Tommy blushed, looking more Irish than ever. "You know what I mean. I'm not good with words. Tell me you understand."

"Tommy, going steady won't change the fact that I still can't take that risk."

He looked hurt. "Eleanor—who do you think I am? I like you."

She tugged her hand away so he wouldn't feel her sweaty palm.

He looked at her for a long time before he shook his head. "You're right. You aren't feeling well. We can talk later. Friday night?"

"Sure."

He leaned down and kissed her. Upstairs, Rosie was listening to music on the radio, stirring a pot of homemade soup.

"Oh no," she said. "Back already?"

She thought of Tommy outside, his shoulders hunched against the cold as he walked to the subway. "I don't want to talk about it. I'm fine. In fact, I'm marvelous."

Rosie looked doubtful. She offered Eleanor the wooden spoon. "Taste?"

"Rosie, it's just going to be you and me on Thursday. Can you make a turkey?"

"What happened?" Rosie asked.

But Eleanor did not want to talk about Tommy anymore. "Can I tell you something? It's about Don."

Rosie looked at her with trepidation. A roll went through Eleanor; she needed to seize the attention, needed to see the momentousness of her feelings reflected in Rosie's reaction.

"Rosie, I'm in love with him."

Rosie dropped the spoon into the soup. "Eleanor. He's . . . how old is he?"

"What does that matter?"

"Don't be silly. You've heard the same stories as I have. A young actress, a director."

"He's a composer."

"Eleanor."

Rosie's suspicion was infuriating. Eleanor thought of all the ridiculous double dates she'd gone on, how many pieces of advice she'd doled out regarding dippy farm boys. Here she was, a Broadway actress with feelings for a real man, and Rosie was pretending she knew better.

"It isn't like that. He likes me. We talk, after rehearsals sometimes. He tells me about his work, his process."

She thought about how close they were growing, circling each other. Don was afraid of his feelings, but Eleanor understood him. That arm around her, at the piano.

Rosie stared. "Eleanor, do you know what you're doing?"

Eleanor spun around the kitchen. "Does anyone, when they're in love? Rosie, he's the most incredible man I've ever known. He's going to fall in love with me. Just give me a few weeks."

Chapter Twelve

After Thanksgiving, rehearsals went on hiatus until they met up in Boston. Charles and Eleanor were the exception; Harry scheduled them private rehearsals in Don's apartment. These excited Eleanor, though she had hardly any alone time with Don. By the time they finished rehearsal, Harry had a list of things to go over with Don, so he stayed behind. No more intimate dinners. No more demo records. A few times, Don called her over on breaks to go over a bit in the score and would watch her so closely she could feel the blood rising in her neck. Boston would come soon, and Eleanor nearly trembled at the thought of so much time together.

When she arrived home, Rosie usually had dinner waiting. She knew all sorts of things, like how to get stains out of clothes or when to substitute canned tomatoes for fresh. When Eleanor tried to help, she got her hand slapped. So she'd come home, accept a glass of wine, and tell Rosie about her day, and Don. Rosie often had a knotted-up look on her face that Eleanor started to despise.

"I suggested a rhyme," Eleanor said one night in December. "He couldn't find the right ending to a phrase and I thought of it."

"Eleanor, that's fantastic."

"It's going in the show. At least for now—things change so fast. He said I have wonderful instincts."

"I'm sure you do—no one knows musicals like you."

"Don does."

Rosie's smile became stiff.

"He's written me beautiful, passionate music." Eleanor knew she was talking about him too much. "I think I inspire him."

"Does Tommy know that?"

Eleanor looked up. "You're supposed to be on my side." She picked up her wine and went to her room to review lines before dinner.

One rehearsal near Christmas ran long. Everyone said she and Charles had chemistry, but Eleanor was still somewhat uncomfortable touching him, and it showed. This rehearsal was dedicated to, as Harry said, "beating that out of" them. Eleanor planned to meet Tommy after, and she would finally have to tell him that she was going to Boston. She'd managed to go two and a half weeks without being alone with him long enough to broach the topic. They met for quick dinners and walks in the park. Tommy attributed her flightiness to the pressures of the show. He was quick to criticize Harry's long hours, which she rebuffed without much passion; it was a good excuse, if untrue. But she would need to tell Tommy the truth that night. So despite how tired she was, she did not want rehearsal to end.

"I'm going to stand here and watch the two of you kiss until New Year's, if that's what it takes," Harry said. "Charles, you've got a wife. Don't you know how to grab a woman?"

Charles did not reply, merely turned to Eleanor and gave her a smile that showcased both his weariness and his commitment to continuing. "Nothing to worry about, Eleanor," he said.

So frustrated that she blinked back tears, she gripped his hands and spoke more to herself than to him. "That's right. We're friends."

"No, you're lovers, and this is the most passionate moment of your lives." Harry slammed his hand on the piano. Don flinched. "I am sick of hearing you talk like you're Charles and Eleanor. You're not some attention-starved actors from New York. This is about passion and true love. This is about people brave enough to shirk the binds of society in favor of love. No one would watch a show about you. You're a bloated, virgin, desperate actor. Not even Don could make that interesting."

Eleanor didn't dare look at Charles, but she was holding his hand and felt it stiffen.

Don was looking at the music. She half expected him to say something. But he stayed quiet. He was focused on what was important: the show.

Harry approached her, getting close to her face. "Are you going to cry, girl?"

If she replied, her voice would crack.

"If something like that makes you cry, I shudder to imagine your reaction when the *New York Times* rips you a new one for trotting out this shit opening night." He sniffed. "Not that I'd let you get that far."

Harry turned away and waved his hand in the air. "Again."

She was almost unable to continue, but she'd rather have died than display such weakness. One day Harry might like her, another he'd think she was garbage, and there was no way to predict it. She couldn't rely on Harry. She couldn't even rely on Don, who would never interrupt a rehearsal for something as trifling as words of encouragement. She had to learn to know when she was good. She straightened her shoulders and focused.

"Luke," she whispered. "What are you doing here?"

"I had to see you."

"If my brothers see us, they'll kill you."

Charles lunged forward and clasped her arms. "I don't care, Molly."

She liked Charles, but somehow his closeness still chafed at her, so she was always aware of her body, dreading his touch. It translated to stiffness. If she kept that up, she'd be fired.

She imagined her mother watching her kiss Charles. She would look away. Her father would cry. Rosie would watch, wide-eyed, entranced that her best friend could kiss a Negro.

Tommy would be jealous. Harry would be proud, if she did it right. What did Don think? What would Eleanor think, watching herself? Even now, after so many times, she could not believe she did it.

But Charles wasn't some stranger; he was her friend, whose face was now as familiar as Tommy's. More so, after all those rehearsals looking into it. Furthermore, Harry was right. This wasn't Charles but Luke, who stirred the inside of Molly enough that she was willing to run off and marry him, leaving her whole family and making a new one. Eleanor understood this kind of sacrifice; she had made it herself.

Eleanor looked past Charles at Don, hands poised over the piano keys. All of this passion existed inside that man. As cold as Don might have been, as awkward and uncomfortable, he had written this. For the first time, it sank in.

Don had written Molly and Luke's love. He'd created this passion, love, surrender. The sound of this music came from his very soul. This was his love. Her stomach dropped, and she went warm.

"Luke," she said, pounding his chest. "I care. If something should happen to you, I'd never be able to go on."

"So we'll run away," he said. He pulled her up close, fitting his body against hers. Eleanor let herself enjoy the warmth of human touch. "Molly Sheeran, I can't imagine God could have brought us together only to take it all away." He swallowed. "Marry me."

Don had begun to play, and the notes resonated in her heart, her bones. "Yes, Luke."

It was so easy. She threw her arms around him, covered his mouth with hers. Luke lifted her off her feet, turning her in a circle and then setting her down once more. His musical entrance was coming up, but she made him pull away, fighting to detach himself.

When he began to sing, she used the measures to catch her breath. By the time it was her turn, she was still panting, but fighting to sustain the phrases made them better. She was desperate to get the words out, to express herself. The music seemed to come from inside of her.

When they finished, Charles kissed her once more. It wasn't in the script, but even before he leaned down she knew he would. It was natural and right.

They kissed for long moments, the excitement from the scene coursing through her, until he broke off, ending the scene.

She was trembling. Charles looked at her, triumphant, and squeezed her arm.

Harry's voice broke through. "Nice job."

It was all they would get, but it was enough.

———————

Don walked them out while Harry finished his notes. "I'm heading to see my mother," he said.

It was the first time he'd mentioned his family. For some reason she'd imagined they were all dead. "Where does she live?"

"New Rochelle, going on three years," he said. "I finally got her out of Indiana, but she says she's never coming to Manhattan."

Charles waved goodbye before splitting off from them.

"Give my best to Gwen," Eleanor said.

She dragged behind, wanting to extend her time with Don as long as possible. Maybe they could walk together as far as Grand Central. As soon as they were alone, she turned to Don, but someone touched her shoulder. It was Tommy.

"You look surprised to see me."

She blushed. "Long day."

He extended a hand to Don, game smile back on his face. "Tommy Murphy."

Don looked him up and down, observing the details of Tommy's uniform, checking his rank. He finished by glancing at Tommy's shoulders, jaw, and hairline, beard ready to grow behind his skin. Eleanor felt caught between the urges to distance herself from him and to show off his youth and vigor.

She felt a lurch. What if Don hadn't warned her off Tommy because he was afraid of her getting pregnant, but because he was jealous? It was preposterous, but as Don looked at Tommy, Eleanor noticed a hardness in his eyes.

"Don Mannheim." He shook Tommy's hand.

"Don, this is Tommy, my . . ." She fell quiet.

Tommy's hand clinched her shoulder. To anyone but Eleanor, the grin looked friendly. "Eleanor chatters on and on about rehearsals."

"This show is so important," she said. "I can't get it out of my head even after rehearsals are over."

"For those of us who love the theater," Don said, his eyes flicking behind the two of them, "it isn't merely a job. Eight hours would never suffice."

He looked at Tommy until the younger man looked at the ground, then up again.

"I don't know about that. I'm not much of an artist."

Don smiled. "No."

The air was tense. "Tommy, I'm hungry."

"Well. See you soon, Eleanor," Don said, eyebrows raised as he turned away.

"So that's the fellow you go on about," Tommy said as Don walked off. "Odd one."

Eleanor watched his back, somehow vulnerable in his dark wool coat. "I don't know what your problem is."

"All I said's I think he's off."

"Have you even seen one of his musicals? You don't know anything."

"I didn't know we were talking about his musicals. I was talking about him."

"They're one and the same."

"There's something weird about that guy. I can't picture him, say, getting a beer with anybody."

"Some people care about more than beer with the guys."

Tommy snorted.

Eleanor tried to look fierce enough to cover her blush. "He wouldn't be able to see the things he does about people if he was just like everybody else. And for that matter, neither would I. You do know I'm good in this show, don't you?"

Tommy had the sense to look repentant. "I didn't say anything to suggest you weren't."

"Do you understand that it's not some school play? This is a masterpiece. It's going to be on Broadway. It's about justice. It's about equal rights."

Tommy laughed again. "Oh, honey, don't pretend you're in this because of equal rights. You might be friendly with that Negro you work with, but you know the moment the show's over you'll say your goodbyes and never see him again."

The tears she'd been fighting finally arrived. Emotions flooded her, too numerous to analyze. "I knew you had a problem with Charles!"

"This has nothing to do with him. You want to be on Broadway. You want people to see you and say, 'Wow, isn't she special. What a star.'"

Eleanor had never seen Tommy angry before. He didn't raise his voice, but red patches appeared on his cheeks.

"I know this is important to you, and I've been a nice guy about all this. But I thought you were my girl and I haven't hardly seen you in weeks. And when I do get a chance to see you, you're giggling over some fruit because he can string together a nice sentence."

"He's not a fruit." She couldn't catch her breath. "Did your friends say that too?"

Tommy ran a hand over his face.

"You would never understand how much I love this, because you don't love anything like I love this. I don't just care about being onstage." She struggled to find the words, her throat closing up. "I love the theater. I want to be at the center of it. Maybe it's not about equal rights, but it's not about being the star. It's my life. It's me."

Tommy put his hands in his pockets and looked at her. "You know, I thought maybe I could love you. But how can I love someone who doesn't care about anyone else?"

She opened her mouth to argue, but he held up a hand.

"I hope you get everything you want from this," he said. His eyes were wide and pained, and she got the sense that he wasn't trying to hurt her. "I hope the theater loves you back."

Eleanor was still shaken when she got to Don's apartment for rehearsal the next day. It was just her in the morning, and Charles had solo time in the afternoon.

"Tea?" Don wore a midnight-blue sweater with the sleeves pushed to his elbows, showcasing his forearms, taut from piano playing. The blue made the gray in his eyes seem soft; he was so handsome that her body tightened at the sight of him.

"No, thank you."

"Problem with the yeoman?" he asked, turning to his rehearsal notes.
She'd wanted the sadness to come, but it hadn't. "I think I'm a monster."
Don looked up at that.

"Tommy and I are finished," she said. "I tried to explain how much I
love the theater. He said I don't care about people."

"He isn't an artist. You can't expect him to understand."

"That's not even the problem," she said. "He doesn't know how hard
it is. I can't get distracted."

Don said nothing, but he kept his eyes on her.

Eleanor sat down on the couch, dropped her head in her hands. "I
hate that he thinks I didn't care. I didn't love him, maybe, but I cared. But
as soon as it became a threat to this"—she gestured at the piano—"I
didn't want him anymore. And every time I think of him I just remember
how much more time I'll have now to run lines."

"The first time we met," Don said, "you told me you understood what
it was like to feel alone. But did you?"

Back in Wisconsin, she had felt alone, even with Pat and Rosie. But
she had been truthful with Don, even if she expressed it poorly; she remembered her desperation, the feeling that if she'd stayed, she would
have lost herself. "I could never have had the life I want in Wisconsin."

"But you didn't know you'd be any happier here," he said. "It's easy to
turn against your hometown, say 'No one understands me,' and assume
it's because they're fools. It's harder in New York, surrounded by different
people and education and culture, theater lovers, to still find yourself lost.
Now it's not them. It's you."

"I thought you were trying to make me feel better."

He played a chord. "I thought we were just talking."

She couldn't sit still; she opened her binder and paged through the
music from the show, an agitation growing inside her.

"You told me we were alike," Don said. "I thought you were crazy. You
think it's hard to feel alone? How old are you—twenty?"

"Twenty-one."

He snorted, but she felt the dry humor directed at himself, not her.
"I'm forty-two. I've never not felt lonely. Ambition has always come first—
it doesn't even feel like a choice. Imagine how it feels to go through this

for twenty more years. I had to write the musicals, just to get the pain out of my own head."

Eleanor crossed the room, recognizing the magnitude of his confession.

"I didn't believe you because I'd been alone so long," Don said. "I didn't think it was possible that I could meet someone like me. At the audition, or in the theater that night at *Charades* . . ." He shook his head. "I didn't know what I was seeing, but I certainly saw it."

She stepped closer.

"You're really an artist, Eleanor. Because you can't do anything else. It's a lonely life," he said. "But you understand that already. And you aren't a monster. It's just how you're built."

"Neither are you."

He laughed, a frightening sound. Eleanor sat beside him on the piano. Don did not move away. His hands were on the keys, curled with tension. With all the courage she had, Eleanor reached out and placed her hand on top of his.

Don looked at her. Eleanor met his gaze. Up close, she examined his eyebrows, the heavy bone beneath, the masculine lines of his face. Barely breathing, she watched his pupils move as he took in her expression. She wanted to kiss him, or twist away. Staying still was too much sensation.

Don moved his hand out from under hers, then took her chin in his hand. "You have a special mind, Eleanor. I know you will do something interesting to the theater."

Eleanor felt his words move her and knew that this would be one of the most significant moments of her life.

"I have never said that to an actress before." Don smiled like he'd told a joke.

Don coached Eleanor for three hours, not stopping again. He made her speak the lyrics of songs like a monologue, then repeat them as fast as she could as she ran around the room in a circle. Once she was out of breath, he would begin to play, and she delivered the song fighting for air. He taught her to warm up her voice with her thumbs between her teeth, to create enough space for resonance in her throat. In the course of one morning, she learned more than ever before.

He walked her to the door and watched while she put on her coat.

"I have to go to a dinner on Friday," he said. "At Yale. The music department is awarding me an honorary doctorate. Will you come with me?"

"If you thought I was out of place with the producers, imagine me at a university."

Don didn't smile, but nor did he look like he agreed. He stepped closer and hooked her scarf around her neck.

"Think of it as more promotion. I despise this sort of thing perhaps more than you do." Eleanor recognized the truth there. "And I don't think I could find a lovelier date at such short notice."

"What will I wear?"

"I'll find you something."

Eleanor wanted to appear cool but could not keep the eager expression from her face. "It's a date."

Though she had been exhausted, after Don's invitation Eleanor was flying high. She walked all the way down through Central Park and Fifth Avenue. Red bows were tied on the lampposts for Christmas, and the windows at Bergdorf's were decorated. They were elaborate and beautiful, showcasing satin gowns with elbow-length gloves, set into snowy winter scenes like in a fairy tale. The lights twinkling in one display shone on a mannequin's silver gown. Diamonds dripped from her wooden neck. Eleanor knew whatever she wore to this dinner would be far less formal, but what if this was only the beginning? She could see herself on Don's arm at industry parties, by his side at the Tony Awards.

She made it all the way down to Times Square. The place was still so beautiful to her. At the intersection of Seventh Avenue and Broadway, she took a moment to appreciate how far she'd come since she stood there on that first day with Tommy and Rosie. For weeks, she'd been moving so fast that every experience mounted over the last, until her new life barely resembled the one she had left behind. She looked at the theaters all around her and felt tears in her eyes. This was her place now. She had done it.

To celebrate, she stopped at the *My Fair Lady* box office and bought a ticket to the matinee.

She went to her seat and opened her *Playbill*. Her mood drooped; Julie Andrews was no longer in the role. A woman named Sally Ann Howes had replaced her. How had Eleanor not known this?

Perhaps the rehearsals had kept her from being on top of the musical world gossip as she normally was. She was in an awkward spot; she had a large Broadway-bound role and was not yet part of the community. It felt silly to harp on the casts of new shows or pore over reviews of leading ladies; that was the occupation of a girl in Wisconsin. Once they opened *A Tender Thing*, she would be one of those ladies. As the houselights went down, she imagined herself entering the opening-night party on Don's arm. She'd wear a gown like the ones in the window. She'd be in the *New York Times*.

By the time she made her way home, it was dark. High from her encounter with Don and her solo afternoon, she had never felt more like an adult. Look at her; she'd moved to New York and in months she'd snagged a role on Broadway and a date with Don Mannheim.

When she got to the door, she heard Rosie laughing. She stopped and listened; she heard a male voice. Tommy. Eleanor had forgotten they had arranged for him to pick up the belongings he'd left behind in her apartment. She was more than an hour late. Smoothing her hair, she opened the door.

Tommy and Rosie sat on the couch, a beer in each of their hands. Rosie had her legs crossed beneath her and relaxed against the pillows.

"Hello." Rosie's smile was slow to leave her face. "How was rehearsal?"

Tommy stood. "Thanks for the beer, Rosie. Let me know if you need help with those hemlines."

"Get on with you," Rosie said, laughing more.

Tommy grinned, then turned to Eleanor, his face going businesslike. "Eleanor, do you have my things?"

Eleanor had thought it would be painful to see him, but it wasn't. Her plans with Don gave her glimmering strength. "Sorry I'm home late."

Rosie looked between them. "Tommy was telling me about Ned's Christmas list. What an industrious little fellow."

"Ned?"

Tommy didn't smile. "My little brother."

Rosie was peeling the label off the beer with her fingernail, her eyes on Tommy. When she noticed Eleanor's gaze, she looked away.

"I'll go get your things," Eleanor said. "I won't be a minute."

Eleanor could hear their happy chatter pick up once she was gone. In one piece, a plan fell into Eleanor's head. How did she not see it before? Perhaps this afternoon had changed her perspective; she was so happy. Now that she had who she wanted, she could see more clearly.

She opened the door. "All righty then."

Tommy was leaning against the kitchen table. "Thank you."

"You two seem to get along." Eleanor raised her eyebrows at Rosie. "I had a grand idea."

"What's that?" Tommy took the bag from her.

"Well, Rosie, you're my best friend."

Rosie had stood from the couch, her hands clasped in front of her, brow furrowed.

"And, Tommy, I know things didn't quite work out, but you know I think you're swell."

He looked at the clock. "Er, thanks, Eleanor. I really need to get on home, you know—"

"Just listen." She clapped her hands. "I know it's awkward—"

"Eleanor." Rosie's tone was short.

"What?" Eleanor shook her head at Rosie. There was nothing to be embarrassed about. Tommy and Rosie had more in common anyhow; it made sense. "I think you two would really enjoy each other's company. You should—"

"Eleanor!" Rosie was horrified. She turned to Tommy. "I'm sorry, Tommy. We don't want to keep you."

"Stop being silly," Eleanor said. "I heard you talking, and you sounded so happy. It'd be neat if the two of you were a couple."

Tommy shook his head and turned to go. Eleanor hustled after him.

"I promise I mean it in the best way," she said. "She's my best friend. This only proves how much I like you."

Tommy opened his mouth to speak, but nothing came out.

"What?" she asked.

"Good luck in your play, Eleanor."

With a wrench, he opened the door and left.

The sound of his footsteps carried down the flights, until Eleanor heard the front door open and close.

Eleanor turned to Rosie, mouth open, and was shocked to see fury on her face.

"Eleanor, I've never been so mortified in my life." Her eyes shone.

"It's a high compliment to set a man up with your best friend. I want you to be happy."

"Maybe I don't want your leftovers!" She looked distraught. "And if I did, how could you embarrass me like that? Make me sound so available, like yesterday's bread?"

"I thought . . ." Eleanor said.

"If you can't see why this embarrassed me, can you at least see why that was a cruel thing to do to him? He's a nice young man."

Eleanor turned away and got a beer from the fridge. She needed something in her hands.

"I shouldn't have to explain this to you. You two were sweethearts. And you passed him off on me like it wouldn't bother you at all. You can't treat people that way!"

The words hit her, cold. No retort came.

Rosie looked her in the eye, her voice flat. "I'm going out."

Eleanor wanted to make Rosie see her side of things. Maybe she'd hurt Tommy's pride—but when he went out with Rosie and really got to know her, Eleanor knew he'd be head over heels within weeks. Rosie would be, too. But as she watched Rosie gather her purse and coat, her movements clipped and quick, and leave without touching up her makeup, Eleanor knew to hold back.

From the window, she watched Rosie's little form hurry down the street. She caught up with Tommy at the end of the next block, walking slow, shoulders slumped. She touched his arm, her head moving to the side as she spoke rapid words Eleanor couldn't hear.

The window was frosted. Eleanor pulled away, then locked the front door behind Rosie. It had been a long time since either of them went to the grocer, so she pulled together a dinner of cheese, crackers, and pickles. Were Rosie and Tommy talking about her? Almost certainly. The apartment was quiet. She drew blankets around herself but couldn't get warm.

Chapter Thirteen

The advent of musical theater can be traced firmly back to opera."

They were seated around a table in the department head's house in New Haven. It was more intimate than Eleanor had expected—just the department head, his wife, a distinguished student who was to receive a scholarship, Don, and herself. When they'd arrived, Dr. and Mrs. Franklin had brought them into a sitting room filled with books and musical scores. Don surprised her by tugging her to join him on a love seat so their legs were pressed together. He had never initiated this sort of closeness before. She was introduced as the star of *A Tender Thing*, but she wondered whether anyone believed that was her only claim to the invitation. Eleanor was elated—other people's suspicions about their relationship might not translate to any progress between them in private, but Don was behaving with real affection tonight. When it was time to sit down for dinner, Don had pulled out her chair and smiled in a way that flipped her stomach.

"Opera. Think of *The Magic Flute*," Dr. Franklin said. "Mozart used unaccompanied dialogue."

"An easy mistake to make," Don said. "Many people believe musicals evolved from opera. Yet the earliest roots of musical theater are found in ancient Greece, and again in the Renaissance, with commedia dell'arte. It has always been its own form."

He turned to Eleanor.

"Miss O'Hanlon is our newest star, but she's also something of an aficionado. What do you think?"

Add to this discussion? She made eye contact with George, the student at the table. He looked at her through pulled-together brows, until she was conscious of her party dress and painted lips, and that she was the only person in the room without any sort of degree. If Rosie had been there, they would have poked fun at him as soon as the party was over. Eleanor and Rosie hadn't spoken since the incident with Tommy. She wished Rosie were there now.

"Who have you studied under?" George asked, before she could speak.

She chose instead to address Dr. Franklin.

"*The Black Crook* seems to be one of the oldest direct ancestors, I believe. Eighteen sixties? That's when the form began in earnest."

"*The Black Crook.*" Don looked delighted. "I don't hear that title enough."

George frowned. "I haven't heard of it."

"It's less a masterpiece than an ancestor," Eleanor said, her words coming easier now. "But it started something marvelous."

She could see that Don was still looking at her. She raised her glass for more champagne, then smiled across the table.

Dr. Franklin filled her glass, then raised his own. "It is truly an honor to have you here, Mr. Mannheim. I don't believe anyone is pushing the bounds of popular music the way you are."

"Copland has more in him yet."

"Don't be modest. You're bringing real art to the masses. I never thought the sheep would stand for it, but here we are." He raised his glass. "To Don Mannheim." He looked at Eleanor. "And to his newest work."

She caught Don's eye when she raised her glass to him, and drank.

Don took her arm when they walked to his car.

"*The Black Crook,*" Don said after a long time of silence. "You amaze me."

"I told you, I had nothing to do in Wisconsin but obsess." Amazed him?

"I've never met an actress who knew her history."

"You must not have been paying attention," she said, but she took his words with pride. She was different. Maybe everywhere else this was pathetic, but to Don, it was a wonderful thing.

"I think young George was struck rather dumb by you."

"He thought I was a ninny."

"At first. But between your knowledge and that dress"—Don nodded at her body, covered with a coat, where she felt the green velvet slipping against her thighs—"I think he had something other than condescension on his mind. Perhaps for the very first time."

Eleanor laughed. She was glad the sidewalk was icy; it made walking difficult enough to be a distraction, especially in her high heels. It also gave her an excuse to cling to Don's arm.

"You seemed more at ease tonight than usual," she said. They reached his car.

"I'm always up for an intellectual debate."

She wanted to believe it was more, as if her presence had given him confidence.

"I think we make a good team." It was more of a suggestion than a statement.

He walked around to her side to unlock her door. "Why else do you think I cast you?"

They drove back along the Long Island Sound in near silence. Gold reflections floated on the water as they drove past large-lawned Connecticut homes. Away from the city, Eleanor felt more intimate with Don. The white lines on the road glowed under Don's headlights, and the exit markers looked the same as all the ones back in Wisconsin. The wide lanes and rush of the car reminded her of the long drives to Milwaukee. They might have been close to New York, but the highway system felt the same throughout the country. It was, Eleanor realized, a part of her old life that Don also knew. It was so small, she felt embarrassed to treasure it. But seeing Don outside the rush of Manhattan, behind the wheel of a car, comforted her. He existed apart from the city, from musicals. He had favorite foods, places he liked to vacation, knew how to drive. She felt an urge to ask him more things, personal things, but resisted. It was enough to be his guest. Eleanor leaned back against the wide leather seat and stretched out her legs, full of good food and wine, conscious of how her dress rode up on her thighs. Don had said George found her attractive—surely that meant he'd noticed her himself?

"It's late," she said.

"No rehearsal for you tomorrow." He looked across at her, taillights glowing red on his face. "Your reward for being my date."

"You know I don't need enticement."

"But you should ask for it." His voice became formal. "Eleanor, I know we have something of a friendship, but this is a difficult business."

"I know."

"For the girls, the turnover is ruthless. Who's the prettiest, who can belt the brassiest."

She watched the scenery outside rush by, feeling outpaced.

"I want good things for you." He tapped the steering wheel with his palm. "This show won't run forever. And then you'll be just another actress in the audition pool. And, please hear this for what it is, but, Eleanor, you're not the best."

She felt his words hit her in the middle of her chest. "I'm only starting out."

"You're fantastic in this show. But there are girls who can tap-dance, who can do a split and hit a high C while spinning a plate. The point is, you're here for another reason. You have a unique mind. You need to secure your place in this business, or it will be gone. No artist is safe, Eleanor."

"Not even you?"

"The winds could change for me, too. At any moment, people might decide to stop buying what I'm selling. We're all posturing, Eleanor, don't forget it."

He made a sound like he was about to explain more, then shook his head.

"You've got to look out for yourself."

Eleanor watched the car eat up the lane dashes below.

"A piece of unsolicited advice," he said, and the intensity faded from his voice until he sounded casual once more.

Her heart was going quickly, and the ease of the dinner had slipped away.

"I want to spend my life in this business," she said.

"Then make Eleanor O'Hanlon an indispensable ingredient."

An hour later, Don pulled up in front of Eleanor's apartment. Her lights were dark—Rosie was asleep, or out, and even if she was awake, they would not speak. Eleanor slipped her feet back into her shoes and turned to him.

"Thank you for bringing me."

"Eleanor, I very much appreciated your company tonight."

She felt desperate to prolong the evening, not to let the car ride sour the success of the dinner. She invited him up for a drink, hoping her voice didn't betray her longing.

"Better not," he said. "It's late."

He leaned across the middle and kissed her on the cheek. His whiskers brushed her skin and sent a shiver all the way down her body.

"Good night, Eleanor. Flick your lights when you're up."

She tried to think of something more to say but couldn't, and she opened the door. Once inside her apartment, she flicked the lights and went to the window, where she watched Don's car reach the end of her block and turn north. Rosie was asleep on the couch, a blanket hiked up around her neck.

Eleanor pulled her suitcase out from under her bed. She folded everything she could think of into it: rehearsal shoes, leotards and tights, all of her makeup, her warmest clothes for a Northeastern winter. At least she had Boston to look forward to.

ACT THREE

The Rehearsal Sequence

Chapter Fourteen

Their first night in Boston, Harry hosted a company dinner at an Italian restaurant. Eleanor had expected Boston to be a smaller version of New York but immediately felt it was different; the waitstaff showed their feelings about the mixed party with heavy sniffs. Charles ignored them with his usual aplomb, but Eleanor saw he was alone in this. The restaurant was split along Harry's rehearsal lines: the black cast, the white cast, the creative team, Charles and Eleanor. Most of the cast were friendly within their groups, since everyone had been rehearsing together without Eleanor and Charles for months. When the waitress filled up the white cast's water glasses and left the glasses on the Negro table empty, they began to chatter behind her back.

"Bad run-in with bleach?" a woman named Penelope, who played Luke's sister, whispered in a voice the waitress was meant to hear. Four of the ensemble women chatted together, eating and laughing. Eleanor watched them. Something about the dinner, and the large communal table, loosened everyone up. She was used to Charles's being the only black man in the room during rehearsals with Don and Harry. When she saw the ensemble during rehearsals, they were focused on their work. It was different seeing people relax instead of having to be on their best behavior, like she knew Charles was conscious of being. That night, everyone was ready to have a good time, waitstaff be damned.

She and Charles sat alone at their own table, which felt ridiculous. Harry, Don, and Len Price were at a table along with the conductor, Frank Taliercio, who often partnered with Don on his projects. The rest of the cast sat at two long tables laden with pasta, meat, salad, and wine, laughing and telling stories. At their table for two, Eleanor felt like a stuffy old couple. Their conversation often lapsed as they looked at the laughing groups of actors.

Before she'd left New York, Eleanor had had a meeting with Geoffrey Bennett, her agent, where she signed the contract for the run. He'd finagled her a higher salary than any of the other women in the cast. Duncan, who played her father and had a quarter of her scenes, earned twice what Eleanor made. But still, it was a raise. "Easy as cake," he said. "Cast full of Negroes, it's hardly worth writing home about." But she did write home about it. She'd yet to explain the integration of the show to her parents and pushed it farther down the road. Her parents understood a good paycheck. With her raise, she settled the last of her debt. They didn't acknowledge this, but it made Eleanor feel like she could finally fully appreciate her journey. Up until now, guilt about the bonds had tinged her triumph. Now she sent money home not out of guilt, but because she could.

She was doing a decent job not looking at Don across the room, but she could feel him nearby like the heat of a fire. They hadn't spent any time together since their dinner at Yale, and she longed to speak with him.

After dinner, Harry gave a speech meant to rouse the cast.

"We've made it this far," he said, "but the work isn't done. We've got to prove ourselves to these chilly Bostonians, or we'll never be able to tell our story in New York, where it counts. And if we bring this show to New York, we bring it to the world."

After dinner, Charles insisted on walking Eleanor back to her hotel. The white actors stayed in a different hotel than the black actors, the only bit of segregation not imposed by Harry.

"I think Harry would've put us in a room together if he could have," Eleanor said.

"He tried," Charles said. When he saw Eleanor's shocked face, he grinned. "I told him this show is controversial enough."

"Are you angry you have to stay in a different hotel than the rest of us?"

"That's like asking a man whose house burned down if he misses his favorite pen."

As often happened with him, Eleanor realized only after she'd spoken the silliness of her words.

Inside their hotel, the white actors were celebrating the out-of-town kickoff. Freddie invited her to join them in his room. Harry would be livid, but Freddie only had to ask once; Eleanor hadn't yet had freedom to socialize with the cast and longed to know what actors were like on their nights off. The rest of the company sprawled on the floor or bed, drinking wine out of paper cups. Eleanor perched on the side of the couch, feeling too young to be invited.

"I can't get a read on him," Lucille, who played Molly's mother, was saying when Eleanor arrived. "He gives me the creeps."

"He's just shy. I've worked with him before," Freddie said.

"Are we talking about Harry?" Eleanor asked.

The chatter in the room stopped, and various reactions confirmed her mistake. Lucille laughed.

"No, dear. We're talking about Don," Freddie said. "Handsome, broody, strange Don."

"Don?"

Freddie cocked his head. "Harry? Harry may be an ass, but he's a genius."

"So's Don."

"Sure," Duncan, the actor playing Molly's father, said. "But not in the same way. Harry's a general, which is good for a director. Don's a strange man." He looked around, gathering confirmations from the other actors.

Eleanor tucked her feet up on the couch, something creeping into her stomach. She shouldn't defend Don so much; it was one thing with Charles, whom she trusted, but this group was still new to her. If she appeared too close to Don, she'd look like she'd slept her way to the part.

"You're right," she said. "Harry really whips us into shape."

"With a barbed lash!"

Eleanor accepted a cup of wine from Freddie. The dancers were all about her age, some younger, but they had begun performing professionally before legal adulthood. For an hour, she listened to their stories of other shows—ridiculous directors, horrific flops, even an actress who wet her pants during the opening number. None of it was plausible, but then again, they were performers, so they carried the stories off. The group lounged together with startling physical intimacy. Even the older actors. Lucille lay with her head in Duncan's lap while he played with her hair. The dancers, a group of five young men, were all homosexuals. Eleanor knew this—the dancers were jaded and shrewd, and she gathered their unapologetic sexuality was a point of pride. But she'd never seen such unabashed affection before. When Freddie, gripped by a moment of exhilaration, did an impression of a famous actress known for her public drunkenness, his friend Gregory rose to play the suitor and dipped Freddie in a tremendous kiss. Eleanor watched, riveted. The room was relaxed and warm. They laughed at bawdy talk. At one point the conversation traveled to whom in the industry they'd slept with. She listened, but Don's name wasn't mentioned. When Freddie asked for her turn, she waved a hand.

"A lady never tells."

"Sure, but an actress does."

It felt like her moment. "If you must know, I lost my virginity to a randy Irish sailor. I couldn't walk the next day."

She downed her wine and elaborated lies, until Tommy was a captain at sea instead of an admiral's yeoman. It served her well. By the time she was done, the group had warmed to her. She knew then that, before this, they had all thought her a priss.

When she excused herself for sleep, the smile was still on her face.

"Bye-bye, little one." Freddie kissed her on the cheek. "Honored you could join us."

She smiled. "Tomorrow night?"

"By the time the show opens, we'll know everything about each other."

"You'll be sick of us," Lucille said.

"Never!" Eleanor said, throwing her arm in the air.

Freddie steered her out the door. "Someone's had too much wine."

Eleanor swayed in the hallway. She pressed the elevator button a few too many times, and when it came, she realized she'd pressed up instead of down. The doors opened and she saw Don inside.

She skipped into the elevator and hugged him.

He sniffed her. "I see you've been breaking Harry's rules."

"Are you going to fire me?" Eleanor thought this was the funniest thing she'd ever said.

"Where is your room? It won't do to have our star pass out in a snowbank."

Once inside her room, Eleanor hurled herself onto the bed.

"Drink some water. Protect that voice."

Eleanor heaved herself off the bed and went to the bathroom, filled a glass, and drank it in one go. "I've only stayed in a hotel once, and it wasn't nearly this nice." She took off her shoes and dug her toes into the carpet. "What are you doing up so late?"

"Meeting with Harry and Len." He sat in the chair by the window and rubbed his palms on his trousers before crossing the room. Don glanced at her, then away. "I have work to do."

Eleanor had seen him uncomfortable, but never so restless. He tugged at his hair until it was mussed and approached the door.

"What's going on?"

"Do you have any idea how much work it is to put on a musical?"

She patted the spot next to her on the counterpane. "I can help."

"When I need help from a drunken little girl, I'll know it's time to retire."

"I'm only tipsy," she said, "not drunk. And be nice to me."

He returned to his armchair. "There are protests," he said. "Outside the theater. Harry and I expected them, but not this early."

"Protests? Really?" People were protesting something Eleanor was involved in? "Because we're integrated?"

"You and Charles have given New England quite a shock." Don leaned toward her, elbows on his knees. "Puritan fools. We wanted a bit of noise—but it's starting too early. Harry's worried it'll grow out of hand."

"You wanted protesting?"

"How will anyone know we're doing something groundbreaking if there aren't people there to condemn it?"

Something about his words stirred her in a way she found unpleasant.

"But you aren't doing it to make waves," she said. "It's because you want to tell the truth. That's why you always write your musicals."

"I need a drink."

"You want to be groundbreaking because it's what's right, isn't it? You want to show audiences that a Negro and an Irish girl can fall in love."

He smiled at her. "I'm going to call for whiskey. Want anything?"

"Don!"

"What?"

She wasn't sure; goodness knew Eleanor struggled when it came to Charles and other Negroes. But this felt different, at least to her. Don's words suggested something more insidious than ignorance.

"Don, why did you write this show?"

He sighed, one hand on the phone. He made eye contact so seldom that whenever he did it was arresting. That pale gray gaze had a way of seeing right through her and making her go still, like he was spearing her to the back wall.

"I wrote it to be on the right side of history." His body took on the tension she saw when he was in social situations. "Next year, we're in a new decade. Integration is coming. I can feel it. If you look back, things always move that way, slow as it might be. The guy who writes a requiem for slavery doesn't end up in any hall of fame. Eleanor, I'm investing in my legacy."

Her face was hot, and she wasn't sure what expression to make.

"I think everyone will remember you," she said, "already."

When she fell silent, he spoke with the air of a father. "It takes more than a few good reviews to become immortal, Eleanor. The truth is no one truly understands my work, nobody, and they just sense that it's pushing the boundaries. Most people can't even put their finger on why my stuff is good. I brought humanity to the theater. I brought conflict, messy endings."

"Loneliness."

"I am ahead of my time," Don said, not really hearing her.

"You're a genius." Eleanor rolled her eyes. "I know. Trust me."

"Well, everyone else won't, so I have to spell it out for them. I'm going to give them something no one else would think of, something that pushes the boundaries enough to make even New Yorkers angry. I'm going to be the man with the first truly integrated musical."

It was a stunning display; Eleanor was unsure if she even believed him, or if he was trying out some speech on her that he would later deliver to Harry or Len Price. But the entire thing left her cold.

"And you need protests to prove how good you are?" Eleanor felt like a fool; of course *A Tender Thing* would be a lightning rod in the press, attracting integrationists and segregationists alike. She had been an idiot to think she wouldn't be dragged in. Charles had warned her. "How bad could the protests get?"

"Right now they're just a few deadbeats out in the snow," Don said. "Hillbilly fools. Let them freeze their balls off, I don't care. But if there's any violence, the producers won't like it."

Eleanor averted her eyes. Violence? "How likely is that?"

"Who knows. But if actors are getting beat up on our watch, it doesn't look good."

Charles. Gwen, and their baby on the way. "So what are you going to do? To make sure they don't get violent?"

"You'll be fine, Eleanor."

"What about Charles?"

"He's tough." He waved his hand. "Been dealing with this shit all his life. Now, big day tomorrow. Time for bed."

He crossed the room and kissed her on the forehead, then let himself out. Eleanor knew there was intimacy in the act, but she was too upset to enjoy it.

That night, she woke in the dark, having dreamed of Rosie and Wisconsin, and realized she'd missed Christmas with her parents. She looked out the window at a city she had never seen before. Blue light came through the curtains, and the entire effect carved out the very center of her, until even breathing hurt.

Months ago, she would have said she didn't care about anything other than the role, and that was still mostly true. But Eleanor imagined protests—what would those even look like?—and felt the significance of what she was about to do. She was about to cross over into something her parents and Rosie would never understand. If she was afraid, then how did Charles feel? It was one thing to upset her family, to break the bonds of propriety. It was another to be Charles, every day.

Their first rehearsal was on a Tuesday. Eleanor arrived at eight thirty in the morning. It was snowing, and she wrapped her face in a scarf so the air would not dry out her throat and harm her voice. The ground was slick. She was focused on her steps, or else would have seen the crowd gathered outside the theater. But when she stopped across the street to cross, she heard them.

Two dozen or so people were gathered outside the theater. A few held signs. One read, SAVE SEGREGATION. She looked behind her; she didn't recognize anyone near. Don and Harry were eating breakfast in the hotel, and the other actors were probably arriving later. The crowd had a relaxed air to them, like they were early for something and saving their energy for the main event. A man and a woman were speaking to a child holding a tiny American flag.

Eleanor waited on the corner a long time, heart racing. She didn't feel ready. Minutes passed, but she could not gather her courage to cross through the crowd and go into the theater. Every time she was about to take a step, she began to fear what might happen. Would they scream at her? Hit her? Beg her to join them? A young woman close to her own age noticed that she was lingering and shouted.

"Are you one of the actors?"

Eleanor swore under her breath. *Hillbilly fools*, Don had called them. They could still hurt her.

More people began to turn. She looked behind her once more. She was alone.

"I am." Her voice sounded stronger than she felt.

The protestors perked up; signs that had been held at sides went into the air. But no one screamed or chanted. Were they as afraid as she was? It roused her; they felt comfortable behind their signs but did not have the courage to speak to her face.

Everyone in the crowd was white. Eleanor had seen the photographs of the white protestors at the school integration in Little Rock just over a year ago. She remembered watching on television as army soldiers walked the students through the doors, the hard creases in the pressed gingham of one of the girls' dresses, the cool look on her face as she traversed the fury. Then, Eleanor had taken for granted that the girl was brave. Now she wondered at the emotions that must have been storming beneath her level expression.

Those whites were hicks. On television, they had looked furious and wild. Her father had turned the television off, calling the screaming groups undignified, vulgar. Even in her Wisconsin town, there was a sort of put-together appearance that belied how people really felt. No overalls over naked chests; no chewing tobacco in public, at least not among the men she knew. And what did they care—it wasn't as though they had to share space with those people. It was just so in Boston. These people were dressed for white-collar work, the children for school. They looked just like Eleanor. But as she approached close enough to see their eyes, a familiar fury burned in them.

She bent her head down. "Excuse me," she said. "I need to get through the door."

"Aren't you ashamed of yourself?" A woman her mother's age said this and grimaced.

"I'm a working actress," Eleanor said, "in a brilliant new musical. No, I'm not."

"Are you the star?" a little girl asked, unable to contain her excitement.

She wasn't sure what she should say. "I play Molly," she said. "One of the lovers."

A ripple went through the crowd.

"What does your daddy think of you?"

Eleanor whipped her head around. She expected more fury but saw an old man with a face like a basset hound's. He stepped forward, softened his voice.

"A pretty girl like you?" He shook his head. "What a shame."

"My daddy wouldn't make trouble like this," she said. "Like you."

"We're not making trouble," the woman said. "We're defending our rights."

"Rights? Jim Crow isn't here," Eleanor said. The words felt foreign to her, like something she'd read somewhere. She tried to speak like a girl who knew her way around these sorts of interactions.

"We're not talking about Jim Crow," the man said. "Just a basic level of decency. What you're doing onstage—it's pornography."

"Someone could get hurt here," she said.

"If someone gets hurt it'll be because one of them loses their temper," the woman said.

Eleanor tried to walk forward. Again, the crowd closed around her.

"I'm going to rehearsal now," she said, making her voice as strong as she could.

"Where are you from, miss?" Another man shouldered his way through the crowd. When people swarmed them, he held out an arm, urging them back until Eleanor's breath returned to normal. He was her own age, with brilliant red hair and broad shoulders. He smiled at her, showing off pretty lips and straight, white teeth. "There's no reason to be afraid." He leaned in. "They're just angry. Don't you take them too seriously."

She stood straight, a shiver going down her neck. "I'm from Wisconsin."

He grinned again. "A fine place. Beautiful land."

"Yes."

"You got a fella? A girl like you . . ." He trailed off like he couldn't complete the sentence.

She gripped her bag. Nearby protestors gathered to listen, closing in, outnumbering her. "I—I have a boyfriend."

"You love him?" His voice dropped. Eleanor couldn't help it; she returned his smile.

"Lucky man." He held out a hand. "My name is Connor Morris."

"Eleanor." His palm was rough, his grip assured. "You should wear gloves in this weather," she said.

"I'm all right." He grinned again, his eyes on her face. She felt conscious of every tiny expression and what he might find in them. "Lifelong Bostonian—our blood runs thick. But you should know that, coming from Wisconsin.

"Eleanor O'Hanlon, isn't it? The star? Irish." He smiled. "My family's from Cork. My granddad came through Ellis Island forty years ago."

"So did mine."

"Maybe they shared a cabin on the boat." He grinned again. She wasn't sure if he was joking.

"Look, Eleanor, I gotta ask. What's your fella think of this?" Connor gestured around him. "I understand where you're coming from—my sister loves the theater. Big important show, right? Great way to get your name out there. But you say you've got a man. Don't you think this puts him in rather a tough spot?"

Connor's eyes tracked her face like he was reading her.

"No."

"Take it from me," he said, touching his heart. "A spirited girl—there's nothing better. But while that's great to catch a man's eye, how do you think he's going to feel when his buddies start asking about you? Thinking you're a certain kind of girl, going to the theater every day and kissing God knows what—"

"Who."

"Pardon?"

"God knows who." Eleanor glared at him.

"Very brave," Connor said, now with a mocking tone. "You think you can take care of yourself, don't you? But out there kissing a Negro for everyone to see . . . you're going to get a reputation."

"I'm a Broadway star," she said.

"What's going to happen when one of them gets handsy? You think you can defend yourself?" He stepped close enough that she could smell cigarettes on his breath. "No woman, however spirited, can fight off a grown man."

Her heart picked up once more. "Are you threatening me?"

Connor grinned again. "No. Not me. But I can't tell you what someone else might do. Someone less polite. If anything happens to you, we're the people you can count on." He gestured vaguely at the people around him. "That's the gist of it—no matter who you spend your time with, you're one of us. If you get in a tough spot, you have to rely on your own people."

"I need to get to rehearsal now." Something about him set off a warning in her belly. "Let me through."

He held out his hand once more. "Connor Morris, remember. If you need anything, I work at the *Herald*. Ask for me. What's my name, now?"

"Connor Morris." He worked at the *Herald*? With calluses like that?

"Remember, even after all this"—he looked up at the theater, shaking his head—"you're always welcome with us."

Eleanor pushed past them, right through the stage door.

Chapter Fifteen

Eleanor had found rehearsals difficult in New York, but in Boston, they punished. In the rehearsal studio, the show had seemed ephemeral, but it became reality in the theater. Still flustered by the protestors, Eleanor hurried inside, then felt a hush in her body the moment she stepped onto the carpeted aisle. The houselights were on, but the stage was lit, illuminating the partially assembled set. The proscenium was enormous and gold leafed. Eleanor gazed from the back of the house. She would stand at center-right on her entrance; the lights would brighten her face. Charles, who must have come in behind her, approached and, smiling, brought her onto the stage. They stood center, hand in hand, and looked out. Eleanor's heart pounded. She tried to think of a detail to tell Pat about what it felt like, standing there, but the emotions all rushed by. Her eyes were wet, but she didn't notice until she reached a hand up to cover her mouth and felt her cheeks.

Soon the rest of the cast joined them. Even the stage veterans shared a moment of reverence as they took in the theater for the first time. No matter how many shows they'd been through, all the cast members were united in their devotion to the art form. These people would surround her in the most important moment of her life.

She'd known their names in New York, but as rehearsals commenced, individual traits began to peek out. Penelope was skilled with makeup and lent Eleanor a hand in this subject where she was unfamiliar. Duncan, playing Molly's father, introduced her to an entirely different dynamic than she'd ever known: flamboyant, middle-aged, insolent. Freddie was gruff when he gave notes on the dance numbers, but preserved the actors' humanity with more care than Harry, and turned out to be funny as well. He could even make Don laugh, and often did, before rehearsals, as they talked near the piano. Though Harry still kept Eleanor and Charles away from the rest of the cast in Boston, the fact that they spent their days in the same rehearsals, restaurants, and hotels as their peers naturally softened the restrictions.

Several times throughout rehearsals, she stopped to take in the moment. She received a dressing room—her very own, with her name on the door. The cast spent an hour learning the spacing in the theater. The stage was larger than their rehearsal studio, so they spent most of the day tweaking the blocking and dancing to use the extra space. It could have been tedious, and was to other actors, but something so mechanical was entrancing to Eleanor.

While in the rehearsal there had been room for experimentation and play with the characters, their time in the theater was limited. Eleanor found that she had even less freedom for creative expression. Once, Harry and Don needed to solve a problem and asked her and Charles to run their meeting scene repeatedly. In between, Eleanor craned, trying to hear what they were saying. The behind-the-scenes work was so fascinating to her that she wanted to switch places with them. But most of the time, she was too busy. They had three weeks to space the production, run it with lights and microphones, introduce costumes, and then run dress rehearsals. Each day Eleanor rehearsed in a wig—real human hair!—so she'd be used to the thing. It was hot and so tight she could whip her head around without its budging.

Casual relationships became close. They began changing costumes backstage. When they ran the first act, Eleanor had to do her first quick change. A dresser named Franny helped her. The woman had a pack around her waist with necessities like needles, tape, water, and bandages. Eleanor would make her exit from the stage and stand with her arms out like a scarecrow while the woman stripped her of her dress. She was uneasy standing in her brassiere, stockings, and slip, but the other actors didn't seem to feel that way and walked right by. The sight of a naked chest or stockinged leg was part of the furniture.

Eleanor was spellbound by the theatrical professionalism of the crew. If she hadn't had so much to do onstage, she could have sat back and watched them work. The men who climbed the scaffolding without a glance down, operating the spotlights; black-clad runners who nipped out to dress the stage between scenes; Dan, the sound designer, who treated microphones with as light a touch as a violinist tuning his instrument; and Otis, the props master. He was a heavy, bald man who'd been working with Harry for three decades. He knew what every actor needed at every moment, handed it off, then replaced the pieces in numbered sections on a table. Everything was accounted for and prepared. Eleanor never worried about forgetting something; Otis handed props to her just before every entrance. The crew was so good at their jobs that Eleanor didn't have to worry about her costume, her shoes, her props—all she had to do was perform.

The best day of the entire process came the week after they arrived in Boston. It was the sitzprobe: "sit and sing." It was their first rehearsal with the orchestra.

They ran through each number so that Frank Taliercio could calibrate tempos and the actors could get a sense of singing with more than the piano accompaniment. Frank was good at his job and anticipated when she wanted to sing faster or slow down. She'd imagined she would have trouble hearing the musical cues, but Frank knew how to watch singers, and Eleanor had no trouble finding the melody.

Don's music was incredible. When played by a full orchestra, layers and details that had been absent in the piano accompaniment revealed them-selves. The score blended Chicago jazz with classical orchestra sounds. Many of Molly's songs had a heavy brass section with a driving piano and rhythm section—fast, tough music. Luke's music was softer, woodwinds and strings, soaring legato lines. It was disarming, hearing such delicate beauty come out of a man. Eleanor wondered if any woman could watch this show without falling in love with him.

When the cast sang as one—near the end of the first act and a number early in the second, and the finale—chills ran down her spine. Their voices blended into a rich texture. The mix of sopranos, mezzos, tenors, and basses, and the cross-section of light and heavy voices, produced a thick, vibrating mass of phonation.

Standing in the middle of the cast, Eleanor heard the sound differently than the audience would. From where she stood, she identified individual voices and could distinguish the harmonic lines. In the seats, the audience would hear the fully blended finished product. For a moment, Eleanor felt a pang—she would not be able to enjoy Don's music in its full magnitude. But then she heard Charles beside her, and Penelope behind him, and she felt a shiver. No one else in the entire world would hear Don's music as she did. In the finale, a trumpet soloist whined a lonesome countermelody beneath the cast's voices, and Eleanor was in tears. She and Charles sang over the top of the rest: "My love, with you / Forever now, with you / For every night and every day."

"Take five," Harry said when they finished.

Don approached. Things had been tense since that night in her room, but when he saw her face, he smiled.

"This day gets me every time," he said.

"How do you do this?" Eleanor gestured to the orchestra. He'd written every instrument's line, every harmony. "Do you hear it all in your head?"

"I don't hear it," he said. "I know what it should feel like, and I write that."

"Then you can't be the monster you say you are. Not if you felt this score."

Don held her gaze. She noticed gray strands on his head, illuminated by the houselights. He kept his hands in his pockets like a boy. The contrast made her want to rumple his hair.

Don made a noise in his throat. "You adjusted to the orchestra brilliantly."

His compliment felt as precious as a pearl. She sucked her lips into her mouth, unsure how to continue. But she should not be so meek; she had worked hard and earned the praise. She slipped her score into her bag. "Thank you, Don."

✳

As they approached dress rehearsals, Eleanor dreaded the crowd outside
the theater more and more. With her red hair, she was easily discernible.
The protestors knew she was the star. Every morning she stopped a few
blocks away to take in the situation before gathering the strength to pass
them. The moment they saw her coming, they would call out to her.
Connor Morris, the *Herald* reporter, was there every day, offering coffee
from his thermos to other protestors, handing out markers to add more
cruel phrases to the signs. She took to using the box office entrance instead of the stage door to avoid them, though she had to pick her way
through the administrative wing on her way to her dressing room. One
night as she was leaving, she encountered a slew of horrible words scrawled
on the stage door, which she tried to rub out with her sleeve. She was
afraid that one night, one of the protestors might follow her home. Something about Connor Morris's charm frightened her more than the rest
put together. Part of her wanted to mention this to Charles, but she wasn't
sure what to say. They had formed a good friendship, but mentioning
that the crowd was singling her out for her whiteness might jeopardize
that. She felt implicated. She didn't want to be likened to those people.

The day of their first dress rehearsal, she applied her makeup and
wondered whether denouncing the protestors was better than keeping
silent. She wished she had someone to talk to about all this. Since their
fight, her only communication with Rosie had been a few bills stuffed
in an envelope for rent. After a few weeks, she had sent her a postcard,
inviting her to visit with a ticket to the show. Eleanor did not receive a
reply.

A knock came on her dressing room door. She glanced at the mirror—
she looked ridiculous, clad in a wig cap, stage makeup, and fake eyelashes.
But this was the theater.

"Come in."

Harry strode through and leaned against her dressing table, riffling
through a pad of paper.

"Do you think we're ready?" she asked.

"Could be in worse shape," he said, then looked up. "You're doing well."

Harry's compliments were even rarer than Don's—especially when she felt that he meant them. She let it hang in the air a moment, ears warming. "Thank you."

Harry looked around the room, his eyes stopping on a box of tampons she'd set near the mirror. He wrinkled his nose. "Put that away. Everyone doesn't need to know your sordid issues."

Eleanor's mouth fell open. Before she could think of a response, she scrambled to grab the box. It slipped from her hands, but she caught it and stuffed it in a drawer. She could not look Harry in the eye. Normally when he corrected her, she apologized, but this time she did not find the will.

Harry had already moved on. "Yesterday, your entrance in the first act came a moment too early. Listen for the cue and don't move until you hear it."

He continued for a few more minutes. Eleanor wrote down his critiques. He told her to get something to eat before they ran the show again in the evening, and left.

Eleanor waited until he was gone and then opened the drawer and retrieved the box of tampons. She put them right in front of her vanity mirror. This was her dressing room, after all.

A few minutes later she knocked on Charles's door. A tall young woman with a round face and a rounder belly opened it.

"You must be Gwen," Eleanor said.

"Sure am." She held out her hand. "I've heard a lot about you."

"You ready?" Charles was powdering his face so it wouldn't shine under the lights, a towel around his neck to protect his costume. He wore just a white shirt, blue jeans, and sneakers.

"I think so," Eleanor said. "As I'll ever be."

"Charlie says you've got real chops," Gwen said.

Eleanor shrugged but inwardly glowed. "Even if that's true, it's still my first show."

"We should go down," Charles said. He looked at Gwen. "How are you feeling, babe?"

"I've been better." She looked at Eleanor. "Whoever said nausea only happens in the first trimester hasn't met my baby."

Charles leaned forward and kissed his wife on the temple.

"Are you going to watch the rehearsal?" Eleanor asked Gwen.

Charles laughed. "You think Harry would allow anyone's eyes on this before he's deemed it perfect? No way in hell." He looked at Gwen's belly. "Sorry, Baby."

Gwen shrugged into her coat. "I think I'll go for a walk. Fresh air helps."

As she watched Gwen pull on her gloves, Connor's face came into Eleanor's mind. "Don't go out through the stage door," Eleanor said.

Gwen looked up at her. "The protestors?"

"Yes," she said.

With Gwen's steady gaze and pregnant belly, she looked powerful. Eleanor felt like a little girl, crying about bullies. "Eleanor, I've dealt with bastards like that my whole life."

Eleanor shook her head. "But there's one in particular—I got a bad feeling."

"They all give you a bad feeling," Gwen said. "That's the point."

"Please don't go that way." Eleanor was still shy around Gwen but wanted to be sure she made her point. She suspected that if Gwen met Connor Morris, she would know exactly what Eleanor meant. "There's something off about him. Please believe me."

Gwen looked her in the eyes. "All right then." She looked at Charles, and Eleanor caught something private in their eye contact. "That goes for you, too, Charlie. You be extra careful tonight."

Charles promised and took Gwen's arm as they went down to the stage.

The cast and crew scurried around backstage, animated by anticipation. The theater still smelled like sawdust from the construction of their set. The orchestra was warming up. Everyone wore costumes that resembled street clothes in their simplicity.

Eleanor expected a speech from Harry to kick off the dress rehearsal, but he was all business. He was onstage with the stage manager, testing the doors on the set himself to make sure they worked. The dancers gathered for fight call, practicing the lifts and stage combat to avoid injury. At ten o'clock, Harry nodded at the stage manager, who went to a microphone on the side of the stage. "Places in five."

The cast dispersed. The commotion electrified Eleanor. She felt like she wanted to do a backflip. A man went to the front of the stage and checked all the microphones on the floor. Franny, Eleanor's dresser, zipped her dress—a pale blue A-line—and retied her sash. In her fantasies, she'd imagined her Broadway debut would involve dazzling costumes, but she had only the one she was wearing, a nightgown during "Morning 'Til Night," and a cream sheath for the elopement scene. The simplicity made her feel more focused. It was all about the story. Nearby, Charles shook out his muscles, closed his eyes, and prepared mentally. Dancers stretched. Otis, the props master, checked over everything on the table backstage: Molly's house keys, the flowers that Luke gave to her in the elopement scene, a picnic basket, and a safe that housed the gun she held in the finale. No one knew the combination except him. It was a real gun, filled with blanks.

"Union rules," Charles had told her back when they started working with the props. Eleanor was excited to learn this; any theater-industry detail was fascinating to her. "No one touches it but Otis, until it gets handed to you."

Eleanor watched everyone prepare all around her. She hadn't yet found what she needed to do to ready herself for a performance and made an exaggerated show of touching her toes and rolling her shoulders. She felt a hand touch her back. Don.

"You look like you're preparing to run a race."

She shrugged. "I like to loosen my muscles."

Don's mouth twitched. "Break a leg today."

She longed to hug him, and since it was such an important day, she gave herself permission.

"It's been a hectic few weeks. I'm sure you're tired, but I know you'll push through. It's everything we've worked for." He twisted out of her embrace. "You never stop surprising me."

"Don." But she didn't know what else to say. "Thank you. That means so much to me."

"Show Harry what you're made of."

Eleanor smiled, hoping to prolong the moment.

"Places, please." The stage manager's voice came over the microphone like a god's. The lights went down. All was black until the lights went up onstage. The first notes of the overture came from a solo trumpet, lonely and true. The hairs on her arms rose up.

Eleanor might have lived weeks in the following days. The long rehearsals were packed with last-minute costume changes and line edits. The show would continue to change daily, until the Broadway opening. It was ever elastic, so their brains had to be as well. On breaks, she and Charles ran lines over and over. With this many rewrites, even Charles made mistakes.

At night, Eleanor returned to the hotel and soaked her feet in ice. After their second dress rehearsal, she woke up in her room with the lights still on, her feet dunked in tepid water. She was struggling to keep up with all the changes. As they approached opening, everyone else in the cast seemed to step into a professional mode, where they could both play and present good work. Eleanor went farther into herself. Her anxiety ratcheted up to a point where she could hardly even talk to Charles during rehearsal.

They had one more dress rehearsal before they began preview performances, which ran for a few weeks before the show opened officially, to give the cast time to perform before critics could review the show. Despite the protests, or—perhaps Don was right—because of them, the tickets were selling steadily, and they expected most of the orchestra seats to be full, along with the best rows in the balcony.

"Why don't you go out and enjoy the city?" Charles asked on their last day off while they ran new lines. "Gwen and I were going to walk to the water, maybe get something to eat. Come with us."

"It's freezing."

"Wear mittens. I have to do something other than rehearse or I'll go nuts. Come on. You can't come to Boston and not even eat a cup of clam chowder."

"Clam chowder? Are you insane?" Eleanor gaped. "You know we can't have that stuff on a show day. Have you ever tried to sing after a cup of that sludge? Phlegm city."

Charles laughed—she was right, every singer knew it—but didn't relent. "If your whole world is this show, you can't be a good actor. Molly is a human being, you know, not a costume."

"Screw you."

"Have a delightful day, Eleanor."

Eleanor delivered a terrible final dress rehearsal. Maybe it was exhaustion, perhaps it was anxiety, but she missed an entrance. She was in her dressing room, thinking she had a long break, when a stagehand banged on her door.

"You're onstage, miss!"

She leapt up, not even seeing who it was who'd come for her, and ran down the stairs. She heard Charles onstage. It was the scene where Luke came to find Molly in the night. Charles stood center calling, "Molly? Molly?"

It would have been funny if she weren't so mortified.

With her missed entrance still on her mind, and in the quest to be perfect, she crashed through the show leaving errors in her wake; she even forgot to bring a letter onstage that Molly's father would need to find, so he could discover the illicit relationship between Molly and Luke. Backstage, she got a scolding from Otis. He had his hands on his hips and glared at her through heavy-rimmed glasses.

"I was right there," he said. "Handing it to you."

"I didn't see."

"I can't do my job if you don't pay attention," he said. "Actors!"

After the dress rehearsal, she packed up her bag and decided she would not obsess over her script all night. A bath, then sleep, and in the morning she would look at the show fresh for the first performance. On her way out, she passed Penelope, who played Luke's sister, and Charles on the stairs, heads bent together, Penelope fingering the edge of her scarf.

"See you tomorrow," Eleanor said. "First performance."

Charles touched her elbow. "Not that way, Ellie."

"There's a better view from my dressing room," Penelope said. "C'mon."

Eleanor glanced at Charles, but he had already moved past. She followed Penelope into the dressing room she shared with Norma, the woman who played Luke's mother. A group of ensemble girls were clustered around the window, still in their slips and false eyelashes.

"Holy cow," Penelope said. She took Eleanor's arm and brought her to the window.

A crowd had gathered beneath the theater. It had swelled since the morning. Two dozen or so marched, while dozens more looked on with flashlights and signs. From three stories up, Eleanor heard the rumble but couldn't discern words. A man's red hair was caught in the blaze of the marquee, his arm in the air, his face twisted with shouts.

"It's that *Herald* reporter," Eleanor said. "Connor Morris."

Charles looked over the top of her head. "He seems insane."

Penelope made the sign of the cross.

"We should all go out together," Eleanor said.

"No," Penelope said, her hand covering her mouth. "No, we have to go another way."

"Surely with a group this large, they wouldn't bother us," Eleanor said.

Charles met her eyes, shook his head. "I'll go down and talk to security. We'll figure out a way. Everyone stick together. Don't let anybody leave."

Penelope went to gather the rest of the ensemble. Eleanor waited on the stairs, stopping people before they went outside.

"I've walked through this group before," Eleanor told Freddie, the dance captain, when he came, annoyed, out of the male ensemble room. "They're awful, but surely they won't attack us?"

Freddie shrugged. "I just want to get some sleep."

Charles returned with three of the theater's security guards. "They're calling us taxis," he said. "Let's get in groups of four."

Eleanor followed his lead. She was grouped with him, Penelope, and Norma, whom she had never actually spoken to. The group waited with nervous energy.

"We'll go last," Charles told her. When the first group opened the stage door, Eleanor heard screams and shivered all the way down. Her stomach went sick. A man's yell ripped through the crowd before the door shut.

Eleanor looked at Charles again. "You seem to know what to do."

"I have no clue," he said. "But part of being a principal means leading offstage as well."

Eleanor looked at her shoes. She heard no judgment in Charles's tone, but she was a lead too and had no idea how to help. But Charles didn't even seem to register her inaction, let alone her embarrassment; he was counting the cast members and, in a low, even voice, giving out instructions that he must have been making up on the spot. Eleanor was too frightened to do anything but appreciate his cool head. When it was their turn, Norma and Eleanor linked arms. The guards returned and ushered them through the door. Like before, the crowd closed around them. Eleanor kept her grip on the back of the guard's coat, her eyes shut tight, hearing the yells and profane words around her. She felt Charles's hand on her back. The chants swelled when some recognized her. The guards on either side of her had to push protestors away, but one of them reached through, gripping at her sleeve. Eleanor cried out when she finally touched the cool metal of the car door.

"Everybody all right?" Charles asked from the passenger seat.

Penelope slammed her door shut, turned her back to the crowds. Two men approached and slapped their hands on the car, their breath leaving damp clouds on the windows. The driver had to go slow to avoid hitting the people who jumped in front, fists punching the hood. Eleanor ducked her head against the back of the driver's seat, pushing the heels of her hands into her eyes.

"Anybody hurt?" Charles asked once they were free of the crush.

"Only my coat," Penelope said, showing the torn seam connecting her sleeve to the shell.

Eleanor couldn't answer. Her hands were trembling. Charles looked across the car at her, reached his hand back, and gave her a shake. His palm was cold. He looked ahead and watched the traffic go by, his eyes wide and unblinking, his chest rising and falling with each breath. She realized she hadn't been truly afraid until she saw Charles's fear.

✳

That night, Don came to her room to give notes. While normally she might have tried to engage him in conversation, she was so exhausted from the day that she longed for him to finish so she could sleep in preparation for her first performance the following day. It would be the first time she performed in a show in front of an audience; she could scarcely eat. With all of her mistakes on her mind, and her body still reeling from the intensity of the protests, she felt near tears. She took the edited lyrics from him and promised she'd have them memorized by morning, then asked him to leave. The truth was, his presence still distracted her so much she could hardly stand his watching her in rehearsals. This was unavoidable, of course, but she needed to keep her mind on the show. For the first time since they'd met, Don was coming second.

Eleanor woke at four in the morning, heart pounding. Her stomach was so upset that she ran to the bathroom and vomited. Then she pressed her cheek to the cool tile floor. No fever; this was pure nerves.

By eight, she hadn't gotten more sleep. They had a short rehearsal from ten to one, to clean up some things before the show that evening. Eleanor struggled into her clothes, her mind racing over Harry's notes, new lines, the entrance she'd missed the day before.

When she arrived at the theater, the crowd of protestors was still outside. Right away she spotted Connor Morris. Doubling back, she went around the block so she could enter through the box office.

No costumes that morning; she sat in the theater and exchanged greetings with cast members.

"You look rough," Charles said.

"Nervous stomach."

He clicked his tongue. "You'll forget your nerves once the curtain rises."

"Yesterday, Charles. What if something happens next time?"

"We can't think of that," he said. "Just do the show."

"I was terrible in rehearsal." Her eyes burned. "You're going to be great. I'm just some girl from Wisconsin. If I mess this up, that's it. I'll be on the train back in a week."

He smiled. "Surely by now you can afford a plane ticket."

"Stop it."

"You won't ruin this," he said. "You've got the head of a bull. It's just you and me up there." He nodded at the stage. "We'll take care of each other."

Charles's words helped. She managed to get through the rehearsal and adapt to the little changes without becoming distracted. At one, she left and went back to the hotel. Her anxiety retreated enough for a nap, and she fell onto the bed without removing her shoes.

Eleanor woke to a knock on her door. She was surprised to see Don through the peephole with a bouquet of yellow roses. "I thought you might need bolstering."

She took the flowers and pressed them to her chest, her stomach swooping. "Stay a minute?"

Don had brought a vase; he walked to the bathroom and filled it with water. "I'm nervous too."

"You?"

"Every time is brand-new."

"You have nothing to worry about. The show is extraordinary."

His smile left his face. "Something's wrong with it."

"I'm sure you always say that."

"Yes. But this one nags at me. Something about it isn't truthful. But I can't see what's the matter. I'm too close to it." He kept his gaze on the ceiling.

Eleanor picked at a loose thread on the counterpane. "Don? Why did you write this show?"

He turned to her. "I told you the other day."

"But all your musicals are about the same thing. People wanting love and not finding it. Missed connection. But this is about people who find each other and don't let go. Why?"

He exhaled. "Eleanor, I'm not sure myself."

"That can't be true." Had Don ever been in love? It was difficult to imagine him as anything but a complete unit. She tried and failed to picture him as half a couple. She thought of his holding a woman's purse while she shopped and nearly laughed.

"I suppose I wanted to know what it felt like."

He hesitated. She hoped he would continue but feared if she prompted him he would close up.

"I knew if I wrote love, I would be able to feel it, if only for a moment."

What he was suggesting was too much; if it was true he'd never felt love before, then the cavern between them, already so foreboding, would become nonnegotiable. "Why, it's not the same, but you love your parents."

He laughed. "My mother is a bitch."

Eleanor was shocked at his language but fought to control her expression. She wanted him to confide in her.

"The woman never cared for anyone but herself a damned day in her life. My father spent every night in a bar, until he lost his job and skipped town. You're not going to find a happy story with me, Eleanor. I'm not young anymore, the wounds don't bleed. But I was a lonely child. That's why the shows exist. They were born from the cavity inside of me."

The words were melodramatic, but his voice was so low, it chilled her to the very bone.

"I just wanted to feel it for a few moments," he said. "And you know, when I was writing . . . I did. In little flickers, I felt it, as the notes passed through my fingers."

He held her gaze for a long moment, then exhaled.

"I'll fix it." He looked at her. "I'll fix the show. I promise. I'm going to give you a hit."

Chapter Sixteen

The moments before the first performance felt heightened. Everything from her vocal warm-up to applying her lipstick felt momentous, like she was about to walk to her demise. But inside, she was still. Her body thrummed with energy, not fear. The minutes passed, each one taking her closer to curtain, but she moved steadily. Voice warmed to her satisfaction, she stretched, then put on her costume. She checked the wig and reapplied her blush. Her stomach, normally so nervous that she could not eat, was quiet. It was as if her body knew how much depended on it and had fallen in line. When the orchestra began to tune, Eleanor felt her body quiet as if in prayer. That one note, an A, could settle her like nothing else. She had never imagined she'd hear it from the wings. The audience recognized it too and quieted. The hairs on her arms rose up.

Duncan, costumed in his suit and tie and looking every bit the middle-class businessman father he was playing, rather than the boisterous, caustic actor he was, came by and kissed her and Lucille on the cheeks before finding his place. Freddie, who led the dancers onstage during the first beat, took Eleanor by the hands. As the overture turned to a bright arrangement of "With You," he danced with her, nearly knocking Franny off her feet. Neither could laugh in case a microphone picked it up. Eleanor's cheeks burned with the exertion of keeping it in. Then, just in time for his entrance, Freddie released her and bounded onto the stage like an adolescent lion.

Ever since Pat had played her that first Gershwin record, she'd wanted this. And as much bravado as she might have put on, she'd barely allowed herself to imagine it. But thanks to Pat, and that advertisement, here she was. She saw the black void of the audience, the glow on the stage. Now that it was happening, she took a moment, determined to remember it.

Charles had been right. *A Tender Thing* was in her body and bones. As dizzying as the rehearsals had been, they had cemented the show into her. All her mistakes were out of her system. It wasn't only the lines that were familiar. Her first dress rehearsal, she'd elbowed Franny during a quick change and drunk too much water, and ended up fighting her bladder for most of act two. Now she knew to stay still during her changes and to time her hydration so she wouldn't need the ladies'.

She entered as Molly, lost in the wrong neighborhood. Unwelcome on the South Side, she felt her otherness and grew afraid, until a young man came up and offered to escort her home. It wouldn't be smart; he would be in more danger in her neighborhood. But he insisted.

She even felt butterflies when Molly pulled Luke around the side of a building and kissed him, meaning for it to be sweet but finding more than either expected. He stopped, afraid for them both, but when she kissed him again he couldn't refuse her. When he walked her home, she sang "With You" with all the wonder she felt in her heart; both Molly and Eleanor were astonished by their circumstances and frightened that their new sources of joy would end and leave them destroyed.

The torrent of their love carried them through the show. She was glad, immensely glad, for Charles. His kindness and generosity throughout the process paid off onstage; she trusted him completely. In the act one finale, when Luke climbed through her bedroom window, she felt true joy in her heart when she turned and saw him there.

When they sang "Morning 'Til Night," they grasped hands and sang better than ever before. It raised her pulse, even aroused her. When she looked at Charles, his face, which had grown so dear, moved her. She felt so attuned to Molly that it was easy to substitute her feelings, until Eleanor clung to Charles—Luke—with real desire. The music was alive in her like a flame, burning her until she released it. They professed their love, and as Molly, Eleanor felt it. She kissed his palm. She felt swollen with love, desire.

"I pray all day / That I can be with you again / From night 'til morning / Morning 'til night."

He pulled her into him, and she began to sob. It was then that she knew she had never felt this in real life. It was as Don had said—she felt flickers of true love as the material passed through her.

She promised to meet him the following night, and he kissed each one of her fingers, then pulled her into his arms. It was a charged moment. Molly and Luke planned to leave each other, but—Harry had directed this carefully—at the last moment, couldn't bear to part. Luke looked at Molly, slow, afraid to even speak the words. Then Molly tugged him down by the shirt collar and kissed him. He pulled away, looked at her again.

She pulled him to the floor. The lights faded to black. Intermission.

When the curtain fell, Eleanor sat up and exhaled.

"Nice job," she mouthed, afraid to speak in case the mics were hot. But Charles had a strange look on his face. "What's the matter?"

"It's quiet." His mouth was tight. "No applause."

Eleanor hadn't noticed because she was so accustomed to not hearing applause in rehearsals. But Charles was right. It was silent.

"Perhaps they're thinking."

After a few moments, a smattering broke the silence.

Charles helped her to her feet. Harry was already waiting backstage.

"What's going on?" Charles asked.

"In case you hadn't noticed, people usually clap after the curtain goes down." Harry paced. "Damn idiots. They hated it. Damn cold-blooded Bostonians."

"So they just . . . walked out?" Eleanor asked. "Will they come back?"

"We'll find out in about twelve and a half minutes," Harry said.

Don appeared behind his shoulder. "We knew they wouldn't like what they saw. They just liked it even less than we thought."

"I thought we could convince them," Harry said.

"I don't think one hour is enough to convince a man of something he doesn't want to see," Charles said.

Don shook his head. "I need to write better work, then."

Eleanor had assumed people might object to the subject matter, but surely they would come around when they saw the show. Apparently not.

"I'm just saying they're white folks," Charles said, "and they don't want to see a guy like me touching her."

Harry took Charles and Eleanor by the shoulders. "By the end of this run, I want the audience in tears. I don't want them comfortable with the idea of you two . . ." He waved a hand suggesting amorous activities. "I want them desperate for you two to be together. I want them praying that you run away and have a happy ending, caramel babies and all."

"Do you think a musical can undo everything this country was built on?" Charles asked.

Harry tightened his grip on their shoulders.

Don looked at Charles for a long time. "I think a musical can do anything—for one evening, at least."

Eleanor could see his mind working. He was already rewriting the show. This was how it happened—in both long hours at the piano and moments of inspiration backstage.

Eleanor wanted to contribute but was afraid of angering Harry. "Won't the New York audience be more receptive?"

Charles laughed. "They'd certainly like to think so."

"What does that mean?"

"It means sure, they're better," Charles said. "But they're still white."

"If we can't at least convince this crowd, we won't have a hit in New York." Harry made a fist. "Damn it if this ruins my streak." He turned to Charles and Eleanor, pointing wildly. "Get your heads straight. If you let this ruin your second act, you're fired."

The performances became experiments; the rehearsals during the day were for the adjustments. Every morning, they received edits to the music, lyrics, and lines, and during the performances, Harry and Don would sit in different places in the audience, listening to the reactions. The following day, they'd repeat. They could spend an entire rehearsal learning a scene that would be scrapped the next day, or else have nothing to change but a few lines. Sometimes the smaller changes were the most difficult to remember. Don and Harry found an endless amount to change in the musical.

Don rewrote the opening number into a rousing group song that illustrated the cross-section of cultures in one mile of Chicago streets. But the applause after that number was lax; it was too much information. They restored the original opening.

Don thought maybe the show needed comic relief and added jokes.

"I feel ridiculous," Eleanor told him after the tenth show, when all her punch lines fell flat.

They swapped out "With You" for a song called "Walking Home" that Don thought would do more work to establish their living situation. To Eleanor, it sounded like a funeral dirge transposed into a major key. Charles, whose pitch was normally precise, kept falling flat. Don told him to get it together, but the key just did not agree with his voice. The song went in for one performance, and then, after they'd rehearsed it half a dozen times the following day, Harry stood up. "Enough! This is out!" He swatted the air. "Back to the original!"

So Don banned the idea of any more "quick fixes" and went back to old-fashioned musical theater writing: late nights at the piano, dissecting rhyme schemes and fiddling with individual words. More than once, he invited Eleanor to join him. She had ideas, plenty, for reshaping the show. Don didn't always agree, but these suggestions provoked vigorous debates that often produced a compromise that was worked in the following evening.

She often stayed late in the theater after rehearsals, elbows on the edge of the stage, looking into the orchestra pit while Don fiddled over the piano.

"How's this?" He worked well with instant feedback. "What would Molly say here?"

Eleanor had a sense of Molly that Don couldn't grasp. He often expected her to be more cautious, but Eleanor knew the central fire of her character. She understood Molly's will, the hard strength inside her, how the girl was given to blunders when not careful. They spent long evenings in the theater, Eleanor's confidence growing each time she told Don something and he nodded. She loved to watch him work, his left index knuckle in his teeth as he scrawled out a lyric, his shoulders moving under his ubiquitous sweaters as he thundered on the piano. She loved being this close to him. Their minds seemed to fuse in these sessions. Don would speak the lyrics, his voice trailing off, until she picked up the sentence and suggested a word, his eyes lighting up, his hand going to the page. The hours added up until her nerves around him waned into more of an awareness than a fear. He stopped inviting her and instead just told her what time he would start working. Every evening, they took a cab together back to the hotel, and he thanked her for her help and praised her instincts. She felt like a mixture of a pupil and a partner.

Her relationship with Tommy had not afforded her any experience in moving forward with a man like Don, but she sensed that this intellectual relationship was the beginning of an even greater intimacy. Don would not flirt—the way to his heart was through his mind, through the vitality that linked them, the music, the lyrics. She was meeting him in his territory and sensed that he was waiting for her to flinch. She would not.

No matter what she said, Don always kept the original ending: Molly and Luke escaping from the picnic. Molly's parents chased after them, but Molly brought the gun, waving it wildly at the crowd. They would get away. At the very end, they sang a reprise of their first love song while waiting for a train. But instead of beholding each other with wonder, the verse was tweaked to reflect triumph: "My love, with you / Forever now, with you / I believed we'd find a way / And now, we're one / The two of us are one / For every night, and every day." Luke kissed her. They boarded the train to their future.

"If we make the audience sit through two acts of despair, we have to reward them for it. We can't expect them to suffer for nothing," Don said any time someone suggested a change to the ending. "These characters have to end up together. This story is about love, people, not tragedy!"

Eleanor wanted the show to work more than anything, but no matter what lines they changed or songs they added, people hated it. When people saw Luke put a ring on Molly's finger, they hissed. It was such an ugly, disturbing sensation, being hissed at by a crowd. Eleanor began to internalize it, leaving the stage hyperventilating. The daily protests outside the show made her angrier, until being in the show started to matter less than the message. Performing the show again and again, and her friendship with Charles, made her more comfortable with the subject matter. She felt herself changing. With each performance, she felt herself sink deeper into Molly's love for Luke, until her character's journey was pushing her own. Their love began to feel as natural as breathing. Each night, she lived as Molly, who, each night, chose Luke. When the curtain went down, she could not entirely leave Molly behind.

One morning, the theater was on the cover of the arts section of the *Boston Herald*: BROADWAY-BOUND "A TENDER THING" STRUGGLES TO FIND FOOTING. The article detailed their poor ticket sales, how people walked out at intermission. It used clumsy summaries from audience members to spoil the plot. The article concentrated on the sex, the scene in which Luke steals money to run away with Molly, and the image of Molly with the gun. Unsatisfied customers provided quotes like "upsetting," "inflammatory," and "vulgar." The byline: Connor Morris.

Eleanor read the article and seethed but could not dispute one fact: people did not like the show.

"If people don't want to like something, there's nothing you can do," Charles said when they walked to the theater that evening.

"Why are you so resigned?"

"I'm not," Charles said. "You think I want the show to flop? You think I like performing for a group of bigots every night, knowing they wish me dead?"

Eleanor blushed. "No. I shouldn't have said that."

"Some people will never be able to look at me and see anything but a threat."

"What can we do?"

They reached the theater. The crowd had swelled to over a hundred people. Charles looked at her, held out his hand.

"It's safer through the back way," she said. "Otis lets me in every morning."

"I'm not taking the back door." He looked at her steadily. "It's the stage door or nothing. I'd love if you joined me."

She thought of the headline in the paper. Was she proud of the show or not?

She took his hand. The voices in the crowd swelled as they approached. Protestors raised their signs, seeing that they had an audience. RACE MIXING IS COMMUNISM. Eleanor had crossed the protestors before, but never with Charles. She held on tight to his hand as the yelling got louder. Usually, people screamed at her, but this time, the words were directed at Charles. She heard filthy words lobbed his way. Eleanor held her head up, refusing eye contact with the protestors, even though tears burned behind her eyes.

Finally, a white-haired man spoke to her. She recognized him from the first day. "You should be ashamed of yourself."

Charles tugged her on, but someone gripped his arm, wrenching them apart.

"Get your hands off that girl!"

She grabbed Charles once more and pushed through the crowd. Whoever had touched Charles had broken an invisible barrier, and the screams went louder, the people pushing and trying to separate them. Charles grabbed her shoulders and covered her back with his body, moving through the crush with as much efficiency as he could without shoving.

When they reached the stage door, Eleanor cried out and touched it with both hands. She hauled it open and Charles pushed her inside, following behind. Together, they slammed it in the protestors' faces.

"Can Harry do anything about the protests?" Eleanor asked Don that night. Anxiety riddled her body and she knew she wouldn't sleep, so she'd decided to speak to Don. She couldn't let go of the idea of violence erupting outside the theater. "This could get dangerous. You should have seen the way they treated Charles."

Don's eyes tracked a lyric on the page. "I had the exact rhyme in my head this morning but forgot to write it down. I hate that."

"Don."

"Eleanor, don't validate those idiots by paying them attention."

"What about Charles? You weren't there, you didn't hear them."

Don opened a folder of notes and spread them out in front of him. "I expected this musical to ruffle feathers. But I'm beginning to think I've plucked the whole chicken."

Eleanor sat in the only available seat: on his bed.

He spread out the music, the crossed-out script pages and blank staff paper. "I confess I was a bit naïve. For this to work, I'm going to have to write the best musical of my career," he said. "No, I'm going to have to become a better writer than I am. Charles was right. If people don't want to see something, they won't. There is no more powerful flavoring than dislike."

"Don, would you have written this musical if you didn't think it would cement you in history?" She felt a sudden need to know.

Don ran his finger over the second woodwind line in the score.

"I would never have started it," he said. "But I will finish it. Even if we never make it out of Boston."

Despite the bad performances, that had never occurred to Eleanor. She'd won a part in a show with Don Mannheim. Would she really be thrown back into the sea of auditioning girls so quickly? She imagined a chorus call, standing in a line of sopranos. Even if she booked another part, what would the experience be like? Surely no other composer would share his piano bench. The thought of losing this side of the process made her anxiety kick up again.

He looked up at her. "I've always found Charles to be magnetic. Toss him into any role and he'd charm an audience. I thought if we combined him with a good story, a girl people believed in, and beautiful music, that we could change hearts. But every night, when the show ends, hundreds of people are still stuck on the first step. They don't want to be moved by him."

"What are you going to do about it?"

"I'm going to change people's minds in the only way I can," he said.

Eleanor looked at the music. For the first time in her life, she struggled to see how it could possibly be enough.

✳

Eleanor liked to eat breakfast at the hotel restaurant alone so she could review the changes to her scenes. Duncan and Lucille ate calmly nearby. They probably escaped the bulk of the protests. The black cast members were usually the targets, with the rest reserved for her.

Eleanor had turned her attention back to her script when someone approached her table.

"Mind if I sit?"

It was Connor Morris, the *Herald* reporter. She pulled the script closer so he could not read it. He interpreted this as her making room and sat down.

"I'm busy."

"Just a quick chat." He held a pad of paper and pen.

"We're not supposed to speak to the press," she said. "So—no comment."

He smirked at her. He really was very handsome.

"Your show is flopping."

"Thanks to your horrible piece."

"I let the audience speak for itself." He turned his head to the side as if he was examining her. "Tell me about your costar. Charles Lawrence."

She shook her head. She wasn't going to say anything that he could twist.

Connor flipped through his notebook.

"Eleanor O'Hanlon, straight from Wisconsin." He looked up. "Quite the gig for a girl from a pig farm."

"Who told you a pig farm?"

"I took a trip to New York," he said. "You know a guy named Tommy Murphy?"

"What on earth did he say?"

"Calm down. Tommy made it clear your amorous history is over, but as soon as I started digging he told me to go 'stuff' myself."

She felt a rush of affection toward Tommy.

"I got the basics out of him before he figured out I wasn't a buddy of yours. Smart guy. Why did you break up?"

"I had to focus on the show."

Connor wrote that down. Eleanor slapped her hand on the table. "I didn't say you could write that."

"Your friend Rosie was even quicker," he said. "Wouldn't give me your parents' names. I had to find those on a parish registry."

She stopped chewing. "You met Rosie?"

"I went to your apartment. That's also where I met your Tommy."

Connor watched her. Eleanor felt her cheeks grow hot, even worse for trying to tamp down the reaction, but she managed not to say anything. So, she'd been right. A flicker went through her, of satisfaction and sadness. Rosie hadn't told her.

Eleanor set her expression. "I'm not going to tell you anything."

"I was right about your parents," he said. "They said I was asking about the wrong Eleanor. Said . . ." He riffled through his notepad. "'She wouldn't be involved with that trash; we raised our girl better than that.'"

Eleanor tried to wrench it away. "Did you even tell them you were putting that in print?"

He shrugged and laid his pen down. "Now, Charles. Are the two of you friends?"

Connor's mention of Charles made something rear up inside of her. She wanted to scratch his face.

"Are you aware of his violent history with women?"

Connor spoke like he was asking the time.

Eleanor gripped her coffee to avoid hitting him. "You're lying."

He gave her a patient look and then riffled through his notebook until he pulled out a folded clipping from the *New York Times* from 1954.

NEGRO STRIKES WOMAN IN HARLEM BAR.

Less than a hundred words, stating that Charles had broken a woman's nose during a riot.

Eleanor read it, read it again. Her hand shook, so she put it under the table.

"If that's true," she said, speaking slowly, "then why isn't he in prison?"

"She didn't press charges." Connor took the clipping back. "God knows why. But you know what they say about men who hit women."

She didn't respond. The banana was coming back up.

"It's never just once."

She stood. "I have to get ready for rehearsal."

"Remember what I said." He stood with her. "If you get in trouble."

She handed him back the article. "I'll never come to you for help."

"You say that now." He tapped his notebook. "But blood runs thicker than water."

She knew she'd think of plenty of comebacks as soon as he was gone. For the moment, it was all she could do to leave the restaurant.

She arrived at the theater early and went straight to Charles's dressing room. She had no plan; she was not even positive she would have the nerve to ask him about what Connor had shown her. But when she arrived, Charles was not there. Gwen sat on the couch in his dressing room, her feet up on his vanity chair.

"What's the matter, Eleanor? Sit down." Gwen had one of those faces, the kind Eleanor trusted at once. Big eyes, round cheeks.

"I don't know how much longer I can keep this up. The protestors. Everything. It's so much pressure. Everyone wants us to fail."

"You probably will."

Eleanor looked up. "How can you say that? I thought you liked the show."

"I do. But I'm in the audience every night, and I hear what people say. I've been telling Charles from the beginning, it's too big a pill to swallow." Gwen leaned forward and adjusted her skirt over her knees. "You can't go from segregation to marriage in two hours."

Eleanor wanted to prove her wrong. But she felt inept. "People should be able to see what's possible."

"If this could be solved in two hours, Eleanor, I have to hope someone would have done it already. It's all so complicated. But I think you can make people care about Molly and Luke."

"How, when the audience is against us?"

"Do you really understand how hard it would be for them?"

But it shouldn't be hard, she wanted to say. If it's about love, like Don always said, then they would risk everything. It shouldn't be a hard choice for Molly and Luke. It was hard for the world to accept, not hard for them.

A stagehand down the hall called for costumes. Eleanor excused herself to get ready, grateful for the chance to leave before she had to answer Gwen's question.

After the show, Eleanor tracked Harry down to tell him about Connor Morris. She found him in the empty audience going over his notes. Eleanor hadn't removed her stage makeup, and her face felt hot and muddy under the pancake. She told him about the protest the previous day and Connor's attention that morning.

"So you're scared."

She would never have admitted this to Don, but Harry was her director. He solved problems all day long. "Yes."

"Stay away from the protestors." Harry swore. "I thought the coverage would be more mixed," he said. "We need to get out ahead of this. Don't give any comment."

Compared with Don's dismissal, Harry's acknowledgment of her worries felt like an embrace. She thanked him.

"It's my job. I need you all not to be distracted and to give the best performances you can." Harry moved a stack of notes off the seat next to him. "You're doing well," he said, as he had the other day.

Eleanor blinked. "Do you really mean it?"

"Don was right about you: You're green in the right ways. You're strong in the others. You've surprised all of us with your performance."

"I thought you hated me."

"If I give too many compliments you might stop trying to impress me." He tapped the list of notes on the pad in his lap. "I love this show, too, Eleanor."

Harry had never offered her any glimpse into himself; he met her eyes now, his face open and unguarded.

"I made Don a promise when we were twenty-one: I'd work on any show he wrote. That's how much I believe in him." He shook his head. "I don't know much about this race stuff, I really don't. But I do know a good story when I see one."

Eleanor didn't know what to say.

He was already turning back to his notes. "Go home. Drink water, you sound dry. No snacking."

Harry's solution became apparent two days later, when a photographer and a reporter appeared backstage before a performance.

"Are we being interviewed?" Eleanor asked.

"No." Harry turned Eleanor around and tightened her sash. "You're the faces, we're the brains."

"Where's he from?" Charles asked.

"The *New York Times.*"

Charles looked unfazed, but Eleanor had more questions.

"Where will the piece go?"

"Somewhere in the arts section, maybe the front. This is a big deal, we're letting them in early." Harry nodded at them. "Right. Break legs."

Eleanor looked at Charles. "I haven't told my parents about the show."

Charles's eyes went wide. "What do they think you've been doing with your time?"

"They know I'm in a show. They don't know about . . . well . . ."

"Me."

"Right."

Charles gave her a long look, then breathed in and out. "I'm gonna look at my notes," he said, turning away. "Don't forget the new lines during the picnic."

"We're going to add a flash-forward," Don said the next morning. He, Eleanor, and Harry sat in a café near the theater. Don ordered coffee; his skin was pale and he had lost weight. If Harry hadn't been there, she would have told him he needed to order something solid.

"The audience needs to see them married," Harry said. "See their happy ending, see how they're just like everyone else."

Eleanor opened the new pages.

"How on earth are they just like everyone else?" Charles asked.

"Son, that's the fucking point of the show," Harry said.

The new scene was sweet and domestic. Molly and Luke eating breakfast, shown before the end of the first act. Molly was reminding him to drop a car payment in the mail on his way to work. She straightened his tie; he kissed her cheek and then—to Eleanor's horror—her belly.

"We'll be fitting you for a new dress," Harry said, "to make you look pregnant."

Eleanor paged through the lines.

"What do you think?" Don asked.

Charles took the pages. "What does this tell anyone? That Luke can get it up?"

"Don't be crass," Harry said, standing up to leave. "We're seeing what sticks. Sometimes you need to experiment. Keep everything the same tonight; we'll first need to fix the lighting for this. We'll run a rehearsal tomorrow."

Charles gave the pages back to Harry. "Insert: domestic bliss."

After Harry left, Eleanor looked at Don.

"You hate it," he said.

Eleanor took the pages back, hoping to find something in them she liked. "It's a bit pat."

"It's ridiculous," Charles said. "In what world do these two end up in a three-bedroom house with insurance and a baby?"

"Where do they live?" she asked. "Chicago, still?"

"No," Don said. "Somewhere more rural, private."

"Where the hell is their kid gonna go to school?" Now that Harry was gone, Charles dropped some of the coolness he always carried in professional company. "What do you think would happen to a black guy on a farm with a white wife? Eleanor—you're from a farm. What do you think would happen?"

She didn't know, not having met any black people outside of Green Bay.

"I don't recall either of you having writing credits on the show," Don said.

Eleanor felt admonished; had those evenings over the piano just been placation?

Charles held up his palms. "Look, Don—I don't mean any disrespect. You know I know you're a genius. But this—this isn't genius."

"Also—" Eleanor stopped when both men turned to her.

"What?" Don's voice had an edge to it.

"Never mind."

"Stop that." He crumpled the pages in his hand, then, thinking better of it, tore them in half. "Obviously this is shit. Eleanor, say whatever the hell you were going to say."

"I don't think we should cut the suspense so soon, but build it up even more than we have," she said. "The audience shouldn't see them happy in act one. See—what if the point isn't what happens to Molly and Luke, but what happens to the audience?"

Charles was watching her. Don turned to look out the window, but she could see he was listening.

"By the end, the audience should want Molly and Luke to be together. They'll leave the theater with a sense of injustice if the couple doesn't get together. Through suspense, we'll trick hundreds of people into wanting a black man to marry a white woman."

Don sniffed. A feeling of waiting on a precipice overcame her. This could be her biggest contribution yet—it would reshape the whole show.

He patted her hand. "Very clever. Now put on your makeup and let me work."

Don took her out for dinner after the show. "I could use a night off. Join me?"

She was surprised and pleased by the invitation; he took her to Revere's Diner, open all night and filled with nocturnal characters. They slid into a booth between two cops and a couple drooped over coffee. They'd only eaten fancy meals before, and she was glad he'd brought her to this place. She felt the plastic booth against her shoulders and did not even mind the scent of bacon from his BLT. She was reminded of home.

"Are we still going to Broadway, Don?" she asked.

"The producers have already sold weeks of tickets on Harry's and my names," Don said. "We'll open. After that, who knows."

She pushed mashed potatoes around her plate. Shoulders hunched, Don looked up at her with red eyes and nodded.

"In the future"—he wiped his mouth with a napkin, did not look at her—"I'd rather you didn't undermine me in front of Charles. I'm glad to let you watch me write, since it interests you, but please keep your opinions to yourself in company."

Opinions? He'd asked for her help. "I didn't mean to embarrass you, Don."

"You didn't. But keep that in mind next time."

"I thought . . ." She felt stupid. But Don had invited her to write with him. And hadn't he told her to look out for herself, that night in his car? "You asked for my help, many times."

Don wiped his mouth again, took his time before answering. Eleanor nearly backtracked. But then he met her eyes, and she felt right for speaking up. She could see he regarded her with respect, maybe even admiration.

"You have unteachable instincts," he said. "And I like spending time together. But, Eleanor, I think we should keep this part of our relationship private."

She felt heat in her cheeks, her chest, and knew he could see the blush rising in her skin. So he had noticed it, too. The attraction between them. The bond that they had built during those intimate rehearsals and long conversations.

She wanted to reach out and touch his hand. Those hands had written the works that shaped her life. Those hands were the reason she was here.

"So what do you think is wrong with it?" He swirled the ice in his glass. "I can barely see the show anymore, I've made so many changes."

The stern tone in his voice was gone; he seemed almost sheepish. When he looked up at her again, she saw he was apologizing, in his way.

She thought through Gwen's words and remembered Penelope's torn sleeve. "The show hasn't absorbed the danger quite yet."

Don's face changed as the words hit him. There it was, that link between them. He already knew what she meant. "Every moment they have would be fraught with sick fear. And all the sweeter because of it."

He brought his hand to his face, thinking, and ran it over a day's growth of beard. Finally, he turned his gaze to her, but it was as though he was surprised to see her there, like he had been far away and come back.

"Maybe I can't write this story," he said. "It's not mine to tell."

She thought about the protestors outside, Gwen's words, even Charles's words from their day in Central Park—how not even he could see himself loving a white woman. She was aware of the risks that might come with debuting this story too soon or somehow getting it wrong. She couldn't shake the *Herald* reporter and his allegations about Charles from her thoughts. She decided to ask Don.

He sat up and looked at her. "Where did you hear that?"

"Someone in front of the theater showed me a cutting from the paper."

"There's more to the story. All I know is those charges were dropped. Charles wouldn't hurt a fly. You can't believe those people. They'll do anything to bring us down."

"Don, if it's dragged up again, no one will care if it's true or not." She twisted her napkin. "They're arresting writers, actors, on nothing charges, saying they're communists. They could say anything to lock Charles up. This could ruin his life."

"I should have known all that would come up again, in this show." Don laid a hand over his eyes and rubbed his temples. "People might call me a genius, Eleanor, but sometimes I think I'm the densest person in the world."

Eleanor reached her hand across the table. He didn't pull away from her touch. "You're not dense," she said. "You want people to believe in the work and not think about everything else."

"But the work is everything else," Don said. "I didn't realize that. It's calling everything to the surface. Danger."

The word conjured the image of the bar, the protestors, Charles in a jail cell. Danger.

Chapter Seventeen

Eleanor should have called her family after the *Times* photographer came. She should have gone straight back to the hotel and called. But she didn't. She should have at least written a letter. Each time she thought of doing one of these things, there were lines to learn, scenes to rehearse. Anyway, who knew what the article would even say?

She found out on Sunday at breakfast. She opened to the arts section and saw the photograph. The oatmeal in her mouth suddenly tasted like mud.

The spread took up most of the page above the fold. It was her, in Charles's arms, her body bowed back by his kiss. His hands were on her waist, fingers spread wide to hold tight and feel her. They were so close that their cheeks, noses, and foreheads touched. Their names were printed directly below:

Eleanor O'Hanlon and Charles Lawrence during a performance of A Tender Thing.

The article was less interesting than the picture. Don talked about how he wanted to write a show about integration and racism, and how the idea had always been important to him. *Investing in his legacy*, Eleanor thought, in a flash of resentment. Harry brushed off questions about the "sordid" scenes: "People who love each other want to be together. This relationship wouldn't be any different." He focused on his methods of rehearsal. Both men said the show was the best they'd ever collaborated on, how proud they were of it, how vital the message was.

"At the end of the day, it's about love," Don said. "What is more universal than that?"

Though the words were attributed to Don, Eleanor could not imagine them in his voice. Love might be universal to everyone but Don—but he knew how to mimic how others saw the world. It made her desperately sad.

She picked up the newspaper. Her parents didn't get the *Times*, but that bought her only hours. Eleanor had already shamed them with her desertion; this now surpassed shame. It was humiliation. She pictured them in church. Neighbors would sneer, shudder; they'd consider her a slut. Most wouldn't heed anything in the article. The talk of love and kindness would be lost. Her neighbors would not see past the picture.

She needed to call her parents. She went up to her room, and her phone was already ringing. It was Charles.

"Did you see it?" His voice was bright.

"Sure did."

"You sound strange."

"It's quite a photo."

"Did you think no one would see? We do that in front of hundreds of people every night."

She couldn't say anything to him without admitting her shame. But her silence betrayed her; he hung up. Almost immediately after, she got another call. This time the front desk connected her to Rosie.

"Eleanor! Are you all right?" Rosie's voice brought her close, like they hadn't been fighting for weeks. She sounded worried. "Your parents saw the paper. They called and asked if I knew. I'm sorry, I told them."

It was so good to hear Rosie's voice. It brought her back to childhood, and she wanted to cry. "Oh, Rosie. Are they very angry?"

"I think that picture was hard for them to see."

"Was it hard for you?"

Rosie hesitated. "I'm worried about you."

"It's perfectly normal, you know." A venomous edge came into her voice. "We do that in front of an audience every night, so the picture isn't a big deal."

"All right, Eleanor."

"I'm just saying it's nothing to be ashamed of."

"I didn't say it was."

They were quiet. Eleanor hated that she had snapped. She didn't want the phone call to end but could not think of anything to say.

"Anyway," Rosie said after a few awkward seconds. "I'm glad you're okay. Let me know if you need anything." The wall between them came back into her voice.

"How are things there?" Eleanor remembered Connor Morris's bit about Tommy and Rosie in the same apartment and longed to ask. "I miss you."

Rosie sounded uncomfortable. Was she winding the cord around her arm? "I have to get going. I'm meeting someone."

Eleanor wanted to tell her everything. But all she said was, "Talk to you soon. Thanks for calling."

"Goodbye, Eleanor."

Eleanor held the phone for a long time, then hung up. She dialed her parents.

Her mother answered. "O'Hanlon residence."

She was quiet.

"Hello?"

She couldn't make herself speak.

"Hello?" A note of panic came into her mother's voice. "Who is this?"

Eleanor wondered if her mother thought people could trace their phone from the article. She tried to speak, but instead of words, a quiet sound escaped her throat.

"Eleanor? Is that you?"

She tried to hear compassion but only heard panic and anger.

"Eleanor, if that's you, I hope you're ashamed. Your father is out working the fields. He went there after church and hasn't come back. We had to find out from Mr. Browning. The look on his face. I've already gotten calls from grocers that won't buy our pork anymore. Did you even think of that? That we'd lose business? Of course you didn't, you've always been so selfish."

Tears began to fall. She kept a hand over her mouth so her mother wouldn't hear.

"You have no idea of the shame." Her mother's voice broke. "I can't describe . . . When that reporter called last week, I didn't believe him. Imagine how humiliated I was when I saw that awful picture. I thought, *That can't be her. That can't be the girl I raised.* But it was. Did you think of us at all when you decided to perform in that filthy play?"

She'd imagined hearing a rejection from her parents many times and had thought she was steeled for it. But it was so much worse than she'd prepared for. Eleanor knew that voice so very well but had never heard it twisted with revulsion.

"And that man—seeing his hands on you! I swear your father had a heart attack. If I could forgive you for myself, I'd never forgive you for what you did to him. No father should have to see his daughter with a man like that."

Eleanor didn't have anything she could possibly say; the room was blurred through her tears.

"We supported you when it was harmless, nice shows, but we won't have this in our house. So if you came home and gave up all that, he said he could find a way. You're still our daughter. That's what he said. Me, I don't know. I don't know."

Eleanor had never thought of this. Her parents' threatening to make her pull out of the show—well, they couldn't make her do anything.

"You or the show?" she asked. Her voice cracked midway through.

Her mother's breathing was loud in the phone. "Yes."

Eleanor thought of her father, sweating outdoors, tiring his body until he didn't think of her anymore. More than a minute went by with only the sound of her mother's breathing. Then, once more, she started to cry.

"Mom—"

"Don't call here again."

Mrs. O'Hanlon hung up.

Eleanor sagged on the bed. For months she'd avoided her parents. She couldn't even claim they were close! Yet now she could not breathe.

All her life, she had wanted one thing. Every birthday, she had made the same wish; every pearl, eyelash, shooting star, and coin had been dedicated to the cause. Along the way, she had promised that she would do anything for one chance. She had never thought to expect that her dream might come true—or that she would need to make good on her debt.

✴

She was putting on her wig when Don and Harry rushed into her dressing room without knocking. Don's face was reserved as usual, but his eyes were bright and his step was lighter than she'd seen it in days. He had avoided her since the night at the diner but now looked so enthused that he neglected to be uncomfortable.

"What's going on?" She'd spent the rest of the morning crying. She'd had to use extra concealer beneath her eyes to mask the puffiness. When she'd walked to the theater, she'd felt as though she were underwater. Even watching Don and Harry bluster in now was overwhelming.

She should have known better. Her mother was right; she was selfish. But in her pain, she also felt real anger. If only her parents weren't so small-minded, if only her town weren't so pathetic, she wouldn't have needed to make such a choice.

"We've got forty-five minutes," Don said, dropping six pages of handwritten music on top of her pressed powder. "New song."

Eleanor picked up the music. "Now?"

"I was thinking about the protests and had an idea," Don said.

Harry perched on her table. He pressed his hands together and pointed at her. "So far it's been all about love. Now we're going to make it about danger."

Eleanor paged through the music. It was a solo for Molly.

"We're adding this in at the top of the second act," Harry said. "Molly and Luke have just slept together and decided to elope. Curtain up, you're packing. Only now, instead of excitement, you're terrified. The song comes after you put the picture of your mother in the suitcase. Now you sing this."

Eleanor read the lyrics. It was a simple AABA ballad; two verses, bridge, verse. "But this is about how she doesn't want to go with him."

"Exactly."

Eleanor looked up. Don was nodding. He tapped a finger on the bridge. "Until here. We modulate from minor to relative major. She starts to remember Luke. The last verse, she chooses him."

"But she chose him in the scene before. When they made love."

"She chose to fuck him," Harry said. Eleanor flinched. "They're attracted to each other and he's right in front of her. It means so much more that she chooses him all alone. She has to doubt first."

She looked over the lyrics. "Every morning over coffee / I'll see him looking at me / And know it's just the two of us / Not even a few of us / Just him and me / A table and chairs, one window and a TV."

She looked at the bridge.

"Can I look back and be happy to be / This man's wife, his family / Say, I found love / And hope it sticks around?"

"But . . ."

"Trust me on this," Don said.

Eleanor paged through the rest. "She doesn't want to go with him," she said. "How can you do that? She loves Luke. If she loved him, she wouldn't sing this."

Harry and Don looked at each other. Eleanor's insides leapt; she didn't know what the look meant, but it was about her. Don tapped the music.

"Molly is made up of more than just love for Luke," he said. "She's leaving everything behind, her family, everything she was raised with. It's all right for it to be difficult for her."

Eleanor looked at the music again. She didn't want Molly to be afraid. Eleanor was afraid enough. Even looking at the lyrics felt too personal, and she worried about singing them out loud without crying. Her mother's voice, twisted with cruelty, was still in her mind. "Don, I can't do this. Not today."

"Come downstairs, we have to run the music before we open house."

As soon as the curtain fell, she rushed to her dressing room. She had never been so affected by a song; it was as if Don had pulled out the fears she had not even articulated to herself. Molly's worries about sacrificing her family for Luke were too close to her own; Eleanor had to push all thoughts of her mother away, or else she would panic. Molly nearly chose to stay home, to keep her family. To perform the song well, Eleanor had to really entertain the possibility of giving up. She had to feel the pain of the loss of her family. Accessing that onstage felt dangerous, like she was a breath away from losing control.

Eleanor feared breaking down completely. Instead, she approached that chasm, then backed away. She concentrated on singing beautifully and making pretty, sad faces.

If she were the sophisticated girl she pretended to be, she would not have been so torn by her choices. Broadway would be enough for her. Don had always known how deep her farm roots ran; she pretended that Wisconsin was where she came from, not who she was. Don knew better. He had put all of that into Molly—all of Eleanor's weaknesses and fears that she wanted to leave behind.

Except that Molly chose Luke. Even with her fear of losing her family. Molly still chose Luke. Did that mean he thought there was hope?

It was late, and she was hungry. She changed into her street clothes.

She realized she'd left her music backstage and went there on her way out. When she opened the door, she heard Don and Harry talking. She hid behind a curtain, listening to their conversation.

"I don't know, Harry."

"She'll get it."

"Maybe this is too much for her. The girl never even met a black man until a few months ago."

"At first I thought you were crazy, casting her. But I see it. The girl has fire."

"Still, she doesn't understand."

"Why would she? She's from Wisconsin." Harry's voice grew tired. He spoke through a sigh. "Give her time."

"Harry, we don't have time."

She wanted to hear more, hear it all. She picked her music up off the floor and strained her ears.

"It's like she was blank, up there," Don said. His words confirmed every doubt that she'd ever fought about her performance. "She has no idea what she's talking about. I thought it should be obvious—an Irish girl, a Negro. But she's just singing away, totally empty."

"She's scared. Don, she's learned this much."

"Can you teach someone this?"

Eleanor reeled. This was Don, who had said she would do something special for theater. And now he didn't believe in her?

"Harry," he said, "she's just a little girl."

A hand touched her arm. She jumped and turned. It was Charles.

"Time to go, Eleanor."

"But—"

"Now."

Charles led her outside, where she caught her breath in the cold air. It was snowing, the flurries catching the light of the streetlamps.

"It's all right," he said. "Don't take it personally."

"How could I not?" she said. "They think I'm awful."

"I heard them say you didn't seem to understand what you were singing about."

"They're wrong." Eleanor's voice was too loud. "The entire time I was singing, all I could think was how angry I was with Molly, that she was even considering leaving Luke. I was so angry with her. And with Don, for writing that."

"You can't judge your character."

"Molly loves Luke. Only weak people would let something like that stand in their way. Charles, they changed the show so Molly nearly gives up on him."

"But she doesn't."

Eleanor felt her emotions getting away from her; she hated it but couldn't stop. "She's supposed to see beyond all this color garbage. She wouldn't be conflicted, wouldn't be scared. Molly is better than that."

Charles took her shoulders in his hands. "That's wrong. You're wrong."

"What?"

"Maybe they were right." Charles's voice was light, infuriating Eleanor. "I don't think you understand how hard it would really be."

"Well, I do!" Eleanor watched him shrug and then raised her voice. "Stop it!"

"Things aren't so easy, Eleanor." Charles pressed his palms to his temples. "Your parents disowned you this morning and you still don't get it."

The wound was so fresh; when he mentioned it, her insides went white-hot.

"Eleanor—it's all right if you're sad about your family. That doesn't mean you don't care about the show. It doesn't mean we aren't friends."

Her horrible performance was now playing in her head. "I'm going to be fired."

"Don's comments in that article were bullshit. It's not about love. It's about race. They just threw some love on top so the audience could see it."

"I think love should be enough." She still heard the coldness of her mother's voice on the phone. The idea that even Molly and Luke—whose love she had started to believe in completely, as if they were real—might reject each other was terrible. "It has to be enough for someone."

"Would it be enough for you?" Charles asked. He looked her in the face. "You asked me if I'd ever be with a white woman. Would you ever be with me?"

She took him in, conscious now of his height, his smooth skin, the way his voice stirred something in her. What would it be like, being with Charles? All his warmth, his beauty, his intense capacity for love that she saw glimpses of, concentrated on her?

"It's not an option," she said.

"You're right."

Desperately, she tried to find proof that he was wrong. "Love was enough for me."

"Love for musicals. Not for people."

"Losing my family wasn't easy just because it wasn't for a person. I'd say it was even harder."

"Well, let's see," he said. "You think you know how hard this would be? Come on. We're going out."

———

"Are you sure this is . . ."

"Safe?" Charles grinned at her. "It might not feel safe, but that's the point. In any case you don't have to worry. Nothing's going to happen to you."

The cab dropped them off in a neighborhood far from the theater. Most places were closed; there were few streetlamps. Eleanor stuck close to Charles, hands in her pockets.

"See that man?" Charles nodded at a figure across the street. "He's looked over here half a dozen times. He's wondering if I kidnapped you."

"That's ridiculous."

They walked a few more blocks until they reached a building with darkened windows. They descended to a basement door, through which Eleanor heard music.

"How did you find this place?"

"Gwen and I came last week to hear music," Charles said.

"Where is she tonight?"

"She wanted to sleep. Besides, this needs to be just you and me."

She was nervous already; his words made her more so.

He took her hand. "Do you trust me?"

She thought about the newspaper article. A knot formed in her throat. But she said yes.

"Good." He pushed open the door. The whole place was filled with smoke. She heard a saxophone and smelled beer.

"How do you breathe in this place?"

Charles rolled his eyes and tugged her inside. "Hold my arm."

He took her to a table and pulled out her chair. She looked around; the place was racially varied, but the integration did not extend to the tables. Eleanor and Charles were the only mixed couple sitting together. In New York, one would see couples who looked different, but not often in Boston. Charles removed his coat. Eleanor wanted to keep hers on; her dress underneath, calico and normally her favorite for its swishy skirt, seemed girlish. But Charles gave her a look, and she shrugged it off. The air was hot and pleasant. The place was dark, with bluish light on the musicians onstage and votive candles on the tables. The flame's glow flicked across Charles's face.

"Tonight," he said, "we're Molly and Luke, testing out a night together."

Eleanor opened her mouth to ask questions, but Charles motioned for her to wait.

A young Negro waitress came up to them. She smiled at Charles slowly, sticking her hip out. He smiled back, then nodded at Eleanor. The girl turned and her smile froze on her face.

"What can I get you, miss?"

No champagne here. "Gin and tonic."

"Jim Beam." Charles smiled at her as she left, then looked around the room. He touched her wrist. "Here. Hold my hand."

They'd held hands in rehearsals, but it felt different this time; without the context of the show, he felt more like skin than usual.

"So what exactly did your parents say?" he asked, his voice so quiet she had to lean closer.

She looked away. A white woman was staring at her, chewing her food. Eleanor caught her gaze. The woman raised her eyebrows, looked back at her plate, and shook her head like she couldn't believe the price on a melon at the market. When Eleanor turned back to Charles, he looked expectant. She fought off an instinct to lie.

"My mother says I'm not welcome home."

He caressed the back of her hand with his thumb. "Because of me?"

She thought again about lying. "They don't understand that it's all fake, onstage."

"Is it fake?"

She withdrew her hand. Gwen came to mind, home and large with child. "Charles."

"You're misunderstanding me. Things are different between us than they were when you started. You're close with me now. We may not be Molly and Luke, but the show has changed you. What did your yeoman say about me? Did he like what we were doing?"

She turned away.

Charles took back her hand. "There's a man checking you out like you're on the bargain rack."

Eleanor turned around. A white man with shaggy black hair was watching her, unblinking. "Why is he staring?"

"He thinks you're easy."

The waitress returned, setting the drinks on the table. Charles's was a double. He eyed it, raised his eyebrows. She smiled at him, moving her hips back and forth. Charles put his left hand over the glass, so the votive shone on his ring. She blinked, looked at Eleanor, stood up straight. "Yell if you need anything else."

Eleanor's mouth fell open as she watched the waitress leave. "That wasn't fair."

"What?"

"You made her think you and I were married."

Charles leaned forward again. "And how did she react?"

"She didn't like it. But that's because she wants to go to bed with you."

"Maybe. But girls like her don't look at me like that when they see Gwen."

"She didn't like us together."

"Bingo."

"Why should she care? It's not as if she thinks you're dangerous. I mean, she's also . . . she would know."

Charles took a sip of his drink, swirled it in the cup. "Eleanor, maybe she's unhappy with *you*."

Eleanor leaned back in her chair and drank the liquid. She was beginning to realize she didn't really like gin; it tasted like fermented Christmas trees. But it was the drink she'd learned to order. She took another pull to stay away from Charles's gaze.

He tapped her arm. "Let's dance."

"No."

He took another drink and then stood up, offering her his hand. The music was slow blues, long plucks on a bass. Eleanor realized her hands were sweating.

"I don't know—"

"Lean against me."

Charles put a hand on her waist. She wrapped her arms around his neck. His embrace shielded her from the room. An empty place opened inside her, dull and lonely and sweet. The blue light glowed through her eyelids, until it seemed the very color of her thoughts. She was no longer Eleanor; she was Molly, and glad to be. They danced like this in the show, and her body recognized the position. She melted against him, joints loose, buzzed. Charles held her close, his body warm under his sweater. He smelled like clean sweat, whiskey, and the smoke that clung to his skin.

"I feel like Molly."

"Yes, that's right." He whispered in her ear, "It's sweet."

"The music."

Charles didn't reply, but she felt him turn his head and rest his chin on her temple. It was intimate and wonderful, warm. She held him closer, feeling not a romantic connection but a profound one; she wrapped her arms around his slender waist and felt closer to him than she had to anyone in a long time.

"I could fall asleep like this," she whispered.

Charles bent to her ear. His whisper was hot and ticklish, and it took a second before she realized what he'd said.

"People are staring."

She looked around the bar. The spotlight blinded her for a moment; she blinked and saw an orange impression. The bass player glanced away when she caught his gaze, his expression closing like a door. The woman she'd seen chewing earlier stared, her mouth tight. Eleanor thought of ways to ease the situation, came up with none.

"What do they think?"

"Who knows?" Charles said. "Some might think you're a slut. Or maybe you're innocent, and I'm a rapist. Others think you should leave me for someone else, you've got enough. You could be a brat trying to upset Daddy. The point is, none of them buy we're in love."

"Well, we aren't."

"Baby, any of this crowd saw you holding a white guy like that, they'd get all misty."

Eleanor didn't like standing in the middle of the room; there was a lot of emotion running through her, and she couldn't get a grasp on it. She pushed Charles away. Her stomach was sour, jumpy.

"You said yourself you felt like Molly," he said. "And still they don't believe in us. They fill it in with something wrong, dirty."

Eleanor looked around again; she met the shaggy-haired man's gaze, bleary with drink. Her eyes burned, maybe from the smoke; she hid her face on Charles's shoulder.

"I want to go home." Eleanor went to the table and sat down to finish her gin.

He sat closer to her this time, nursing his whiskey. "I do love the music here. Let's just listen."

She began to feel warm, the sides of the room growing fuzzy. The music lulled her, rocked her like she was a child, or at least that's what she wanted it to do—she could not concentrate. She felt eyes on her like fingers scraping down her spine.

She said, "Charles, I'm tired."

Charles looked at her. "Are you afraid?"

"Yes."

"Hmm."

"Did you pick this place because we'd be treated like this here?"

Charles looked at her, hurt touching his eyes. "I picked this place because we could come together. Here, they stare. Eleanor, other places, it's worse."

"I have to go to the bathroom."

"I'll walk you."

The idea of his walking her to the bathroom was far too intimate; it would egg on their audience. "You'd better not."

The ladies' was disgusting: paper littered the floor, a tampon floated in red water, and the mirror was so spotted with an unknown substance that she had to turn her head a few times to find an open space to reapply her lipstick.

She pushed open the door, ready to go home. The shaggy-haired man was in the hallway. She kept her head down. Somehow, she walked right into him.

"Pardon."

He caught her by the arms. "That's all right, baby."

She stiffened; he didn't let go.

He stared a beat too long, eyes narrowed in a kind of smile. When he didn't look away, Eleanor thought he must be very drunk, until he dug in his nails.

"What are you doing with him? Don't know how you stomach it."

"Leave me alone. My boyfriend is waiting."

"Bullshit."

"He is."

"How much?"

She flushed. "You've got it wrong."

He pushed her against the wall. The bricks were freezing.

"I'll be your boyfriend tonight." The man leaned forward and covered her mouth with his; she tasted beer and dankness from cigarettes. Eleanor squealed and smacked him on the back. His mouth was limp and wet, and it traced down her neck, leaving behind the beer smell.

"Stop it."

He pulled back without removing his hands. Eleanor slumped against the wall. Her heart pounded, and she waited for it to be over. The man kneaded her breast in his hand. In a fleeting rush, she realized that this was a situation unlike any she'd been in before. He was not just grabbing a feel; he wasn't going to stop. An instinct flared up, her pulse speeding to a race.

"Let me go." Her voice was weak coming out, and she didn't recognize it. "Get off."

He pinched her thigh, then her ass. "You're fat for a whore."

"Get off me!"

He reached between her legs, moving up until he grabbed her in his hand. She froze. He smiled at her and raised his eyebrows in an expression of smug amusement. Eleanor felt a wave of hate so powerful that it infused her veins, then her muscles. She snapped her teeth toward his face.

He jerked back. She managed a wrenching movement that dislodged his grip, then raised her knee and shoved against his groin. He crumpled.

"You fucking bitch!"

She ran.

Charles was already halfway down the stairs. "Eleanor! I heard shouting—are you all right?"

"We're leaving. Now."

Charles did not stop apologizing until they reached her hotel.

"I know you didn't mean for it to happen," she said, her voice tight. "Just almost, right?"

"No!"

They pulled up to her hotel. Charles paid the fare. The cabbie kept the car idling on the curb, watching.

"Thank you," she called out. "I'm fine!"

The man gave her another look and then drove away.

Eleanor kicked a piece of ice on the sidewalk. Charles, maybe trying to win her favor, kicked it back like a child playing soccer. "Did that serve your fancy, Charles? You got to tutor me for the night. Am I going to be a good actress now?"

"I told you I didn't mean for it to happen." His mouth was tight. "But don't you see—if I'd gotten to you, if we brawled . . . who do you think the barkeep would think attacked you? Me, or him?"

"You would know."

"Excuse me?"

"Charles—did you . . . did you hit a woman? In a bar?"

He swore under his breath.

"Charles."

"How can you even ask me that?"

"I saw the article."

"You know me. That's what you think of me?" He looked sickened. Eleanor couldn't respond, already recognizing that she'd been wrong. Connor had tricked her, somehow, and she'd fallen right into it. Charles's eyes were wide, pained. "You think I beat the shit out of some old bird?"

Eleanor took a breath. "I don't think you—meant to. But I need you to tell me."

He took her arms in his hands. "You shouldn't have to ask."

A streetlamp cast his shadow long and slender on the sidewalk. Eleanor wanted to be better, wanted not to care. She waited for him to speak. Cars passed them, but Charles did not seem to notice. He swore again. She broke apart from him and wrapped her arms around herself.

"You know Gwen and I sing in clubs sometimes." He faced away, one hand cupping the back of his neck. "There was one, Benny's. They had a popular jazz combo. Even whites came out."

His voice was quiet, but it was a still night and she didn't struggle to hear.

"By the end of the night it could get rowdy." He saw her look and explained. "Bar fights. Stupid men, drunk off their asses, who'd throw a punch for no good reason."

"Is that what happened to you?"

"I don't slug anyone without a reason." Charles turned. The lamp cast shadows over his face so his eyes and mouth were dark voids. Eleanor still felt his glare and was ashamed for having asked the question. She wanted all this to stop. She wanted to extract this entire conversation from the air until their friendship was untouched by it. "I don't slug anyone, for that matter.

"The white folks called the cops one night," he said. "Some girl screamed that a 'darkie' grabbed her breast and they raided the place. If there wasn't a fight before, there was when the cops arrived.

"It was madness. Cops shoving their way through. Cuffing fellas who hadn't thrown a punch. Lou, our bass player, got hit with a nightstick.

"I wanted to get us out of there, but it was a riot. I got a arm around Gwen and shoved my way through the crowd. At one point, someone grabbed me, and I didn't think. I swung my elbow back, to get them off."

Charles bent his head in his hands. "She was an old white woman who liked music. She'd been sitting with Gwen and tried to follow us out. God knows what she was doing all the way up in Harlem, but there she was. And I broke her nose."

"Oh my God."

"I spent the night in jail. Cops beat the living shit out of me. The woman came up the next day. She told them someone swung a door open on her nose. I don't know why she did it. She told them to let me out. I went home, but couldn't walk for days. I thought that was the end of it." He met her eyes. "But even you don't trust me."

Eleanor looked down at the concrete.

"I thought that maybe, maybe you were starting to get it."

"Charles. I'm sorry."

"No shit." He paused, considering his next words. "You think I've been keen on you this whole time?" Charles had clenched his fists at his sides. "I have to explain every damn thing to you, from stage directions to entrances. I took you to that bar tonight because you didn't even understand what the musical was about. You think the theater is some glamorous fairyland."

"Well, I'm sorry I haven't been in the business my whole life—"

Charles continued as if she hadn't spoken. "But I'm your friend, and I stood by you when Harry made you cry. You even criticized me for not being a pure enough artist. 'It's just a paycheck to you.' Screw you, Eleanor. Maybe I can't put my blind trust into this bullshit. And this is why. Some friend you are."

Eleanor took her face in her hands. She wanted to cry but felt like if she did, she would lose control, and that would be the wrong move here. It hit her on two sides: everyone who had once loved her now hated her, but if she pled for sympathy, she would be worse. This was her problem to solve, alone. She gathered her breath and approached him. She wrapped her arms around his shoulders.

"I'm sorry."

He kept his hands at his sides. "Well?"

"I understand."

"What do you understand, Eleanor?"

"That it's hard! That Molly had a real decision to make. That love isn't enough."

"Their lives would be a battle every single day."

"I couldn't handle one night, and I wasn't even really out with you."

"You saw how people treated us. Imagine if we married. Imagine trying to buy a house. Imagine enrolling our child in a school."

Eleanor wanted to crumple to the ground.

"Don's show is good," Charles said, his voice going tender. "I'm the first man to say. Sometimes I still don't understand how a white man could write something like this. But it's too pleasant, too happily-ever-after. That's not the way it's going to be."

Eleanor watched car beams sweep the salty winter streets, then pass. "Maybe Don wants it to be that way."

"Were you scared tonight?" he asked. "That—what you felt all night, all those eyes, wondering who was going to try to do something to us— that's what's missing from the musical. You, Don, Harry, want the show to prove things aren't as bad as they look. That two people could defeat the system. Eleanor, that's not for the white man to say."

"Do you think it can get better?"

"Things are changing," he said. "But not yet, Eleanor, no. And when they do change, it will be damned tough. So Molly and Luke . . . they're scared. But they're not scared enough."

Chapter Eighteen

I hate writing romance." Don tore another sheet of paper and threw it onto the orchestra pit floor. "It always sounds fake. All that hand touching and I-can't-live-without-you. It's private. When you watch it, it looks ridiculous."

"Perhaps because that's not what people really do," Eleanor said. "Gaze into each other's eyes and that."

He chuckled. "I'm told they do."

Eleanor lounged in the first row of the theater. She loved being there with only Don. Empty, it felt like a church. It was her day off. Eleanor had planned on extra sleep, but Don had informed her she was to accompany him to the theater early in the morning so he could try out new material. They'd already been at it two hours—though Eleanor had scarcely done anything. Whenever Don looked at what he'd written, he made a disgusted face and began scratching out lyrics.

"People don't really do that." She looked over the lip of the stage down into the pit. "At least, I've never seen it. It's just something they do in movies. People kiss and such, but goopy stuff like playing with hair and pet names—that's drivel."

He gave her an odd look. "My dear, I thought you had some experience."

Eleanor leaned back so he couldn't see her. She could hardly imagine such intimacy—her relationship with Tommy had ended too early for any of that.

"Have you ever had a pet name, Don?" She was glad he couldn't see her.

"Eleanor, I'm working."

"'My little quarter note'? 'My cuddly fermata'?"

She was being cheeky at best. But she thought Don could do with some needling, and after all, he had interrupted her sleep.

"Which rhyme rings better to your ear?" He read her two options. She told him. He made a noise in his throat.

"How do you know pet names are real if you've never experienced them? They could be like fainting. In my experience, people faint far more often in fiction than in real life. Pet names could be equally over-represented."

He didn't answer. She waited several long moments, growing more nervous as each one passed, and then peeked at Don in the orchestra pit. He was engrossed in his work.

"Lovers create their own language," he said after a long time. "Pet names, secret jokes—like a bubble of intimacy. It's evolutionary. The stronger the bond of the parents, the greater the chances the offspring have of surviving."

"Don, I had no idea you were so romantic."

"Luke and Molly will have only begun this stage when the musical ends." He spoke slowly, and when Eleanor looked she saw he was reading his lyrics. "So their dialogue will still be focused on declaring their love."

She imagined Luke's struggling to find a place to take Molly out. Would he pick somewhere similar to the place Charles had taken her? Would it backfire just as badly? Charles had been devastated when she was hurt; what if that night hadn't been about learning to act but was a dress rehearsal for an entire relationship? How would Molly and Luke feel if they stepped out for one night and learned their love was impossible?

"I don't think it would only be about love," Eleanor said slowly.

"How do you mean?"

"Molly and Luke aren't like other couples." Eleanor leaned her arms on the edge of the stage. "They might move faster," she said. "They depend on that intimacy stage more than other lovers. If they don't feel united, even to the two of them, they'll never stand a chance."

Don looked up, waiting for her to continue. Eleanor, nervous, did just that.

"They have less in common than lovers who come from the same background," she said. "If they loved each other, I think they would try— maybe even without knowing they're doing it—to create a bubble around themselves. Make the relationship as strong and as real as possible before taking it out into the world."

"Build intimacy faster." Though he didn't look away from her face, she knew he had stopped seeing her and had already begun rewriting things in his head.

"They should plan their life together," Eleanor said. "Give them a dream."

"Like what? Molly is your character. You know her as well as I do."

What an astonishing concept. She almost held back. But he was right; she knew the answer.

"They should plan their future. Their house. Children. They have no role models, so they have to dream it up themselves."

"Come down here," Don said. "Will you help me?"

By evening, the stage manager delivered Eleanor sheet music to a song called "Sunday Evening." It would come near the end of act two, right when Luke and Molly were losing faith. In it, they imagine their home together in the quiet hours at the end of the week, when they belong to each other. They dreamed not of passion but peace. She already knew the lyrics by heart. It had taken six hours, but she and Don had written a song. Well, mostly Don—he wrote until he was stumped, then looked to her for suggestions. Eleanor recognized three of her rhymes and one full line in the chorus. Her own words, paired with Don's music. No one but Don knew she'd contributed, but she didn't care. This felt different than her little opinions, tossed off when Don needed encouragement. This song was her idea. She'd been part of creating a new musical—not only through interpretation but through text. She ran her finger over the words on the sheet.

The melody was simple, almost like a church hymn, but with more dissonance in the accompaniment. Don had concentrated on strings, so light the song shimmered.

They had an emergency rehearsal that night, even though they were supposed to be off. Frank Taliercio even wrangled the orchestra. When they finished singing it through the first time, Charles didn't say anything, only nodded.

Harry rose out of his seat. "That's it! That's the money, right there!"

"This is beautiful, Don," Charles said finally. "How did you come up with it?"

"Old-fashioned brainstorming," he said. "You sit with something long enough, you'll get a breakthrough."

Harry hoisted himself onto the stage and began to walk Eleanor and Charles through the blocking. When he returned to his seat, Eleanor couldn't contain herself.

She tugged Charles's sleeve, bending him toward her. "It was my idea."

"Really, Eleanor?"

She nodded. "Thanks to you."

"Trust Don not to say anything."

"I don't care. Charles, some of these are my lyrics. I'm going to perform my own material."

He grinned. "Attagirl."

They went to the wings to wait. Eleanor should have been tired after her late night and her day of work, but she bounced on her toes. When the underscoring for the change before their new song began, she turned and threw her arms around Charles.

When they finished, Don took her out for a cocktail. They found seats at the end of a quiet bar, and he ordered an old-fashioned. Eleanor asked for a glass of champagne. Neither felt festive; they didn't toast. They were exhausted and too nervous for celebration.

"I think this new song might be our secret ingredient," he said. "Between 'Sunday Evening' and 'A Table and Chairs,' I think the show has more gravity."

"I hope it's enough."

"The song is good. But I'm not a fool. It can't fix the other two and a half hours." He drained his glass. "I suppose this night is more of a wake than a celebration."

"We still have the pre-Broadway rehearsals to work it out."

"At least you understand how much we poured into this." He drained his glass. "I don't know how I can limp back to New York."

She was surprised; she had not expected his shame to run so deep. "Don, if the show isn't a hit, that doesn't mean it's a failure."

"That's what 'flop' means." He moved his hand on the bar like a dying fish.

She gripped his wrist, shook it until he stopped.

"I'll see it through to New York. But I wish I'd never even started."

Eleanor tried to feel sorry for him, but it was impossible. "Don, I've lost my family because of this show. Don't tell me it wasn't worth it."

"And it was worthwhile to you, Eleanor?"

She thought of her days writing with him, her night with Charles, the incident with the drunken man, everything she'd learned, everything she show had given her and might give someone else. She thought of the following day, when she would perform "Sunday Evening" in front of hundreds of people.

He was shaking his head before she answered. "Why did I even ask you? I brought you from Wisconsin and gave you a shot at Broadway. No matter what happens, I got you out of that miserable place. Of course it was worth it to you. But me? I have a reputation, a career."

"I came to New York on my own."

He jerked his head. "You might think I'm old, Eleanor, but I've got at least twenty, thirty more years to produce work. This is the only thing I've ever known how to do well. If this show fails, it will all come down around me. And then who would I be?"

Eleanor felt nervous, even frightened, as he broke from her grasp and ordered another drink.

He shook his head, his eyes closed, his lips pulled into his mouth. "I couldn't make it work."

They were quiet a long time. Eleanor saw his hands tremble as he held his drink. His eyes flicked to her once. It occurred to her, in a glowing moment, that Don had come to her for support.

"This show means something to me, and to Charles. If we get it right, it can cause change. Even if it isn't a hit, Don, one person will listen and understand Molly and Luke."

He didn't answer. She left her hand on his arm. "Don, even if it's a flop, it will still be the most brilliant thing you've ever written. That will always be true, long after people remember *The Birds and the Bees*. Don't you dare call that your best. Please. You couldn't even convince me."

He laughed, patted her hand, left his over hers. "Eleanor, you are a good friend."

He turned to her. His collar was unbuttoned, sleeves rolled, hair mussed. He looked more casual than usual, and tipsy. He met her eyes. That had been happening more and more lately; today, after their long hours of work, he didn't even seem to prepare himself before looking straight at her.

"Don." She met his gaze, held it. "You aren't just a writer to me. I don't just admire your work. I admire you."

She tightened her grip on his sleeve.

"Eleanor, don't do this." He stood. He looked sure and sad, and she knew that he had been aware, all along, of how she felt.

She was silent.

For a moment, his expression was pained, before he hid his face, looking through his wallet. It took several tries for him to separate two fivers.

"Let's go back to the hotel," he said, then met her eyes. "Separately."

She got to the theater early for their last performance and once again went through the side doors, afraid that if she encountered the protestors, or saw Connor Morris, she would lose control.

Charles came by with a postcard painted with a rose and smiled as if their show were a hit. "Real flowers wouldn't last through the trip home."

"I got you something too." She produced a bakery box. "I went to Mike's this morning."

"Did you have one for yourself?" He pulled on the red-and-white string, opening the box and revealing a half-dozen fat cannoli. "Gwen will have a fit."

"I've one saved for after the performance. Couldn't risk the phlegm."

Eleanor was jumpy at the thought of seeing Don later but vowed to enjoy the performance for herself and relish the time she could spend singing with Charles. He had one of the most beautiful voices she'd ever heard, and a comfort and charisma onstage that could not be learned. That night, they'd perform her own number. That night, at least, she would get to live her dream.

She left Charles to get ready and went backstage to have a moment of peace before they opened the house. Onstage, staring at the empty seats, she thought about everything that had changed since she'd auditioned for Don. Was she still that farm girl who didn't have a proper headshot? Somewhere between renting her own apartment and swallowing the failure of A Tender Thing, she had begun to feel a hardness inside of her chest. Broadway no longer carried the fizzy excitement of years past. Instead, when she thought of the shows, they seemed like exquisite, complex puzzles. She lost her sense of worship without losing any fascination. Even if "Sunday Evening" couldn't save the show, she knew there was truth in the song, and her contribution improved A Tender Thing.

"You're not going back to Wisconsin," she said out loud. "No matter what happens. Even if you never do another show."

She waited for the words to be enough. She took a breath.

"Maybe one day, you'll write your own show."

The idea was still small, but when she said it, it rang against something in her. She looked into the orchestra pit, where she'd sat beside Don as he wrote "Sunday Evening." That had been a thrill that was as powerful as it was unexpected. But it made sense: She hadn't fallen in love with musicals because of the ingénues. She'd fallen in love with the melodies, the symmetry, the marriage of words, music, and dance. She'd wanted to climb inside of them, and from her place in Wisconsin, acting was the only entrance she could see.

In minutes, the cast would gather together for their preshow ritual. They'd tell each other to break legs. Charles would pat her on the shoulder before going to the opposite wing for his entrance. Freddie would finish up his elaborate stretching routine by resting his foot on the shoulder of the tallest person nearby. Eleanor would close her eyes and visualize Molly's moment before she walked onstage.

But right then, she didn't think about Molly. She thought about how far she herself had come.

It was her best performance. She spoke without thinking. When meeting Luke at night, she discarded the theatrical looking-over-her-shoulder in favor of a real fear. Throughout the performance Eleanor felt the weight of her parents' rejection, and it grounded her, gave her something for Molly to risk.

She threw herself against Charles, meeting his kisses with vigor and leaning into his touch. For the first time, she began to crave him. By the end of the first act, when he lowered her onto the ground for their love-making scene, she was trembling.

Usually, she had finished by sliding up from the leading tone to the tonic of the scale, resolving the tiny dissonance against Charles's held note. But Don had changed the harmony, so now she leapt up to the fifth, in a glorious high note. Don wanted Luke and Molly to end each song in different places. It sounded beautiful; Eleanor's high notes had improved in the rehearsal process, and this one rang out true and clear. She got chills, then reached for Charles, bringing him to the floor.

After the first act, Harry approached with his pad of paper. "Your meeting scene was fantastic. Magnificent, lady. God, more of that. Hold on to it for New York."

She swallowed; would they make it in New York?

From what she could sense, "Sunday Evening" worked. The audience was silent. While Charles sang, she tried to hear coughs or rustles but came up with nothing. Their voices floated above the orchestra. When they kissed, there was a full three seconds before people began to clap. Then the applause swelled along with the underscoring. Eleanor clung to Charles, her face hidden in his chest, and listened. It was the most glorious sound she'd ever heard.

At the end of the show, they ran downstage right, where the lighting was darker and they were illuminated by a spot. The crowd behind them was still singing, searching for them. She touched Luke's cheek.

"We got away." A train whistle sounded. The music from "Sunday Evening" swelled up, triumphant, with brass instead of strings, brighter, happier than before.

"Our love can do anything," Luke said. He kissed her. Together, they sang the final lines. He brought her hand up to his lips and kissed her finger, now dressed with a gold band.

"And now, we're one / The two of us are one / For every night, and every day."

Her high note floated above the orchestra. The spotlight narrowed. Luke cupped her face and kissed her. Just before blackout, he pulled her onto the train.

Eleanor and Charles held hands in the curtain call. For the first time, they received applause from the entire crowd. It was a sparse house, but no one walked out. There were no cheers, no flowers, and no one stood up, but they clapped.

Because she could not stop herself, Eleanor burst into tears.

ACT FOUR

The Eleven O'Clock Number

Chapter Nineteen

In Wisconsin, the winters were silent. The frost rolled heavy over the farms, snuffing out the noise of the animals. Only when Eleanor sat outside, plowing a path to the center of a field, could she hear the snapping of twigs or the falling crystals. In bed at night, the moonlight reflected off the snow, which froze over in an impenetrable blanket. The world turned blue. The thaw didn't come until April, the noise of the birds and squirrels returning with the grass.

New York was different. Winter amplified the sounds. The pavement was salted and too frequently crossed for any snow to pack, so it turned to brown muck that cars kicked up as they passed. People's shoes were filthy, crunching over the sidewalk. On Eleanor's first day back, she stepped into what she thought was a sheet of ice—it turned out to be a muddy slush puddle, six inches deep.

All this made her excursions out dreadful, but still, she was glad to be back home. Eleanor would not miss Boston, with its crumbling buildings and the chilly demeanor that hung from every brick and citizen.

It was Monday, one week after she had returned to the city. On Friday she'd had a meeting with her agent, Geoffrey.

"I think it's time you attend some auditions," he said. "One can never be too prepared."

She didn't want to think about what she needed to be prepared for. So he set her up with a string of appointments. Unlike the open calls of the summer, creative teams brought her in along with a small selection of actresses. She supposed that was what "making it" meant.

That day, she was called in for a new musical by Rodgers and Hammerstein. Something about a singing nun; it sounded inane. But a Rodgers and Hammerstein audition was nothing at which to turn up her nose. *A Tender Thing* was a masterpiece in her eyes, but tickets had sold in New York only on Don's and Harry's reputations. They had four weeks of healthy audiences. After that, it was all up to word of mouth. She could be unemployed by June.

There were two other women there, each with her headshot and résumé in her lap. One woman looked familiar. Eleanor peered over her shoulder to read her name at the top of the résumé—Sally Anne Howes, the woman who had replaced Julie Andrews in *My Fair Lady*. Eleanor's stomach lurched; not three months ago, she'd watched the show, smug that she was a star and Sally a replacement. Well, here they both were.

The elevator doors opened. Eleanor felt the wave of dismay before she recognized her.

Maggie Carmichael's mouth opened in surprise. Her eyes were bright; Eleanor imagined how she must look, waiting to audition when she was supposed to be the star of a Broadway hit.

Maggie sat beside her. "The gossip says Boston was a true experience."

Eleanor was quick to change the subject. "How's *Charades*? Why are you at an audition?"

"This is what we gypsies do, isn't it? Go from show to show?"

Eleanor had thought about a life of this. She'd grown so attached to *A Tender Thing* that she was afraid to move on to something else. This experience, albeit punishing, was special. Would she attach to every show, then be wrenched free, only to do it all over again?

A young man came out and called in Sally Ann.

"She's in *My Fair Lady*," Maggie said. "A Broadway baby one day. But who knows about tomorrow?"

"I'm going to look over the sides." Eleanor pulled out the script cuts they'd been given the day before. "I can't talk now."

Maggie raised her eyebrows. "Break a leg."

In the room, a man in a gray sweater sat in the middle, younger men on each side. He was reading Eleanor's résumé and looked up when she came in.

He waved a hand toward the center. "What are you singing today?"

"'Morning 'Til Night.'" When he didn't reply, she added, "From *A Tender Thing*."

She handed her music to the accompanist—another young man, though a part of her expected to see Don behind the piano—and stood center. She anchored herself, thought of the scene before, imagined Charles in front of her. The accompanist began to play, and she sang.

It was a different experience than it was with Charles, but they had performed together enough that she felt him there. After weeks with an orchestra, the piano sounded skeletal. He played too fast and she couldn't get her bearings. She didn't breathe before the high note, and it came out strangled.

"Thank you," the man said.

She blinked, smiled, and left.

As Eleanor struggled into her coat and scarf, Maggie approached her.

"You sounded great." Maggie bit her lip, looking uncomfortable. "You know," she finally said, her eyebrows pulled close together, "we're each other's competition, but you don't have to hate me. We're just two people who want the same thing."

The experience of the audition still hung around her. Would that be her life from now on? A series of rooms with strangers, bare cuts of songs she had once sung with a full orchestra?

Maggie was looking at her, and her face managed to show two expressions. She looked supportive, but behind that, she showed the gleam of a predator who knew she was closing in. A predator who wanted a real opponent. Maggie wanted a friend in the waiting room, so she had an equal to beat in the audition studio. Her expressions were transparent, and both were convincing. Eleanor finally appreciated why Maggie was compelling to watch.

"I know we're competition," Eleanor said. "So forgive me for not wanting to chitchat before an audition."

Maggie rolled her eyes but did not seem angry. "Eleanor, this is painful enough. No one is pulling for any of us."

Eleanor felt foolish. "You're right." This wasn't where she wanted to be. She didn't want to audition again and again or learn parts like a model trying on clothes. She wanted theater, the real creation of it. Maggie had something else, something barbed that allowed her to navigate the pool of talented girls, pushing them aside without hurting herself. Eleanor didn't even need this job, not yet, and she was already anxious. Instead of feeling inadequate, though, she felt grateful. She nodded at Maggie, smiled.

"Break a leg. I hope it goes well."

The radiator was screeching when Eleanor got home. She needed to get it bled. They would start New York rehearsals the following week; three weeks of those, and then the show would begin preview performances. Opening night would follow in early May, after four weeks of previews. If they flopped, she could afford rent for six months.

At eight, the door opened. It was Rosie, her hat and shoulders covered in snow. She met Eleanor's eyes and nodded.

For the past week, Eleanor had barely seen Rosie. Between her shifts and evenings out, Rosie came home to change clothes and sleep. Hot rollers and cold cream were the only evidence that Rosie was even there. When they shared the space, they bumped around each other squeaking out "Pardon" and "Do you want the light on?" The night she returned, Eleanor had expected either an empty apartment or a blowout fight. Instead, they left each other extra coffee and saved the hot water. Rosie slept on the pullout in the living room. Eleanor didn't know if it was a truce or a cease-fire.

"How was work?" she asked.

"Fine." Rosie hung up her wet things and set off for the bathroom, washing off her makeup. "A woman came in today with the foulest-smelling coat I've ever encountered."

"How long did it take to get out?"

"Haven't yet. Look at my hands—I've been scrubbing with baking soda since noon. I look like I clawed my way out of a burning building."

"Oh no. Here."

Eleanor joined her in the bathroom and perched on the sink. She scooped a dollop of Vaseline, rubbing until it was warm. Rosie held out her hand, and Eleanor took it between her palms. She massaged the ointment over Rosie's chapped skin, taking care to cover the backs of her hands and nailbeds. She gripped Rosie's hand between her own until it was warm. Rosie's fingers were small, the knuckles like smooth pearls.

"Your hands are like ice," Eleanor said.

"Outside's colder than a well digger's ass," Rosie said.

Eleanor flushed. She'd only heard that expression once before. "So, Rosie Hughes, you can keep a secret."

Rosie looked down. "I'm sorry."

Eleanor washed her hands, then, when she was ready, faced Rosie. "You're sorry? I thought you hated me."

"I did," Rosie said. "But I should have told you about him and me."

Eleanor shrugged. "I meant what I said, setting you up. Even if I made a mess of it." She looked at Rosie but couldn't catch her eye. "I'm sorry."

"You embarrassed me," Rosie said. "I didn't want to look desperate."

Eleanor stared down at the bathroom tile. "I wanted you to be happy."

Rosie blushed. "You aren't mad? He was your boyfriend."

"In name only. I don't know if you two've ever talked about me. There's no love lost there."

Rosie made a face.

"Does it bother you? Tommy and me?" Eleanor was nervous to ask; doing so suggested that Tommy still held feelings for her, when she suspected he didn't.

Rosie smiled, like she was trying not to hurt Eleanor. "Look, it's like you said. I don't think there's any love lost there. He's not yours, Eleanor. I don't think he ever was."

The words hurt; he was the first man to look at Eleanor as a woman. She remembered his hands on her waist and his smile in the morning light, then let the feeling pass. She put an arm around Rosie.

"Shall we have a drink?"

Rosie held up her shining hands. "I don't think I'm in shape to go out."

Eleanor went to the kitchen and fished out a bottle of gin.

"I don't have to sing tomorrow." She swished the bottle. "Want to get tight?"

Reparations with Rosie went a long way toward bolstering Eleanor's mood. When Don invited her to a performance of *The Music Man*, she dressed up. After their last evening in the bar, Eleanor was surprised by the invitation. She rewore the green dress he'd purchased for their Yale dinner, remembering the effect it had had back then. Don rang the bell at six forty-five, and when he came up, she saw his eyes widen.

"Smashing," he said.

Each time he looked at her body, she felt like she'd done something much more impressive than exist. "Would you like a drink?"

"One. I don't like to be drowsy in the theater."

Don took his place on the couch, in that way he had of not noticing other people's discomfort, and picked through the belongings on her coffee table.

"'Eyelashes—the new rave.' I wasn't aware those were a recent invention. And you find this sort of reading compelling?"

Eleanor returned with two glasses of gin. She set his down on top of the *Vogue*. "They're my friend Rosie's. She copies all the patterns."

Don raised his glass. "Thank you for accompanying me tonight."

When they clinked, Eleanor wondered if tonight might be the night something passed between them. She wanted to discuss the show and how his revisions were coming—but he stuck to politics, which she knew nothing about. He had strong opinions on Castro, called Eisenhower weak for recognizing him. Eleanor hoped her blank look read as interest. Eleanor wondered when Don had time to read the newspaper. He talked quickly, happy to have an audience. With her legs crossed beneath her,

Eleanor rested her arm on the back of the couch so her fingertips touched his cashmere sleeve.

Eleanor was too aware of him; he was so close, but she had no idea how to bridge the divide. She was as stricken as she had been in the library months earlier. At five after, Don placed his glass down and announced they should be on their way.

"You're like my mother before church," Eleanor said. "'We have to be there early!'"

Don put his hand on her back. "This is church."

"People say musical theater is in a golden age," Don said in the lobby during intermission. "I hope that isn't the case. I want to believe I haven't lived through the best of it."

Right then, a balding man with heavy eyebrows approached Don.

"Dick." Don shook his hand, then turned to Eleanor, again placing his hand on her back. "May I introduce you to our new star, Eleanor O'Hanlon? Eleanor, this is Richard Rodgers, a man who needs no introduction."

She worked her way through several sentence beginnings before finishing one. "Mr. Rodgers, it's such an honor. I adore your musicals."

"Dick is a good friend of mine." Don pulled Eleanor closer. She could feel the sweat from his palm. "This man taught me how to write a song."

"Are you a singer, young lady?"

Don tapped her hip with his fingers. "I snapped her up to star in *A Tender Thing.*"

"Lucky man." Rodgers winked at Eleanor. "The gossip says you're good."

Though she knew this wasn't a real compliment—he had never seen her himself—Eleanor could not speak.

She listened as Don and Rodgers discussed the performance, as well as rehearsals for their new productions. Don was speaking very quickly, laughing often. She had never seen him in a subordinate position; it might have been endearing, but he was making her nervous. Eleanor didn't mention that she'd auditioned for Rodgers's newest project. Rodgers noticed Don's hand, which never left her waist.

The bell rang, signaling the end of intermission, and Rodgers kissed her on the cheek.

When they returned to their seats, Don gripped his program until it creased.

"Do you dislike him?" she asked.

"Hush. You never know who's around." Don reached for her hand and held it for the remainder of the show.

On their way home, Eleanor asked again. "You seemed uncomfortable."

"We have no hard feelings at all." Don seemed surprised enough by her question that she believed him. "I'm sure you've noticed I don't like small talk. I was glad to have you there."

"He's a genius. I'm sure he's intimidating."

Don made a noise. "Hammerstein, his partner, is really the brains."

Eleanor was insulted that he thought she didn't know who Hammerstein was. "Don, I think he believes we're a couple."

Don walked quickly, his eyes scanning for an available taxi. "I'm sure he does."

Eleanor hesitated.

"I'm not so cold that I don't enjoy being seen with a pretty young woman." Don's eyes flicked to her. "Though of course our relationship is strictly professional."

She blushed, as if he was rejecting her all over again. "But he'll think I slept with you to get the role."

"Everyone gets the role somehow." He turned to her, and she was startled by the stony expression on his face. "A composer out with his star is nothing new. Tongues will hardly wag. It's almost expected nowadays. I'd much rather people spend their time thinking about my work—especially people like Dick Rodgers."

"But you touched me that way, knowing it would cause gossip."

He was quiet. "Being out with you, my dear, doesn't cause gossip. My solo appearances are what have always interested people, in the most invasive of ways."

He met her eyes and she saw something hard there that alarmed her. But then he turned away, searching the downtown traffic for a cab with its lights on. She watched him for a long moment. Most people Don's age were married. For the first time, Eleanor allowed herself to imagine that he had been truthful—that he had never become so close with another person. Until now, she'd attributed his words to artistic hubris. But what if it was more? This realization came as if she were tripping over a stone; her stomach swooped, and she recognized the certainty of her misfortune as much as the suddenness of it. It frightened her to imagine him so separate. She went back through her memories, seeing his touches in a new light, his flirtations.

"Don," she whispered, approaching him and laying her palm against his back. His sweater was soft and warmed by his skin. "Did you mean it when you said you never felt love?"

She prayed that he would turn and do something out of a musical—take her in his arms, profess his affection. He stayed facing the passing taxis.

"I've never told you an untruth."

She didn't understand. "But how could you write the show? Every note carries such yearning. Even if I wasn't playing Molly, I'd feel it. How did you know how to do it?"

He sighed. "I told you before, Eleanor. I wanted to know what it was like."

"I think you do know what it's like," she said. "That feeling must be real to you." She looked up. "Wanting someone that much. I know what it's like."

He held her gaze. His eyes were pale as a Wisconsin winter pond.

He raised his arm. A cab pulled against the curb. He helped her in and kissed her cheek. He handed the driver a bill and patted the roof of the car before shutting the door and stepping back to the curb. Eleanor watched him on the corner as they drove away.

At home, Eleanor sat with Rosie, who was exercising her arms with soup cans.

"How was your date?" she asked.

Eleanor curled her feet beneath herself. She explained the strange moment with Rodgers and how Don had rejected her at the bar in Boston.

"So it was a date," Rosie said, "but only for people to see."

Eleanor blinked. "Why would he do that?"

"He wouldn't be the first man to bring a date just to show off."

"Show off what? I'm just an actress, and there are far prettier ones if that's what he's after."

"Stop it. You're lovely, you're young." She twisted her mouth. "You're female."

She hated to prove Rosie right about something. But she did understand men. "I don't think he's being honest about something."

"If you think so, you're probably right." Rosie adjusted the cans so she pushed them out in front of her. "Makes your bosom firmer," she said.

Eleanor left her to it. She went to the kitchen and opened a new jar of pickles. Don had always been strange, but she had always assumed she understood him. They had so much in common. As she undressed for bed, Eleanor wondered if she knew him at all.

Chapter Twenty

Eleanor took the Broadway local up to 125th Street. As the train climbed, more and more whites got off, until she was the only one. She sat, knees together, crossing off the stations in her mind. She thought that she was going to get a nosebleed, up so high.

People stared—or at least she thought so. She'd worn a navy scarf over her hair, which Rosie said made her look like a nun, and did nothing to hide her complexion. It was lunchtime. People were out despite the cold, doing their shopping or getting a meal, shouting greetings across the street, smoking under store awnings. Everyone was black up here, as far as she could see. She felt as conspicuous as—well, as the only white girl on 125th.

Charles and Gwen lived on 130th. Once she was moving, she felt better. The shops did not look so different from the ones downtown: groceries and delis, liquor stores, cigar shops, and in the distance, a church; like the rest of New York, the streets were an intersection of everything a person might need.

On her way north, she passed a school at recess, the road closed off. Girls played hopscotch on the sidewalk, and boys were playing stickball in the street. She passed a girl with skinny knees sitting on the curb, watching the boys with a knotted mouth.

After crossing Columbus, Eleanor reached Charles's brownstone. She rang the bell for number 3.

A large woman with hair pulled into a gray-patched bun opened the door. Her eyes widened when she saw Eleanor, but she otherwise did not speak.

"I'm here to see Mr. Lawrence?"

"Who are you?"

"My name is Eleanor O'Hanlon. I work with him in the show."

The woman held open the door, and Eleanor stepped inside.

Three young children barreled down the staircase, a girl and two boys. They nearly knocked over Eleanor's escort, who wrangled one by the hood of his coat.

"Where do you think you're going like that, Bobby?"

The boy stopped, eyes going wide. "Outside."

"You'll break your neck going down those stairs," she said. "Or mine."

"Sorry, ma'am."

"If I see you like that again, Bobby, I'll tell your mama."

She gave them a stern look, holding each pair of eyes long enough to make sure they received her point, before dismissing them. Once they were gone, she smiled.

"You must have children," Eleanor said. "You sound just like my mother."

"I'll take you in," she said, pulling out a key.

"You wouldn't happen to be Charles's mother?"

"Yes. Mrs. Lawrence."

"How is Gwen?"

"You'll see her for yourself. She's out for a walk but should be back any minute."

Mrs. Lawrence opened the door, calling out Charles's name as she did.

Eleanor stayed at the threshold, looking in. The apartment was tidy, with windows that did not catch the afternoon light. The radiator clanked in the corner, the room too hot. A couch sat against the wall, covered in a crocheted blanket. A gray cat lounged on the back. Something was cooking on the stove. Mrs. Lawrence left Eleanor waiting and went back to preparing the evening meal.

Eleanor removed her hat and gloves and held them in front of her. As soon as Charles emerged, she switched to one hand, thinking she looked foolish with her hands clasped like an unfaithful husband.

"Eleanor." He kissed her cheek, surprised to see her. She nodded at an upright piano in the corner, sheet music spread on the stand.

"Practicing?"

"Just singing," he said. "What are you doing all the way up here?"

Eleanor removed the scarf from her hair and folded it in her lap. "Can I tell you something even I can't believe?" She glanced at him; he was listening. She was nervous, but she had come all the way up to Harlem for someone to talk to, someone who would understand. She told him, "I don't think I want to be an actress."

Charles softened. "Don't get blue on me now, Eleanor."

"It's not that. I can't stop thinking about the show, about how to fix it." She heard him click his tongue against his teeth.

"I know it's silly." She'd thought Charles might understand, but he seemed dubious. "But I think I could be a writer."

"Have you spoken to Don about this?"

The mention of Don had her blushing. Charles's eyes took in her face, and she felt like he could see every thought she'd had.

"He's an odd one," Charles said. "Tough as he is, he might not laugh at the idea of a lady writer. You never know."

"Maybe." Eleanor had no idea what Don would think; he surprised her again and again, opening up, then slamming back closed as if she'd humiliated him. "He is odd. He can be . . . kind. There's something about him, Charles, that makes me think he understands Molly and Luke better than all of us. He's captured their love, at least. The furtiveness, the fear."

"It seems Don Mannheim has asked these questions before," Charles said. "I've been in a lot of musicals and plays, and I've never played a character who feels like a real man. Always . . . clowns before. He's done something right with the show, even if it's not perfect."

She looked across the coffee table and caught his smile; she cared for him quite deeply. He'd been a true friend throughout the process. Now, with everything between them, she felt a depth of esteem for him that she carried for no one but Rosie.

"Are you in love with him, Eleanor?"

She went hot; she covered her mouth with her hand.

Charles clicked his tongue. "You're smarter than that."

"How did you know?"

"You're the only person who would call him kind."

"Don wrote the pieces that made me who I am," she said. "Of course I love him. But he doesn't love me."

"Then I think you know how it was he came to write this musical."

But she didn't know.

"He confides in you, asks you for help. I know you two have been out together. No one can claim to know him so well."

She thought of Don on the street the night before, the look in his eyes. "I still don't think I understand him."

He raised his eyebrows. "You don't want to understand."

She picked up the corner of the blanket, examined the crocheted squares. She could feel Charles looking at her.

"Eleanor, when he first saw me in the club, he bought me a drink. I didn't know if he was propositioning me for a job or something else."

Eleanor's face warmed. "Charles, whenever we go out, he treats me like his date."

Charles didn't reply, just kept his eyes on her.

She knew what he was trying to say and felt humiliated. She struggled for her words. She continued to examine the blanket.

Then the front door opened, letting in the hallway draft. Gwen entered, followed by a boy of about fifteen who was so tall and thin he looked stretched out. When he saw Eleanor, he narrowed his eyes, then offered a smile so resembling Charles that she knew him to be Davey, his little brother.

"Hi, baby." Charles kissed his wife. "Look who came for a visit."

"What are you doing all the way up here?" Gwen asked.

"So this is the white lady." Davey held out his hand. His arm was so thin that Eleanor imagined a noodle.

Gwen leaned against her husband. "You know, I heard about all that business with the article."

Eleanor knew how much Gwen loved Charles. She felt that she'd made a larger error than she was aware of, no less dangerous for her ignorance. "It was a horrible mistake."

"Charlie forgave you, so it's put to rest." Gwen hesitated. "If you have any more questions about my husband, you're welcome to ask me."

Eleanor felt hot. "I will."

Davey was raising his eyebrows like he was enjoying the scene before him. Gwen smiled at Eleanor. "So let's catch up."

Charles held out his hand to help Gwen as she descended toward the couch, palm on her stomach. She groaned when she landed.

Davey stared at Eleanor. "You ever been up this far?"

"No."

"You know Gwen was a maid, as a girl," he said. "She cleaned up after women like you."

Eleanor blushed again. "I've never had a maid."

Davey shrugged, then turned to Gwen. "I'm going back out."

Charles stood. "Where?"

"Meeting friends in the park."

"Be back by dinner." Charles's voice took on a paternal tone. "We're going to—"

"Seven."

Davey loped from the apartment without another word. Eleanor heard his footsteps all the way down to the street.

"He's a good kid, but he makes me hope to God this one isn't a boy," Charles said, nodding at Gwen's womb.

Eleanor did not know what to say; she had no brothers, and growing up in Wisconsin was very different from growing up in Harlem.

"I hope the show will have a better run in New York than Boston," Charles said.

Gwen gave him a look like he was naïve. "A few hundred miles won't change much."

"At least in New York we've got protestors on both sides of the issue," Charles said.

Gwen heaved herself off the couch with a pained expression.

Charles stood. "Are you feeling all right?"

"I don't like this talk." Gwen went to the piano and played middle C.

It needed a tuning; little ripples muddied the pitch. "The protests could get out of hand quickly."

"I thought you weren't afraid," Eleanor said.

"Maybe my maternal instincts are kicking in. I think you two are playing with fire."

Eleanor watched as Charles walked over and rested his hand on his wife's hair, cupping the back of her head. She watched their tenderness with an empty, aching feeling. Gwen rested her forehead against Charles's chest.

"I don't see how those characters could have a happy ending," Gwen said. "But wouldn't it be wonderful if life worked that way?"

Chapter Twenty-One

The night before the first Broadway rehearsal, Rosie made dinner.

She pressed a glass of champagne into Eleanor's hand. "You did it. Everything you said you would."

Rosie had roasted a chicken and mashed potatoes, and it wasn't until the bell rang that she announced that Tommy would dine with them.

"You're my best friend," Rosie said. "So we need to make this work. Go get the door."

Tommy stood straight, like he might get a prize for his posture. He handed over a bottle of wine.

After a minute of tense hellos, Rosie dropped flatware into Tommy's hands. "Why don't you set the table?" Then she left to check on the chicken.

"We've been dismissed," Tommy said once he and Eleanor were alone.

"I think we're supposed to be friends again," she said, narrowly missing the phrase "kiss and make up."

"I figured as much."

They fell quiet. Eleanor wondered what they could talk about—the show seemed taboo, like it would drag up their old fights. "So how're things with Rosie?"

Tommy's shoulders tensed.

"She tells me you two are swell."

"Well," Tommy said. Eleanor waited for him to continue, but that appeared to be it.

Eleanor poured more champagne. "I really am happy for you."

Tommy adjusted the forks and knives with more care than was necessary. Eleanor picked up her glass and drank too much in one gulp. "We could just pretend you and me didn't happen."

Tommy backed away from the table and sank into the couch.

Eleanor tried again. "We always got along. Why don't we pay attention to that?"

He drank from his glass, looking unhappy about it.

"I'd offer beer, but . . ."

"It'll disrupt her menu." Tommy caught her eye, and seeing her grin, offered one of his own. "I'm sure the production in the kitchen is even fancier than what you're up to all day."

"And you'll lose a finger if you go investigate," Eleanor said.

It was a new set of roles; friend of Rosie, Rosie's boyfriend. Eleanor felt her importance level shifting, going from principal to supporting, in Tommy's eyes. But then she realized that shift had already happened, months earlier.

"Will you meet her parents?" Eleanor asked.

"Not sure," he said. "I don't think they'll visit."

Eleanor laughed. "Mr. Hughes isn't the New York type."

"Will he like me?"

His voice betrayed only a touch of self-consciousness, but he wouldn't have asked unless the concern ran deep. Eleanor smiled.

"Why don't I tell you about them?"

"Did you have fun?" Rosie slipped on a nightgown.

Eleanor was already dressed for bed, having escaped to the bedroom to allow Rosie and Tommy to say a long goodbye in the living room. "I did."

The night had improved after they each downed some champagne. Once it became clear that Tommy and Eleanor would not break out into a fight, Rosie relaxed and began to show off her usual sparkle. She told stories Eleanor hadn't heard before, about evenings out with Tommy's friends and Sunday family dinners. She talked about the clashes with Tommy's mother over how to cook a casserole, and then how they bonded over Billie Holiday. It was then that Eleanor knew how much Rosie had been holding these stories back, afraid of showing her happiness. But though she felt some jealousy, it wasn't over Tommy, and then even that passed, and she began to laugh with them.

Rosie knelt on the edge of the bed, her long hair rolled into curlers. "I have something to tell you." Her hands were clasped in her lap. Eleanor couldn't see her left fingers but understood immediately.

"Rosie."

Her friend smiled, her eyes moist. "Oh, Eleanor. He asked me yesterday but I couldn't say yes until I knew you and I would be all right."

Eleanor felt steeped with dread. Marriage would change everything. Rosie was leaving, for good. She wanted to throw off her blankets and make a scene. Rosie waited. She looked apprehensive, but underneath, very happy.

Eleanor took a deep breath. "I'm going to miss you," she said. "So much."

Rosie wrapped her arms around her. Eleanor began to cry, surprising, desperate sobs. She felt Rosie's cool skin against her cheek. They had spent so many years together.

"This is what you always wanted."

"Both of us now."

"Yes." Eleanor pulled back, wiped her eyes. "Oh, I'm such a bad friend."

"You're being a bad friend because you're a good friend."

"I suppose you'll be moving out?"

"We found a place. Tommy's moving in next week; I'll join after the wedding."

"Wow. You've never even stayed over at his," Eleanor said, realizing as she spoke.

"I know," Rosie said, her face going red. "We haven't yet. But now, I think we will."

"Rosie!"

She squealed and kicked her feet against the bed. "I'm getting married!"

Eleanor pulled her in again. They stayed awake a long time, arms around each other, as Rosie designed her dress out loud. Eleanor listened, alternating between smiles and a falling feeling in her chest.

At their first Broadway rehearsal, all the bitterness from Boston washed away for a few hours. They had been on a break for six weeks between the end of the Boston run and the beginning of Broadway rehearsals, and in that time, much of the tension of their quiet crowds seemed to have eased. The cast was spirited and laughing. At one point in each of their lives, Broadway had beckoned like an impossible dream. They were all grateful, and it showed. Even the veterans like Duncan and Lucille seemed to appreciate the good fortune. A job in theater was never counted on. Everyone was happy to be able to do what they loved one more time. Eleanor saw that even Don had noticed the cast's mood; he smiled as Freddie did a series of pirouettes, then fell over, grasping the corner of the piano, breathless with laughter. Don nudged Freddie's hands away from his music, and Freddie, in a gesture of startling bravery, grasped Don's nose between his forefinger and thumb. Eleanor waited for Don to admonish him. Instead, he laughed.

They rehearsed in a studio on Eighth Avenue, far above the city. The protestors hadn't gotten wind of their location, so Eleanor enjoyed an uneventful walk through the front doors. She sat against the mirror with the newest copy of the script in her lap, running her finger over the line that read "A Broadway Musical." One of the producers had provided a breakfast. The entire cast was there, along with investors and designers. It was an important morning, she knew, but she didn't allow herself to get excited.

In Boston she'd shared the cast's excitement, joined in the exaggerated stories, the playful singing over breaks, the air-kissing. But that day she felt preoccupied by the coming rehearsal. Freddie greeted her with an embrace, and she returned it without enthusiasm. She was concerned about the show and had been waking up in the night with ideas on how to fix it. But she stopped short of asking Don. She did not know if their conversation after *The Music Man* had negatively affected their relationship.

Don stood over the piano, talking to Frank Taliercio about some new additions to the music. Frank was testing tempos, conducting and listening to Don's corrections. When Don saw her, he stopped.

"Eleanor."

"My first *real* Broadway rehearsal." She leaned against the piano. She loved seeing him in the rehearsal studio, where he was most comfortable. Even his clothes seemed to fit with more ease. He gave her a kiss on the cheek with the performed deference of a creative powerhouse greeting his star.

As she watched his face, she didn't see any hint of the intimacies they'd shared in the last months. He barely looked at her, instead concentrating on the score in his hands. She felt wrong, like she had imagined their friendship. She waited for him to acknowledge her more meaningfully; he did not.

"You're busy."

Don nodded. "Have a good rehearsal."

Eleanor waited for a real smile, for him to meet her eyes, for him to show her a piece of the score. Instead, he turned to Frank and resumed their conversation. She stepped away, as self-conscious as she'd been on her very first day. Don's walls had gone back up, and she had no idea how to proceed.

By then, Charles had arrived. He poured himself coffee from the breakfast table. She seized the opportunity to escape. Doing so, she caught Harry's approving look; he loved to see evidence that his forced bonding had created genuine feeling between the two leads. Eleanor nodded at him, feeling like a cog in Harry's great machine.

They had three weeks in New York to fix every problem on Harry's list.

Broadway was all about sticking to the budget. Every evening, Harry passed around notes to each of them scrawled on steno paper. *Faster delivery, scene four* or *Turn to the right, not left*. If they didn't incorporate the notes the following day, Harry demonstrated how much his temper had shortened. During the Broadway rehearsals, she saw Harry at his best. They had just eight hours in a day, during which he accomplished at least twelve hours' worth of work. He split them up and rehearsed scenes simultaneously, so no time went unused. He noticed every cast member, even fired a chorus boy for checking his shoelace in the back of a crowd scene. That spread Freddie even thinner than he had been. As dance captain, he had to spend extra time going over the choreography with one of the swings, a young man who understudied multiple roles in the ensemble, so he could be the chorus boy's replacement. Eleanor watched them working over lunch.

"I don't know how you have the energy," Eleanor said. "I'm exhausted, and I don't spend my days dancing."

"Stamina," Freddie said.

"Harry really puts you through it."

"He was in the military, you know," Freddie said. "That's why he runs rehearsals like this."

"Half artist, half machine."

"I think that's how he makes all of it work in his personal life. You know, since he's a fag. Balancing the wife, his boys—everyone knows, maybe even her, but since he shot a rifle in Germany they don't care as much."

Eleanor had considered this before. Most of the men in the cast were homosexual, but it was as if they shrugged on a cloak the moment they walked onto the street.

"I thought people in theater were open-minded."

Freddie laughed. "Maybe inside the building. But you never know who to trust. In my experience, some people are quite another way in public."

In March, three weeks before they would start previews, Harry pulled Charles and Eleanor aside during a rehearsal break. "What have you heard about *A Raisin in the Sun*?"

Eleanor had never seen a straight play before. She knew this was the first play to hit Broadway by a black woman. "I want to go."

"And you will. Both of you. Opening night tonight. It'll be great press for us."

"Can we have an extra ticket? For Gwen?" Charles asked.

Harry shrugged. "But I want to see a photo of my two stars in the *Times*."

He sent a girl from wardrobe to Bergdorf's. She returned later that day with three dresses for Eleanor. Harry picked a light blue silk that brushed the floor, with a white fur stole she looped around her elbows. Eleanor had never felt more elegant; large, borrowed diamond teardrops brushed cool against her neck.

She and Charles got ready in the rehearsal studio and met Gwen in front of the Ethel Barrymore Theatre. She wore peach satin over her round belly and had painted her lips red.

"I had it ready for your opening," she said, pulling the skirt out to display it, "but I decided to use it tonight. I couldn't miss this."

Charles offered one arm to each of them and they entered the theater lobby, which was filled with men in tuxedos. Flashes from the photographer's bulbs glinted off women's jewels.

"I've never seen such elegance," said Eleanor.

"I've never seen so many white people lined up to see a cast full of black people," Gwen said.

"I was thinking the opposite," Charles said. "When have you seen so many black people in a theater?"

Gwen smiled, the flashbulbs reflected in her eyes as she looked around the room.

A photographer captured them. Eleanor blinked over a green blob. She clutched Charles's arm, feeling a rush of nerves similar to what she'd felt at the investors' party. Charles gave their names. "The stars of *A Tender Thing*," the photographer wrote down.

Charles whispered in her ear, "If this play's a hit, it's good news for us."

Gwen paused by the ladies' room, hand on her swollen belly. "I don't know how I'm going to make it through a full act."

Charles kissed her cheek. "Better hope these're aisle seats."

Eleanor followed Gwen into the ladies'. The skirt of her gown was too formfitting to lift up, and she struggled with the zipper. After a while, she heard Gwen's voice, by the sinks.

"I'll wait right here, Eleanor."

She won the zipper battle and emerged to wash her hands. Beside her, an elderly white woman was having trouble with the soap dispenser.

Gwen reached over and fiddled with the spout for her. "There you are."

"Thank you, dear," the woman said. She finished washing her hands and opened her purse. She offered Gwen a quarter.

Gwen pursed her lips, then laughed. She took Eleanor's arm. "Enjoy the show."

Eleanor was unsure if she should say something, to tell Gwen she'd noticed what happened. But Gwen had already moved on, was telling Eleanor about the gown she was sewing for the baby's baptism.

The play was very different from what Eleanor had seen before. She'd worried she'd be bored without music, but Eleanor found herself sinking into the characters, more enthralled with the tighter focus. She'd expected the play to be more like a movie, but it was another thing altogether; the scenes were tense and intimate, and she felt as though she were inside the family's kitchen. Eleanor was surprised by the simplicity of the plot. As she watched Sidney Poitier's performance, she was amazed at the strength of the empathy he evoked from her. It made her wonder if she had been missing something by limiting herself to musicals.

On their way to the opening party—another trip to Sardi's—Charles had to adjust his gait to accommodate two women in high heels, one seven and a half months pregnant.

"That's what our show needs a bit of," Charles said. "Reality."

"The play was grounded," Gwen said. "I know those people."

"Even I felt like I knew those people," Eleanor said.

Charles stopped them in Times Square. "Look at you, pretty ladies."

Gwen bent one knee into a bevel and pursed her lips. Eleanor laughed. "We do look nice, don't we?"

"Gorgeous." Charles carefully twirled Gwen under his arm and then held her, her back to his front. He rubbed his face on the feather trim on her cape. "Achoo!"

Gwen swatted him away, then turned back and kissed him. Eleanor watched them from the curb. The lights above them shone down multicolored, turning the white of Charles's tuxedo shirt purple and yellow. He took his wife's hands and spun her again. Gwen tossed her head back, her mouth open as she laughed. She walked away but kept her hold on Charles, until the smooth line of her arm was long and straight. He kissed her hand.

Eleanor approached. "With this much sugar I'll never stomach the cake at the party."

Charles offered her his other arm.

All three linked up, Eleanor skipped and sang a line from *The Wizard of Oz*.

"Am I the lion?" he asked.

Gwen touched her belly. "I believe that would be me."

Eleanor looked around Times Square, buzzed by the show, her clothes, the company of her friends. "A year ago I'd have been in bed already, so I could wake up to feed the pigs."

"Is it true that farms are all in sepia tone?" Charles asked.

Eleanor laughed, then turned somber. "Where do you think Molly and Luke go, after the show ends?"

"On the train?" Charles thought about it. "New York, maybe. I want to see a show about them after they go. I want to see their lives together, in an apartment. I want them to be happy."

Gwen widened her eyes, shook her head. "In New York they'd find more people to accept them—and more people to make their lives hell."

"You see mixed couples around here," Charles said. "I see it all the time."

"Well, sure. But do they have children?" Gwen asked. "It's quite another thing, having a family."

"Maybe that's the compromise," Eleanor said. "They don't have kids."

Charles shook his head. "Don thinks it's a happy ending all the way through. The kids, the house, all of it."

They were nearing Sardi's. "What a night," he said. He was smiling wide; Eleanor had never seen him so elated. "Two more weeks and this will be us!"

"Well, after another month of previews," Eleanor said, but only because she felt the need to temper her emotions. Attending a Broadway opening—she was overwhelmed. Through the restaurant windows, she saw flashbulbs, a crowd in black tie. Her stomach twisted. "Oh my. We're actually going to be on Broadway."

Charles watched her, still smiling. When she looked at him, he pointed to her face. "That? That expression? It's going to feel like that every time," he said. "Opening night never gets old."

"I thought you couldn't give it your all," she said. "I thought it was a job."

"I never said it wasn't the best damned job there is." He pulled Gwen into him again. "How does it feel to be married to a Broadway star?"

She rolled her eyes, then stood on her toes to kiss him. "You're going to charm the pants off this town."

Eleanor felt another twist. She thought of all the protests. "You will, Charles."

Charles caught her eye. The joy slipped from his face, and she saw her own fear mirrored back. They stood on the sidewalk across the street, watching the cast of *A Raisin in the Sun* arrive at the restaurant, their expressions reflecting the triumph of their performance. Eleanor hoped that, when she stepped out of her cab on opening night, her face would shine like theirs.

Charles tugged their arms. "C'mon, ladies. Let's enjoy it while it lasts."

With two weeks left until their Broadway performances, they moved into the Winter Garden Theatre on Broadway and Fiftieth Street. It sat fifteen hundred people. Eleanor's hand shook when she touched the cool stage-door handle for the first time. Everyone rushed about, running to dressing rooms, trying their dancing shoes on the stage floor to make sure they weren't too slippery, locating costume accessories that had gone missing in travel. She stood in the wings. The set was hung backstage: Molly's room, the backdrop that showed the streets of Chicago at night and during the picnic, Luke's mother's kitchen. In the orchestra pit, a man was tuning the Steinway. She smelled sawdust and walked to center stage. The house-lights were up, and the designers had a table set up in the middle of the audience, ready for note-taking during their technical rehearsals before they added costumes. Eleanor opened her arms as if to take every empty seat in her hands.

With their new address came notoriety. Groups of protestors began camping outside, but this time, opposing groups joined in. The police cracked down on the protesting after a fight broke out between one group supporting the show and the segregationists. Protestors on both sides gathered every morning, and every afternoon, the cops did a sweep of the sidewalk.

"Almost makes me more nervous," Charles said on their way back from lunch one day, eyeing the empty sidewalk. "I like knowing where those guys are. You know they didn't just go home."

Journalists began covering the New York production. Photographers waited outside and tried to grab cast members before they went into rehearsals. Once, Eleanor had been buying coffee at a deli and was approached by a stranger claiming to recognize her from the papers. Only after a few probing questions did she realize he was a reporter.

Connor Morris appeared only once, all the way from Boston, just before they began dress rehearsals. Eleanor was crossing Broadway and saw him standing on the corner of Fifty-First Street, his red hair gleaming in the morning sun. He saw her and raised his hand. She ducked, running across the street to the stage door, but when she touched the handle and looked back, she saw he hadn't made any move toward her at all. Unnerved, she went inside.

Once during these hectic weeks, Charles asked her to go for a lunchtime walk in Central Park. It was newly spring; the magnolia trees were blooming.

"Will your family come to the show?" he asked as they began their stroll.

Her parents had not reached out to her, though she continued to send money home. The thought of them was like a wound in her belly.

"Gwen has started praying the rosary every morning." He glanced at Eleanor. "For you, too."

She didn't want that to be necessary. "I'll tell her thanks next time I see her."

"All those reporters have got her nervous," he said. "The other shows weren't covered like this."

"The protests drew them in," Eleanor said.

"Prayers won't do much." Charles was stiff, his hands in his pockets, head down.

"Is something wrong?"

Charles swallowed. "You said this was just a paycheck for me. I have a wife, and soon, a child. I have to think of it like a job. This show, especially, Ellie. We're making people angry. I have to be careful, for my family." He pulled a newspaper clipping from his pocket. "But I'm taking the risk for them, too, you know. It's not about money. I want you to know I'm all in, when we bring this to Broadway. This show is important to me."

Eleanor unfolded the clipping. It was from the *Times* that morning. A fourteen-year-old black boy had been killed in the Bronx, found on a playground with his throat cut. His name was Johnny Randall. There wasn't a picture, but there didn't need to be; Eleanor thought of Davey, Charles's brother. She skimmed lines about how he was armed, how he spent time with alleged street gangs. "He was just a kid."

Charles took the clipping back, folded it in his pocket. "By tonight, it'll be pinned on someone who looks just like me. This happens every day, all over the city."

Eleanor didn't know what to say. She apologized.

"Who knows who killed this boy? The cops aren't going to find out." Charles rubbed his palms on his jeans. "That won't be my son."

His voice provoked something in Eleanor that had her looking away, blinking.

"Luke is a good man," Charles said. "Do you know how rare it is for me to play a good man?"

"He's no better than you."

Charles shrugged, then started toward the duck pond. Eleanor watched his long shadow on the sun-drenched path, the article crumpled in his hand, and realized that her pulse was elevated. She took a breath and quickened her pace to catch up with him, wiping the sweat off her brow with the back of her hand.

Chapter Twenty-Two

Eleanor smeared cold cream on her face. She reached for a sponge and foundation and painted over her freckles. The sounds of the theater rumbled around her. It was night of the first preview. The first time anyone in New York would see the show. In the female ensemble's dressing room, girls were shrieking and chatting, warming up their voices and helping each other with makeup. It was a strange, happy din. To anyone listening it would not have sounded extraordinary, but Eleanor knew it was. Tomorrow's *Times* would feature an article showing the different makeup stations, where every white girl shared with a Negro girl. It was Harry's final step; after separating the casts throughout rehearsals, he'd integrated them before the final dress rehearsal.

"We're in this together," he'd said that morning, standing on the lip of the stage with his slender arms spread out. The words were a cliché, but Harry was such a dry man that the truth rang through. "I want every audience member to leave this theater knowing what this show is about."

Eleanor gelled back the fuzzy hairs that tended to slip out from beneath her wig, then slipped on the cap, pinned it down. The tasks focused her mind and calmed her body.

Eleanor had received flowers from many of the leading ladies in town. She looked at them all, amazed. One year ago she would have foamed at the mouth to be where she was. It was as though she had climbed to a momentous height and was now looking down at the drop. Only by recalling every step could she believe she'd done it. She heard the orchestra warming up downstairs, and it gave her more confidence.

One card lay open on her dressing table, a watercolor hydrangea from a drugstore.

Dear Eleanor,
  None of us back home can believe it. You really did it, honey.
I wish I could be there. I'll be first in line to buy the recording.
    Your friend,
      Pat

This card had brought on tears, which ruined the makeup that she was now replacing. She slid a program from the stack in the lobby and sent it around the cast to be autographed. She imagined Pat framing it under glass, hanging it behind his register, telling people he'd given her the notice for Don's open call. Eleanor wished there was a way she could express her gratitude; she wouldn't have been here without him, and not just because of that notice. He'd introduced her to this world, shared his love of it with her.

Though it hadn't turned out the way they'd planned. Back in Wisconsin, she'd believed that the people who created those beautiful musicals must be as beautiful inside. They must love the art like she did. Now Eleanor was one of those creators and didn't know if she was fulfilling her dream or proving that it couldn't come true. The facts of the dream were all true—here she was in a Broadway dressing room, about to premiere a Don Mannheim show. She had imagined something glittering and fun; instead, she'd gotten *A Tender Thing*. She looked around the dressing room, at the naked bulbs framing her face, the industrial carpet, the lights of Times Square shining through her window, and committed them to memory. Tomorrow she'd write Pat a letter, telling him everything. That way he could pretend he'd been there.

A knock sounded at her door.

"Come in," she said through a bobby pin in her teeth.

It was Don, carrying a heavy paper-wrapped package.

He was back to avoiding her eyes. But she didn't feel pressure to make him meet her gaze. She continued pinning her hair. "As though I needed something else to remember tonight."

He passed her the package. It was a framed piece of sheet music, the first page of "Sunday Evening." On it, Don had written, *To Eleanor, my Molly: Thank you for bringing my dreams to life, and for holding me to a higher standard than I would have asked for. Your friend, Don.*

She stared at it for a long time before she could look up. When she did, Don was focused on her makeup, his face red. If he were anyone else, she would have poured out her heart; it was right on her tongue. Instead, she kissed his cheek.

"You have no idea what this means to me," she said, looking at the music again. "I will always treasure being in this musical."

"Do you think I got it right?"

The show had not changed much in the few weeks leading up to Broadway. Eleanor believed in it. But she did not tell him all she thought he could change. She hoped the audience would give them a chance.

Eleanor touched Don's face.

"To the day I die," she said, "this will be the most important thing I do."

Rosie and Tommy were in the audience. Eleanor had seen much less of them since they got their own place, where Rosie lived in all ways but the official. "I'm saving my address change for my wedding night," she had begun saying in a conspiring tone.

"No one I know has ever seen me perform," Eleanor said to Charles backstage.

"Gwen's here, with my mother and Davey."

Eleanor had too much energy. She hopped back and forth to shake some of it off, until she bumped into Freddie as he stretched. He poked her, laughed. "Watch it, starlet."

"This feels so much more real than Boston." Tears once again filled her eyes, adrenaline or emotion. When she turned toward Charles, tenderness for him welled up inside of her, and she thought of their night out in Boston and all the hours onstage, all their lunches. She threw her arms around him.

"There, there, farm girl," Charles said, but was laughing. When she pulled back, he took her hands once more. "Of course it's different. This is Broadway."

She squeezed his hands. "We did it."

"I'm glad I did this with you," he said.

Since Freddie had the most Broadway credits out of the cast, he led their preshow congregation. They held hands in a circle. Freddie offered a sort of prayer, with no mention of God—they were united by the art, by music, and they had a mission to tell a story. He kissed the hands of the dancers on either side of him. Then the stage manager called places. Charles squeezed Eleanor's hands and went behind the back flat so he could enter stage left.

She heard the crowd quiet as the lights dimmed and the orchestra tuned to an A.

The hair stood up on the back of her neck, on her arms, even on her legs. All her nervous energy rose up, knotting into an unbearable peak, and then faded away. Her fingertips stopped trembling. Her eyes dried. She bit her tongue so moisture could flood her mouth, then swallowed; her throat was in good shape.

Eleanor tried to hear the overture as if for the first time. When the dancers entered, the audience had never seen the choreography before, the clever way Harry had blended teenage movements with dance. Soon, Luke entered, singing with his brother. No one had seen Charles like this before. Then, taking one last breath, Eleanor walked onstage.

For a moment, she let herself feel the lights of Broadway. Then she began.

She sang her first song, introducing herself to the audience as a girl on the verge of womanhood. And then she turned around and locked eyes with Luke.

He looked so handsome there, but it was more than that. It was his face, or his movements, the way he inhabited his body. She stilled as the orchestra began to play under them.

Luke stared at her. Molly blinked, turned around, wondering if he would still be there when she turned back. He was. She held out a hand to him. He pressed his palm to hers. Meanwhile, the music played low and sweet.

Someone passed by, upstage of them. Both jerked their hands back. Molly smiled, embarrassed, then looked up. Asked him for directions.

After their kiss, the music changed to something else, dark and beautiful, deep brass and cello, a minor key. It made Eleanor's stomach churn in delicious apprehension.

Eleanor could feel the audience with them. Her energy twisted, and she felt electrified. They held the kiss for another beat, feeling the suspension of the moment, and the audience's eyes. Many of these people had never seen a kiss like this before. She felt her blood pound through her heart, felt the triumph of the moment. She knew then that no matter what love came into her life, this would be her most momentous kiss.

When they pulled back, Luke quivered. They could not stop staring at each other. Molly couldn't feel her feet and hands. Luke touched her lips.

The music changed again, this time to something exciting, bubbling up with lots of percussion and strings and staccato brass.

They began to sing.

Before the act one finale, Eleanor waited backstage. She was hit with a wave of anxiety so horrible that she had to grip her stomach to keep from heaving. Her breath was short.

"You're just nervous for the next scene," Franny, her dresser, said. She helped Eleanor into a chair and directed her to hang her head between her knees.

They were approaching the scene where Molly invites Luke to stay in her bed.

Eleanor breathed deep. This was more than nerves. It was a wave of dread so severe that she fought not to moan. She imagined critics writing about her, articles that would go all the way back to Wisconsin, about her sordid actions onstage. They would write about how she kissed without a hint of chastity. How she directed Luke's hand to her breast. How her nightgown slipped up to her thighs as she lay back on the bed. She imagined her parents reading the article over the breakfast table. She imagined them in church, the glares of parishioners.

Another wave of nausea.

"This scene has not bothered me in a long time," she whispered to Franny.

Franny gave Eleanor's shoulder a squeeze. "You're an actress, remember."

It was time for Eleanor to get back onstage. There was one moment where she was conscious of the audience, but then she heard Luke, calling for Molly, and she focused herself. All that mattered was Luke and being with him.

The opening notes of "Morning 'Til Night" began to play. Her mind flashed to her audition, Don's playing for her. She sang with every ounce of herself. When it came time to invite Luke to stay, she felt no fear.

"It's going well," Charles said during intermission. She heard rumblings from behind the curtain. Harry stood backstage in his suit.

"The audience is with you." Harry smiled, genuine emotion breaking through his controlled front. He looked ten years younger. "You're all on fire out there."

He gripped Eleanor's hands and kissed them, then did the same to Charles before exiting.

"I never thought we'd get a real compliment out of the man," she said.

"Let's not let it go to our heads." Charles looked delighted. "Still have to get through act two."

Act two was more challenging, beginning with the new song. But Molly's thoughts and feelings came to her so readily. Eleanor understood why they'd rehearsed and rehearsed; she stepped into Molly like a skin. The costumes and music helped; she felt like a new person, and all of the emotions were there. She sang about doubting her relationship with Luke, questioned if she could give up her family.

At the end, she realized that none of the things in her life would matter if she wouldn't fight for them. She decided to run away with him.

Racing backstage, Eleanor held out her arms for her costume change. A rush of cool air hit her back. The door to the alley was propped open.

"Why is that open?" she asked Franny.

"No time for that. You'll miss your entrance," Franny said. "We need to get you back onstage."

Franny zipped Molly's navy dress. Otis rushed over to her and gave her the wedding ring she wore in the finale, which she slipped into her pocket to wait for the last scene. Under her breath, she murmured, "And, with you / Forever now, with you . . . ," while she waited for him to retrieve the gun. The metal was freezing, and heavier than she remembered. Everything felt heightened that night, brighter, sharper, colder, more intense. Eleanor gulped some water and made it onstage in time for her scene with her parents, in which she is caught packing a suitcase. From that moment on, Eleanor had no breaks for the remainder of the show, until the curtain dropped.

She argued with Duncan, her voice breaking as she told him he could not keep her. She wrenched the suitcase from him and raced out of the house, running back to her meeting place with Luke. She threw her arms around Luke and held on for a second, opening her eyes and looking backstage.

Eleanor recognized a familiar shock of red hair. Her stomach lurched. But then the person moved into the shadows, and she had no time to worry about it; she turned back to Luke.

"We're never going to get away." She pulled the gun out of the pocket of her coat. "I don't want to use it. Just scare everyone a bit."

Luke shook his head. "God help us, Molly."

She grasped his hands. "Of course God will help us. God himself brought us together."

Molly pocketed the gun; they exited stage left, in time for the mob to enter stage right and cross. They sang, a layered collage of earlier music, the ensemble broken up into interlocking lines from the white chorus, the black chorus, Molly's and Luke's families. Don had woven together different melodies in an organized clash, so if the listener didn't pay attention it sounded like chaos, but they could just as easily weed out every individual line. It brought chills down Eleanor's back. The music swelled into a moment of cohesion, all the choruses making a magnificent chord.

Molly and Luke ran across the stage, hand in hand. Just then, Molly's uncle pulled out a knife and aimed it at Luke.

Her hands were shaking; she gripped the gun with trembling hands and pointed it back at her uncle. "Don't you dare!"

The crowd went silent, the music cutting off in one staccato note that hung in the house in a ringing echo.

Her father stepped forward, calling for Luke to let her go.

Molly raised the gun again. "Don't speak to my husband that way."

A ripple went through the audience. Molly heard it in the crowd before her, watched her father's face crumple in pain and disgust.

Protests erupted from the crowd, Luke's family or friends, maybe; Molly didn't hear them. The world had begun to blur.

"You're going to hurt someone," Luke said to Molly. "Give me the gun, Molly, let's get out of here!"

She didn't want to, but she reached the gun toward him.

A moment of real life pierced through the scene. In Eleanor's heightened state, her palms had gone sweaty. She fumbled the gun, and Charles lurched to catch it. Instead of gripping around the handle, his fingers splayed like a crab around the barrel and the bottom, grasping where he could. He jerked and was adjusting his grip, fighting not to drop the gun, when his finger pulled the trigger.

It happened so fast that, in hindsight, Eleanor could not say for sure she even remembered it. She had not thought to pay attention.

She felt the force of the explosion before she heard it, right in her abdomen. The sound was enormous, and painful, and it was several seconds before her brain processed it. Her awareness came like jumpy frames of a film, until she realized moments later that something had happened. An explosion, the sound of breaking glass, and then heat.

Sparks rained down from above. Eleanor looked up, in a daze. At first all she noticed was the beauty, the flames around her. Her eardrums rang, and the world had gone quiet. Pieces of glass sprinkled the floor. Too slow, she reached up to cover her face. A shard pierced her cheek, right under her eye.

Moving her arms away from her eyes, she looked at Charles. He was still, his hand on the gun, his eyes on the broken spotlight above them. A spark landed on the curtain behind Charles, then extinguished when it hit the flame-retardant fabric.

Charles looked at her. Their eyes met, and she saw pure terror.

"That's a real gun!" someone yelled.

Eleanor's awareness snapped back into place. Someone in the audience let out a high peal, wrenching beneath her skin like claws. The audience seemed to collectively gasp, something she had only heard on television. After the initial scream, no one spoke. Tiny shimmers of fear ran through the crowd. Eleanor could see the audience members now that the spotlight had gone out, and she looked out into a sea of people gripping their seats, eyes wide and fixed on Charles.

He gripped the gun until the flesh beneath his fingernails had gone white. Eleanor watched him look at the gun and then the broken spotlight above them, and then all around as if searching for a victim. The rest of the cast were all standing.

"What happened?" she whispered to no one.

Sounds began to rumble from the audience, first a sob, then another; before long, the cast had cracked their freeze. Someone screamed again, and then another yell. The petrified atmosphere shattered, and the audience broke into panic.

"Get out of here!"

"He's got a real gun!"

"He's gonna shoot up the whole fucking place!"

The cast began to run off the stage like lost mice, bumping into each other, falling, scrambling to their feet in an effort to get offstage. The audience was pure pandemonium—they were crawling over each other toward the door. Someone was speaking over the house microphone, but she couldn't make out words. The screams masked everything. Charles gripped her shoulder, holding her in place, behind him.

She looked out once more, and saw someone advancing toward the stage, arm raised.

Eleanor screamed, clawed her fingers against Charles's shirt, trying to pull him toward the wing. His feet didn't budge, and they both stumbled.

"Eleanor?" He was clearly in shock.

"Get offstage!" She couldn't speak; she screamed, her emotions coming straight out of her throat. "Charles! Go!"

He was still rooted to the spot. In a fit of panic, she wrenched at the gun. "Give it to me, Charles!"

It was as if he had been waiting for her instruction: he dropped it like a red coal. She caught the gun before it hit the floor and held it between her fingers. She had no idea what to do next; her heart was pounding and she looked left and right.

The man coming toward the stage, was he still there? Was he going to shoot?

She raised the gun up, toward the ceiling. "It's all right!" she yelled. "It was a mistake! He's not trying to hurt anyone!"

Suddenly, someone grabbed her arms with a grip that almost caused her to drop the gun. She screamed. It was Rosie, her face an inch from Eleanor's. She shook Eleanor by the arms and when that didn't work, knocked her back with a slap.

Rosie's grip held fast. "Eleanor, get out of here. Move your feet."

"Give it to me." It was Tommy. In her numbness, Eleanor didn't realize how strange it was to see them onstage, and felt that she could relax now. Like Charles, she handed over the gun at once. Tommy pulled a lever on it, opened it up so metal bullets spilled into his hand. He swore, then slid the gun into his coat pocket.

"Why was it loaded?" Eleanor asked. Rosie gave her another shake and pushed her toward the wings.

Dimly, she was aware of the screaming crowd and police sirens swirling over it all. A voice, spoken over the house microphone, saying words she didn't catch.

Tommy grabbed Charles by the upper arm, wrenched him around, and pointed him toward the wing. "You! Get out or you'll be shot!" Tommy shoved. Charles caught the momentum and began to run, his long legs gummy under his weight, like a foal.

"Come on!" Rosie pushed her again. "We have to go!"

But still Eleanor could not move. She stared out at the audience. Many of the seats were clear by now; red velvet reflected back at her as people pushed and shoved through the aisles to get out. The doors to the street had all been slung open, and beyond that, she saw red and blue lights flashing, spilling into the lobby.

In this haze, she looked across the top of the crowd for Don. In all of this, she had not thought of him, but she could not leave without knowing where he was.

Rosie was screaming her name. Eleanor knew she should move, but her legs did not obey. After another moment, Tommy grabbed her around the waist. He threw her over his shoulder, knocking the wind from her lungs, and carried her off the stage and into darkness.

Chapter Twenty-Three

"Y ou have nothing on him!" Eleanor slammed her hand on the desk.

"He drew a gun on a crowd," the officer said without expression, as if now that Charles was locked away the situation had become boring.

"I had the gun first! You don't even know how the show works," Eleanor said. "Otis, our props master, gets the gun from a safe. He hands it to me. Charles takes it from me, onstage. How could he have gotten to it?"

"Miss, if you don't calm down, I'll be tempted to throw you in there with him."

Eleanor was about to yell again when Rosie took her by the hand and led her to the plastic chairs against the wall.

"I've got seventeen dollars," Tommy said under his breath. "You two have anything?"

Eleanor didn't have her wallet. Rosie only had a beaded clutch with a five-dollar bill inside for emergencies.

At the theater, Charles had had no way of protecting himself against arrest; hundreds of witnesses had seen him fire a gun. Backstage, police officers had taken the gun from Tommy and thrown Charles to the ground. With a knee to his back, the police arrested him despite insistence from a dozen cast members that it had to be a mistake.

"Right now, we know he fired a gun in a theater." Two officers had brought him out through the front door, displayed to a crowd of onlookers. Reporters took photos. The atmosphere was energetic and sharpened by fear and adrenaline, like a hunt. When Charles passed by the crowd, audience members booed and screamed foul things. Charles kept his head down as they pushed him into the car. Eleanor tried to follow, but Rosie held her and did not let go.

It had taken an hour to break through the crowds surrounding the theater, and another forty minutes before an officer would speak to them. Rosie brought up the idea of going home to clean her rainy-day fund from her sock drawer, but Tommy wouldn't let them separate. It was useless—even cleaning out their savings, they wouldn't have enough to bail Charles out.

They heard someone running down the hallway. The door swung open and a sweaty, panting Harry walked through. Eleanor could never remember being happy to see him before.

"That gun was safe before the show," Harry said to the cop. "I checked it myself."

"Who the hell are you?"

"Damn it, I'm the director. Who are you?"

"Language, sir. I'm Officer Heizer."

"Well, Officer Heizer, you think I would allow a gun on my stage without taking all the precautions?" Harry's slender body crouched over the desk like a feral cat. "That man is innocent. Did you even see what happened?"

"Sir, I've been working all night, not attending plays."

"It's not a play, it's a musical. And if you had attended, you'd know that he could have done a lot more damage if he wanted to. This lady dropped the gun, he caught it, it went off and hit a spotlight. Thank God no one was hurt. The question is—who loaded the gun?"

"Someone was backstage." The memory came back to Eleanor as she spoke; the events of the night had jumbled everything up. "I remember, the door to the alley was open."

Harry turned to her, his eyes like lasers.

Officer Heizer sighed. "Why is this just coming out now?"

Harry took a step closer, examining Eleanor. "Has anyone offered this woman something hot to drink?" He turned to the officer, then the clerk behind the desk. "She was onstage, right next to him, when the gun went off. Don't you think she's your best witness?"

Harry didn't wait for a reply and steered her into a chair. He waved a hand at Rosie, who disappeared to find coffee. "Eleanor, tell me what you know."

"Someone was backstage. I have my quick change right before the final scene, you know, and I remember I felt cold air blowing on my skin."

"That door is locked during the show."

"It wasn't tonight. Ask Franny, she noticed it too."

"Otis is the only one who touches the gun until it goes onstage."

Eleanor shook her head. "The gun was freezing. It felt different tonight. Otis always gives me the wedding ring, then the gun. Someone must have switched them when he was giving me my ring."

Harry turned to the officer, snapping his fingers. "Write this down."

"Sir," Tommy said, "I don't think ordering them about is going to help."

"Who are you?"

"Tommy Murphy. I'm in the navy." Tommy turned to the officers. "Officer Heizer, Miss O'Hanlon named someone else who can back her up—Eleanor, what was her name?"

"Francine Garber," said Harry. "I have her contact information at the theater, as well as everyone working on the musical. Otis Johnson, props master. I've worked with him eighteen years."

"Look, sir." Officer Heizer rubbed the bridge of his nose. "People need to see someone behind bars for this."

"And we'll find that person," Harry said. "It's not Charles Lawrence."

"The man has a record."

"It should have been scrubbed," Eleanor said. She felt hot inside, her muscles out of control with fury.

Everyone in the room looked at her.

At that moment, Rosie returned, coffee in hand. "I know you don't take sugar, but I thought some might help right now. You're a bit drawn."

"What record?" Tommy asked.

"It was an accident, even the victim said so."

Officer Heizer turned an appreciative eye at Rosie in her pink satin as she set up Eleanor's coffee on the table. Eleanor glared at him.

"Sir, the man in the cell was framed for a crime," Harry said. "Don't let a retracted incident from five years ago stand in the way of his freedom."

Eleanor knew that incident wasn't what was standing in his way and was about to say so when Harry touched her elbow. She glanced his way, and he gave her a tiny shake of his head.

It took forty minutes of begging, but Harry was able to post bail. Charles emerged a few minutes later, still in costume, his jeans torn and dirty, a bruise forming under his eye.

Eleanor ran up to him. "What did they do to you?" Her breath was hard to catch. Her tremors became overwhelming, and then she was crying.

"Let's go home," Rosie said, wrapping an arm around Eleanor.

It wasn't until they were all piled into a cab, Rosie sitting on Tommy's lap so they could fit everybody, that Eleanor burst forth with what she wanted to say.

"So we aren't even going to acknowledge why Charles was in jail tonight?" she asked. She turned to Harry and Tommy. "Neither of you said anything about how unfair it was. They just locked him away. And why? *Why?*"

A streetlight lit their faces. No one looked at her.

"Give it a rest, Eleanor," Charles said. "It wouldn't have helped."

"That officer needed a good kick in the ass. Whoever loaded that gun," Eleanor said, "wanted something terrible to ruin the show—maybe even get Charles thrown in jail—"

"Eleanor." Charles reached out and took her hand. He sounded exhausted, even annoyed. "I don't want to talk about this anymore."

"Yes, but—"

"I said no more." He held a hand up to his swollen eye.

Eleanor fought back her words. She looked at Charles and felt a rush of affection and pain, like the turning over of her own heart. His wounds looked worse by the minute. Each time she glanced at him, she was reminded of what people had done, what she had been a part of, wittingly or not. A lump rose in her throat and stayed there. "Let's get you some ice. Where are we going anyway?"

They decided Tommy and Rosie's place would be safest and directed the driver there.

"Where's Don?" Eleanor asked Harry.

Harry counted money for fare. A beat went by. "He's at home."

"What did he say?"

"He's devastated," Harry said. The driver pulled over to the curb.

Eleanor swung her feet out of the car, a question on her mind. It knotted her stomach, and she almost didn't ask. But she saw Charles, following Tommy and Rosie into their apartment so he could call Gwen, and felt a wave of fury. "Why didn't he come with you to the station?"

Harry sighed. "Don isn't one for conflict."

"He wrote the show that landed us in this mess."

Harry's face was blank.

"He made a lot of people angry," Eleanor said. "And Charles had to pay for it."

"I understood what you meant."

"He . . ." Emotion was coming over her fast, and she realized she couldn't keep enough of a handle on it and still speak with Harry. She didn't want to have her meltdown there, one foot out of the cab, in front of a man whom she still barely trusted, no matter what had passed in the last two hours. She reached out and offered her hand to him. "Thank you, Harry."

"Stay safe, Eleanor. Don't speak to any reporters."

"You should eat something."

"I had a sandwich."

Rosie touched Eleanor's forehead. "You're not hot, but you're shaking like you have a fever."

"Here." Tommy shoved a glass under her nose. She drank what was inside without looking. Whiskey.

He handed one to Charles.

Charles didn't move. "I need to call my wife."

Tommy kept his mouth shut tight. Charles had called Gwen every five minutes from the hall phone in Rosie and Tommy's new place, but no one was picking up except for Charles's downstairs neighbor, who said she hadn't seen his family return after the show.

"We left the number," Rosie said. "Gwen will know where to call. I'm sure she waited somewhere safe for the streets to clear."

"I have to go."

Eleanor gripped his arm. "You can't go out there."

"You have no idea what could be happening to her," Charles said. He did another lap of the apartment. They all watched him. No one wanted to bring up the baby, the fact that she couldn't walk far in her condition. Eleanor felt useless; she could hardly imagine how Charles felt.

"Charles, it's dangerous."

"The pigs let me go," he said. "So I'm going home to my damn wife."

Tommy added more liquid to Charles's glass. "You have a much better chance of coming home to her if you stay the night."

"I'll get you blankets," Rosie said. She had still not removed her pink silk dress, though hours ago she'd lost a rhinestone clip-on. Eleanor watched her go barefoot into the bedroom and emerge with blankets, her head lopsided with just the one chandelier. Rosie draped each of them in a comforter. She looked up at Tommy. "Would soup help them?" Rosie dug through the freezer.

Eleanor felt the exhaustion in her eyes—they drooped and blurred, stinging, but she still wondered if she would be able to sleep. Thank goodness she hadn't had the chance to drink the sugared coffee.

Seeing Eleanor blink, Tommy gripped Rosie's shoulder. "Time for bed," he said. "All of us."

Eleanor turned out the living room lamp. Charles lay on the floor in a makeshift bed of the comforter and extra pillows, his head propped on his arm. "I should call Gwen again."

Eleanor didn't want to tell him not to, even though she knew another call would make things worse. Gwen wasn't home. The thought was harrowing.

"Gwen is a smart woman. She probably didn't want to get stuck in the crush in midtown and hid out with a friend."

"She's the wife of a madman with a gun. Carrying my mad baby." He rolled onto his back. It was dark, but she could see the light from the streetlamps shining on his eyes. "You don't know what happened."

"Does she have friends in Hell's Kitchen? Maybe someone let her stay."

"She would've found a way to tell me." Charles was quiet. "I think I should go."

If Eleanor loved someone like he did, she would have gone. "Cover your costume."

He shrugged. "On the street, I'm just another black guy."

He spoke with bitterness, but there was a slight tremor to his voice.

It was chilly out; she went to the hall closet, gave him a sweater she had bought Tommy.

Eleanor stood there, watching him. His eyes were wide. She wanted to wrap him in her arms and keep him in the apartment. But he looked at her again and shrugged, picking his keys off the coffee table.

"Be safe," she said.

"I will."

"Call when you get home?"

"Yes," he said, though she knew he wouldn't. If Gwen wasn't home, he'd go out looking for her, and Eleanor would be far from his mind.

He touched the knob, his fingers loose, and stopped. His shoulders made a smooth curve under the sweater, his head bowed. He turned back and met Eleanor's eyes. It had seemed that in the past months, they had built a pocket of safety between the two of them. Eleanor felt as though he were looking back at her from a place far away. Charles's eyes were wide and sad, and he breathed out, his chest going concave. Eleanor felt her anger from the evening shiver and fall away, and in its place, felt a profound and deep grief. She didn't want to let him leave. They looked at each other for another moment.

"I'm sorry, Charles," she said.

His mouth was tight and thin, his nod just one quick jerk. Then he turned away and opened the door.

She watched him go, his slender body lonely in the empty stairwell. When she heard him reach the street, she turned the dead bolt.

She dragged the comforter off the floor and lay back on the couch. Alone, with her friends asleep and Charles out on the streets, she let herself think.

Violent tremors wracked her body. She thought of Don. How could he have left them? If that bullet had hit someone, Charles would never have seen his way out of prison—no matter his innocence. It wasn't fair to blame that on Don. But he had been so callous with their welfare, had known Charles's unstable position without doing a thing about it.

She turned over, facing the upholstery. Of course she knew he hadn't intended the violence to happen. Don didn't plant the gun. But even before that, he had to have known the show would be an enormous news piece. *I'm investing in my legacy*, he'd said. Had he even believed in the show, the way Eleanor had, the way she knew, against his better judgment, Charles had begun to?

Don had known how big this musical would be. Why hadn't he thought about the actors? That he'd put them into dangerous positions, stalked by reporters and abandoned by their families?

Harry had been difficult, but in a way, weren't his criticisms acts of protection? He'd set her up with an agent, tried to instruct her on the business. Hell, he hadn't even wanted a girl this green. But Don had. He'd used her as a date, as a pretty girl on his arm, even as a source of inspiration and the occasional lyric—but Eleanor would never forget the terror she'd felt onstage after the gun went off. Where had he been? He hadn't even checked in backstage. He'd gone home.

For so long, she had thought she and Don were the same, but wondered if that was still true. Musicals had always represented something more to her: tales, humanity, tied up in two-act arcs. She saw the world through them. They'd brought emotion into her childhood bedroom. *A Tender Thing* meant more to her now, after this night, than ever before. But Don? What did he love about musicals? His talent? All those characters under his control?

Eleanor gave up on sleep and went to the window. It was near morning; outside, she could see a man preparing for the commute, stacking papers into his newsstand. Those papers reported the end of something she and Charles might have been foolish to believe in from the beginning. Charles would probably be on the front page, in handcuffs, disgraced. The truth was—and Eleanor felt this deep in her bones—the onlookers wanted someone to blame. They hadn't caught the person who'd planted the gun, and Charles was next in line.

Gwen had been right all along—there was no happy ending for Molly and Luke.

＊

Charles met her outside the hospital waiting room. She'd come as soon as he called, hailing the first cab with its lights on. When she saw him, her breath came out in a rush. He looked drained, but his eyes were relaxed, and his smile lifted every muscle.

"Gwen's resting." His bruise had darkened, made worse by lack of sleep. A vessel had burst in his eye, so when he looked to the side, she saw bright red. "She's healthy. I'm a father."

Eleanor wrapped her arms around him. At first he was stiff, but slowly, the tension left his body, until he collapsed. His usual buoyancy, the life that thrummed through his bones and lit his smile and added that essence to his voice that made him an irresistible performer, was defeated by exhaustion. He caught his breath in gasps, the relief acute and painful. People passed them in the hallway, parting like a current.

He wiped his eyes. "God. I nearly lost her, Eleanor. She fell in the crowd and went into early labor. I got home and found a note to come to the hospital. My mother didn't want to wait for me, in case . . ."

Eleanor gripped his arm. "But she's fine. And your baby?"

"A boy. The worst night of my life turned into the best." Charles's smile split through the fatigue and anguish, turning his tears joyful. "Do you want to see him?"

On the way to the nursery, Charles talked about the baby's loud cry, what Gwen said when she saw him. He asked if the police had come to her apartment, then told her the baby had a birthmark on his tummy. He looked ready to faint.

"There he is." Charles and Eleanor stood by the window. He pointed at a baby in a blue blanket near the edge.

"What's his name?"

"Donald. Donald Harry."

Eleanor widened her eyes. Charles laughed out loud.

"Jesus, no. Your face." He went quiet, touched the glass. "His name is James, for my father. James Luke."

"Luke?"

"Yes. We'll call him Jimmy."

She watched Jimmy, what she could see of him. "Is that him crying?"

"Don't you dare suggest he become a singer."

Eleanor hesitated. "The gun—I think it was Connor Morris. The reporter."

Charles didn't respond and instead rested his brow on the glass, closing his eyes. He opened them again and looked at his son. Eleanor watched the baby twist in his blanket, the little impression from the umbilical cord.

"When he was born," Charles said, "his daddy was in prison."

"His daddy is the bravest man I know."

Charles looked at her, smiled.

At the elevator, a middle-aged white woman stared at them for a long time. She held flowers, probably celebrating a grandchild. Eleanor wasn't sure why the woman stared. Did they look like a couple, or did she recognize them from the papers?

Eleanor was still wearing her costume. The cream sheath was stained with sweat and drops of blood from the cut under her eye. It would need to be replaced—but then Eleanor realized she'd never need to wear the costume again.

"What makes you say Connor Morris?" Charles asked Eleanor once they had some food in the hospital cafeteria.

"I think I saw him," she said. "Backstage. I saw his hair. I didn't even remember until last night."

Charles tore the crust off the sandwich and rolled the bread into tiny sticky balls. Eleanor didn't like it and looked away.

"I already put in word to the police," she said. "I hope they take it seriously."

Charles crumpled the wrapping. "Now what?"

"Time to find another job, I suppose." Eleanor pressed the heels of her hands into her eyes. "I don't want that."

"This might sound crazy, but I don't either."

"There's going to be a news story tomorrow morning confirming that the gun was planted," Eleanor said. "Otis, Harry, Franny, and the stage manager have all given statements to the *Times*."

"Well, that's good. But if audiences weren't convinced before, I don't think a loaded gun did us any favors, planted or no."

At his words, Eleanor felt a fall in her chest. He was right, of course. But that didn't mean she was ready for the show to be over. This entire section of her life, over. They sat in silence. Eleanor closed her eyes, feeling a feverish haze from so many hours awake. Just when she was about to fall asleep, Charles shook her.

"Now you're going to really think I'm crazy," he said.

He was smiling. Eleanor, so tired she felt drunk, was in such despair that she was ready to seize on any happiness. "What is it?"

"What if we fixed the show?"

"How?"

"I have some ideas." He started balling up the paper from their sandwiches. "I know you do, too. Between you, me, and Don, maybe we can come up with something."

Charles was out of his seat before Eleanor could wrap her mind around his words.

"What's gotten into you?"

"I'm not letting that Morris fellow dictate my life," he said. "Or my son's."

"After last night, I thought you'd be ready to retire from the stage forever."

His exhaustion was gone. "I've got a boy upstairs, a healthy wife sleeping down the hall. What can I say? I'm feeling lucky."

She pulled him by the arm until he stopped. "Charles. Are you sure?"

"What'll Jimmy say when he learns his daddy gave it all up when it got hard?"

"You gave it all up for him, and for his mother."

Charles shook his head. "I have a duty now, Eleanor. I have to make this world as safe a place for him as I can. And quitting might keep him safe today. But with this show, I've got a chance to change a few people's hearts for good."

Eleanor's eyes filled with tears. She hadn't realized how much she wanted this, too. "I have plenty of ideas."

"Attagirl."

Eleanor waited while Charles spoke to Gwen. She could see them through the glass, Gwen, dark circles under her eyes, shaking her head and looking at her husband with a mixture of bemusement and annoyance. She patted the bed and he sat, and she took him by the shoulders and kissed him, pressing their brows together. Eleanor turned away until Charles emerged, coat on, grinning, and rushed toward the elevator, beckoning her to keep up.

"Gwen says if I don't come home, she'll kill me," he said.

"If we give even one more performance, I can die happy," Eleanor said. "Connor Morris can't win."

"The show must go on."

Eleanor smiled. "As they say."

His legs were longer, and she had to trot to keep up, her feet stinging with blisters.

On the street, Charles stepped back so Eleanor could hail the cab. She gave Don's address and they drove west, through the park. "It's the ending, Eleanor. It's not right. It's never been right."

Charles tapped his knee with the heel of his hand. "What if the point isn't to get the audience to accept Luke and Molly together—but to get them to *want* them to be together?"

"I've been saying that."

"So what if Luke and Molly don't end up together?" Charles held up a hand before Eleanor could interrupt. "If they end up together, plenty of people start imagining their babies, a white woman shacking up with a black man—it's too much for their delicate little sensibilities. But what if we show them the reverse? Show them what their hatred does? Instead of showing a world where they can be happy, we give them the world as it is."

Eleanor watched the trees outside her window. "So we let the audience have the easy way out?"

"No. I think that's where we're stuck. Don wants to let the audience have it easy, wants Molly and Luke to be happy, no problems, wouldn't that be nice? Most of the audience says hell no, and the rest get to go home happy in the knowledge that the world isn't such a bad place after all. I say, we show those people the exact world they created, the world they defend every time they protest outside our theater or plant a gun backstage. We show it to people, as it really is, and we make them regret it."

"But that's the world they want," Eleanor said. "Those people who boo us, who leave after the love scene."

"And we'll be giving it to them," he said. "The other way, we impose our morals on them. This way, we show them—really show them—who they are."

Eleanor felt swelling in her throat. "Show the world as bad as yesterday?"

"The point now isn't to write a hit, Eleanor. The point is to tell Molly and Luke's story."

The trees were blossoming in the park. She closed her eyes against the pink and green racing past the cab windows. Molly and Luke's story. Gwen had been saying the whole time that, in this life, they wouldn't have the story Don was giving them.

"Don says they have to be together, to give the audience a relief."

"That's nonsense." Charles's fist pushed his cheek up to his eye, in the unself-conscious pose of deep thought. "Don's got his own business to work out, and that's why he wants them tied up, safe and happy."

Eleanor felt a roll of anxiety, then certainty, hard and true as a pebble. "I think we can persuade him," she said. "But he might be resistant."

Soon, the cab reached the other end of the park, and they were pulling over.

Don wore no shoes when he answered the door. The exhaustion had added years to his face. She remembered the hard panic she'd felt on-stage, when she did not know where he was. "Did you get out all right?"

"I managed." He took in her body, checking for injuries, running his gaze over Charles.

"Don, you could have called."

"Harry told me you were safe."

She hadn't been home to answer, but Don's response confirmed he hadn't tried.

"You have no idea how sorry I am that this happened," he said. "I never imagined anything like this. Whoever did it was sick."

His apology chafed at her, even though he seemed sincere.

"We had to go to the jail," Eleanor said. "Harry was there."

"He told me."

"Why weren't you?"

Don looked away. Eleanor took a step forward, toward the door, but Don did not move aside. She felt a flash of fury.

Charles cleared his throat. "Gwen gave birth to our son last night."

Don looked up at that, something like concern in his eyes. "What?"

"She went into labor after she fell in the crowd outside the theater," Charles said.

"Early labor," Eleanor said. "Don, she could have died."

Charles held up a hand. "We're calling him Jimmy."

"Congratulations," Don said, before turning to Eleanor. "I understand you're angry. But this wasn't my fault."

A flurry of comebacks appeared in her mind.

"You should go," he said. "People have been lining the sidewalks. They'll recognize you."

"Too late," Eleanor said. "We passed them on our way in." This time, the crowd had felt more curious than angry; the group was made up of protestors, supporters, and nosy people who wanted to catch a glimpse of Don the morning after his first failure. Eleanor and Charles had pushed through the gatherers without raising their heads or answering questions.

Charles stepped forward. "We have to talk to you, Don."

His knuckles tightened on the doorjamb. "I'm not in the mood for company."

"Are we really company?" Eleanor asked.

"Yes."

She blinked, smarting.

The elevator bell rang. Don stood up straighter, his eyes going wide. "Eleanor, Charles, look—"

The doors opened. Freddie came out, holding a bundle of newspapers, a bottle of liquor, and a pizza box. Eleanor stared. He wore a cotton shirt and jeans. He met her eyes, then looked away.

For a long moment, no one spoke. Eleanor looked between the two men, trying to piece it together. Freddie was just a dancer. What could they possibly be working on?

"I got the papers," he told Don. "It's still everywhere."

She already knew the answer when she asked the question. "Why are you here?"

A vein in Don's temple popped out. At first when she looked at his eyes, their pupils dilated, she thought he was angry, but then she saw the tension in his neck and realized he was terrified.

"Last night was difficult," Freddie said, looking between them. "Don wanted some company."

Charles took the paper from Freddie, shook his hand. "You all right?"

"Not a scratch," he said. "Gregory turned an ankle on the way out, so he can't dance for a while, but that was the worst of the damage." Freddie approached Eleanor and laid a hand on her arm. "Are you all right, Eleanor? I couldn't find you after. You look pale."

But Eleanor couldn't respond to him. She didn't want to cry, and in the effort not to, laughed. How different all this had been from those dreams, how much more complicated, how much crueler. She had come to New York in love with the beautiful shows; she expected the people behind them to be just as perfectly crafted, sparkly, accomplished. They were certainly as fascinating, but at every turn, she felt she'd miscalculated. More than anything, she felt stupid. Don had never been anyone but who he said he was.

Charles cleared this throat. "Don, we'd like to speak with you about the show."

Don shook his head, but Charles met his eyes. Then Don dropped his hand from the door and stepped back.

He didn't invite them into the studio. Freddie slid the pizza onto the coffee table in the living room, and Eleanor, legs still weary, slid right down onto the floor with her back to the couch. Charles sat beside her, resting his elbows on his knees. Don stayed by the front door, his arms crossed over his stomach.

"We want to do the show one more time."

Don swore under his breath.

Freddie's eyes flicked between the three of them. "I'm going to make some tea." He went to the kitchen; Eleanor heard cabinets opening. He knew where to find the mugs.

Don picked up a newspaper, emblazoned with Charles brandishing the gun, his eyes turned toward the ceiling in horror, Eleanor's arms wrapped around him, her mouth twisted in a scream. He dropped the paper on the ground. He picked up another: Charles, in handcuffs. He dropped it. Another: the crowd, rushing through the theater, beneath a headline:

INTERRACIAL SHOW ENDS
IN BLOODY MAYHEM

"Bloody?" Eleanor said through her teeth.

Don dropped the paper, reached for another.

"Stop this." Charles took the papers and threw them aside.

"I'm ruined," Don said.

"Enough," said Eleanor. "You aren't ruined. You're Don Mannheim. You said you wanted controversy. Here we are."

"You're only ruined if you let them ruin you," Charles said.

"So you two came here with a brilliant idea for a hit?" He walked past them toward Sullivan the turtle, his eyes on the glass tank. Someone had supplied him with fresh lettuce. She wondered if it was Freddie.

"We know how to end the show," Charles said. "End it with the truth."

Don laughed. "The noblest of artistic pursuits."

Eleanor wrenched herself from the floor and took him by the arm. "Don Mannheim. Enough of this self-pity. Last night was horrible. It was a tragedy. But it's not just your tragedy."

"It's my show, isn't it?"

She pressed her tongue to the roof of her mouth before she gathered herself enough to respond. "No."

The teapot whistled from the kitchen. Don tensed, as if just remembering Freddie was there. "You won't say a word about him?" he asked, nodding to the next room.

Charles shook his head, but, returned to this subject, Eleanor felt a rise inside her. Before she could stop it, she blurted, "Don, you used me."

Sweat shone on his brow. "You can't tell anyone."

"Why didn't you tell me?" Her voice broke, but she went on with red cheeks. "I would have gone with you to the theater, to dinner, anywhere. You could have told me."

"Eleanor, do you understand? This is my career. This is my life."

Eleanor looked at him. Her heart was broken, no matter how stupid she had been to allow him into it.

Don reached over and took her hands in his. He'd touched her like this before, and she went back through her memories, coloring each touch with platonic feeling. "Eleanor, right now, I'm a genius. If this gets out, I'll become the 'homosexual composer.' I'll be good—for a fag."

She blinked away the tears in her eyes.

"I told you not to want me."

Eleanor felt humiliated. She sat on the couch, took her head in her hands. She was too exhausted; her tears flowed. Charles was watching, but instead of feeling embarrassed, she felt strong. She knew he wouldn't laugh at her. "Don, I thought we were friends."

Don took her chin in his hand. "I never lied to you. I do care for you." His voice was very quiet. "I have come to care very much."

He ran a finger under her chin, along her neck—those long fingers that had produced all those pieces that changed her life. She found she still felt a protective compassion for him, for those musicals that had raised her.

"I won't tell a soul," she said.

He nodded solemnly.

"So this is why you wrote the show, then?" Charles asked. "Forbidden love?"

Don looked at his bookshelf, the scripts and awards and framed programs on the walls. "What I told Eleanor was the truth. I've never been in love. I wanted to feel it. And writing the musical, I finally did."

Charles joined them on the couch. "So you needed Molly and Luke to be happy."

Don jerked his head to the side.

"It's all right," Eleanor said to him. "You said I knew Molly as well as you. Doesn't Charles know Luke just as well?"

"You knew what it would feel like for Luke," Charles said. "The fear, the hiding, the shame of pursuing something the country thinks you aren't good enough for, of rejecting everyone you're raised beside. It's incredible, Don. I never saw the two things together, before, but I see it now."

"The world makes you earn your happiness," Don said. "Only the purest can indulge."

"Put that onstage," Charles said. "Don, the audience doesn't want a fantasy. Put in everything you know about the world, everything you know about love."

"I know nothing of love."

"That isn't true," Eleanor said. "You've been trying to write something you don't know. Your experience of love hasn't had the happy ending. Why are you writing that?"

Don sat up but did not speak. His face moved through reactions, some of which made her furious even if she had expected them: laughter, affront, condescension. But Eleanor waited. She banked on the fact that he would not be able to resist the possibility, however small, of success. Slowly, he faced them. "Tell me what you're thinking."

The Finale

Chapter Twenty-Four

I already wore my good dress on Sunday," Rosie said, a line between her brows. "You're telling me I've got to rustle up something else?"

"I need to know someone in the audience is rooting for us." Eleanor threw dresses from her closet onto the bed. "We're throwing a party after the show. Maybe a funeral. But we're going on tonight."

"I can't go. I have nothing to wear."

"You can wear any of these."

Rosie's eyes went round. She pulled the cherry-red dress Eleanor had worn to the investors' party from the bottom of the pile. She held it in front of her like it was a dance partner. "I want."

Eleanor laughed as Rosie hugged it to herself. "It's yours. I never want to see that dress again."

"What will you wear?"

"I have an idea. But you're going to need to help me." Eleanor pulled a garment bag from the hook in the closet. "We've got an hour before rehearsal. If I promise to love you for the rest of my days, can you make magic happen?"

Rosie's mouth dropped open. "Mr. Rabinowitz—"

"Thinks you have the flu," Eleanor said. "I already called."

"You manipulative little monster."

"How often do you get to go to two Broadway performances in one week?"

Rosie rolled her eyes. "So what are you wearing? Does it have pleats? Pleats take ages."

Eleanor turned away from Rosie so she wouldn't see her friend's reaction when she unzipped the bag.

Rosie's gasp told her all she needed to know.

"Eleanor, no."

"I need to make an entrance." She posed enough to make Rosie smile. "Please?"

Rosie was shaking her head. But, trouper that she was, she waved a finger up and down Eleanor's body.

"Strip, and put that on. I have pinning to do."

Most of the rehearsal was between her, Charles, and Harry.

When Harry read the script, he looked to Don. "This is brilliant, Don."

Don said nothing. Eleanor fumed, but it didn't matter; even if Don was too proud to correct Harry, they'd already called the lawyers and her name was being added to the contract and the program, albeit in very tiny font. Charles hadn't wanted recognition, afraid of looking as though he'd manipulated the situation in his own favor. But he'd insisted at least one of them get credit. The knowledge that her fingerprints were on a real musical touched a deep part of herself. She felt a balance between her past and present, as though she had been preparing her entire life for that night's performance.

Eleanor had seen Harry create a stage picture before, but never so quickly. He snapped his fingers as he read the script, thinking. After about five minutes, he turned to the stage manager.

"Light the front whites," he said, gesturing to the line of lights hanging over the top of the stage. "No spots. Clear the set midway through the riot scene. I want a clean stage."

Eleanor waited as he gave directions for the sound balance and then shaped the ensemble in a crowd upstage so everyone was visible. He didn't have time to try options and trusted his first judgment. Eleanor let herself be awed by him; throughout this process, he had put the work first, every time. He placed Molly's mother downstage from the rest, so she was singled out.

"Luke and Molly, center," he said. Eleanor took her place on the ground, center stage.

They ran through the beats of the scene. It was an easy scene to add in, technically, as it had no singing or movement. The cast made their way into this frieze during the riot scene and held their places until the end of the show. One by one, they walked offstage. Harry gave them all numbers, and the cast led themselves off. They marked it, then Harry dismissed everyone save Charles and Eleanor.

"Eleanor, your part is easy," Harry said. He turned to Charles. "Are you up for this?"

Charles said nothing, just nodded.

"All right then. Let's run it."

Despite everything that had happened to him in the past two days, Charles was a professional. All his lines were memorized. He delivered them without affect. Eleanor aimed her face upstage so no one would see how he brought her to tears.

When he finished, Harry walked up to him and placed his hands on Charles's shoulders.

"Marvelous."

They ran it again, for good measure, then broke for an hour.

Eleanor returned to her dressing room. Rosie was there, holding the garment bag.

"You owe me," Rosie said.

"I already gave you my boyfriend."

"You can make that joke exactly one more time before I pull out your hair."

She hung the bag on the back of the door and came up to Eleanor, placing her palms on her face. "I'm so proud of you. You've really done it now."

Eleanor looked away. "The show's going to close."

"You've fallen in love with a hundred shows that barely played a week on Broadway," Rosie said. "All those recordings, all those scripts you read. It doesn't need a long life, just one performance."

Eleanor thought about all of the shows she'd loved as a girl, even the flops. She'd found the records in the back of the store, dug out the scripts at her library.

"You put in your piece," Rosie said. "No one can ever take that away from you."

Eleanor smirked and sang a bit from the Gershwin song, the first one Pat had ever played her. "'The way you wear your hat . . .'"

Even Rosie knew that one. She leaned up on her toes and kissed Eleanor on the forehead. "This show would have never happened without you."

Eleanor couldn't take any more; the praise hit somewhere weak, and she felt too exposed. She wrapped her arms around Rosie.

"You know I love you more than all this."

Rosie laughed.

"Okay," Eleanor said. "As much."

The news of the shooting had brought a special breed of person to the theater that night. The house was packed. People were wondering if there would be another disaster. Everyone thought the show would close, apparently, but everyone wanted to be one of the few who'd seen it.

"They want a car crash," Don said in Eleanor's dressing room before the performance.

"They won't get one," Eleanor said. "They're going to get a piece of art."

Don touched her face. "I'm sorry I couldn't give you a hit."

Eleanor looked out her dressing room window at Times Square outside and thought of her first day in New York with Tommy and Rosie. She'd wanted to be a Broadway baby, wanted the lights and the costumes and the bright music.

"This is better than any hit," she said. "I think you did your legacy well, Don."

"Not in this lifetime," he said.

"Maybe not," she said. "But wasn't that the point?"

He met her eyes.

"Says the twenty-one-year-old."

"Yes, who finished it for you."

Don let out a laugh, a real bark. "Oh, Eleanor," he said. He stuck out a hand. "Friends?"

"There was a time I would have died to have you call me a friend," Eleanor said. She took his hand, shook it. "Are you going to watch?"

"From the balcony."

She slid her wig cap over her pin curls. "I'll do you proud."

He turned to leave, then stopped. "You already have."

Once he left, Eleanor felt the nerves come in, persistent and strong. Though no one would pay enough attention to the program to realize she'd contributed to the writing of the show, she would know. If they got their closing notice that night, there would always be a part of her that felt it was somehow her fault, no matter how true that was. But it didn't matter, because it was 7:50, and the show would begin in ten minutes.

Backstage, she and Charles held hands. The entire cast was quiet, solemn. Right before curtain, they drew together in a circle, everyone's arms around everyone else's, and said a prayer. Even with such weight hanging over them, the rumble of the audience worked on the group of actors. None of them were immune. Charles had tears in his eyes. Eleanor embraced him.

"Thank you," she said. "For everything."

"And you." He hesitated. The lights were going down. "Will you be his godmother?"

Eleanor was speechless. "Gwen?"

"Agrees." He smiled. "Well?"

She couldn't speak; she nodded. "I won't be helpful with the church parts."

Charles smiled. He drew her close. "One more time, Molly."

By the time the overture began, Eleanor was ready.

It was a good audience. Perhaps because the group was a daring sort, or the bad news made the show an underdog to be rooted for. They clapped, laughed, and when Luke climbed through Molly's window at the end of act one, she heard gasps.

Eleanor avoided Harry at intermission, not wanting to break the momentum of the show. She drank water and freshened the powder on her face, then got ready to begin again.

The second act came easier than earlier. It was like that phrase her mother used: the other night had put the fear of God in her. She sang "A Table and Chairs" with a real weight, feeling the knot in her stomach that had not dissipated since the gun went off on Sunday.

The anxiety carried through the city picnic, where everyone was onstage mingling together. Molly slipped away to get her things, still unsure of her decision. When Luke ran on to meet her for the elopement, his smile was so welcome after such sorrow that the knot loosened.

But then her father spotted them. He gripped her arm, preventing her from joining Luke.

She reared back and spit in his face, wrenched her arm away, and ran after Luke. They met up in the alley behind Molly's house.

The riot scene swelled up better than in any previous performance, the woven voices sounding ghostly and hateful and afraid, lacing together until the fears of Molly's family and Luke's family were indiscernible.

"Luke," she said, her voice cutting above the chorus. "I love you."

She opened her purse and pulled out the gun. This time, it had been locked in the safe until the very last minute. The props master had even fired it at the floor beforehand to check that it was empty. Still, Eleanor heard gasps from the crowd. This was the moment they had come for. Hairs raised on her arms. She held up the gun so it flashed in the lights.

The sound of the riot was still going behind her.

"This will frighten everyone into letting us go," she said.

"Molly, you're playing with fire!"

"They need to know we're serious." Her voice was infused with concentration; no tremble betrayed her fear, though adrenaline flooded her body.

Luke tugged the gun away from her. The audience's murmuring grew louder.

"No," he said. "I won't pull a gun on anyone. Go hide in the church."

"Luke, if you think I'm going to leave you here—"

"I won't risk the gun," he said, dropping it in the garbage can in the alley. "If you want to be my wife, go hide in that church! I'll come find you!"

Molly made to leave, but Luke tugged her back, giving her a kiss so decided and romantic that the audience reacted with a buzz. Too quickly, he let her go. Molly straightened herself, and then Luke gave her a push.

"Go!"

So Molly ran offstage. The riot music picked up again, the crowd milling about. The stained-glass window and pew came up, her hiding place for the rest of the show. She tucked herself behind a pillar, waiting for Luke, heart pounding. The sounds of the riot from the picnic came through the church walls, until Molly was clutching her hands together in fear, waiting to hear screams or gunshots.

The sound of a door opening, then closing. The music cut off. In a moment of clarity, Eleanor realized that the theater was silent. No one rustled a program.

Someone was inside. Molly tucked herself farther behind the pillar.

The person entered the stage; a murmur went through the audience.

Molly did not reveal herself, her eyes wide, afraid to look and see who was in the church. Quietly, she began to sing the last lines of "Sunday Evening," unaccompanied, so that the audience understood Molly was singing inside of her head and not out loud.

One cough went through the audience, amplified throughout the theater. Molly held her arms around herself.

Just then, the door on the other side of the church opened.

Her eyes flew open. A second person was inside, and she was between them.

"Molly?"

It was Luke. Molly whipped around, seeing him standing behind the altar. She couldn't speak for fear, still behind the pillar, and saw her own father standing at the back of the church.

"You!" Mr. Sheeran screamed. He raised his hand. Molly caught the glint of metal, reflected against the stone walls.

Luke's eyes went wide. He held up his hands.

Molly didn't think. "No, Pa!"

She ran out from behind the pillar just as the crack of the gun sounded; she heard it, and then she fell.

Duncan raced toward her, but Luke threw him off. He dropped to his knees beside her, gathering her in his arms.

"Molly."

"Luke." She swallowed, her breath coming fast.

His grip was tight around her, as if he could hold her in the world. He said her name over and over.

Molly closed her eyes, fell back into Luke's arms. He held her close.

All was quiet for several long moments.

Someone stepped forward to put a shawl over her body. Luke's grip tightened, but then his mother's voice: "Someone should cover her."

He allowed it.

Mr. Sheeran stooped, but Luke shoved him away.

"Let me move my daughter."

"No." Luke looked up at Mr. Sheeran. He was shaking, whether from anger or repressed sobs, he didn't know. He retracted his arms from Molly's body and laid her on the ground. He removed his coat and placed it beneath her head. Then he stood.

He turned to the rest of them. "You didn't believe us." He turned to Mr. Sheeran. "You didn't believe she knew her own heart."

He looked at his mother. "None of you."

He looked at the crowd behind him, his back to the audience.

Don's underscoring began to swell, the slow notes of "Sunday Evening" coming through the theater.

"Now she's gone," Luke said, his voice breaking. "Now . . ."

He collapsed, his knees going out until he landed hard, prostrate before her. He kissed her forehead.

One by one, the cast members began to leave the stage. Don's music swelled until it took over the whole theater, the blue notes filling the space with a thick sorrow.

Eleanor felt Charles's head on her stomach, heavy and warm. She kept her face upstage so the audience could not see her tears.

Finally, when the violins bowed the last, legato notes, Charles gathered her in his arms and carried her offstage.

A taxi pulled up as soon as she stepped outside the party; she was conspicuous on the street, a young woman in a fitted tuxedo jacket and trousers before dawn. They sped down Broadway—no traffic—but by the time they reached the East Village, they stopped so that Eleanor could read the headlines in the papers newsboys were unloading outside corner stores.

Don's name was emblazoned on the front page, above the fold. Years later, when Don was doing more ambitious work that failed to grasp the hearts of the masses, Broadway openings would no longer make the front page. The composer's picture would hardly ever be included. This was the only time Don, called a genius for decades after, would have his picture on the front page. When he died, the best he would wrangle was the front of the arts section. Like a true genius—and over the years of her career, Eleanor would never be sure she'd met more than one—he put everything into his work, and his work had a life longer than the man.

But that morning, he and Harry were on that front page, Eleanor between them, beaming. Charles was of course nowhere to be found. Without buying the paper, Eleanor knew the review would focus on the shooting. Would the music receive a mention? What about their one standing ovation, so hard-earned? The article might say New York wasn't ready for such a story, even with the new ending—an ending that punished the lovers for challenging a system that wasn't ready for change. People would always sympathize with the losers.

That night, the audience had left in tears. Some called it a masterpiece. A few still called it vulgar. Lots said it was Luke's fault that Molly was killed. But for the most part, between the new ending and the terrible event that had previously overwhelmed newspaper headlines and changed the audience's sensitivity, the show worked. With Molly's death, the audiences could afford to be generous. People wept for Luke and Molly and the life they could have had. They mourned their lost future.

The taxi pulled up to her destination. She let herself out, feeling the waning champagne in her blood. There was nothing worse than sobering up.

Once in their apartment, she locked the dead bolt. Men's shoes were paired by the door. Rosie's own pumps were probably back in the closet already. This little evidence of them warmed her deeper than anything else that night. She couldn't bear being alone tonight, now that it was all over. Rosie, hugging her goodbye before she left the party, must have seen the exhaustion on her face, and invited her to join when the party ended. After the rush of the last few days, Eleanor needed to be with a friend.

Tommy and Rosie's door was open, the light of the sign for a twenty-four-hour diner across the street shining through the window over their bed.

Tommy still slept on his back, one hand over his heart. Rosie lay on her stomach, hands out like she was proclaiming innocence. Her hair was spread over the pillow, mouth open. Rosie had never been one to tolerate anything other than a perfectly restful night's sleep.

She climbed into the bed between her friends, fitting herself around Rosie.

Tommy stirred. "El?"

He pulled up the blankets to cover all of them.

Rosie, still asleep, rolled over and wrapped an arm around Eleanor's waist, nuzzling into her. Tommy leaned over and kissed her on the forehead before letting sleep claim him again. Between them, smelling them, Eleanor felt her heart rate return to normal. The energy of the show leaked from her body, slow as honey, until at last, her muscles relaxed. The faces she'd seen in the audience, all the moist hands clasping hers in congratulation, the burn in her cheeks from smiling, faded from her mind until it was another night.

She looked at the ceiling. Charles was back in Harlem with Gwen and Jimmy. Don was likely staving off sleep at the piano. Even then, her body ached for him. But it was like a ghost, and gone in a moment. She turned and pressed her nose to Rosie's hair. It was damp and clean. It was a smell she knew better than anything in this city, had known since she was small, even as Rosie changed shampoos or perfumes or bed partners. The smell predated New York, Broadway, her picture in the paper.

The sun was firmly in the sky by the time Eleanor fell asleep, warmed by their bodies. Seventy-eight blocks north, Don Mannheim sat at his piano and started something new.

ACKNOWLEDGMENTS

First and foremost, thank you to my parents, Loretta and Carl Neuberger, whose love, support, and example are the foundation of everything in my life. My grandmothers, Marilyn Carolan and Loretta Neuberger, who nurtured my love of music and stories, and led by example. My grandfathers, Eddie Neuberger and Don Carolan, whose lives shaped mine, and this book. My brother, Will, I love you so much.

This book would not be possible without Christy Fletcher and Sarah Fuentes, who guided this book and me through every decision and leap of faith. Sally Kim and Gabriella Mongelli—editors are book superheroes, and I'm so grateful you're mine. Gabriella, I couldn't have asked for a better teammate for this book. Sally, thank you for sitting with me at LPQ and sharing your wisdom, long before this process even began. Thank you to everyone at Putnam whose work improved this book, especially Aja Pollock, Claire Sullivan, Elke Sigal, and Tal Goretsky.

Thank you to everyone at Viking Books, but especially Laura Tisdel, Pamela Dorman, and Amy Sun, for your advice, ears, and support.

Linda Plym, Bill, Sigourney, Odessa, and Dash Buell—thank you for being my New York family. A good bulk of this book was written in your home.

I have such deep gratitude to all of my writing teachers, starting with Brando Skyhorse. David Lipsky. My teachers at Brooklyn College: Joshua Henkin, Helen Phillips, Ellen Tremper, Sigrid Nunez, and especially Julie

Orringer, who taught me to find guidance through writing, and Ernesto Mestre-Reed, who read this first and asked me the hard questions. My writing community, Chelsea Baumgarten, Garrard Conley, Jenzo DuQue, Sameet Dhillon, Wesley Straton, Jill Winsby-Fein, and so many more, thank you for your reads, companionship, and advice. Special acknowledgment to my friend Jivin Misra, who has read this book almost as much as I have.

Ben Bartels, for my first real home in New York. Navin Raj, je t'aime, I'll take the subway with you anytime. Matthew Campos, for Paris, for growing up with me, and for believing in me. Jenny Poth—*The King and I* brought us together. Rose Bisogno, for your name and wisdom. Laura Boehm, from lunch next to Canal Saint-Martin to here. Danielle Dettling, my sister—Quack! I'll never let go. My life is so much richer for each one of you.

And last, thank you to my voice teachers, Dr. Dorothy-Jean Lloyd, Matthew Ellenwood, and Frank Schiro. Each of you introduced me to a bit of the world through musical theatre. I wish every young artist could be taught with such dignity and joy.